# GIRL ON THE RUN

BY DARYL WOOD GERBER

# Girl on the Run



ISBN-13: 978-09973611-1-7
ISBN-10: 0-9973611-1-5

Cover and Interior Design by SheridanINK

www.darylwoodgerber.com

First Edition

Printed in the U.S.A

## DEDICATION

To my husband, Chuck. *Forever.*


## ACKNOWLEDGEMENTS

"If I didn't define myself for myself,
I would be crunched into other people's fantasies
for me and eaten alive." ~ Audre Lorde

Thank you to my husband, Chuck, for appreciating that I am a strong woman and believing that I can do anything. Thank you for always seeing us as a team, yet separate and equal. I am so blessed to have known you and to have been loved by you. You fill my thoughts constantly and you always will.

Thanks to the two women who have helped me most on this journey. Sheridan Stancliff, you are an Internet and creative marvel. Kimberley Greene, you have no idea how much I appreciate you...or maybe you do.

To my family and friends, thank you for all your support. This is a new adventure for me, and one that I hope you will share with joy.

Thank you to my talented author friends, Jenny Milchman, Jamie Freveletti, Krista Davis, Hannah Dennison, and so many others for your words of wisdom and encouragement.

Thank you to my first readers from the Cake and Dagger Club who inspired me to move forward with this project. Your enthusiasm is infectious.

Thank you to all my readers for taking the journey with Chessa Paxton as she finds her courage and strength, and thank you, in advance, for sharing your love of my newest novel with your family and friends. An author's story cannot come alive without readers!

# CHAPTER 1

Chessa Paxton had dreaded the night, even feared it, but now, dressed as Sleeping Beauty, she quivered with anticipation as she moved with the throng toward the entrance to the Boardwalk Casino. Everything was exciting: the costumes, the eager chatter, the orchestral music being piped through amplifiers. The Happily Ever After Ball was going to be, in a word, *heady*. She stumbled slightly and gripped the skirt of her costume so its sequins wouldn't snag on the other gorgeous princesses' gowns or any number of billowing witch capes—heaven forbid she cause a snafu. A cool summer breeze, typical at night in Lake Tahoe, swirled up from behind. Chessa shivered, wishing she had brought a shawl for her shoulders.

Zach slung an arm around her. "Are you okay, babe?"

Even though Chessa was still seething at her husband, she leaned into him for warmth. "Yes."

Once she entered the ballroom, exhilaration shot through her, and she forgot she was cold or anxious. The lush gold-themed décor—all her doing. Food stations and carving stations set in every corner of the room—her suggestion. Bartenders at the open bars were offering beverages from the finest champagne to the costliest whiskey. Couples were already partying on the dance floor.

Chessa hummed along with "Some Day My Prince Will Come" as she pressed through the exuberant crowd. Ever since she was a girl, she had dreamed of designing costumes for this kind of ball. She had no idea that she, by the ripe age of thirty, would be one of the people running it. Assistant in charge of Special Events. She loved her new title. The ball, which was the Thursday night kickoff party for the three-day Happily Every After Convention, had been designed as a fundraiser for MASK: Making Art out of Sad Kids, a spectacular cause that helped fund doctors around the world so they could fix children's damaged and deformed faces. *A smile is worth a thousand words* was MASK'S slogan. Chessa had no clue there would be so many people willing to help: the rich, the powerful, from land developers to politicians to publishers, comic book mavens, and costume play—or *cosplay*—aficionados. All were here with many wearing, at the very least, masks.

A waiter passed Chessa carrying a tray of savory onion au gratin appetizers. The aroma made her salivate, but she couldn't indulge. Not yet. Maybe later when she was sure everything was running smoothly.

Zach swooped tendrils spilling from Chessa's updo off her neck and planted a kiss beneath.

A swizzle of desire coursed through her, but she quashed the feeling. "That's not getting you off the hook, mister." Not after what she'd seen in the desk at their cabin. "Talk to me."

"It's nothing. Promise. When we get home."

"I don't like secrets." Her father; the pack of lies.

"I know, babe. I know." Zach slipped an arm around her waist and squeezed. "C'mon, ease up. Enjoy the fruits of your labor. We're at the event of the year! An event *you* put together."

"*Helped* put together."

"Enough modesty. Admit it, my love. You are brilliant. A mastermind. Not to mention gorgeous. Look around." Zach gestured to the swelling crowd. "Every man here wants to be me and take you home."

"Well, every woman *doesn't* want to be me," Chessa said, feeling a tad lighter, the stimulation of the event working like a happiness drug. "Certainly not hanging around with you in that getup."

"What's wrong with it?" Behind his goofy mask, Zach's eyes twinkled with mischief. He had begged her to make him a frog prince costume, complete with bug eyes, webbed hands, a lopsided crown, and a fake red tongue hanging down the bib of his green tuxedo. Ridiculous. "Watch this." He hopped ahead—actually *hopped*—and splayed his arms. "I'm a prince in disguise."

Chessa couldn't help herself. She laughed out loud.

A woman called out, "Sleeping Beauty! Hey, Chessa!" Helena Gorzinski, the chief human resources officer for the casino, was dressed as Belle from *Beauty and the Beast*, the Disney gold-gown version. She glided forward and extended the cell phone she was holding.

"I like the wig," Chessa said. "You should consider dying your hair black." Helena had mousy brown hair.

"In another lifetime." Helena smiled but the smile didn't reach her intent gaze; she had been born serious. "Someone named Dr. Fairchild called for you. I'm not sure how he got my number." Her Polish accent was barely noticeable; her family and she had worked hard to Americanize themselves. "He said he tried your cell phone. You didn't answer. He wants you to call him back."

Zach groaned. "C'mon, babe, you don't need to talk to your therapist. You're handling this. You won't—"

"Have a meltdown." Chessa placed a finger on her husband's frog-like mouth. "I agree." *Fragile before, nevermore,* she reminded herself. "Helena, thanks, but I'm not taking any personal calls tonight. If the doctor calls back, tell him I'm fine. Have you seen Ms. Kimura?" Yukiko Kimura, Nevada's Director of Business and Industry, was the woman who had dreamed up the brilliant idea of the fairy tale theme.

"Over there. She's hard to miss in that ruby red costume you made her."

Chessa grinned. "Zach—"

"Go. Do your thing." He swooped in for another kiss.

Before he left, Chessa said, "I'm parched. Would you get me some water?" No wine tonight. She needed her wits about her until the last guest departed.

Zach saluted and walk-hopped toward the nearest bar. A wiry, redheaded man in a black uniform with gold epaulettes stopped him and said, "Szabo, my man."

Hearing Zach's surname shot Chessa back to the time when they met. After a long day of skiing, she and her mother slipped into Alpine Meadows Lodge for a drink. Her mother rarely imbibed, but that day she led the way. She'd had a scare; she had taken a bad spill on a hill packed with moguls. She wanted a brandy. When they entered, Zach was sitting on a stool at the bar, his ankle bound in a cast, his leg propped on a neighboring chair. While waiting for their drinks, Chessa's mother urged her to introduce herself to the dark, handsome stranger. Instead of shutting down, Chessa found the courage. Zach was charming, talkative, and sexy. He said his last name was Szabo, Spanish in origin, but he'd never been to Spain. She fell hard for him. They talked for three hours straight; her mother magically disappeared. Four weeks later, they moved in together. Six months after that, they married. At Zach's insistence, Chessa kept her maiden name. He said it was important for a woman with a career to maintain her own identity, although he had balked when she was offered a better paying job with growth potential at one of the casinos in Las Vegas. *Stay local,* he begged. She acquiesced.

Chessa surveyed the room to catch a glimpse of him and spotted him still chatting with the guard. The man poked him in the chest. Zach flinched and backed up. The guard grinned and strode off. Within seconds, a pasty-skinned witch with a black mouth, prominent cheekbones, and red-and-purple tipped dark hair approached Zach. Her gown of black feathers fluttered.

As if Zach felt Chessa's gaze on him, he turned and twirled his webbed hand, signaling he would return with water soon. Chessa drew in a deep, calming breath and weaved her way toward Red Riding Hood.

"Ms. Kimura," Chessa said.

Normally Yukiko Kimura could appear icy with her no-nonsense demeanor, but tonight, with rosy cheeks and bright red lipstick, she looked sweet and approachable. Chessa had spent a full week on the costume and was pleased with the result.

"Enough with the formality, Chessa. Tonight, call me Yukiko." She took a sip from a bottle of water she was holding and assessed Chessa. "Are you okay?" The woman didn't miss much. She never did. Chessa had enjoyed working with her on the event. "You look pale."

"I'm fine. A little tired." And still ticked off at Zach. She shoved her irritation aside. "But who cares? I'm so happy. You and I…we did it."

Yukiko and Chessa had coordinated every aspect of the function. Chessa had managed the costumes, the décor, and the menu; Yukiko had contacted the bigwigs. Helena had managed the invitations.

"Yes we did. Listen, I need to chat with the senator. We'll catch up later and recap the evening, okay?"

Chessa's stomach churned. The *senator*. One of her least favorite people.

Yukiko brandished her bottle. "Don't forget to drink plenty of this stuff. You've got to keep hydrated."

She hurried away and joined second-term Senator Jeremiah Wolfe who was wearing exactly what Chessa would expect him to wear, a Big Bad Wolf costume complete with vile fangs and sharp claws. *The better to eat you with, my dear*. Standing with him was Captain Hook a.k.a. Wally Evert, one of the most influential men in the Lake Tahoe area and one of the ugliest, with his fleshy toadlike face and his bulging right eye. At first the men seemed pleased to see Yukiko, but within seconds, the conversation turned heated.

Yukiko's red cheeks blended with the rest of her face. She whacked the senator and Evert with the butt of her water bottle and said something. Chessa wasn't a lip reader, but she was pretty sure Yukiko said: *You! You!* What was she accusing them of?

Someone from behind Chessa touched her shoulder. "Nice job, young lady."

Chessa spun around and gasped. Maleficent, à la the antagonist in Disney's *Sleeping Beauty*, grinned at her. The towering black horns made the woman seem eight feet tall.

"Who are you?" Chessa asked. The woman was wearing so much makeup that her face was unrecognizable. Chessa hadn't had the luxury of studying the guest list like Yukiko and Helena had, so she wasn't sure who everyone was.

The woman chuckled. "Mine to know." She swept up the folds of her train and continued on.

A few more guests, including Cruella De Vil, Simba from the Lion King, and Rumplestiltskin, approached Chessa and paid her equally nice compliments.

A waitress in a milkmaid uniform—each of the staff was wearing a costume designed by Chessa—sashayed to Chessa carrying a silver tray filled with skewered ahi tuna appetizers. "Want one?"

A nibble wouldn't hurt, Chessa decided. She took a kebab and downed the treat in one bite. Seconds later, she was even thirstier than before. She spied Zach still hanging out with the witch, her request for water apparently forgotten, and felt a moment of peeve.

Moving in his direction while passing groups of people, Chessa caught snippets of each conversation. Robin Hood raved about the casino's upcoming poker tournament. The Blue Fairy from *Pinocchio* carped about the unbearable traffic that the Glory to God revival at Heavenly Mountain Resort would cause. Peter Pan was upset about the nanotech firm that had taken up residence in South Lake Tahoe. A female Mad Hatter praised the tenderness of the roast turkey and pointed out the carving station to her friends.

Chessa moved beyond them all, her gaze focused on Zach and the witch. Who was she? Why was Zach talking so intently with her?

"Help! Chessa!" Helena raced to Chessa, the skirt of her gold gown rustling. "Costume snafu. My zipper."

Chessa never went anywhere without a few sewing items. She fished in her clutch purse, pulled out a safety pin, and weaved its bar beneath the tongue of the gown's zipper. "There. It shouldn't pop open. But no jerk-style dancing."

"As if."

A woman cackled. Chessa turned toward the noise. The witch was regaling Zach with a story. She dragged a long pointy fingernail down the front of Zach's costume and back up. Then she petted Zach's frog-like cheek. He batted her hand and said something Chessa couldn't make out. Then he stormed off.

Chessa pressed through the crowd to catch up to him but couldn't because Captain Hook—Wally Evert—waylaid her.

"Hello, me lass," Evert said in pirate speak.

The senator strolled up. "Don't scare her, Wally."

Chessa's skin crawled at the sound of his voice. She wanted to flee but knew it was impossible, given her cumbersome gown with its big folds of fabric. Besides, there was nowhere to go. Guests had crammed in around her to allow for more space on the dance floor.

"I'm not scaring her, you blowhard," Evert said, keeping up the pirate pretense. "Her husband asked me to do him a favor." He jutted a bottle of water toward Chessa. "Have at it, lass."

Chessa gratefully accepted the water, popped the top open, and drank half of the liquid in one gulp.

"Nice party, Chessa," the senator said. "If only your mother could have lived to see the success you've become." He reached toward her face.

Chessa tensed. How dare he mention her mother.

"Sorry. I merely wanted to help." The senator signaled with a finger. "You have a hair sticking to your cheek."

"I don't need—" A flush of heat rose up Chessa's throat. She felt like she was going to vomit. Not from his touch. From something real. She'd eaten an ahi appetizer. Had the fish turned? "I need the ladies' room."

Evert said, "Are you okay?"

"Not sure. I—" Her stomach rumbled. She raced to the restroom and barely found the sink in time.

After cleaning up, another wave hit her. She had to tell someone. Yukiko. Or Helena. She felt along the wall to the door. She clutched the jamb. *Don't fall*. She opened the door of the ladies' room. The glare of lights in the hallway disoriented her. Which way to the ballroom? Images were blurring.

"Chessa!" Zach appeared. "There you are." He swooped her into his arms, unwieldy skirt and all.

She rested her head against his shoulder and thought about the last few moments with Zach at their house. What she saw. Their spat. She didn't want to be mad at him any more. "So tired," she whispered.

"I know, babe. I've got you."

He carried her through the hotel's rear access. Her right arm dangled over his. She couldn't move it even if she tried. He deposited her into a casino vehicle—a van—and climbed in beside her.

*"Te amo,"* he whispered as he attached her seatbelt. *I love you,* in Spanish.

Chessa wanted to say she loved him, too, but her mouth wouldn't move.

## CHAPTER 2

"Get away from me." Morning sunlight pierced the sheer curtains and made Chessa wince. A man in uniform was reaching for her. She scuttled backward crablike, her heart stabbing her ribs. The sequins of her gown snagged on the jute rug. The smell of fear replaced the scent of pine as she crashed into something hard, wooden. The bed. *Her bed.* "Who are you?"

"Ma'am, you called us. Emergency response."

Chessa tensed. She couldn't remember calling them.

A second man in uniform appeared. "What's going on?"

"She's a little freaked."

The first pointed a harsh light at Chessa. She shielded her eyes then squeezed them shut. A riot of metallic stars collided behind her lids. Why was she barefoot? Why did her feet ache?

"Who's the man on the floor, ma'am?"

Chessa peered between spread fingers and reality came rushing at her. Zach's Frog Prince costume rested in a heap on the tile in the bathroom. Zach, beautiful Zach, lay prone on the rug, a towel cinched around his waist, his black hair wet, arms outstretched and hands fisted, as if he had tried to defend himself. A pair of Georgian scissors with lions' heads handles jutted from his back. Blood oozed from the wound. A vase of pansies lay in shards beyond his head.

"Ma'am, who is he?"

Chessa covered her mouth to keep from screaming. She stifled the urge to gag. "My husband." She glanced at the EMTs, at their grave faces. "Is he...?"

"Dead? Yes, ma'am."

"Oh, no!" Tears flooded Chessa's eyes. Just last week, on the eve of their anniversary, Zach had chased her around the house in a silly game of tag. She had let him catch her at the top of the stairs. They had tumbled into bed and spent the afternoon there.

The first man gently lifted her to her feet and guided her down the stairs. Her sequined gown rustled as they went. He sat her on the floral sofa in the living room. "Want some water?"

Chessa couldn't answer. Her throat was constricted with terror. Perspiration peppered her skin. She peeled away sticky curls clinging to her neck and watched men and women in uniform orbit the rooms of her cabin, the beams of their flashlights slashing the area even though it was daylight. The green and blue décor swirled together like a nightmarish Van Gogh painting. Doors slammed. Walkie-talkies crackled. She caught broken phrases.

"Scissors."

"Rage."

"Late twenties, maybe early thirties."

A pockmarked deputy said, "Guilty as sin."

Chessa caught him gaping at her. Did he think she had killed Zach? She wanted to scream, *No*. Why couldn't she? Because she couldn't remember anything. She grabbed a throw pillow, shoved it against her stomach, and slumped forward.

Someone laid a hand on her shoulder, a man with a gravelly voice. "Miss, we'd like to ask you a few questions."

Chessa struggled to a sitting position, the effort demanding all her strength, and locked eyes with a gnarled older man, striking silver hair, brown skin crisscrossed with age lines.

"I'm Detective Tallchief from the Washoe County Sheriff's Department. What's your name?"

A deputy handed Chessa a glass of water and a tissue.

"Chessa." She drank the liquid in one long gulp and mopped her eyes with the tissue. "Chessa Paxton." The words sounded garbled, indecipherable. Why was she having trouble forming them? She could do better. She had to.

A man grunted. Chessa gazed in his direction. He was muscular, in his late thirties. He was leaning against the knotty pine wall beyond Tallchief, arms folded, looking like he wrestled mountain lions daily and enjoyed it. When he lasered her with a stare, alarm scudded through her.

"Where do you reside?" Tallchief asked.

"Here." Where she had lived with Zach for the past year in a two-story log cabin with few neighbors and a flower garden. They had planted the garden together. Zach had rubbed potting soil in her face. She had sprayed him with the hose.

Tallchief hitched his baggy trousers up over his slim waist and offered a reassuring smile. "What do you do for a living?"

"I'm"—she licked her lips—"a special events coordinator. At the Boardwalk Casino in South Lake Tahoe."

"Did you kill your husband?"

"No!" At least the word made it past her lips this time. A shockwave of grief spiraled through her. A funeral. She would have to plan another funeral. She swallowed hard. "We were in love."

Mountain Lion Man snarled.

"Can it, Newman," Tallchief said.

Chessa clenched her teeth. Didn't they believe her? Did they think she was guilty? She wasn't. She couldn't be.

*My father.* Goosebumps crawled up her arms. *They know what he did.* She wanted to curl into a ball. Hide. *Wait!* She sat a little taller. *Maybe they don't know. It's been over twenty years. Maybe they haven't made the connection.*

"Tell us what happened here."

"Zach—" Chessa glanced at the front door. She recalled it was ajar when she returned home. Zach never left the door open. Sunlight flooded the front path. The sun was just rising when she entered earlier, wasn't it? "What day is it?" she whispered, as flashes of memory whizzed through her brain, nothing more than wisps of color and blurred images, but they hung there, beckoning her to remember.

"Friday," Tallchief said.

"What time is it?"

"Seven A.M."

A clearer image began to form. She had been home less than an hour. "When I got here, the door was open. I went inside. I picked up the letter opener from the desk."

"To defend yourself?"

"I don't know."

"Did you think someone was inside the house?"

What didn't Tallchief understand about the words: *I don't know.* "I tiptoed upstairs."

"You tiptoed? So you *did* think someone was here. Why did you enter if you thought—"

"I saw—" Bile crept up Chessa's throat. "I saw Zach."

"No one else?"

Chessa shivered. Why did she go inside if it wasn't safe? That wasn't like her, taking risks. She must have heard Zach moan. She couldn't have killed him. She couldn't have. She massaged her forehead. Her feet ached as if she had carved her soles with sharp stones. Where were the gold slippers she had worn to the ball?

"Is there somebody you'd like us to call?" Tallchief asked.

"Jeremiah Wolfe."

"Why?"

"I'm his stepdaughter."

Mountain Lion Man—Newman—cursed. Someone else whistled.

Chessa's nerves jangled as if they were on fire. These people would find out about her father. It didn't matter that she wasn't like him, that she couldn't have done what people said he did. They would throw her in jail. She braced for the assault.

Tallchief said, "I'm sorry about your mother. What a tragic accident."

Chessa felt like he had socked her in the gut. The car crash that killed her mother a year ago had ripped Chessa's world to shreds.

"You don't have any siblings," Tallchief said.

She had a big huggable Labrador retriever named Jocko, but he didn't live with her. He lived with her stepfather. Zach was allergic to dogs.

"Did you and your husband fight?"

Chessa sucked in a breath. "Last night. But we made up." Or had they? She couldn't remember. Before then, the worst thing she had ever called Zach was *jerk* because he had wanted to see a guy movie when she had wanted to see a chick flick.

"Why is there blood on your face and gown?"

## CHAPTER 3

Chessa gaped at her dress. The folds were caked with blood. Lots of blood. She started to tremble. Had she...? Impossible. She loved Zach. Adored him. He was her soul mate. "I...I felt my husband's neck for a pulse."

"Why are you wearing a gown?"

*Because every woman wears a gown to a ball* Chessa wanted to blurt, but refrained. Her mother would have been proud. A lady holds her temper.

"I attended the Happily Every After Ball." Flashes of it came to her in spurts, like images through a kaleidoscope: Zack in his ridiculous costume, ogres, princesses, witches.

"I heard of that," Tallchief said. "Put on to raise money for MASK. Making Art out of Sad Kids, right? The doctors fix up little kids' faces."

Chessa jolted as another memory came to her. She was running. Along a moonlit path. Someone was chasing her. A man in a ski mask. Why was he wearing a ski mask in June?

"Have you been drinking, Ms. Paxton?"

"No." She never drank liquor when she was working. Only water.

"How about after the ball?"

Chessa rubbed the hollow between her eyebrows. Why couldn't she remember what happened afterward? Why was she so thirsty? Her mouth tasted metallic.

"Are you on something, Ms. Paxton?"

Chessa clasped fistfuls of her dress as another memory slammed into her. Red hair had protruded from beneath the ski mask. A redheaded man dressed in a black uniform had chatted with Zach at the ball. Could it have been the same person? Had he been a guest at the ball or security? No, the casino's regular security wore maroon uniforms. Chessa whimpered. Why couldn't she remember more?

"Ma'am," Tallchief said, "I repeat—"

"I feel dry-mouthed." Her hands started to shake. "Is it possible that someone drugged me?"

"Uh-uh. That's it, Tallchief," Newman said. "I'm tired of this two-step. Lady—" He eagle-eyed Chessa as he donned a pair of latex gloves and strode across the room. He stopped at the desk and with his pinky lifted a gold slipper. "Why is there only one shoe? Did you lose one getting into your pumpkin, Cinderella?"

A snappy comeback lodged deep in Chessa's throat. Was he blind? She wasn't Cinderella; she was Sleeping Beauty!

Newman tossed the slipper aside and lifted a passport. "Is this your husband's?"

Chessa's insides knotted up.

"Why does it say Szabo?" Newman asked.

"My husband's surname was Szabo. I kept my maiden name because of my career."

"And what about these?" Newman waved three more passports while eyeing Tallchief, who had his cell phone out and was talking to someone in muted tones. "One's Russian. Another's Swedish. The last one's from Spain."

Chessa chewed on her lip. Last night, right before leaving for the ball, she had found the additional passports. She asked Zach about them. She would never forget the way his eyes turned black. *When we get home,* Zach told her. He would explain then.

"Ma'am, I'm talking to you."

"My husband traveled a lot. He was a venture capitalist."

Newman ambled toward her, his feral gaze never leaving hers. Chessa felt fury building inside her. She was not the criminal. She was the victim. Didn't he see that? She glanced at Tallchief who was still talking on the telephone. Why wasn't he making this cretin back off?

"How many guys do you know who have four passports?" Newman asked.

Chessa shuddered. She didn't know any. Not one.

"Didn't your good old stepdad vet this guy?"

"Yes." According to Jeremiah, Zach was gold. Zach had graduated from UCLA with a degree in economics. He had never been married. Chessa's mother had welcomed him wholeheartedly, too. They had been one happy little family.

"Seems he might have missed a detail or two, don't you think?" Newman crowded her.

Chessa recoiled. The room whirled.

*Gunshots. The keen of a hawk.*

She could barely breathe. A heavy weight was on top of her. *Snow White's dead body.*

She pushed up.

*Her fingers tangled in folds of taffeta and silk and metal-studded suede.*

"Lady!"

Rough hands clinched Chessa's wrists. She forced her eyes open. Newman was prying her fingers off his shirt.

"Dang it, Newman!" Tallchief yanked Newman away from Chessa and lost hold of his cell phone. It clattered onto the hardwood floor. He snatched it and muttered, "Ingrate."

Newman said nothing. His hard-edged jaw ticked with tension for a long time and then he walked away. When he did, Chessa let out the breath she had been holding.

"Miss Paxton." Tallchief massaged his neck. "How long have you been married?"

"A little over a year." An imaginary cinch tightened around Chessa's lungs. Zach—her *husband*—was dead. Murdered. "Please, I need some air." She clambered to her feet.

"Hey, Cinderella—"

"I'm Sleeping Beauty!"

Newman cocked his head, a smug grin on his face. "Whatever. Don't forget your purse, just in case you want to freshen your makeup."

Chessa's heart rate kicked up a notch. The spangled purse that matched her gown was jammed into one of the mail slots of the desk. At the end of a day, she always placed her purse on the counter in the kitchen, checked her calendar, and then put Post-it reminders for the next day on the refrigerator. *Always.* Who had put it in the cubbyhole?

"Can I make a phone call?" she asked, trying to control the panic that was swelling inside her.

"Yeah, sure, you're not under arrest yet," Newman said. "Make two. Make three if you like."

Chessa froze. *Three.* Last night someone said: *Three days.* Who? She shuddered as the memory slammed into her: the redheaded man in the guard uniform. The rest of what he said echoed in her mind: *The witch said, 'Be ready; the firestorm happens in three days.'* He hadn't been talking to Chessa.

# CHAPTER 4

Nothing ticked Marcus Newman off more than liars. Sure, he'd lied as a kid, but once he found the straight and narrow, he toed the line. He expected others to do the same. On the other hand, Chessa Paxton looked freaked out. Why? He reviewed what he'd said to her. Did the number two or three have significance to her?

"Ma'am"—Marcus moved toward her—"just so you know, we can retrieve your phone messages, if you have the impulse to erase them."

Chessa shrank back as if he'd slapped her then shuffled to the porch and perched on the swing.

Tallchief strode to Marcus's side. "Geez, you can be a jerk."

Marcus rolled out the kinks in his neck. "You, too."

"Yeah, but I'm running the investigation."

"Good, then run it instead of running for office," Marcus said, irritated that Tallchief had wheedled control of all homicide cases for the past few months. He was no better than an ambulance chaser. "You were on the phone covering your rear because she's Jeremiah Wolfe's stepdaughter, and the press is going to be all over this."

"Wait a second—"

"Look, you want to become mayor, that's fine, but you're being too nice to this nut-case. Beautiful or not, our sweet Ms. Paxton probably just offed her husband. She might have had an accomplice."

"Where did you get that crazy idea?"

"Trust me on this. Don't fall for a pretty face."

"Me? You're the one who's partial to women with curly hair and curvy bodies."

Marcus gritted his teeth. His life was not going under the microscope today, not if he could help it. He'd served fifteen years on the force. He had an exemplary record. That was what was on the line today. There was no call to dredge up his mess of a relationship with Ginnie. He'd loved her, and she left him for reasons he still couldn't understand. Okay, he understood them, but he didn't like them. She sent an annual Christmas card. He tore up each one.

"Chessa Paxton has got a lot more than a few bruises," Tallchief said. "She looks like she tumbled into a briar patch. Did you notice the scratches?"

Marcus nodded.

"Maybe she's telling the truth. Maybe she passed out someplace on the way home, then woke up to find this bloodbath. I want you to back off."

"Aw, c'mon. Tell me you're not buying the memory loss crap."

"I'm buying whatever I want. Back off, do you hear me?"

Marcus didn't respond well to authority. He never had. As Tallchief rattled off the facts, as he knew them, Marcus ran his hands down his neck feeling edgier than he had in years. Maybe it was the weather, which was wildfire-dry for June. He preferred the cool of fall and a long hike, or sitting on his balcony, beer in hand, with the sounds of Dave Brubeck channeling through the speakers.

"You listening, Newman?"

"Yeah." While Tallchief droned on, Marcus flipped through Zach Szabo's investment portfolio. *Passive resistance is the best way to achieve a goal,* Gandhi said. The portfolio looked pretty blank. And those passports. Marcus stifled a laugh. Sven Svenson, a.k.a. the Swedish equivalent of John Doe. Was Szabo a total idiot?

Marcus glanced out the window. A crowd of gawkers had arrived. All on foot, each with a cell phone. Neighboring houses stood a half-acre away with dense forest in between, but somehow the word was out. The gawkers collected behind the yellow crime tape. A Toyota Highlander stood in the carport. Chessa Paxton sat on the porch swing, her face averted from the group. She was whispering into the cell phone, fingers of her left hand gripping the phone tightly, her other hand twirling curls of her blonde hair. Marcus experienced an uncommon moment of sympathy for her but squelched it. She was probably talking to her stepfather, a man he had never admired and never would. He was too far right politically for Marcus's taste.

Tallchief scowled. "You haven't heard a word I've said, have you?"

Marcus definitely had moments of tuning out. He didn't like that aspect of himself, but he couldn't curb it. Way back when, after his mother died from an overdose, he learned how to block out his father. At the age of twelve, when his old man split—the jerk just up and left—Marcus moved himself and his little brother Eddie into a cardboard box behind a restaurant and learned how to tune out the rest of the world. If not for his foster mother and his stint in the army, Marcus might have taken the route his mother had.

"I'm not sure what happened here," Tallchief said, cutting into Marcus's musings, "but she's definitely freaking out. Tread softly is all I'm saying. I don't want one of Wolfe's fancy lawyers telling me we overstepped our bounds. She's not a delicate little flower, but the lawyers will make her look like a lost soul, and we can't have that. Got me?" He jammed his hands into his pockets. "So, how's the new partner?"

Marcus drew in a long, slow breath. His last partner quit a month ago. His new one— "Raw. A greenhorn." Most likely Captain Armstrong had put him with the kid, hoping Marcus would quit. He wouldn't; he'd stick. The Captain couldn't bully everybody into early retirement.

"You know, we weren't too bad as a team."

"Are you joking? We lasted five weeks." Those were Marcus's first weeks on the job. "Any longer, we might have drawn blood."

The screech of tires on dirt ended their conversation.

Marcus peered through the front window. "Well, I'll be. The infamous Reverend Davey Diggs has arrived."

"The televangelist?"

"The same."

"Short and ugly, isn't he?"

"Bad genes." Diggs didn't suffer from dwarfism, but he was smaller than the average man, built like a cork, and as white as a lily. Despite the drawbacks, women swooned for Diggs, which Marcus didn't understand. Maybe the attraction had something to do with women feeling more beautiful around ugly men. "He's a media hound. He turns up whenever he senses drama in the making."

Diggs scrambled out of a white Mercedes and snaked his way through the gawkers to the front of the crowd. "Chessa!"

"Swank car for a pastor," Tallchief said.

"He has a big flock."

"Get rid of him fast." Tallchief chucked Marcus on the shoulder. "When you're done with him, tackle the princess, but go against your nature and be gentle."

# CHAPTER 5

Chessa sat on the porch swing, her skin itching with uneasiness. People had gathered beyond the crime scene tape. Some held up cell phones and snapped pictures. Disgusting ghouls, all of them. Reverend Diggs, too. He called to her. She didn't want to talk to him. He couldn't save her. His prayers were worthless. He hadn't saved her father or her mother or Zach. She sucked back a sob. *Zach.* Why did he have so many passports?

"Chessa!" Diggs called a second time.

She ignored him. Unless the reverend could divine what had happened last night, he was useless to her.

To the right, off at a distance, she spied a man in a baseball cap peeking around the ponderosa pine. Was he from the media? One of the sheriffs caught sight of the guy, too, and headed toward him. The guy bolted.

Chessa tucked her chin and drew her hair around her face as she stabbed a telephone number on her cell phone.

At the same time, Newman stepped out onto the porch. Through strands of hair, Chessa saw him glance her way. He looked concerned. For her? Not likely. She squelched the nausea roiling inside her and listened as an answering machine picked up her call.

~ * ~

Marcus marched down the path toward Reverend Diggs. Gravel crunched beneath his boots. He breathed in a lungful of crisp morning air to keep himself in check. He believed in God, but he didn't attend church. Religious extremists drove him nuts.

"Officer," Diggs said, smoothing the lapel of his blue jacket.

*Who the heck wears a wool suit in Tahoe in the summer?* Marcus wondered. He bit back a knee-jerk comment. "Don't cross the line, sir," he said. "In fact, all of you, get out of here," he ordered. Some were the press. Why weren't they descending upon Diggs? He loved giving interviews. "Go. This isn't a dog and pony show. When we know something, we'll alert the proper authorities." Many obeyed and disbanded.

Diggs didn't budge. "Officer," he repeated. "A minute of your time."

"It's Detective."

"Please, I'm a friend of the family." Diggs held his stubby hands out as an appeal.

Marcus worked his tongue inside his cheek. "Are you here on behalf of Jeremiah Wolfe?"

"One of my parishioners texted me." He held up his cell phone. "May I speak with Chessa and possibly pray with her?"

Marcus eyed Chessa sitting on the porch. She looked as tense as a coiled spring ready to pop. *She should be tense, jerk. You laid into her, but good, and everybody's looking at her like she's guilty.* He remembered Tallchief's words to cut her some slack and made a vow to try.

"No, sir, I'm sorry," Marcus said. "Not until we've sorted through the facts. You can tell her stepfather we're taking good care of her."

"I haven't come to do his bidding."

Yeah, like Marcus believed that. He folded his arms across his chest and waited until Diggs left the premises, the roar of his Mercedes rousing the creatures in the pines to riot.

As Marcus returned to the cabin, he paused near Chessa. Her chin was tucked protectively into her chest, her cell phone pressed to her ear, her other hand kneading the folds of her dress. Something about her bothered him. It wasn't that she was good looking, though Tallchief was right. Marcus liked curvy blondes with soft features and full lips. And it wasn't the fact that she hadn't cracked under his verbal attack, either. It was the vacant thing he'd seen in her eyes, like she was having difficulty processing information. Was she simply in shock, or was something else at work? Had she stabbed her husband? How much force would that require? Marcus had learned to kill in the army. A pinch to the neck, that's all it took. But Chessa Paxton? She was a costumer for a casino—correction, a *former* costumer, now special events coordinator. Her biceps, visible through the splits in her ribbon sleeves, were strong, but she didn't seem to have that killer's edge.

Chessa said into the phone, her voice breathy, "I've got to see you. I don't know where else to turn."

Marcus wondered whether she was talking to her stepfather or a lover. A woman as good looking as her might have a few of those.

"I can't remember anything after the ball," she added.

Marcus snorted. What kind of whackos attended a Happily Ever After Ball? Comic book conventions, he understood. He liked Marvel heroes as much as the next guy. But fairy tales? What a crock. Many fans had arrived a week ago with the first flock of summer tourists, which also included families, bikers, sun-worshippers, and gamblers. At least, from what he could tell, the fairy tale fans were respectful of the environment. Marcus loved Lake Tahoe and hated when the area catered to ill-mannered jerks.

"Hey, Detective Tallchief, sir," one of the team yelled from inside the house. "Are you down here? You've got to see this!"

Marcus charged through the front door and nearly crashed into a younger version of himself, barrel-chested, brown hair—his new partner, Keegan, who was holding a bottle of pills.

"What's that?" Marcus demanded.

"Diazepam."

Marcus seized the bottle from him. Chessa Paxton's name was on the label. He snarled. He marched outside, snatched the cell phone out of her hand, and dragged her by the wrist inside the cabin. "Upstairs, Princess!" He wanted to grill her with her husband's lifeless eyes staring up at her.

"You're hurting me."

He released her and shoved her ahead of him. "You said you weren't on drugs."

"I'm not."

"You take diazepam. That's for alcohol withdrawal. You got a drinking problem? Maybe that's why you can't remember what you did last night."

"No." Chessa twisted her head to look at him. "It's for..." She hesitated. "I sleepwalk."

Marcus scanned her face. Her eyes looked less hazy. Had she been faking disorientation earlier, or was she coming out of a stupor? It didn't matter. Sleepwalkers were capable of murder. The Reitz murder in 2004 had made a case for it.

Chessa paused near the top of the stairs. "Look, I don't feel any aftereffects from diazepam. Ever. And I have memories when I sleepwalk. Tactile memories. The feel of the doorknob. The breeze if I open a door."

"How about the feel of a pair of scissors in your hand?"

When they reached the top of the stairs, Chessa stumbled over a catch in the carpet. Marcus braced her, his arm around her waist. She twisted away and shuffled into the bedroom. Short of her husband's feet, she sucked back a sob. What was she staring at?

"The bracelet," she whispered.

Marcus noticed the antique charm bracelet in the deceased's hand. "Is it yours?"

"My mother's. She gave it to me when—"

"Hey, Newman," Tallchief said, cell phone next to his ear. "The Captain wants us to check out all those A-list attendees at the ball."

Marcus grumbled under his breath. Did the man ever stop campaigning? He was glad he hadn't needed to attend the ball and listen to blowhards talk about taxes and the state of the economy. The guest list would have included the usual: Nevada's high rollers, wealthy business owners like that nanotech guy and the pizza chain entrepreneur, real estate moguls and Republican fat cats.

"Wally Evert was there," Keegan said.

"Swell," Marcus muttered. Wally Evert, the boat king and renowned local gambler, was a good friend of Jeremiah Wolfe's.

Marcus returned his focus to Chessa. She hadn't budged. Maybe she really was in shock. She lived in a cabin in a forest like a princess in one of those danged fairy tales. Murder didn't happen in those stories. Correction, maybe it did in the Brothers Grimm versions. Marcus had never read any of those.

Slowly he surveyed the room again. Tidy yet quirky. Dream catchers hung on the walls, as did drama masks and stone-faced marionettes. Multiple candles, a stack of books, and a collection of framed pictures sat on the bedside tables. Home sweet home, except for the dead body. He was about to grill Chessa again, from the top, when someone whistled from the bathroom.

A female deputy dashed out and shoved a set of papers at Tallchief. "Sir, you've got to take a look at these."

Tallchief skimmed the pages then whacked the sheaf of papers against his leg and stomped toward Chessa. "Well, well, Ms. Paxton, cut the damsel in distress act. You and your husband were getting a divorce."

Marcus took the papers from Tallchief, examined them, and swooped upon Chessa. "Is this your signature?" He flapped the document in front of her.

The color drained from her face. She stumbled across the room and sank into the blue velvet armchair. "I feel sick." She dropped her head between her knees.

"Uh-uh, Princess, lift your head. Is this your signature?"

"No."

"Maybe that's why your husband is clinging to your precious charm bracelet."

"No."

"Maybe he wanted to give us a clue as to who killed him. He wouldn't give you the bracelet until you signed on the bottom line."

"No."

"You signed, and in a rage, lashed out and killed him."

## CHAPTER 6

Chessa gripped the arms of the chair. Everything in the room became blurry. Her heart thudded so hard she thought it might explode inside her chest. This couldn't be happening to her. "We were happy. We were—" Early on, her mother had taught her never to discuss the family business outside the house. She squeezed her eyes shut to keep herself from passing out and flashed on Zach at the ball, talking with the redheaded guard. "Zach argued with a man last night. The man poked Zach's chest."

Newman said, "What did he look like?"

"Red hair, flat nose, black uniform with gold epaulettes. At first I thought it was a costume, but he might have been a security guard. Not regular security. The casino uniforms are maroon."

Tallchief sniffed. "Some of our guys work special events; we call them rent-a-cops."

"Zach..." Chessa moaned. She had to get a grip. She had to make sense of what was happening. "He told me he loved me right before I passed out."

"Apparently he lied," Newman said.

"When did your husband present you with divorce papers?" Tallchief demanded.

"He didn't." Chessa hadn't meant for the words to come out so loudly, but she couldn't help herself. "I've never seen these."

"Is that, or is that not, your signature?" Tallchief butted in front of Newman.

Chessa examined the handwriting for a second time. "It looks like my signature, but"—she chewed on her lower lip—"the P isn't right. It's too loopy." The letters looked the way she used to write them back in grade school, when she had needed her mother's signature on an excused absence slip. Too often kids taunted Chessa about her father. She believed he was innocent, but she had no comebacks, so on occasion, she would cut school and wander the beaches of Lake Tahoe. "I did not sign this document."

"Hey, Detective Tallchief?" A deputy who looked like Newman but younger held up his iPhone. "I got something you should see. About her father." He displayed the screen to Tallchief, whose eyes went wide.

Chessa's stomach churned. The time had come.

Tallchief lifted his gaze and grinned at her. "Well, doesn't that beat all? There's already a murderer in the family. This is going to be a slam dunk."

The haze clouding Chessa's mind cleared. She remembered the day the sheriff took away her father. *I'm innocent, sweetheart!* her father yelled. What had he done? He was a craftsman; he made artisan tiles. *It's all lies. I'm being framed.*

Was she being framed, too? The bracelet, the divorce papers. Someone must have planted them. Why? A month after her father went to prison, Chessa overheard Jeremiah and her mother talking. Jeremiah said someone high up in the sheriff's department was making sure the murder charge stuck. Would that happen to her? Did Jeremiah think it would? Was that why Diggs had come to the house? To plead her case? Or had he come on his own, thinking some Divine Hand was at work in Zach's murder?

*Stop it,* Chessa chided. *God had nothing to do with Zach's death.*

Her breathing grew ragged. She had to escape. Had to prove herself innocent. She couldn't do that from behind bars. But where could she go dressed in a ball gown with no shoes? And how could she prove anything if she couldn't remember events past midnight?

*Run!*

She glanced at the door. A sheriff would grab her before she could fly through.

"I feel sick." She forced herself to burp. "I'm going to throw up."

"Not here, you're not," Tallchief said. "This is a crime scene."

Exactly what she hoped he would say.

She moaned and covered her mouth.

"Keegan!" Tallchief pointed at the brawny deputy. "Take Ms. Paxton downstairs. Stand outside the door. Bring her back when she's done."

Though her body thrummed with nervous energy, Chessa pretended to struggle to her feet and let the deputy sling his arm around her shoulders. As they hobbled downstairs like an awkward team in a three-legged sack race, Keegan turned his head to the side, probably scared she would puke on him.

"Deputy Keegan"—Chessa deliberately made her voice weak—"I need to swing by the front closet. I need a change of clothes."

Keegan didn't argue.

Chessa purposely stumbled off the bottom stair and grasped the officer's elbow for balance. "This'll just take a sec."

Inside the hall closet, she found a pair of mesh running shorts, a paint-splattered microfiber shirt, a sports bra, and an old pair of sneakers. In April, Zach and Chessa had repainted the kitchen, stained the knotty pine, replaced window screens, and oiled all the springs on the windows. Would a man planning a divorce do those kinds of things? Yes, if he was planning on selling the house and dividing the assets.

As Chessa lifted the items, her body trembled with grief. *Zach. How could you?* She pushed the painful thought from her mind, slipped inside the guest bathroom, and took her first full breath since the sheriff's department had arrived. Catching a glimpse of herself in the mirror—eyes haunted, mascara leaking down her cheeks, curls matted to her head and neck—did nothing to inspire courage. She twisted the knobs on the sink, filled her hands with water, and splashed her face with it. The icy coldness tamed the fear roiling in her mind. She blotted her skin with a towel and rechecked her image. A slight improvement but not much.

The bathroom was situated at the back of the house. Leaving the water running, Chessa stole to the window. Birds of all shapes and sizes crowded the various bird feeders in the yard. A family of squirrels dined at a munch box. A twinge of worry pierced Chessa's heart. Who would restock the feeders while she was gone?

*Don't think about them. Run!*

Chessa refocused on the grounds. She had a clear path and plenty of thick trees for cover. None of the sheriff's men were scouting the backyard. The guy in the baseball cap and the few gawkers that had doubtless remained were nowhere in sight.

To mask the sound as she unhinged the lock on the window, Chessa grunted loudly. Then she tiptoed to the door leading to the living room and listened.

Keegan was tapping his foot on the floor, probably trying to block out her sounds of distress.

*Perfect.*

Chessa removed her gown, every hook and eye on the bodice difficult to undo. She let the gown slide to the floor and noticed a silver grommet clotted in a splotch of blood on the skirt. The sight sent a shiver through her. Where had the grommet come from? Not from her gown. Not from Zach's costume.

*Don't think about it. Move!*

She threw on the bra, T-shirt, and shorts, shoved her sore feet into sneakers, climbed onto the toilet, and eased out the window.

# CHAPTER 7

For the first few hundred yards, Chessa zigzagged from tree to tree, focused solely on keeping hidden. In the shadow of a pine, she paused to catch her breath. Her skin crawled with dread. What was she doing, running from the law? Because of her father's history, she had spent her life obeying the law: full stops at stop signs; crossing at crosswalks. But, now, because of her father, she was fleeing. Guilt swept over her. What kind of wife was she? How could she leave her husband at a time like this? She considered turning back, seeking her stepfather's help, and throwing herself on the mercy of the court.

A chorus of *guilty* rang out in her mind, the children from her youth taunting her, their words tearing into her soul. No, Jeremiah couldn't save her. He had tried to pull strings on her father's behalf, but to no avail. She had to run. Had to learn the truth. She couldn't be naïve any longer. Her fantasy life with Zach was over.

The passports. Why did he have them? If he had been involved in something terrible enough to get himself killed, she needed to know what it was and confront it.

She tore ahead, thigh muscles straining with each stride, and urged herself to dredge up memories of last night. She had to have been drugged. When? By whom? Had the person who dosed her killed Zach and planted the bracelet in Zach's hand and the divorce papers in his costume?

Pine needles crunched beneath Chessa's feet as she flashed on a run earlier in the day. At daybreak. Before sunrise. Heading toward home. From where? She was barefoot, which explained the damage to her feet.

The spit of gunfire. The screech of a hawk.

Chessa remembered looking up. Seeing the bird. No trees had blocked her view, which meant she had been standing in a clearing. A meadow possibly. But which one? There were so many around the Lake Tahoe area.

The last time she had stood in a meadow was with Zach on their anniversary. He had released doves from a cage, dropped to one knee, and proposed all over again.

Angry tears pressed at the corners of Chessa's eyes and blurred her vision. *Zach. Did I ever know you? Why did you want to divorce me? I didn't take the job in Las Vegas. I stayed in Lake Tahoe. I did everything you said. Always.*

That ended now. She wouldn't be a puppet any longer. Not for Zach. Not for her stepfather. Not for her mother.

Anxiety swelled in her gut as she darted across a gravel driveway and through a neighbor's pine cone-riddled yard. Ever since her father turned out to be a killer, she had doubted herself. His betrayal had shaken her to the core. Her mother had told her to move on, but Chessa hadn't been able to. In high school, she hadn't dated at all. In college and into her twenties, she had dated a few men, but not one was someone with whom she wanted to spend the rest of her life. And then she met Zach, her Prince Charming.

Last night he said he was a prince in disguise. Had he been trying to clue her in to his deceit?

~ * ~

Marcus stomped down the stairs of the cabin, irritated that Chessa Paxton was taking so long. He found Keegan leaning with his back to the wall near the bathroom and curbed the urge to shake the kid. Ever since his brother Eddie died, Marcus had tried to take it easier on young officers, and he'd done a pretty good job. "Hey, deputy, is she okay in there?"

Keegan pushed off the wall, struggling to yank his hands from his pockets. "I think so, sir. I haven't heard her puking for a while." He stretched his neck. "Nice little cabin, huh? What do you think it goes for?"

"Nothing you or I could afford." Lake Tahoe housing prices had soared in the past few years. Even a one-bedroom cabin like this went for over half a million. Maybe, in a year or two, Marcus could afford to buy instead of rent. He wondered how Chessa and her husband had afforded this place. "Ms. Paxton?" He rapped his knuckles on the bathroom door.

She didn't answer.

He knocked again. "You okay?" He placed his ear to the door and heard water spilling into the sink but nothing else. Not a breath. Zip. He tried the doorknob. Locked. She hadn't expected Keegan to enter, so why the heck had she—

Using his shoulder, Marcus banged against the door. It didn't budge. He rammed it until the lock ripped from the jamb. The princess gown lay in a heap on the floor. The window was open. He dashed to it. The scene in the yard looked like something right out of an animated movie. Squirrels and birds were eating to their hearts' content. The only thing missing was a singing princess.

"Dang it!" He fished Chessa Paxton's cell phone from his breast pocket and stabbed in *69. The last number she had called was a local number. He pressed SEND and waited.

"Senator Jeremiah Wolfe's office," a woman answered. "May I help you?"

# CHAPTER 8

Chessa spotted a shed beyond a brown chalet, its doors open. A small truck with a snow shovel attachment, dusty from disuse, stood inside. Desperate for a rest, she stole behind the shed and leaned against the rough wood. Detectives Newman and Tallchief had to be having conniption fits about now, she mused. *Good*. She placed her hands on her thighs, closed her eyes, and drew in gulps of air.

As if transported through time, she saw herself hurrying into the ballroom at the casino last night, the issue of the passports nagging at her, her anger at Zach fresh and righteous. But the buzz of excitement in the room threw her off. So did Zach. His kisses. His apology. She needed to chat with Yukiko Kimura, so he—

Chessa's eyes blinked open. She remembered Zach chatting with the redheaded guard, whom he appeared to know, and afterward he met up with a witch. Who was she?

*The witch said, 'Be ready; the firestorm happens in three days.'*

Chessa's throat tightened as anxiety turned into jealousy. Sure, some people considered Chessa attractive, but a lifetime of worrying that her father's madness resided in her made her wonder whether, pretty or not, she was worthy of love. Had Zach fallen for someone else? Was that why he'd wanted a divorce?

*Stop it. Zach loved you.* His last words were: *Te amo*. And after a while at the ball, he stomped away from the witch. What had she said that made him angry? Did she give him orders? Did Zach refuse? Did she kill Zach and forge Chessa's signature on the divorce papers?

Chessa could barely breathe. She needed to crash. She needed to regroup. She couldn't let doubt rule her. She peeked around the corner of the shed. No sign of the sheriff. No posse. No scent-sniffing dogs. No media.

Fighting off fatigue, she sped from her hiding place and raced toward the highway as she figured out her next move.

~ * ~

Marcus steered his weather-beaten Toyota Tundra south on Highway 28 through mid-morning lake traffic, cursing any driver who got in his way. He understood why Chessa bolted. With her history, he would have run, too. Who would she contact? What was her plan?

Keegan sat in the passenger seat, his cell phone locked to his ear. The kid looked pasty enough to puke, but Marcus didn't care. He wouldn't let him off the hook. He'd messed up.

"Any sightings?" Marcus asked.

"We've got units looking in a wide radius. One of the guys still on site at the Paxton/Szabo house found an address book for Chessa with less than six personal numbers in it and a handful of clients' numbers. All have been called. No one has seen her."

"What about the contacts on her computer?"

"They match the address book."

Marcus swore under his breath. For all he knew, Chessa had made it to a major road, stuck out her thumb, and hitched a ride to Alaska. He pulled up to the gated entrance of Senator Wolfe's private estate near the Glenbrook Golf Course, rolled down his window, and presented his badge to the guard. The other sheriff's vehicles lined up behind him.

Once admitted, Marcus drove up the circular driveway and parked. He climbed out of his truck and approached Tallchief in his gunmetal-gray Explorer. "Keegan and I are going in."

"You're not—"

"—in charge. Yeah, I know. But I'm motivated. Why don't you take a breather? An altercation with a senator could mess up your political future."

Tallchief glowered at Marcus, but he didn't argue.

Halfway up the azalea-lined path, Marcus threw out his arm and blocked Keegan. "Yo, hold up!"

Keegan removed his gun from his holster.

"Put it away, deputy, and take a moment to drink this in." Marcus gaped at what could only be described as a mind-blowing estate forged out of cedar, natural stone, and multi-paned windows as tall as cathedral windows. The pitched roof jutted out over the cobblestoned porch.

"Nice," Keegan said.

*Better than nice.* If Marcus had the talent, he would have become an architect. He loved this kind of stuff.

He tramped to the heavy pine door and peered through the etched glass panel on the right. Lake Tahoe, in all its deep-blue glory, lay just beyond the back porch. At the end of the pier bobbed a forty-foot Chris Craft Roamer, its sleek blue-and-white body gleaming in the sunlight.

Oh, yeah, Marcus was envious, but he wouldn't give up his soul, not like Wolfe had. The senator had succumbed. He had sold out to hobnob with the rich and infamous. After his first term, Wolfe, the son of a miner, took up with entrepreneurs like Wally Evert and a battalion of land developers. He used to vote his passion; now he voted theirs.

Marcus pressed the doorbell, its deep-toned chime as grand as the house. The door opened, a security system beeped simultaneously, and a severe looking woman with inch-long black hair appeared. Marcus wasn't quite sure where the woman's pallid skin ended and her tweed suit began. Her one extravagance—a hint of perfume.

"Detective Newman and Deputy Keegan, ma'am."

"I'm Patience Troon, Senator Wolfe's personal assistant. How can I help you?" She regarded Marcus with disdain, her gaze running from the top of his head to his feet.

He wished he had polished his boots, but then scrapped the idea. The woman's name was Patience, after all. No one except prudes and people who came to America on the Mayflower had that name. "Sorry to disturb the senator, ma'am, but we're looking for his stepdaughter."

"She's not here." Troon would have made a good knuckle-cracking nun. Those steely eyes.

"May we speak to Senator Wolfe?"

"He's in a meeting." She folded her hands primly in front of her while—Marcus was pretty sure—mentally polishing her imaginary halo.

"He'll take a short break to talk to law enforcement." Marcus leaned forward, forcing Troon to inch backward. As she did, he strode into the handsome entry decked out with expensive wood paneling, Persian rugs, and huge bouquets of fresh flowers in gargantuan crystal vases. "Nice place. Stuff dreams are made of."

"It's home."

*Not yours,* Marcus wanted to say, but didn't, because he didn't presume to know Senator Wolfe's private business. The guy could be screwing Troon, but Marcus doubted it after what he had read in the news about Wolfe since Chessa's mother died. According to gossip magazines, the man had turned celibate.

"Please, ma'am," Marcus said, stressing the *ma'am,* which seemed to drive a stake through Troon's snooty heart, "if you'd tell him we're here. Thanks very much."

She turned on her sensible heels and strode from the room, every clacking step a reinforcement of her loathing. As she passed a young woman in a starched white uniform, she said, "Fetch some coffee for these gentlemen and show them to the library."

Marcus cuffed Keegan on the shoulder. "Eyes open, mouth shut, got me?" From his new vantage point, he surveyed the rest of the house, its antique furniture, countless antique clocks, and fussy art, all originals he guessed and not to his liking. He preferred shabby chic, easy-care stuff like Chessa Paxton had in her cabin. He listened for movement on the second floor, perhaps sounds of a young woman running from the law, but heard nothing, just the incessant ticking of the clocks.

# CHAPTER 9

Chessa broke though a clearing of pines, sweat streaming down her face and neck, her feet stinging from newly formed blisters, and skidded to a stop on the shoulder of the road. The sounds of morning traffic made her head throb. Exhaustion threatened to overtake her as reality sank in. She had run off in a panic, half-cocked, without a plan other than needing to find out why Zach had so many passports. What had he been up to? Who was the redheaded guard? If the casino had employed him, even as a temporary guard, maybe Helena Gorzinski would know who he was. Perhaps she would know the witch's identity, too.

First, Chessa needed to find someplace where she could collect herself. To her right lay undeveloped land. To her left stood a series of billboards advertising hi-tech sunscreens, a casino in Reno, and *new, new, new* homes! Beyond the advertisements, a sign welcomed visitors to Incline Village, and she thought of Ferguson Fairchild, her friend and therapist. He lived nearby and worked out of his home. He knew about her sleepwalking forays into the weird, how much she hated losing portions of her days, and the loss she felt for her father as well as her mother. Maybe he could make sense of everything that had happened in the past twenty-four hours.

Keeping to the far edge of the pavement so she would be less noticeable, Chessa sprinted toward town. After a few turns, she reached Pinion Lane and veered right. When she saw a Volvo standing in the carport of Ferguson's cottage, she smiled. Back in high school, he told her he would own a Volvo one day. Not a Mercedes or a muscle car. A Volvo, just as steady as he was.

Chessa mopped sweat off her face, hurried to the front door, and entered without knocking. Ferguson never locked the door. He believed in the ultimate goodwill of man. She strode across the *neutral space,* as Ferguson called it, the furniture done in beiges and grays to emphasize the neutrality. She drew up short at his office door.

An IN SESSION sign hung on a hook.

~ * ~

Marcus eyed the scones on the tray that Wolfe's white-starched maid carried in, and his stomach growled. He had skipped breakfast.

"This way, gentlemen," the maid said.

Marcus followed her through an ornately carved archway into a library as grand as the rest of the house. Floor to ceiling bookshelves were crammed with leather-bound books. A ladder on casters allowed for easy access to the upper shelves. He spied a few authors' names, including Dickens, Fielding, and Greene, and wondered how many books were first editions. And there were more clocks. Dozens of them. The ticking made his teeth ache.

The maid set her tray on a pushcart and said, "Do you require anything else?"

Marcus shook his head.

She had barely retreated into the foyer when Keegan said, "Hey, did you know Senator Wolfe is an amateur photographer?" He plucked a book from an eye-level shelf and flipped through it. "The guy's good."

"Put that back." Marcus nabbed a scone and downed it in three bites. While wiping his fingers with a napkin, he spotted camping gear tucked into the far corner of the room, gear that should have been stowed in a closet somewhere. He wadded the napkin and plopped it into the wastebasket near Wolfe's desk as he took a closer look at the gear. Was someone planning on going camping? Chessa? He looked for telltale signs of her in the room but found none.

Keegan waggled the topmost book. "This one is all about Lake Tahoe, and he's added tidbits of info, like, did you know Tahoe is the highest lake in the U.S.? Or that it was formed over two million years ago?"

Marcus did. Thanks to his foster mother and her love of Lake Tahoe, he was a walking encyclopedia on the area, but for the moment, he was more interested in the empty tumbler sitting on the desk and the near-empty decanter on a side table against the wall. He had heard a rumor that Wolfe was a tippler. Was it true?

Keegan whistled. "Will you look at Ms. Troon?" He displayed the photo book to Marcus. "She's a blonde."

"Women change their hair color all the time."

"Yeah, but she's prettier now. Think she had a nose job?"

Marcus whipped around. "Put the book down, deputy."

"Yeah, sure." Keegan replaced the book and headed for one of a pair of tooled leather armchairs. "These look perfect for the Inquisition, don't you think?" He started to sit.

Marcus cleared his throat.

Keegan remained on his feet. "Smells good in here, doesn't it? Female. You know"—he snapped his fingers—"like cinnamon."

"Probably Wolfe's wife's scent lingering around." It wasn't Troon's, which was tart, like the woman. When Marcus was assured that Keegan had settled down, he continued his tour of the library, noting the dozens of framed photographs of Wolfe with powerful people. Many included his wife Adriana, who was night to Chessa's day. Dark hair, intense eyes, and a challenging smile. Gauging by the way Wolfe and she stood in each photo, bodies turned toward each other, neither looking off as if wanting to be someplace else, a couples' psychologist might say they were madly in love.

How would Wolfe, less than a year after his wife's death, handle his stepdaughter being accused of murder?

## CHAPTER 10

Chessa stared at the IN SESSION sign and alarm cut through her. In her haste to enter, she must have missed seeing the patient's car. Was the fact that Ferguson was with somebody an omen? Should she flee? She tore to the window and peeked through the split in the curtains. There wasn't a second car in the driveway. Maybe Ferguson had hung the sign on the door in error, or the patient had gotten a ride or come on foot. Chessa listened at the door and heard a woman sobbing. *Shoot.*

Despite the strains of Beethoven's *Eroica* playing from a state-of-the-art stereo system, Chessa couldn't find her calm. Stay or run? Were there other choices? The glass and brass clock on the mantle by the fireplace read five to nine. Ferguson took patients on the hour, starting at eight A.M. She could wait five minutes.

Not keen on bumping into anyone other than him, Chessa slipped into the den on the opposite side of the living room and slid the door closed. She eyed the overstuffed beige chair with yearning, wanting to sink into its comfort, but she knew if she did, she might drift into a dark sleep. Whatever drug she had been given—she was convinced she had been dosed with something—was still working its bitter magic on her. Had Zach drugged her? Her soul ached at the notion.

The door to Ferguson's office squeaked open. Chessa heard the requisite good-byes and the click of the front door shutting. She drew near the connecting door, her heart banging in her chest. Would Ferguson help her or dismiss her? Believe her or think she was guilty? With trembling fingers, she twisted the doorknob and slipped into the living room.

Ferguson whirled around, looking as GQ as always, his goatee trimmed, his gray silk shirt wrinkle-free, and the pleats in his gray trousers precise. He smiled. "I thought I heard somebody enter. What's—"

"Zach's dead," Chessa said, unable to hold back. "Murdered. The sheriff thinks I did it. I couldn't have. Not even if I was—"

Ferguson strode to her and wrapped his arms around her.

The warmth and closeness ruptured the dykes. Tears spilled from Chessa's eyes as she told him everything: waking up next to Zach, alerting 911, the bursts of memory. "I had to have been drugged, right?"

~ * ~

Marcus set the picture frame down as Senator Wolfe strode into the library looking like he had just returned from a day at the beach, his salt-and-pepper hair sopping, his jogging shorts and Grateful Dead T-shirt equally wet. A big, slow Labrador retriever trailed him and settled on the carpet beside the desk. The dog looked up at the senator with sad eyes.

"Detectives, forgive me." Wolfe's basso voice suited his gigantic frame. Not many senators weighed in at six-five, two hundred-plus pounds. He offered his hand.

Marcus shook it, noting the odor of Listerine and fine red lines of rosacea that marred Wolfe's otherwise handsome face. Had he indulged in a late-night drink or an early-morning one? With his stepdaughter on the run, was he craving a belt?

Wolfe inadvertently glanced at the tumbler on his desk then offered Marcus a bemused smile. "Ms. Troon told you I was in a meeting. I was actually finishing my workout. *Shh*. Don't tell the press."

"Being a triathlete takes dedication."

"You look like you work out, too, Detective."

"Purely recreational."

"I don't believe that. An army man wouldn't let himself decline." Wolfe jabbed a finger at him. "Lieutenant, right? Two combat medals. No injuries. If I've got my facts straight, a preacher found you at the age of thirteen and put you into foster care service, and your foster mother turned you around."

After moving into his foster mother's house, Marcus learned to trust people. *One foot in front of the other,* she had drummed into Eddie and him. She made him get involved, do community service, think about people other than himself. *Tune in*. While in the army, he did the same. Until Eddie offed himself. Then Marcus found himself questioning authority. Once he returned stateside, with foster mother's help, he found his path: *Make the law matter*.

"Ms. Troon works fast," Marcus said.

"She's a wizard with Google."

"Me, too," Keegan chimed. "I love the Internet."

"Ms. Troon didn't Google me, deputy," Marcus sniped. "She got her hands on my personnel file."

Wolfe grinned, and Marcus disliked him even more than he thought he would.

"I work out three times a week," Wolfe said as he strode to his mahogany desk. He cursorily read a few papers. "Swimming, running, biking from 4:30 to 7:30 A.M., like clockwork."

Was he giving Marcus his alibi? How guilty was he? Or was it Wolfe's habit to fill in the blanks?

"Heaven forbid I put on a pound. The constituency won't allow it."

Marcus shifted his feet. They wouldn't appreciate a drunkard, either, he was pretty sure.

"Why are you here, detective?"

"Sir, I'm sorry to tell you this, but your son-in-law was murdered."

"Zachary? No!" The man faltered. "When?"

"Didn't Reverend Diggs tell you?"

"Davey? What does he have to do with this?"

"He came to your stepdaughter's cabin this morning, while we were investigating. He said one of his flock alerted him to the situation. Chessa—"

"You can't possibly think Chessa has anything to do with Zach's death."

Marcus hadn't said that. Interesting that the senator would leap to that conclusion. "Sir, it's highly possible. She was there, covered in blood. She called 911. While we were questioning her, she skipped out."

Wolfe sank into the ergonomic desk chair. "Oh, lord, she must be scared to death. She didn't do this. She adored Zach."

Marcus had seen lots of adoring wives pop their husbands. "Sir, she takes diazepam."

"For sleepwalking."

Wolfe glanced toward the floor above. Was Chessa hiding upstairs?

Marcus took a step closer to the desk. "Sir, is she here?"

Wolfe met his gaze. "No." Not a hint of deception.

"She called you this morning. What did she say?"

"She didn't call—" Jeremiah Wolfe leaped to his feet; the chair squeaked. "Patience!"

In an instant, Troon came into view.

"Did Chessa call earlier?" Wolfe demanded.

"She left a message."

"Why wasn't I informed?"

"You were"—she wove her hands together—"busy. All Chessa said was, 'It's me. Call me.'" Troon pursed her paper-thin lips, looking as sour as if she had sucked the juice from a dozen lemons. "She's left messages like that before."

"Leave us."

Troon stepped backward until she exited the room.

"My stepdaughter"—Wolfe licked his upper lip—"is a high-strung young woman, Detective. She's been lost without her mother."

Marcus would bet Wolfe was, too, hence the drinking. "Your wife was active in a lot of Nevada's affairs," he prompted, hoping that talking about her might make Wolfe let down his guard.

"Adriana was my better half for over twenty years. She was tireless. She wanted me to strengthen our schools and clean up Lake Tahoe, both physically and culturally." Wolfe left the safety of his desk and paced the room, his gaze locked on the lake beyond the window.

Marcus followed his gaze. Was Chessa Paxton somewhere in the backyard, prepared to make her escape across water?

"Last year, my wife and I were in Geneva." Wolfe spun back to face Marcus. "I sit on a committee that studies global warming." A pained expression crossed the man's face. Marcus didn't know where he was going with the conversation, but he didn't want to stop any train of thought that might lead to finding Chessa. "We had the afternoon off. We were headed for the Musée de l'Horlogerie. My wife collected clocks." Wolfe gestured toward the timepieces. "I got waylaid by a colleague, so I told Adriana to go ahead. Seconds later, the taxi she was in exploded. It was a freak accident. A faulty gas tank." He shuddered. "Chessa and I were devastated. Chessa's sleepwalking episodes started after that. She..." Wolfe's voice faded. He faced the lake again.

Marcus hated when people didn't finish sentences. He didn't like guessing games. But he waited.

Wolfe grimaced. "Adriana wanted Chessa to become a lawyer, to follow in my footsteps, maybe even become president." Before serving in the senate, Wolfe had been a well-respected litigator. "She—"

"Chose another path?"

"Exactly."

Marcus frowned. *Enough with the walk down Memory Lane.* "Sir, where is Chessa? It will help her chances if she comes in willingly."

"Chessa hated law," Wolfe went on as if he hadn't heard Marcus. "She worked at a law firm through college as an intern, to please me, but she truly hated the law. She tried journalism for a bit, but she found it grueling, especially when her mother or I didn't agree with her slant." He smiled sadly. "She always dreamed of becoming a costume designer. She said art was in her blood. You see"—Wolfe coughed once into a fisted hand—"Chessa's father was an artist. A craftsman by trade, but he also painted. Oils, specifically."

"Get to the point."

The telephone rang once. The intercom crackled. Through it, Troon said in her crisp voice, "Senator Wolfe, Reverend Diggs is on the line. He called earlier, while you were exercising."

Wolfe lifted the telephone receiver and depressed the button. "Hello, Davey."

Another button on the panel of telephone lines lit up. Marcus glanced toward the hall, his ear attuned for sound. Was someone listening in on the conversation? Chessa? Or was the hands-on Troon monitoring every move Wolfe made?

"Yes, terrible news, Davey, just terrible." Wolfe's face was as fixed as a wax statue's. "She hasn't been arrested, but she's on the run. Calm down, Davey. There wasn't anything you could have done." He listened and nodded. "Thank you, yes, I appreciate your concern. I'll call Wally myself."

As Wolfe hung up, the other light on the console went dark.

"Davey's a dear family friend," Wolfe explained as he strolled to Marcus's side of the desk. "Very concerned."

*How about Wally Evert?* Marcus wondered. *Why do you need to call him?*

Wolfe said, "So, where were we, Detective?"

"Chessa's father."

"That's right. Art is in Chessa's blood. I assume you know about her father."

"He's in prison for murder."

"That's why she fled, of course. He claimed he was framed, and she fears she will suffer the same fate. At least that's my take."

A muscled ticked in Marcus's jaw as he thought of his brother, Eddie, and how he had been accused of a crime that he didn't commit. Eddie would have run, too, if the rod-up-his-rear sergeant hadn't held him at gunpoint.

A security beep cut the air; an exit had been breached.

Marcus shoved thoughts of Eddie aside and charged out of the library. Instead of finding Chessa leaving, he bumped into Tallchief entering.

"A hiker just found a massacre in Spooner Meadow," Tallchief said, out of breath, his eyes blazing with fury. "And get this? All the victims are wearing fairy tale costumes."

## CHAPTER 11

Chessa sat on the sofa in Ferguson's living room and tilted her head back. It was barely nine thirty in the morning, but she was too exhausted to keep her eyes open. Ferguson was roaming the kitchen, noisily pulling dishes and silverware from the cabinets and drawers. He'd offered to get her something to drink and eat. Despite the clatter, Chessa willed her muscles to relax.

Suddenly she couldn't breathe, couldn't move. She was there, in the meadow.

*The scent of Shalimar and pine trees and death smashed together. Revulsion churned inside her. A heavy weight lay on top of her. If she didn't get out from under it, her chest would explode. She shoved the body off and dared to look at the others. Snow White lay beside her, eyes wide, brown wig halfway off her head, two bullet holes in her chest. Prince Charming lay beyond Snow White. Plus there were eight dwarves and Red Riding Hood. Blood was everywhere.*

Chessa jolted upright. Her fingernails were digging into the chair arm. Had she fallen asleep? No, it wasn't a dream. The massacre was real. She willed herself to remember more.

*Bullets slammed into Snow White; she tumbled backward, knocking Chessa to the ground. Chessa's fingers tangled in the laces of Snow White's dress. They fell backward as one unit.*

Chessa leaped off the couch. That was why she hadn't been shot. Snow White had protected her. The grommet Chessa had found in her gown had come from the woman's costume. "Ferguson!" She raced to the kitchen. "I remember. I was kidnapped. Zach. The guard. All these people."

Ferguson set the teapot leaking steam out of its spout onto the stove and braced Chessa's shoulders. "Slow down."

"I was pushed. Into a van. A security guard was the driver. Zach..." She told him about the meadow, the massacre. She gave a list of the costumed characters that were murdered.

"Are you sure? Maybe you're remembering a nightmare. Did you drink too much at the party?"

"I didn't drink anything other than a bottle of water." Chessa broke free and paced the room. "It had to have been laced with something."

"Who gave you the water? Zach?"

"Wally Evert." Chessa recalled how Evert and her stepfather swaggered up to her. Wally claimed Zach gave him the bottle of water. Seconds later, she felt sick. She ran to the restroom. Zach met her at the door. "The sheriffs." She raked her hair with her fingers. "They'll think I did it. They'll think I killed all those people."

"Don't be ridi—"

"What if somebody planted something of mine there?"

"You've got to get over this paranoia of being framed."

"My father—"

Chessa would never forget when she was ten years old and her mother caught her calling prisons in Nevada, searching for inmates with the last name Paxton. Adriana wrenched the telephone out of her hand and told her to forget about her father. But Chessa couldn't. Her past with him was like a favorite film she replayed in her mind: tumbling on the floor, swimming in the lake, his hand on hers teaching her how to draw. The day the sheriff came to take him away, her father and she were sitting at the kitchen table, a bowl of soup in front of each of them. Neither lifted their spoons.

"Ferguson, what if my father wasn't lying? What if he was framed? Jeremiah said someone high up in the sheriff's department made sure the murder charge stuck. What if an officer in the Washoe County Sheriff's Department plans to do the same to me?"

Another memory niggled at the recesses of Chessa's mind, about Zach and the redheaded guard, but she couldn't piece it together.

Ferguson clasped her arm. "Let me give you something to calm you down."

"No drugs." Chessa pulled free. Her breath snagged. "You. You called me last night. Why?"

"To see if you were okay. You get anxious at functions. C'mon, take one Ativan."

"No." She had to stay clear-headed. No masking her pain. No going *dull.* "I've got to leave."

"You need to call an attorney."

"The only one I know is Jeremiah's." Chessa glanced at the door. "I can't stay here. They'll find me. I need cash. I have to go paperless until I can find out the truth."

"*Paperless*?" Ferguson coughed out a laugh. "You sound like Jason Bourne in the Ludlum novels."

That was exactly how Chessa felt. She had a faulty memory and no future if she didn't figure out the truth. Except she didn't have the skills Bourne had to survive.

"The sheriff will demand you tell them everything you know about me, Ferguson." Chessa's breathing came out short and staccato. "They'll want to know what we talked about in our sessions." How she had wondered, over and over, whether she could kill like her father had.

"I know an attorney. I'll call—"

"I need a change of clothes."

"I don't have anything that'll fit you."

"One of your girlfriends has to have left something here."

"I'm girl-free of late."

"You're never girl-free." Chessa bolted toward Ferguson's bedroom at the back of the house. Its chaotic state was a far cry from the order in the rest of the place. Shirts were thrown on the silk chairs, laundry tossed on the floor, the bed unmade. She whipped open the folding doors of the closet.

"I'm not kidding," Ferguson said from behind. "I cleared out everything female a month ago. I'm starting over, although I could make room in my life for you."

Chessa spun around, her throat suddenly thick. In high school, Ferguson had declared his love for her and she had rebuffed him. Now there was something in his tone. Deep concern registered in his eyes. Could he have killed Zach so he could win her heart?

No. Insane. Zach's death was linked to the massacre. It had to be.

"That was insensitive of me." Ferguson's face flushed. "You know I only want your happiness. That's all I've ever wanted." He pulled a shirt, a pair of chino shorts, and a belt from the closet. "Here. I'm afraid I don't have a pair of shoes that will fit."

"That's okay. The ones I'm wearing are fine. But I'll need something to dress my blisters."

"In there." He pointed to the bathroom.

Chessa hurried inside and closed the door. The room was tidier than the bedroom by a mile, its granite counters and floors sparkling clean, towels neatly hung. She switched clothes, tied the long-tailed shirt in a knot at her waist, and cinched the shorts with the belt. While hunting down a tube of ointment and a box of Band Aids, she caught a glimpse of herself in the mirror: hollow cheeks, scratches and bruises, matted curls. At least she could fix the hair. She opened drawers and found a pair of scissors. Her hands trembled as she reached for them. She breathed easier when she touched them and had no tactile memories of stabbing Zach. Granted, they were not the scissors the killer had used to murder him, but Chessa was certain that the last time she had held scissors was to make minor alterations to Zach's costume before the ball. And she had used big-handled scissors, not the antique ones with small finger holes. Since the age of twelve, Chessa had collected sewing gear. Her mother picked up items for her whenever she traveled. The day before she died, Adriana called Chessa from Geneva to tell her she had purchased the most adorable Victorian doll pincushion. Chessa was going to love it.

Tears pressed at the corners of her eyes. She swiped them aside and lopped off clumps of her ringlets. She dumped them into the stainless steel garbage basket. In minutes, the front half of her head was trimmed.

Ferguson knocked on the door. "I called the attorney but reached an answering service."

"Come in."

He pushed open the door and his mouth dropped open. "Wow. Big change. Want me to catch the back?"

"No thanks, I can—" Chessa shook her head and the room began to spin. She clutched the rim of the sink as a memory that had nipped at the edges of her mind came into focus. When Zach deposited her in the shuttle van, he pushed her hair off her face. His touch. The love in his eyes. No way did he want to get divorced. But after he buckled her seatbelt, he climbed into the passenger seat up front. Why didn't he sit with her?

"The guard!" she blurted. "He called Zach a pansy. There were pansies strewn on the floor by Zach's body."

"I'm not following."

"He must have killed Zach because Zach was part of it. Don't you see? There were two men in the clearing. Two. The guard spoke to someone else. It had to be Zach. I can't picture him there, but it had to be him." Chessa swallowed hard. "They killed them all. With guns. I...I was protected by Snow White."

Anger swelled in Chessa; anger at Zach for being involved and anger at herself for blocking his participation from her consciousness. "How could he do it, Ferguson? He hated guns. Hated them." A couple of months ago, she had wanted to go to a shooting range. Zach had forbidden it.

Ferguson took hold of her. "Chessa, let me hypnotize you. We'll figure out the whole picture, and then we'll try the lawyer again."

Chessa shuddered beneath his touch, feeling like the human equivalent of high-powered electrical wire, flailing about with spastic energy. She twisted free. "I've got to go. I need some money and a cell phone."

"I can't lend you my phone. My patients' confidentiality—"

"Can I borrow your car?"

"And then what? Where will you go? How can I reach you?"

Chessa wasn't sure. A special events coordinator, even a costume designer, always has a plan in mind. Step one is always followed by step two. But right now? Living moment to moment? She had never felt so unfocused in her life.

## CHAPTER 12

Marcus paced Senator Wolfe's office, angry at Tallchief for ordering him to stay and finish what he'd started with the senator. There were eleven dead in a meadow, each wearing fairy tale costumes. Was the massacre related to the death of Chessa Paxton's husband? Was she involved? Man, he wanted a fresh look at the crime scene before officials and media trashed the area.

Wolfe was talking on the telephone, looking like a boxer in his fifteenth round, ash-white and whipped. He had been making requisite calls for ten minutes. Marcus understood damage control was necessary before the whole Lake Tahoe area went berserk, but Wolfe was pressing the limits of Marcus's patience.

When Wolfe hung up, Marcus cleared his throat. "Sir, no more delays. I want facts."

"We don't know if those people were at the ball," Wolfe said, his voice hoarse with emotion, "but if they were, I might know some of them. I should speak with their families, their loved ones."

Marcus was impressed that Wolfe would consider someone else's feelings at this moment, seeing as his stepdaughter was on the run. On the other hand, maybe the guy's interest was self-serving, designed to thwart Marcus from pursuing his investigation. He folded his arms. "We were discussing Chessa's possible whereabouts. Her friends. Her associations."

Wolfe sagged. "There's one person she might trust. A therapist who works out of his house in Incline. Chessa and I—" Wolfe eyed the empty tumbler on the desk. "We haven't spoken much since her mother died."

"Name of the therapist?"

Wolfe provided the information then slumped in his chair, fingertips kneading his temples.

Marcus smacked Keegan on the shoulder. "Let's go, deputy." As they neared the door, he noticed the camping gear again and whirled around. "Senator. The backpack. Why is it here?"

"I returned from an outing a few days ago. I like to reorganize my pack before I stow it. Why do you ask?"

"Is Chessa an experienced camper?"

"Chessa?" Wolfe grimaced. "She despises camping. I took her to Marlette Lake when she was eleven. The first night, a dozen spiders crawled into her sleeping bag. The next night, a raccoon came into her tent looking for food. In a word, she was traumatized. The forest will be the last place you'll find Chessa."

~ * ~

Jeremiah Wolfe waited until the front door of his home slammed before pouring a stiff drink. "This is all your fault, Adriana," he muttered as he took his first sip. If only he hadn't fallen for her. If only he'd lived a cleaner, healthier life, maybe his heart wouldn't feel like it had shattered into a thousand sharp pieces with the loss of her. "Patience!"

She didn't answer.

He scrubbed a hand through his hair and downed the drink. He wiped his mouth with his forearm and pressed the intercom button on the telephone. "Patience!"

Jocko raised his head and whimpered.

"Quiet, cur. Patience, answer me!"

A crackle split the air. Through the intercom, Patience said, "What?"

"Get in here."

Jeremiah released the button. What would happen to his career? His stepdaughter was wanted for murder. Reporters would pounce on her father's past. They would dredge up the sordid details and probe until they drew blood. Didn't they realize some secrets were better left buried?

Fury tore at the seams of Jeremiah's tolerance. Pushing the liquor aside, he rose from his chair and paced the room, urging himself to get a grip. Good old Davey Diggs would advise him to get on his knees and pray. Wally Evert would tell him he could buy his way out of any problem. They had no clue. Jeremiah wondered what surrounding himself with fools said about his character. Adriana had introduced him to Evert and Diggs. From this point forward, he would blame his poor choice of acquaintances on her.

Patience strode into the room and struck that patronizing pose she had mastered so well.

If she tapped her toe, Jeremiah would fetch a hammer and nail her foot to the floor. "Get me my personal attorney on the phone."

"The state provides—"

"This is not a matter of state. We've got a media onslaught to ward off."

"Sir, I told you one day Chessa—"

"I don't want a lecture."

"Her mother—"

"Patience, do as I ask." He whacked the desk with his palm. No one, especially Patience, was allowed to denigrate Adriana.

Patience nodded curtly and turned on her heel.

Before she exited, he said, "By the way, where were you last night?"

"I'm sorry?"

"You heard me. I got home from the ball and wanted a telephone conference. You didn't answer my page."

"I went on a date."

"You?" Jeremiah couldn't imagine who would date the Ice Princess.

Patience snarled. "I am not your beck-and-call girl, sir. You were at the ball. I went out. Later, when I got your message, I phoned, but you didn't answer. Were you too drunk to do so?"

Jeremiah had hired Patience straight out of college. She was amiable back then, even cute. When had the transformation to ball-breaker occurred? He swallowed a nasty retort and said, "After I talk to my attorney, get me Wally Evert on the phone."

## CHAPTER 13

Marcus turned north onto Highway 28 and called the precinct. He needed boots on the ground in Incline Village. A clerk asked him to wait as she patched him through to the appropriate person. Keegan, who was sitting in the passenger seat, continued to run his finger along the screen of his iPhone, boning up on Chessa's father's history. He had asked if he could read what he'd discovered to Marcus, but Marcus told him to wait.

Man, how Marcus wished he could crawl inside Chessa Paxton's brain. Was she hoping to pin down last night's sequence of events, maybe flesh out an alibi? Would the therapist—Dr. Fairchild—help her do that? Would he convince her to stay put and wait for the sheriff to show up? Maybe plead insanity? If she hadn't gone to her therapist's, where was she?

Via the rearview mirror Marcus spotted a guy in a dark sedan riding his tail. The guy's baseball cap created a shadow and made it difficult for Marcus to make out his features, but he felt like he'd seen the guy before.

"Keegan," he said to the deputy. "Behind us. Recognize him?"

Keegan swiveled and faced front again. "No, sir."

The driver backed off, probably because he noticed Keegan's sheriff hat and decided his hurry to bypass officers of the law, even in an unmarked vehicle, was not worth risking a speeding ticket.

The clerk came back on the line and said she was patching Marcus through to the person in charge of traffic. Quickly Marcus ordered units in the Incline Village vicinity to approach Dr. Ferguson Fairchild's house with caution. He provided the address. Marcus also ordered units to assemble at either end of town and lay down Stop Strips, their spikes ready to tear out tires in case Chessa found some way to obtain a car.

He ended the call and said, "Keegan, recap that article."

Keegan turned the phone sideways. "Per a reporter out of Reno, 'Philip Stewart Paxton was living life in the fast lane. The thirty-four-year-old craftsman was a regular at the bars in Tahoe City.'"

"What exactly did he do as a craftsman, do you know?"

"He made artisan tiles for house kitchens and bathrooms."

"Go on."

"The whole thing went down in the early nineties."

Marcus blew out a long stream of air. "Chessa must've been about seven or something."

"Yep. According to locals, Paxton was dabbling in drugs, although his wife swears that he wasn't. 'Few suspected that this charmer would turn into a vicious killer.'"

"*Charmer*?"

Keegan laughed. "Yeah. The Placer County sheriff added that, 'He comes across as an easy-going guy.'"

"Placer County. Good group of people. Where did this happen?"

"Truckee."

Marcus dodged two teens cutting across the road at Zephyr Cove and plowed ahead. "Continue."

Keegan dragged the scroll bar on the cell phone. "Seems Paxton got into an argument with the victim, a car salesman who sold the Paxtons their Honda."

Back when Marcus bought his truck, he had wanted to level the salesman because he'd lied about the interest rate, but Marcus wouldn't have killed him. "There's got to be more to it than that."

"It says Paxton slayed the man in his apartment."

"The salesman's?"

"Paxton's. He stabbed him twenty-six times."

"Whoa! That's some kind of anger. Why did the salesman go there? Was Paxton's wife home? Witnesses?"

"Doesn't say." Keegan toggled down the screen. "One official said, 'Paxton was found passed out, the weapon in his hand. He swore he was framed."

Marcus's stomach roiled. His brother, Eddie, had said the same thing to his sergeant. The guy told Eddie to curl up and die. Eddie did him one better.

~ * ~

Chessa sat in the driver's seat of Ferguson's Volvo, but she didn't turn on the car. She hadn't even inserted the key into the ignition. She felt tense and brittle as doubt threaded its way into her psyche. Could she prove herself innocent? Could she do it alone? One step at a time. First, she had to contact

Helena. Yes, she had a weekly lunch appointment scheduled with Helena tomorrow, Saturday, but this couldn't wait until then. Second, she needed to learn more about the passports.

And after that?

Ferguson leaned on the driver's window frame. "Storm's coming."

Usually the greatest risk at Lake Tahoe in the summer was getting a severe sunburn, but occasionally big boomer thunderstorms formed over the basin, and authorities warned hikers and boaters to head for cover. Bloated gray clouds were gathering overhead.

"The storm is the least of my worries," Chessa said, forcing herself to sound chipper. By the look on Ferguson's face, he clearly didn't believe her bravado, but she held strong. "Thank you. I don't know what I would've done without you."

"What about the attorney?"

"I'll contact you." Chessa jammed the key into the ignition. Her fingers shook as she twisted the key. The engine turned over.

Ferguson kissed her cheek. "Be careful. If the rain turns to hail, the roads could get messy."

~ * ~

As Marcus passed the first roadblock leading into Incline Village, his cell phone jangled. He answered, hands free. "Newman."

The officer at Dr. Fairchild's house spit out his report.

"She what?" Marcus carped. "What's the license plate number of the Volvo? What do you mean the doctor doesn't remember? What kind of idiot doesn't—" Marcus ground his teeth together. "Great, yeah, hold on." He tossed his phone to Keegan. "Call the DMV and track down this vehicle."

# CHAPTER 14

Chessa drove toward South Lake Tahoe, her body thrumming with energy. She didn't look forward to the resistance she would get from Helena about handing over the list of ball attendees and employees. Privacy was a major issue for an immigrant like Helena. Chessa hoped she could drum up a convincing argument before she reached the casino.

Just past Country Club Drive, Chessa was forced, along with other drivers, to pull to a stop. They had to wait while a slew of pink-shirted ten-K *Runners for the Cure* moved west. When traffic didn't move minutes later, even though the tail end of the throng had passed by, she craned her neck to see what was the hold up.

Terror seized her when she spotted a burly officer swaggering down the median checking inside cars. Just beyond him Detective Newman was walking with Deputy Keegan. Jeremiah must have told them about Ferguson. Either that or Newman was psychic. Not likely.

Chessa jammed the car into park, opened the passenger window, and slinked across the console. She peeked over the dashboard and through the windshield. The officer stood six cars away. Newman and Keegan were nowhere in sight.

Quickly Chessa scrambled out the window and landed awkwardly on her heels. A twinge shot up her right ankle. Pinpricks of pain riddled her shins. She crouched down, gave her legs a shake, and, staying low, weaved between cars to the side of the road. She darted through a thicket of gorse that divided the highway from the residential neighborhood. Manzanita nicked her arms. Blood spurted from each scratch. She ignored the pain and burst through to the street and then searched for a route that would keep her in the shadows. Running in the open wasn't an option.

The distant rumble of boats on the lake drew her attention. During high school summers, Chessa had earned money by scrubbing the walkways and polishing the boats at Evert's Marina. The marina was located a few miles away, northwest of Incline. Wally Evert's speedboat was always juiced up.

Granted, it was a risk to go anywhere near Evert's. If he had a hand in drugging her, he was her enemy. But she had to. A boat might be her only means of escape. How to get there undetected was the challenge.

~ * ~

"Detective Newman!" The burly officer beckoned Marcus and pointed at an idling Volvo.

Marcus raced to it. The license plate matched what the DMV had provided, but the car was empty. There were no maps on the seats, no notes giving an indication where Chessa was headed.

Keegan said, "Passenger window's open."

Marcus dashed around the car. He wasn't a tracker and wouldn't presume to be one, but the only way Chessa could have disappeared was through the mass of bushes leading to the residential area.

He barreled through them, thorns ripping his skin, as he wondered how stupid Chessa Paxton was. As a full-blown fugitive, a sheriff could shoot her any time, anywhere. So why did he suddenly feel the irrational need to protect her? After being adamantly against her and ready to arrest her, did he actually believe she might be innocent? Yes. He had his doubts. Could she possibly be guilty of a massacre? She would have had to herd eleven victims to Spooner Meadow in the dark of night. By herself? No way. Something wasn't skewing right.

Marcus paused at an intersection and cupped his hands around his eyes. Not to block the sun's glare—the sun was pretty much obliterated by clouds—but to block out distractions. Dozens of A-framed houses lined the streets. A couple of kids rode bicycles. A third aimlessly kicked a pinecone. Where was Chessa? She couldn't have gained that big a lead on him. He had arrived at the Volvo seconds after traffic came to a standstill.

Keegan pointed east. "Think she went back to her stepfather's?"

Marcus shook his head. Traveling south on the highway would make her too visible, although going to Senator Wolfe's estate made sense. Chessa could hide behind her stepfather's battalion of attorneys. So why hadn't she gone there first? Was she concerned about tarnishing his reputation? Was she that honorable? Or had her stepfather come to the rescue in some other way? When Reverend Diggs called, another light on the panel of telephone lines had lit up. Maybe Troon had cut in to give the senator a hint where Chessa was headed. Before hanging up, Wolfe told Diggs that he would call Wally Evert. Was that code? There had been something shifty in the way Wolfe had looked at Marcus afterwards.

Evert owned a marina a couple of miles northwest on Lakeshore Boulevard. Would Chessa dare go there? Would Evert provide refuge? Worse, would he give her a boat to escape across the lake?

"Keegan, send one of the guys to search the beach. Describe Chessa to him."

The mass onslaught of early morning beachgoers would make it hard to see her, but Marcus wouldn't let the opportunity slip from his grasp.

"Then move the blockade to the westernmost end of Incline."

## CHAPTER 15

Chessa sprinted down Selby Drive and turned right onto Lakeshore. She tore past the Hyatt Lake Tahoe and kept straight, proceeding west on Billionaire's Row, so nicknamed because of the gorgeous, broad-beached properties that were among the most expensive in all of Lake Tahoe.

A minute later, as rain drizzled from the clouds, Chessa darted left through gates that led to a beach area maintained by Incline Village residents. Breathing high in her chest, she dodged people who were leaving due to the imminent storm, but there were plenty of hopefuls remaining: athletes, vendors, and more. She rushed past a pack of teen girls playing volleyball and felt a tug on her heart. How could they be so carefree when her life was unraveling? Grit filled her shoes and wormed its way beneath the Band-Aids. She couldn't stop and fix it. She didn't have time.

The blare of a siren to the east pierced the air. A rumble of thunder sent a shockwave of terror through Chessa, as if God himself was hot on her trail. A second rumble quickly followed the first. She glanced behind and didn't see anybody trailing her, but she couldn't let up.

More rain leaked from the sky as Chessa sped past a woman who was picnicking with a short, milky-white man. The way the man was lecturing the woman in a booming voice made Chessa think of Davey Diggs, and a horrible notion shook her to the core. Diggs had worn a Rumplestiltskin costume to the ball. Had the killer kidnapped the dwarves hoping to capture the reverend who, thanks to his holier-than-thou sermons, had made a lot of enemies? If so, the killer had messed up. Diggs was alive.

As Chessa neared the area where optimistic artists were setting up easels for an art festival, her thoughts about Diggs were quickly replaced by thoughts of Zach. The two of them had planned to attend the festival. He told her he loved art as much as she did. Was that a lie? Was everything, even the way she had met him at the ski resort, a lie? The broken leg? His excuse about waiting for friends that never showed up? Chessa questioned whether her mother, who always worried about Chessa's lack of a love life, had met

Zach previously and paid him to be waiting at the bar.

Chessa tripped over a tin can buried in the sand and cursed, but the pain to her toe was nothing compared to the ache in her heart. If only she could ask her mother to fill in the blanks.

Another explosion of thunder rocked the area. Rain began to pelt the ground. Distracted, Chessa slammed into a lemonade vendor's pushcart and tumbled to her knees.

The vendor yelled, "Watch it, lady!"

From Chessa's new vantage point, she caught sight of a man in a sheriff's uniform darting toward her—not Newman or his partner. Thicker, heavier. He was shielding his eyes from the rain and didn't seem to have spotted her yet. He was about fifty yards away. Also, beyond the park fence, she spied a sedan moving slowly on the street. Her breath caught in her chest when she got a better look at the driver. He was wearing a baseball cap. Was it the same guy who had kept tabs on her at the cabin?

Chessa crept to the backside of the pushcart and crouched out of view. She glimpsed herself in the cart's warped Mylar panel and grimaced, barely recognizing herself. Maybe the sheriff or the driver wouldn't either, but she couldn't bank on that.

About ten feet from the pushcart, a mother was changing an infant while two towheaded children played in a circle around them. On a nearby fold-up chair hung a pink T-shirt and a Thomas the Train baseball hat. Chessa didn't approve of stealing, but her life had turned so topsy-turvy that rules had to be broken. She crawled toward the chair. As she neared, thunder grumbled again. The mother looked up at the sky. Chessa didn't hesitate. She leapt to her feet, seized the clothes, and dashed toward the public restrooms.

One of the children let out a wail, but no one blew a whistle. No one shouted *Thief*!

Chessa disappeared inside the cinderblock bathroom and locked herself inside a dank stall. Quickly, she removed Ferguson's shirt, wedged it between the toilet tank and the wall, and threw on the pink T-shirt. She exited the stall and assessed herself in the damaged mirror by the sinks.

*Not bad.*

She tried to put on the child's train hat. It was too small but adjustable. She unsnapped and lengthened the plastic band, jammed the hat on, and peeked out of the restroom. The thickset sheriff was talking to the lemonade vendor. Neither was looking in her direction. The reporter, or whatever he was, had vanished.

A pack of sullen beach-goers were heading to their cars. Chessa slinked from the restroom and slipped in among them. In seconds, she would need a fresh escape plan. The pack would disperse in the parking lot, and she would be exposed. She almost cheered when she heard the sound of tennis shoes smacking pavement. The ten-K runners she had seen earlier were charging toward her on Lakeshore Boulevard.

Pumping her arms, Chessa joined the ranks and zigzagged into the center of the group. She wasn't wearing a race bib, but nobody seemed to mind.

~ * ~

Marcus wiped rain from his eyes and muttered as he read the sign: *Evert's! The Best Marina in Lake Tahoe.* Beneath those words, Evert boasted that the repair shop employed the most knowledgeable staff. All Marcus cared about was who was entering the area. No one remotely resembled Chessa, but that didn't mean squat. According to the sheriff who had questioned Dr. Fairchild, Chessa had changed her look, not that the doctor was forthcoming about that. The sheriff had found discarded clothes and hair clippings in the bathroom.

The crack of lightning over the northern crest of mountains followed by a crash of thunder did nothing to help Marcus's nasty mood. He scanned the horizon to the east. Chessa hadn't passed through either of the blockades on foot, and officers were checking cars, pedestrians, and every single one of those ten-K runners.

Four fresh-faced deputies, including Keegan, jogged toward Marcus from different directions. Tallchief had taken the more seasoned faction with him to the meadow to investigate.

"She's not here, sir," Keegan said. "We've searched the locker room and the shop and the pier."

"Look again." Marcus signaled for them to make another tour, and then he marched toward the sales shop, prepared to tackle Evert himself.

## CHAPTER 16

Pushing aside the pain that was shooting up her legs, Chessa ran with the pack of ten-K'ers and tried to dredge up more details of last night. Why had Wally Evert drugged her? Had Zach put him up to it? Why would Evert, one of the most powerful men in Lake Tahoe, have done Zach's bidding? Granted, he was one of Zach's newest investment clients, but that wouldn't give Zach carte blanche to boss Evert around.

Rain cascaded down on Chessa and the race entrants as they neared the marina, but the moisture didn't blur her view of three sheriff's vehicles in the parking lot. Four deputies paced the grounds. At the end of the T-shaped pier where Evert's boat was moored, another deputy stood guard.

Chessa cursed. Newman had outwitted her. Quickly she abandoned her goal of escaping via boat; she would run until her legs gave out. Continuing west on foot, she eased in behind a pair of broad-beamed women who were having an argument about Johnny Depp's acting ability.

Seconds later she noticed a roadblock ahead. Officers were stopping cars as well as race participants.

Heart pounding so hard she could feel its pulse in her throat, Chessa doubled back and darted into the parking area of the aging Tahoe Motor Court Motel. She splashed through rain puddles to the registration office and hid on the far side of a soda machine.

Seconds later, she peeked out. No one seemed to have noticed a runner leaving the pack, but she couldn't count on that for long.

Twenty feet of underbrush, dirt, and gravel stood between her and the marina. Seeing no deputies in the immediate vicinity, she tore across the narrow expanse. She flattened herself against the wall of the building, skirted to the door marked Employee Entrance, and slipped inside. A moment passed before her eyes adjusted to the artificial light in what employees called the *bulletin room*. Notices about local events and races, OSHA warnings, and an employee-of-the-month photograph were plastered on the wall opposite the entrance.

Without warning, the door to the outside opened. Chessa raised her hands to defend herself. She dropped her arms when she realized the intruder was only a teenaged girl dressed in the marina's uniform of light blue T-shirt and shorts.

"Hey," the girl said, not making eye contact. She rushed into the locker room on the right, opened a locker, slammed it with a clang, and skipped passed Chessa down the hall. "See ya." Life was too rosy for her to slow down.

Chessa slipped into the locker room. The scent of Lysol seared the lining of her nose and revitalized her like a whiff of smelling salts. Energized, she sorted through a pile of soiled T-shirts that lay on the wooden benches. She selected one and changed into it and then tossed her shirt and the child's hat into an empty locker.

Dressed as an employee, she headed for the sales office, bypassing the mini-lunch room where three employees sat at a metal picnic table. They were talking about their weekend plans while playing cards and waiting for something that smelled like pizza to finish cooking in the microwave.

Up the hall on the left, the glass door to the sales office stood ajar. Chessa crept to the door, peered through the glass, and stifled a gasp. Over the past few months, she had seen the *Evert's Marina: Bigger Is Better* construction signs as she drove along the highway, but she had no idea how huge the place had become. A spiral staircase led to a newly built second floor. The main floor was packed with oars of all sizes, lifejackets, beach toys, and clothing. A few customers roamed the aisles.

At the register, a petite clerk with whom Chessa had worked—Chessa couldn't remember her name—was ringing up a sale for a customer. Unless Evert had moved everything around, the safe that held boat keys was located on the counter behind the register—difficult to access, but not impossible if the clerk left her post.

Chessa inched the door open but shrank back at the sound of raised voices. Marcus Newman, sounding as mad as a German shepherd on a tight leash, marched down the stairs with Wally Evert and a ravishing ash-blonde. Evert, dressed in his customary black shirt and slacks, didn't look much happier than Newman. His fleshy toadlike face was flushed a deep shade of red that matched his hair, and his wandering, strabismus-inflicted right eye practically bulged from its socket. He was talking over his shoulder to Newman. Chessa couldn't make out the gist. She caught: *Detective, Chessa,* and *no idea.*

Again she wondered whether Evert at Zach's command had drugged her, but she pushed the niggling thought aside when she noticed Evert was bouncing a set of keys in his hand. Had he already gone for his daily boat ride or was he going on one soon? If he kept hold of the keys, Chessa would never be able to borrow his boat. She'd have to take another one. No matter what, she needed the kind that could outrun the Coast Guard or any of the other official agencies that Newman might dispatch to apprehend her.

"Hey, Missy, catch." Evert tossed the keys to his sales clerk.

*That's her name,* Chessa thought. *Missy.* Her father owned a restaurant in Tahoe City.

"File them. I'll be going out later."

"Mr. Evert, I'm sorry about—" Missy twitched her head in Newman's direction. "I told him you were busy."

"No big deal." Evert glowered at Newman. "Look, Detective," he said, the words clear as a bell, "all I'm saying is Chessa's a good kid."

"I'm trying to believe that." Newman's tone didn't convince Chessa, nor did his tight jaw, which was ticking with tension. "But humor me. Give me a personal tour of this outfit. Show me any possible hiding places."

"Sure. Whatever rocks your boat." Evert laughed at his apparent use of humor. "Since your men have been all over the inside of the building, let's check out the perimeter, then we'll visit the hangar. Sugar"—Evert caressed the ash-blonde's chin—"I'll be back soon. Pick anything in the store. My treat." He led Newman out the front door.

Twirling the keys around her index finger, Missy the sales clerk returned to her spot behind the counter. She set them down and opened the combination safe.

From across the shop, the ash-blonde said, "Hey, Missy, can you help me?"

"Sure." Missy left the keys on the counter and the safe open and crossed the floor.

Chessa grinned. What was that Chinese proverb? *Luck never gives; it only lends.* She eased the shop door open and stole to the counter. The keys felt warm in her hand. She eyed the rest of the keys and an idea came to her. Hastily she plucked all of them from the safe, tossed them on the floor, and fled.

Near the door to the repair hangar, she heard voices. She paused. Inside, Newman and Evert were grilling a pair of teens that were working on one of the kayaks. Beyond the hangar doors, outside on the pier, two of Newman's men paced in the rain like sentries waiting for the enemy.

A motorboat zoomed past the end of the pier. Water mushroomed from the boat's wake and lapped the pylons beneath. Evert's speedboat, a Baja 40 Outlaw, bobbed at the end of the dock, its white-and-black body defiant and restless as rain bombarded it.

How Chessa itched to get her hands on the wheel, but if she tried to reach the speedboat via the pier, the officers would nab her.

On the shore to the right of the pier rested six canoes, each turned upside down to avoid collecting rainwater. Stealing one wasn't an option. The movement of turning the canoe right side up would alert the officers. But seeing the canoes gave Chessa an idea.

She fled down the hallway, through the locker rooms, and out the side entrance of the building. Flattening herself against the wall, she sidled to the corner nearest the lake and peered around it. Fifty yards stood between her and the speedboat. The sound of water lapping the shore sent a shiver through her. She had only started her twenty-minute swims last week, and she had worn a short-sleeved wetsuit to keep warm. After each, she had needed a hot shower, three cups of coffee, and an hour of sunshine to thaw out.

*Fifty yards,* Chessa told herself. *You can manage fifty.*

She hurried toward the shore and slid into the water. Needles of pain shot through her. She inhaled and dove under the surface. Her chest felt sucker-punched from the cold, but she continued on. She emerged beneath the dock and treaded water while drinking in big gulps of air. Just as she was going to submerge again, she heard a man overhead shout, "Sir, she's here. On the premises. An employee saw her in the locker room."

Chessa cringed. So much for thinking the teenager hadn't paid attention to her.

Footsteps pounded above.

Officers ran to the end of the pier and returned.

"She's not in Mr. Evert's speedboat," one yelled.

"This way," a man said. Newman. Chessa recognized his voice.

Footsteps retreated. The pier went silent.

Careful not to create a telltale ripple that would reveal her position, Chessa did a head-above-water breaststroke. Five feet. Ten feet. The water was so cold she could barely feel her fingertips. She came alongside Evert's boat and fumbled to unhook the tethers holding it to the dock. She gave the Outlaw a shove, driving the tail end away from the pier, and dove beneath the surface again. She came up on the far side.

Staying low, she scrambled onto the ski platform and crept into the craft. She crab-walked to the helm, inserted the key into the ignition, and twisted. The engine sputtered at first and then roared to life. She shoved the gear into forward.

The boat pitched and stalled. Chessa cursed.

"Sir!" a man yelled. "There she is!"

"Stop!" Newman cried while charging down the pier.

He looked oddly receptive, like he might listen to reason. Four more deputies stampeded down the pier behind him, guns raised.

"Don't shoot!" Newman warned his men, even though his hand was on his firearm.

Would he draw it? Chessa wondered. He looked ready to leap into the water in front of the boat. If he did, would she run him down? No, she couldn't. She ground the gear into reverse, backed up ten feet, and then plowed forward, swinging wide of the pier.

Newman kept coming. Faster. He intended to jump. But then he skidded on the slick surface and slid as if he was stealing second base.

Chessa squared the nose of the boat and pulled back on the throttle. As the craft lurched ahead, she yelled, "I was framed, Detective. I'll prove it. I promise."

She wasn't sure if he heard her. She didn't care. The promise was meant as much for her ears as his.

## CHAPTER 17

Marcus couldn't believe he'd lost Chessa Paxton again. Two hundred and sixty-five days out of the year, Lake Tahoe boasted remarkable weather. How had he rated one of the few stormy days to go chasing after a fugitive? Tallchief would throw a fit when he learned Marcus had failed. Chessa was probably having a good laugh.

He turned to the youngest of his deputies. "You. Keep an eye on the speedboat."

"But, sir, visibility's—"

"Watch her."

"Yes, sir."

"You," he said to Keegan. "Get the Coast Guard on the line and give them some bearings."

"Where are you going?"

"To get a key." Marcus hurried to the marina's shop and flashed his badge at the wide-eyed salesclerk. "I need the key to your fastest boat."

"I can't."

"Why not?"

She pointed.

Marcus cut around the counter and saw the clutter of keys on the floor. Chessa was proving to be a clever girl. "Aren't those ID tags attached to them?"

The clerk brightened.

"Help me," Marcus ordered.

They dropped to their knees and pawed through the tangled mess.

"How about this one?" Marcus held up a set of keys with a red-and-white ID tag.

The clerk shook her head. "It's a cruiser. Too slow."

"This one?" He hoisted a key with a miniature blue buoy attached to it.

"That's the Harper's old woody."

"Vintage?"

She nodded. Marcus cursed. A woody wouldn't go over thirty-five miles per hour at best. The delay Chessa had caused was providing her with a hefty lead. Given the swiftness of the Baja 40 Outlaw, she could make landfall in dozens of places inside of ten minutes. He would bet she wasn't stupid enough to choose one of the twelve launching sites or other marinas around the lake. Where was she headed? To a friend's house? To a spot where she could climb to the road and thumb a ride? He abandoned the idea of chasing her, leaving the job to the Coast Guard, and said, "Where's your boss?"

"Upstairs. He doesn't want to be—"

Marcus stormed up the stairs and barged into Evert's office. Evert was standing at the window that provided a magnificent view of the lake. Was he watching Chessa escape? In a matter of seconds, Marcus took in the office. A desk. A well stocked bar with stools. A seating area. Dozens of photographs of Evert shaking hands with the most influential people in the state of Nevada hung on the walls. A photo of Evert with his arm around an extremely disfigured woman caught Marcus off-guard. Ex-wife? Relative?

"Mr. Evert."

Evert turned, his face revealing nothing.

"You disappeared in a hurry." Marcus moved closer. "Did you plan that?"

"Plan what?"

"Don't play coy. Chessa Paxton escaped in your boat."

"I had nothing to do with it." Evert raised his hands, but a smile played at the corners of his mouth.

"Your girlfriend," Marcus said. "Where is she?"

"She left. She had a hair appointment."

"Did you tell her to distract your salesclerk?"

Evert shook his head. "C'mon, Detective, you guessed what would go down. Chessa showed up here and she stole my boat. But that's as smart as she'll get." He left his post at the window and sauntered toward Marcus. "My bet, she's headed for her stepfather's as we speak. She'll throw herself at his feet and beg for help. Why? Because Chessa has had a rough life. She's not equipped to do much more than follow orders."

That didn't sound like the woman Marcus had been tracking. In fact, she was proving to be much more resilient than anybody seemed to know. She fled the cabin, eluded the sheriff, changed her look, abandoned the car she'd borrowed, and thought ahead enough to know she needed a high-speed boat to make her getaway.

~ * ~

Jeremiah Wolfe stood at the window of his home office and watched the rain hammer the lake. The reflection from the dark clouds made the water look pitch-black. His mood felt equally dark. He picked up the phone and dialed.

The person on the other end answered, "Phoenix."

*What crap,* Jeremiah thought. *Code words.* Except it wasn't crap. The phoenix bird—adopted as a symbol of early Christianity—always holds sway over underlings because of its ability to rise, unscathed, from the ashes. This Phoenix was no different.

Jeremiah bit back bile and continued. "I just spoke with Wally. Chessa drove off in his boat."

"They're not going after her?"

"They've dispatched the Coast Guard."

"Where's she headed?"

"I would imagine where she always winds up. Here."

"I'll contact our man. He'll know what to do."

"Did you forget that a sheriff is stationed at my place?"

The line went dead.

# CHAPTER 18

Cutting through the choppy water, Chessa became wetter, her clothes soaked from the rain as well as the spray of the lake. She endured the chill and switched off the boat's radio deck. Tracking one boat on a span of water the size of Lake Tahoe would be difficult, but there was no sense letting the GPS system or the emergency locator transmitter make her an easier target for the Coast Guard.

How had it come to this? If only she could turn back the clock. But she couldn't. Where could she go? Who could she trust? If she went to Jeremiah's, would he turn her over to the sheriff? Would the sheriff anticipate her decision and station his men around the perimeter? Maybe they had all gone to Evert's Marina, or perhaps they had learned about the massacre in the meadow and had convened there.

Keeping a sizeable distance from land, she headed southeast. As she neared the estate, she slowed the boat, raised a hand to shield her eyes from the rain, and scanned the shoreline. Visibility was limited in the downpour, but she could make out the dock and the boathouse.

And then she caught a glimpse of something. Metal? Glass? Maybe binoculars. She noticed a lone figure in the hills, short of the dock. Was it one of Newman's men, searching for her, ready to alert the others?

She didn't wait to find out. She tugged the steering wheel hard to the right.

At the same time, a sound pierced the storm. A crack.

Something hit the boat. A bullet?

Pulling out all stops, Chessa raced the Outlaw toward the California side of the lake. As the speedboat forged ahead, she glanced over her shoulder. No boat had launched from the dock. No one was chasing after her. She wiped rain from her eyes and wondered whether she had imagined the attack.

Minutes later, she realized she hadn't. She heard a chug-gulp noise, like the engine was stalling. She eyed the gas gauge and moaned. The bullet must have hit the tank because the gauge read nearly empty.

Chessa considered new landing options. Public beaches could be rocky and unpredictable, but Newman wouldn't expect her to make that choice. She stared into the wet gloom and shuddered, not from the cold that was clutching her core, but from a memory. During high school, her girlfriend Jewel and she had made it their mission to discover every beach spot in Lake Tahoe: the ways in and the ways out. They'd had such joyous times exploring. A year later, Jewel was dead. Killed by a mugger. Chessa didn't have a clue whether Jewel's parents still lived in the Rubicon Bay area, but if they hadn't moved, maybe she could beg them for help. Newman wouldn't know about Jewel. Her name wasn't in Chessa's address book, only etched on her heart. Could she go fifteen miles on a gallon or less of fuel?

With Maggie's Peak as her navigational point, Chessa motored toward Rubicon Bay. Twice she held her breath as larger boats crossed her path, but neither turned out to be a Coast Guard vessel.

Near the famous Fleur du Lac estate, its gazebo memorable from *The Godfather Part II*, the engine sputtered. Chessa coaxed the Outlaw forward, but it coughed and died at the bend near the public beach known as Meeks Bay, a good two miles from shore and longer from Rubicon Bay.

As if mirroring Chessa's dilemma, lightning slashed the sky and thunder boomed, and then hail—as Ferguson had predicted—began to pelt Chessa and the craft. Through the noise, she heard the thrum of an engine. A powerful engine. It had to be a Coast Guard vessel.

Chessa couldn't remain on the idle speedboat. She strode to the stern and rummaged through the holds beneath the padded seats. She swore under her breath as she searched. There wasn't a wetsuit and there weren't any life preservers, either. Didn't the law require them? How could Wally Evert be so lax? Chessa snagged a tube of greasy sunblock and a pair of men's swim trunks. A thick layer of goo might offer some protection from the cold water, and the trunks would be lighter in the water than the heavyweight shorts Ferguson had loaned her. Quickly she switched into the swim trunks, lathered herself with sunblock, and transferred the cash Ferguson had given her—sopping wet after her foray beneath the pier—to the zipper pocket on the inside of the trunks, and then she settled onto the ski platform at the stern of the boat.

Teeth gritted with determination, she lowered herself into the water.

Thanks to her earlier swim, the chill didn't shock her as much as it had before, but apprehension about the distance she had to swim practically crippled her.

Two miles. Two long miles.

*Go, go, go.*

Chessa pushed away from the boat and swam freestyle. Ten strokes. Twenty. Thirty. The cold stung her eyes. She couldn't see beneath the surface because the dark blue water, thanks to the storm, was inky black.

Switching to breaststroke, she lifted her face out of the water and searched for the shoreline. All she needed was a glimpse to feel a connection to reality.

Her teeth chattered. Her fingers tingled and her arms felt rubbery. She couldn't wiggle her toes. She flipped onto her back and gulped in air. Her lungs felt like they had been shrink-wrapped. Panic threatened to consume her. No matter how much she had prepared herself for the effects of the icy water, she couldn't ward away the terror of death.

She started to sink. Water covered her mouth. Then her eyes.

*Fight!* a voice shouted within her. Her mother's voice. *Fight with all your might.*

Shooting pains cut through Chessa's stomach and her heart.

*Fight!* yelled another voice. Male this time. Zach? No. Her father. Tough, bold. *You cannot drown. If you die, whoever killed Zach and the people in the meadow wins.*

White-hot fury swelled inside Chessa. She propelled herself upward and broke through the surface of the water. A *whoosh* exploded in her ears.

Ahead, she saw Sugar Pine Point.

Less than a mile to go. Impossibly far away, but she had to make it.

Chessa lifted her left arm and sliced it through the water, then her right. Left. Right. Each stroke feeling like she was hoisting a bucket of water.

## CHAPTER 19

Marcus drove toward Spooner Meadow, rain pounding the windshield so hard it made his head ache. As he worked through bits of information, he decided this might be the nuttiest case he had ever handled. Eleven dead in fairy tale costumes and Zach Szabo murdered a few miles away. Were the two events related? Was Chessa the killer? Running from the law made her look as guilty as all get-out. Why was he having doubts?

His iPhone jangled. He pushed the telephone icon on the steering wheel. "Newman."

A deputy from the precinct updated him. The Coast Guard found Evert's abandoned speedboat on the California side of the lake, drifting north of Homewood. It appeared to have had a gas leak. The coasties found no sign of Chessa Paxton and plenty of places she could have made land if she had swum.

Marcus ended the call and muttered, "Swell." He filled in Keegan.

"I'll bet she drowned, sir." Keegan stuffed the remains of their fast food lunch into a paper bag. "The water temp is beyond cold."

Marcus wouldn't make that bet. When he'd seen Chessa in her gown, he had noticed faded tan lines on her bare shoulders, and her biceps were well formed. She was a swimmer. If she had survived, where was she? How long had the boat been adrift? Did she abandon it because she knew someone in the Homewood area? The current was running south to north because of the storm. She might have made land closer to Meeks Bay. What was her next move? Sheriff's men were crawling all over her cabin as well as the casino where she worked.

"Sir." Keegan pointed to the turnoff.

Marcus drove the truck up a well-trampled path and parked in the designated area. He exited the truck and approached a pair of forensic technicians who were taking photographs of tire tracks and footprints, soggy from the spate of rain, some identifiable, others washed out. "Tallchief?" he asked.

"At headquarters over there," a sandy-haired tech said.

"What've you found so far?"

"We've got SUVs, off-road vehicles, dirt bikes, and boot tracks. Lots of boot tracks. A virtual smorgasbord."

Each day, hundreds of people converged at the trailhead and hiked to the backcountry. Heck, Marcus had done it too many times to count, the last time with Ginnie. After she left, he stayed away. He slipped extra-large protective coverings over his Timberlands and tramped between two strands of yellow crime scene tape along a three-foot-wide path of compressed grass. Beyond the tape, lookie loos strained to get a peek, each of them wearing hiking boots, each a possible suspect.

Marcus stopped where the path met Spooner Meadow and inhaled sharply. The intense sunlight hitting his face wasn't as harsh as the view ahead: a mass of people swarming around a cluster of bodies. He counted a dozen sheriffs, the ME, Search and Rescue detectives, and five executive types wearing expensive suits, the kinds that would wrinkle in the rain and heat. Perhaps they were the senator's folks or media. Not FBI. The Bureau wouldn't have been called yet. Captain Armstrong wasn't in the mix. He liked to make an entrance when he arrived. Overhead, RAVEN, the department's helicopter, flew in wide circles. Someone inside the craft was taking photographs of the scene.

With megaphone in hand, Tallchief paced near the white base tent that had been set up as headquarters. He spotted Marcus and yelled, "Get over here!"

Marcus trudged toward the tent, ready for a tongue-lashing.

"You lost Chessa Paxton?" Tallchief said. "She stole Wally Evert's boat?"

"He's not pressing charges."

"Did he aid and abet?"

"No."

Tallchief inhaled then calmly gestured to the bodies. "Eleven dead."

"IDs?"

"On every one of them."

That puzzled Marcus. Why would the killer leave the IDs unless the killer wanted the bodies identified because somehow that would mess up the investigation?

"Who are they?" he asked.

"We're compiling a list. Get a feel for the situation. We'll talk later, back at the tent."

As Tallchief moved away, Marcus wondered why the guy was being nice. Maybe the media was besieging him, and he hoped to cede the mess to Marcus to protect his political future. *Whatever*.

Marcus neared the bodies, and the burger he had eaten on the way over waged a revolt. What a sight. The chests of the victims had been ripped open by bullets. Blood was everywhere. The faces of any that had been wearing masks were no longer hidden. Their eyes were frozen in shock and horror.

Marcus wanted names and details and someplace to heave.

~ * ~

"Doing okay, hon?" the wife that rescued Chessa asked.

Chessa sat hunched by the campfire, a plastic cup of whiskey in her hands. A chill wracked her body despite the warmth of the Patagonia blanket that her rescuers—a tan and weathered couple—had wrapped around her. They were on a camping trip to celebrate their twenty-fifth anniversary.

The wife turned hot dogs on a makeshift grill. "Liquor taste all right?"

Chessa nodded, hating that she was acting like a puppet and answering *yes* whenever someone pulled her strings. She sipped from the plastic cup and let the warm liquor trickle down her throat. She rarely drank the stuff. Both Zach and she had preferred a glass of wine with dinner.

"How about some lunch, hon?"

"Got to keep up your strength," the husband said.

Chessa shook her head and pulled the blanket tighter. She studied the couple and coveted the way the two of them gazed at each other, so obviously in love. She listened to them tell her about the way they had met, their retirement plans, and their college-aged girls who were traveling in Europe between semesters. They didn't press Chessa for answers. She wasn't sure she could provide any. Her tongue was lodged inside her mouth, locked with secrets and fear. She would flee if she could, but she couldn't. She could barely focus. She knew the dull pain in her head would pass when she thawed out, but she worried that she wouldn't defrost before the sheriff showed up and arrested her.

# CHAPTER 20

Marcus kept tight to the designated walking area. Adrenaline popped through his system as it always did at a crime scene. He surveyed the heap of bodies and wondered how Chessa Paxton fit into the picture. The victims at Spooner Meadow had probably attended the ball at the casino. Had Chessa or her husband known these people?

From behind, Keegan said, "Not your typical fairy tale scene, huh?"

Marcus swung around and stabbed a finger at his partner. "If I hear another cute remark out of you, I'll—" He bit back the rest of what he wanted to say. The kid looked green at the gills. "Do not vomit here. There's a spot assigned for puking."

As the deputy hustled off, Marcus decided to pace the perimeter of the meadow. At the line of demarcation where pine trees sprang up, he scoured the ground looking for footprints, discarded candy wrappers, cigarette butts—anything out of the ordinary. He scanned the forest beyond, the pines denser than he'd seen them in years. No broken boughs. No unnatural paths. No recent forest fires. How had the killer arrived? Was he or she nearby, wielding a pair of binoculars to get a close-up look of the investigating team?

Within minutes, Keegan returned with a bag of chips in his hand.

"You must be feeling better," Marcus said.

"Yep."

Marcus shook his head. *Oh, to have an iron stomach.*

"What are we looking for, sir?"

Marcus plucked a piece of grass from the meadow and chewed on it. "Do you see tire tracks?"

"No."

"How do you figure they carted eleven bodies into this area without a car?"

"From the trailhead?"

"Other than the trailhead."

"Haven't the techies reviewed all this?"

Marcus's creed was to look at everything with fresh eyes no matter how many specialists claimed the job was done. "What if the perpetrators didn't enter the meadow from the normal route? What if the trailhead was populated?"

"At midnight?"

"At any time. C'mon, think. Use that brain of yours."

Keegan grinned. Apparently he thrived on abuse. "Maybe they walked in."

"All of them? Walking in the dark?"

"Uh, guess not. Sorry."

"Don't say sorry. It's a good assumption, but I don't think anybody marched in eleven people, and they sure didn't carry them." Marcus raked his hair with his hands. Eleven dead. A spray of bullets. Why not clean individual shots? Less mess, less fuss. Someone was in a hurry. Were the victims ready to rebel?

Marcus glanced at Tallchief holding court near the headquarters tent, the other officers fawning on his every word. It would be an hour or so before the two of them could knock around ideas. He pushed Tallchief from his mind and refocused on the perimeter. Assuming the crimes were related and assuming Chessa was involved, how did that skew his thinking? Was she a liar, a killer, or a victim? Had she been in the meadow? Had she lured the victims there? Would he find tire tracks matching her Toyota Highlander? It wasn't a big enough vehicle to move eleven people. If she herded them in, she would have needed at least one accomplice. Her husband or the redheaded guard she mentioned? No, she had seemed truly frightened of him. If it was Zach Szabo, did he go along with the massacre and, afterward, chicken out? Marcus switched up the theory. What if the guard was the ringleader, and Chessa reneged on the deal? The guard came after her and offed her husband as a warning.

Keegan broke the silence. "You know, in the Snow White story, there are seven dwarves. Why were eight killed?"

"Somebody couldn't count."

"What if only one of these victims was the target and the other ten were subterfuge?"

"Big word, kid."

"College graduate. B.S. Economics at Reno."

Marcus dropped out of UNR his senior year, twelve units shy of a degree in criminal justice. He had intended to finish college after the army, but the war had messed with his head. He had wanted a few years of civilian life before he made any major decisions. A few years had turned into twelve.

"I considered joining the Treasury Department," Keegan went on, "but I gave up when I realized I didn't want to leave Tahoe."

"And law enforcement?"

"I'm a rules guy. I like rules."

Marcus liked order. "So, back to what you were saying." He moved along the perimeter. "Do you think one of the dwarves was the target? Which one? Got their real names?"

Keegan shook his head.

"Sure you do. Spill. I saw you kibitzing with Tallchief after you puked."

"This is my idea, not Tallchief's."

"I repeat, got names?"

Keegan pulled a list out of his pocket. "The eight dwarves are doctors."

"Associated with MASK?"

"No, sir, although they were guests at the ball. Red Riding Hood was Yukiko Kimura, Nevada's Director of Business and Industry."

"That means Senator Wolfe knew two of the victims if we include Paxton's husband." Marcus thought of that last minute at Wolfe's house. The senator had looked smug and in control until Tallchief came running in and announced the massacre. "Weren't the senator and Ms. Kimura at odds lately?"

"Yeah," Keegan said. "She liked growth for Nevada and he was against it, but any one of a bunch of radicals who doesn't like the skyrocketing prices in Nevada might have wanted her dead. She wasn't popular."

Marcus was starting to appreciate his well-informed partner. He snatched the list from Keegan. "This guy, Spitzer. The name sounds familiar."

"He's that nanotech guy who opened a facility in South Lake Tahoe. You know the one, where all the picketers march outside."

"Sure, I've seen them. The fanatics, the homeowners, each with a different agenda."

"You got it. Spitzer's work is very controversial. He was interviewed about a month ago in the *Tahoe Quarterly*. I get it sent to me online. He—"

"I saw the article. Didn't quite understand it."

"There's a lot of good coming from nanotechnology. Those things they call nanobots help detect cancer and AIDs."

"Layman's terms."

"It's molecular manufacturing. Creating things from the bottom up. They combine chemistry and fabrication"—Keegan weaved his fingers together—"to produce precise machines at the nanometer scale. You see, these buckyballs—"

"Bucky what?"

"Carbon molecules with sixty or more carbon atoms. Little nanobot machines. You find them in clothing and creams and medicines and—"

"Did you memorize all this?"

"I read a lot of e-magazines."

Marcus sniffed. He couldn't wrap himself around some of the techno-stuff. He liked the feel of paper in his hands. He had stacks of magazines at home. Each time he looked at them, he wished he had more time to devour them. And e-books? Not a chance. Maybe Ginnie was right about him; he was a renaissance guy. It had a better ring to it than dinosaur.

"That's why you have all these people who are calling nanotechnology freaky science," Keegan said. "They're spooked that nanobots will invade their bodies. You know, like *The Blob*."

Marcus frowned. Would frightened people kill to put an end to cutting-edge science? "Didn't the media make a big to-do about Spitzer's attending the Happily Ever After Ball because he never went anywhere outside his high-security home?"

Keegan nodded. "He wasn't exactly a hermit, but he liked to stay close to his personal computers and home lab. His wife was camera-shy, too."

"Is she one of the victims?"

"Snow White."

"Rotten luck," Marcus said, but he would bet dimes to dollars Spitzer's wife wasn't important in this scenario. "Back to the dwarves."

"They weren't actually dwarves. They were of normal height. One was a facial reconstructionist. Another was an eye specialist. All of them were probably worth a pretty penny."

Marcus massaged his stiff neck. This case was getting weirder by the nanosecond. What did these victims have in common? How did the killer pick them? Did every one of them matter or were one or two, like Keegan suggested, the targets and the rest collateral damage?

"Uh, sir?" Keegan folded the list and tucked it into his pocket. "I almost forgot. Detective Tallchief wants to talk to you."

"Talk or give me an earful?"

Keegan stifled a smile. "If you don't mind me asking, Tallchief and you don't get along. He says that because you screwed up in the army, we have to suffer through your crap."

"He sure has a big mouth."

"Actually he said that *I'm* going to have to suffer through your crap. Exactly what crap would that be?"

Marcus grinned. "Worried I'm going to hamper your chances in the department?"

"Nah."

Marcus smirked. He'd had the same worries when he had partnered with Tallchief. "I went AWOL for a month."

"Why?"

No judgment, just curiosity. Marcus was okay with that.

"I'd seen too much. I stressed out. I went back, finished my stint, and said good-bye."

"Tallchief said it was because your brother died."

Marcus ground his teeth together. "During my teens, I tried everything in the book to get my brother Eddie off drugs. For one short stretch, he cleaned up long enough to enlist in the army. A couple of months in, some guy called him claiming to be one of his superiors. He tells Eddie he has uncovered a major drug shipment and orders Eddie to watch over the stash. Eddie shows up. The guy isn't there, but Eddie stands guard."

"Oh, man, I see where this is going."

"An hour later, Eddie's sergeant shows up, finds Eddie with the stockpile, and arrests him on the spot. The anonymous guy never came forward. Eddie swore he was framed, but because he couldn't remember who called him and there was no record of any call, he was left to fry."

"Sheesh."

"His army-appointed lawyer presented a lousy defense. The verdict was delivered fast—*guilty*. A week later, Eddie hung himself."

"Whoa."

"A month after that, I shipped home and fell into a funk. If only—"

The shrill bite of a whistle pierced the air. At the headquarters tent, Tallchief was waving his hands over his head—grandstanding—beckoning everyone in the field to gather around.

# CHAPTER 21

Marcus strode across the meadow, squinting into the afternoon sun.

"If only what?" Keegan pressed.

"Nothing," Marcus muttered. Keegan didn't need to know that Marcus would always blame himself for Eddie's death. He never should have let him enlist.

"Move it, Newman!" Tallchief bellowed.

Marcus shook his head, amazed at how political ambition and loneliness could change a pretty regular guy. Tallchief never would have acted like a jerk if his wife was still alive. She had been the heart and soul of their marriage.

"Looks like they found something," Keegan said. "A weapon?"

"Or a suicide pact note." Marcus could drum up a whole lot of possibilities. He never admitted to anyone the horrors that invaded his dreams in the wee hours of the morning.

Tallchief flailed something gold and sparkly. "People, we have a slipper. If I recall, Ms. Paxton was missing one just about this size."

"Man, this is like something out of *Cinderella*," Keegan whispered.

"Or *Nightmare on Elm Street*," Marcus said. "Where'd you find it, Tallchief?"

"Beneath Snow White's body."

"That doesn't prove she was here. If you were the killer, would you leave a shoe behind?"

"Are you defending her, Newman? Got a little crush on the princess? Is that why you let her get away?"

A muscle in Marcus's cheek twitched.

"She whacked her husband," Tallchief continued. "At least grant me that."

"I'll grant you nothing at this point," Marcus said, wondering when exactly he'd switched sides. "What's her motive?"

"I'm working on it." Tallchief turned to an evidence officer and handed over the slipper.

"Sir." Keegan tapped Marcus on the shoulder. "I meant to tell you, Chessa Paxton has written some articles. Pieces against expanding the Lake Tahoe area."

Marcus raised an eyebrow. His new partner was a fountain of information. "When? Recently?"

"In college. They're pretty brazen."

Marcus saw where Keegan was going with the theory. Chessa could have been one of the protestors upset with Spitzer or Kimura. "Until I peruse them, let's keep that to ourselves," he said, though the notion gnawed at him. Had Chessa been at the massacre site? Why not mention that interesting tidbit if she wasn't involved? Could she have blanked out something like that? "Hey, Tallchief, what tests have they run on Zachary Szabo?"

"Toxicology," Tallchief said. "Why?"

"Maybe we should have his hands tested for gunpowder residue."

Tallchief marched to Marcus. "You think he was involved here? You think he planted his wife's glittery slipper?"

Marcus stretched his spine. "Let's also run a check on his frog prince costume. See if there's any blood matching these victims."

"You know, Newman, some people are guilty. Not everyone was framed like your brother."

*Or Chessa Paxton's father,* Marcus mused. He breathed slowly through his nose, refusing to let Tallchief get under his skin. "Who's going to be in charge of following up on all these people?"

"The Cap has called in the forces."

*The Cap.* Marcus sniffed. So that was why Tallchief was being such a sycophant. Well, let him cozy up to Captain Armstrong. Marcus wouldn't.

"A couple of other sheriffs' departments are pitching in," Tallchief went on. "You know the drill. I've scheduled a press conference. I'm posting Paxton's picture on television."

"It won't match." Marcus was pleased that he knew something Tallchief didn't. "She lopped off her hair." He would bet she would change her look again, too. At one time, she had been a costume designer. She probably had a flair for disguises.

"Fine, we'll alter the sketch. She's not going to chop off her nose, is she?" Tallchief turned to the crowd. "Back to work, everyone."

Before leaving the meadow, Marcus reviewed the crime scene one more time. If Chessa was involved, how could she have gotten eleven people to the area with little or no struggle? As he marched toward his truck, it dawned on him. The ball was held at the casino. The casino probably had a shuttle bus or one of those idiotic mock cable cars to take people from place to place. Maybe some of the victims had been on the bus before the killers arrived. Maybe they were collateral damage after all.

## CHAPTER 22

Once she was dry and warm, Chessa mustered the courage to ask her rescuers for a ride to South Lake Tahoe. They readily agreed; they were headed in that direction themselves.

Settled into the Subaru's rear seat, the aroma of a midday campfire clinging to her hair, Chessa thought about her next few steps. She was isolated; there was no one she could reach out to other than Helena or Ferguson. Had he been in touch with the attorney yet? Could she risk contacting him again? By now the police must have grilled him. Why hadn't she developed more friendships over the years?

Chessa flinched, knowing why she hadn't, because she had feared the other children's taunts. Her father's imprisonment became hers. Jewel, the one friend who had taken pains to break through Chessa's emotional fortress, had encouraged Chessa to write to her father and tell him how angry she was. Chessa had followed through with the writing. She scribbled a note daily for a year, but she never told him she was angry. Instead she tried to connect by sharing stories about the art classes she was taking and the costumes she was designing for school plays. He never wrote back. The silence broke her heart.

Pressing the bitter thoughts from her mind, Chessa closed her eyes and rested her head against the seat. As her body gave in to exhaustion, another memory of Zach struck her. When he was putting her in the van, he whispered in her ear and told her to *follow orders*. She started to protest but stopped when she caught him gaping toward the rear of the vehicle. Hadn't he expected to see all the others? Snow White, Red Riding Hood, the prince, and the dwarves were sitting in the last row.

"You okay, hon?" the wife asked from the passenger seat.

Chessa opened her eyes.

"You moaned, dear."

"I'm fine," Chessa replied, but she wasn't. Her stomach was sour, her throat was bitter, and her heart was sick with sorrow. Her husband was a killer. How could she have missed the signs? How could Jeremiah and her mother have missed them, too? Zach and they had gotten along so well. Like old friends.

"We've got some muffins if you're hungry."

Chessa shook her head. The quarter of the hot dog she had finally accepted back at the campfire sat like a heavy lump in her stomach.

"You know, you haven't told us your name."

Chessa hesitated then said, "Jewel."

"Pretty name. Do you work at Evert's Marina?" The woman pointed at Chessa's shirt.

Chessa glanced down and fingered the logo. "Uh, no. I bought this at the Salvation Army store."

As they drove south on SR 89, the wife continued to chat nonstop, regaling Chessa with family stories.

Not wanting to appear ungrateful for their hospitality, Chessa nodded and said, "Wow" or "Mm-hm," but the whole time she was thinking about the ride on the shuttle van. The redheaded guard drove; Zach obeyed his commands. Yukiko Kimura was in the Red Riding Hood costume, Chessa was certain of that. Who were the others? Would finding out their identities help her figure out why Zach killed them?

At the junction to Highway 50, Chessa said, "Stop!"

"What's wrong?" The wife twisted in her seat.

"Let me out please."

The rain had subsided. Sunlight was peeking through a break in the clouds. The area at the junction, which was crowded with souvenir shops, drugstores, and motels catering to customers that fed into the casinos less than a mile northeast, was humming with activity. The Cloud 9 Motel, located on the northwest corner, was where Zach and Chessa had spent their wedding night. They had gotten a great rate because she knew the owner Brandi Hayden, a former showgirl at the casino. Brandi owed Chessa a favor.

"Please, stop the car."

The husband veered to the shoulder of the road and braked.

"It's all our talking, isn't it, hon?" the wife said. "I can be such a chatterbox."

"You've been wonderful. You've gone out of your way for me, and I can't tell you how grateful I am." Chessa unbuckled her seat belt and open the door.

"You're not going to hitchhike, are you, Jewel?" the woman said, her face pinched with concern. "I've told my daughters—"

"No, ma'am," Chessa cut her off. "I'm not going to hitchhike." She meant it. Too many people had taken advantage of her. It wouldn't happen again. Not if she could help it. "I have a friend who lives nearby," she lied and pulled a twenty from the two hundred Ferguson had given her. She offered it to the wife. "Buy a pizza on me. There's a great little place—"

"Uh-uh." The woman waved her off. "We won't take a dime. The kindness of strangers, you know."

Tears crept into Chessa's eyes. She slipped the money back into the swimsuit pocket and stepped out of the car. "Have a great wilderness trip."

"We intend to, hon." The woman winked. "Be safe."

As the couple did a U-turn and drove south toward Echo Lake, Chessa caught the wife watching her.

## CHAPTER 23

Chessa headed in the opposite direction from the Cloud 9 Motel, in case her rescuers later recognized her on the news and contacted the sheriff. Once the Subaru drove out of visual range, she retraced her steps. The warmth of the rain-free afternoon infused her with hope; the scent of the pine trees cleared her senses.

As she drew near the charming but tacky motel with its blinking neon sign, light gray-and-white buildings, pitched roofs and overgrown gardens, images of her wedding night flipped through her mind like pages from a photo album. A snapshot of Zach the liar quickly replaced Zach the lover. When had his treachery begun? Before the marriage? Afterward?

Not eager to reveal herself to anyone other than Brandi, Chessa found a hiding spot between two cars and waited. She cupped her hands around her eyes to block the glare of the afternoon sun. She couldn't make out the people inside the reception office. They were just silhouettes.

Chessa tensed as a Jaguar XKE drove into the lot and parked. Two African-American males climbed out—winning gamblers, she determined, by the way they were gleefully counting their wads of cash. They headed for the office and entered. Soon after, a young couple strolled off Lake Tahoe Boulevard and into the motel. An Asian man toting a stack of books and a family of four carrying a bag of take-out food followed them.

An hour later, with no sight of Brandi, Chessa worked hard to squelch the surging panic inside her. What if Brandi had sold the place? Chessa's sketchy plan would fail before it even got underway. Willing the negative thoughts away, she moved to a new perch between two sedans to wait.

Soon after, a ragtop Jeep swerved into the lot. Brandi Hayden, as beautiful as ever, stepped out of the Jeep in tank top and shorts, her long legs tucked into ankle-high leather boots, her café au lait skin gleaming.

In a stage whisper Chessa called, "*Psst.*"

Brandi whipped her head around. Her waist-long cornrows smacked her shoulders. "Girlfriend." She hurried to Chessa. "I heard on the radio. Your husband."

"I didn't do it."

"Well, of course you didn't."

Chessa sucked back a sob. "I need a place to crash for a few hours." She couldn't make herself say the word *hide*. "Can you help me?" Way back when, Chessa had bailed Brandi out of jail on a trumped up prostitution charge. There was no truth to it. She had a nasty ex-boyfriend.

"Absolutely." Brandi clutched Chessa's elbow and ushered her down a cobblestone path toward one of the bungalows. "Luckily, it's still June. The motel's not yet full." At the entrance to a unit that faced the water, Brandi pulled out a universal passkey, slid it into the magnetic lock, and pushed open the door. "Go in."

Chessa obeyed.

Brandi followed her in and let the door slam shut. "Home sweet home."

The room, in keeping with Brandi's desire to create little fantasy getaways, looked like the one in which Chessa had spent her honeymoon, Hawaiian in style with rattan beds, grass mat flooring, and fake palm trees tucked in the corners. Hula skirts and oil paintings of the Hawaiian islands hung on the walls. A bittersweet memory tugged at Chessa's heart. Around midnight on their wedding night, Zach had demanded she do a hula wearing nothing but bra and panties. The sex after her dance had been incredible.

"You look like crap." Brandi jammed her fists on her hips. "Your hair."

Chessa fingered her hatchet job.

Brandi sat on the bed and patted the bedspread. "Tell me everything."

Chessa spilled it out in a stream: Zach, the massacre, the guard, the witch and the firestorm. "Did I know my husband at all?"

"Lots of men keep secrets from their wives."

"He had three passports in addition to his own." She recounted the countries of origin. "And there were divorce papers, which the sheriff thinks I signed. I didn't."

"Maybe one of his friends could tell you more about him."

Chessa chewed on her lower lip.

"You don't know his friends?"

"I'm not sure he had any." Like Chessa, Zach had been a loner. They had socialized with her mother and stepfather. Why hadn't she considered their insulated dynamic odd?

"What about family?"

"His parents died. His younger brother lives overseas." At some point, Chessa would have to figure out how to contact him. They'd never met. "Zach didn't socialize more because he said he wanted alone time with me." She tried to keep the misery out of her voice but couldn't. She thought of calling Jeremiah and asking him more about Zach's past. He had vetted him. She wanted to know how had he come up with the information he had collected. But she couldn't call. The sheriff's department had probably tapped the line, and even if it hadn't, Patience Troon would listen in, claws primed, ready to deliver Chessa to the proper authorities. She had never liked Adriana and never warmed to Chessa.

"About the passports," Brandi said. "I saw something on the news about how terrorists can get them with no problem."

"Zach wasn't a terrorist."

"Are you sure?"

Chessa wasn't sure of anything.

"You said his was a US passport, but the other three were Russian, Swedish, and Spanish."

Chessa nodded.

"There are gambling casinos in those three countries." Brandi was an excellent poker player. That was how she had earned her down payment for the motel. "Could he have been an international gambler and you didn't know it?"

For six months, Zach had been trimming expenses, fewer dinners out, no wild sprees to the mall. One night he said glibly that the honeymoon was over. Chessa hadn't pressed for an explanation. She made enough for both of them to get by on. And yet he'd had enough cash to purchase some expensive suits—for business, he told her—and a number of bottles of wine he liked from a chic vineyard.

"Maybe he became addicted to gambling and ended up owing more than he could pay," Brandi said.

"But why kill eleven people? Why kidnap me?"

Brandi gripped Chessa by the shoulders. "Girlfriend, you're tired, you're stressed. I know it's only three in the afternoon, but let's get you a glass of vino."

"Uh-uh. I need a clear head." The few sips of whiskey from her rescuers had eaten away at the lining of her stomach. She felt raw and shaky. "And a computer."

"And food. While I'm gone, you take a shower." Brandi pointed to the bathroom. "And feel free to use all the products on the counter. The face cream is yummy. It promises to give a woman firmer, younger skin." She patted the underside of her taut chin. "It slinks under the surface and puffs up all the wrinkles."

As Brandi exited, Chessa gazed at the armoire. A television was housed inside. Normally, she avoided watching TV, but staying current with the news was a necessary evil.

# CHAPTER 24

Marcus sat down at his desk, blocked out the substation noise, and read the articles Chessa had written in college. Sure, they were flagrant, but most read like an exercise in journalism school. Take a topic, pick a side, and lambaste it. Economic growth, gambling, Lake Tahoe's environmental issues. Nothing was off limits. All were e-zine pieces. None of them had been published in notable magazines. The last of record, an article about preserving Lake Tahoe's historical purity, had elicited a quick response from the senator. He was in favor of turning back the clocks. Maybe his approval made Chessa hang up her pen. None of what she had written convinced Marcus she was a murderer.

Mission complete, he checked in with a pair of deputies who were tracking down relatives of the nanotech guy. No luck yet.

Next, he touched base with a team that was searching for the vehicle used to transport the victims. Indeed, a casino shuttle van, the fifteen-passenger kind, had gone missing; the regular driver had been located at home, sicker than a dog and admittedly embarrassed by the fact that he'd left his post last night due to a rapid onset of stomach flu. When Marcus ended that call, he was more than convinced that some of the victims were collateral damage, but which ones?

Afterward he met up with Keegan and drove to Yukiko Kimura's house.

From the onset of the interview in the kitchen, the Korean housekeeper, who was about as expressive as a blank piece of paper, tirelessly polished silver. She had to complete her tasks before Ms. Kimura's brother came to handle the funeral and the sale of the house and so many other things. Occasionally the woman blew loose strands of straight black hair off her face, but she didn't stop her work. She finished each piece, set it on the black granite counter, turned it so the afternoon sun streaming through the spotless windows would gleam off the broadest part, and then took up another.

"Did you like working for Ms. Kimura?" Marcus asked.

"She was the best employer I ever had." The housekeeper rubbed the tooled handle of a pitcher with the towel. "I worked many places. San Francisco. New York. My sister moved to Reno and she told me to come. It is nice at Lake Tahoe."

Marcus wasn't interested in the woman's life story, but he didn't feel he could rush her and still expect cooperation. He shifted feet.

"I do not like the cold weather in the winter," she went on.

"Not many people do unless they ski."

"I do not ski."

"Me, either," Keegan cut in. "I tried once. Fell flat on my face. Almost broke my leg."

Marcus gave Keegan a sign to cut the chitchat. "Ma'am, did Ms. Kimura have any enemies?"

The housekeeper licked her upper lip, as if she knew the conversation would finally come to this. "She was not popular, if that is what you ask. She made decisions that angered people. Some citizens do not wish for Nevada to grow. Many call us to complain."

"Like who?" Keegan asked.

The housekeeper stopped polishing. "I do not understand."

Marcus grinned. He'd bet the housekeeper understood more than she was letting on. "Who called Ms. Kimura, ma'am? Do you have names?"

"One. A man. Ms. Kimura would not grant him a permit to develop some lakefront land. He filed an appeal."

"His name?"

"Billingsley." The housekeeper wrinkled her nose. "He's very crude."

Marcus had seen Billingsley Construction signs around the lake. He made a note in his pad. "Did Mr. Billingsley even threaten your employer?"

She nodded. "He tried to run her off the road."

"When?"

"A few weeks ago."

"Why?

"Ms. Kimura saw him at a restaurant and accused him of bad business practices. Is that the term?"

"Good enough."

"He yelled at her and told her she was crazy. She dismissed him and left. On the drive home, he drove directly at her. She had to veer out of his way. She complained to Senator Wolfe. He said he would look into it."

Marcus surveyed the kitchen, trying to spy something that would reveal the character of Nevada's Director of Business and Industry. Like the rest of the house, the room was spotless. The copper pots hanging over the island looked unused. So did the stove and sink. Other than her career, what had Yukiko Kimura enjoyed doing? "I see wedding pictures. Where is Ms. Kimura's husband?"

"He died three years ago. His heart." The housekeeper sucked back a sob and resumed polishing. She rubbed the silver hard with the towel.

"Are there any men in her life?" Keegan asked.

She tilted her head. "Why do you ask?"

"Jealousy is often a reason for murder," he suggested.

"No." The housekeeper set her towel aside, dunked a small sponge into the silver polish, and scooped out a tablespoon's worth. She slopped it onto the pitcher's lid and swirled it in circles.

"How about women?" Keegan asked.

Marcus cut him a hard look. Keegan shrugged.

"She was dating a man," the housekeeper said. "She broke up with him a month ago."

Marcus took back the lead. "What was his name?"

The housekeeper rinsed the polish off the pitcher and buffed the pitcher dry with a clean towel.

"Ma'am?"

"Wally Evert." She growled out the name.

"He's not your favorite guy, I take it."

Her lip curled up in a snarl. "They fought. People saw them. Lots of people."

# CHAPTER 25

Marcus stood in the reception area of the Belle Vista Hotel, North Lake Tahoe's most chic hotel, the kind of luxury he would never be able to afford, and did his best to remain still. His skin itched like crazy, but it had nothing to do with the weather; the storm had passed. And the sensation had nothing to do with his current conversation with the matchstick-thin concierge, either. She was a professional woman who took her job seriously. So what was bugging him? He suddenly realized it was his conversation with Kimura's housekeeper. Evert's name had kept cropping up. How did he fit into the whole scenario?

"They were wonderful, giving men," the concierge said as she retied the turquoise scarf that was looped around her neck. She was suitably saddened to hear about the deaths of the eight doctors, the hotel's guests—*former* guests. She had arranged their itinerary, their rooms, and their sightseeing trips. "Have you called their families?"

"You were first on our list. Do you have contact information for each of them?"

She opened a program on her computer and printed a list of the doctors' names and room numbers. She included their dates of arrival and their planned departure dates.

Marcus tucked the sheet of paper into his pocket, and his stomach grumbled. He ignored the plea. Food held no appeal. "Tell us more about the doctors' junket, ma'am."

"It was paid for by the MASK foundation."

Marcus turned to Keegan. "I thought you said they weren't part of MASK."

"They weren't, to my knowledge."

"He's right," the concierge said. "I think the MASK people were wooing them."

"Why would they do that?"

"They probably hoped the doctors would provide free services to the damaged children MASK helps." The woman hesitated. She rolled her lip between her teeth.

"Please continue," Marcus said.

"Dr. Smith, the eye specialist. I knew him better than the others. He visited our hotel at least once a month." She glanced over her shoulder and back at Marcus. "We try not to judge at the Belle Vista, but he was a heavy gambler."

"Your hotel doesn't have a casino."

"True. We at Belle Vista pride ourselves on being a hotel that thinks the lake and the environs are enough of a draw. We cater to those who love sports and fresh air. We—"

"Sir"—Keegan elbowed Marcus—"I believe she's hinting he joined the occasional private cash game. My dad—"

Marcus held up a hand and addressed the concierge. "Did Dr. Smith join cash games at this hotel?"

She toyed with the tips of her scarf. "Sometimes he hosted them."

"Aha!" Keegan jabbed a finger in the air. "I was right. See, my dad told me that one time he met this guy, a real famous gambler. He had dinner with him in Reno before a boxing match. Anyway, this gambler told my dad how guys like him got around the tax thing with their winnings by having these cash games. Sometimes in hotel rooms. They all put up a million. At the end of the night, only one guy goes home the winner. Together, they go to the hotel's safety deposit room. The losers take cash from their boxes—each guy has one—and they transfer the cash into the winner's box." Keegan brushed his hands like he was getting rid of dust. "No tax liability."

"It's not illegal," the concierge said.

Marcus wasn't so sure. "Tell us more."

"Dr. Smith had a dinner party in his room the night before last."

"The night before the Happily Ever After Ball."

"That's correct."

Keegan said, "If the doctor won that night, he might have made a few enemies."

Marcus nodded. "Ma'am, please give me the names of people who attended."

"I'm afraid that would be a violation of house policies," the concierge answered, though she looked like she wanted to reveal all.

"Any recognizable faces?"

"One or two," she said cryptically.

"Known gamblers? Wally Evert, perhaps?" Marcus liked the gambling angle as a reason for mass murder. Settling debts the old fashioned way. He also liked Evert's involvement, given the romantic connection to Yukiko Kimura. "A nod would do."

The woman didn't budge, but she didn't deny that Evert was one of the poker players.

"Who else was there?" Marcus asked.

"A celebrity who has been in and out of rehab for gambling."

"Male?"

She nodded.

"Good looking?" Marcus hated playing twenty questions.

The woman's cheeks flushed pink. "Great in a swimsuit."

*The Italian Stud,* Marcus determined. The thirty-year-old had made a blockbuster movie every year for the past five years and vacationed in Lake Tahoe while on hiatus. Rumor was that the Stud owed earnings for his last two films to Paul Tarantino, an independent lender—some might say *predatory* lender—who happened to be a crony of Wally Evert's.

"Was a man named Tarantino at the game?" he asked.

The woman blinked deliberately.

Marcus presented a picture of Szabo to the woman. "Did you see this man at the get-together?"

"That's Senator Wolfe's son-in-law." The concierge shuddered. "He was murdered, too, wasn't he?"

Marcus nodded. By now the Internet was flooded with cell phone footage of the exterior of Chessa Paxton's cabin.

"He wasn't here. I don't think his wife killed him."

"Why not?"

"Because she's a good person. Her name is often in the Lifestyle section of the paper, helping out with this or that cause. People that give freely of themselves aren't usually killers."

Marcus grunted. "Ma'am, I can give you a long list of good people who have been known to kill, if provoked."

## CHAPTER 26

Chessa opened the doors of the armoire in the hotel room and switched on the television. She found early afternoon talk shows and soap operas, but no news covering the massacre or Zach's death or her flight from the law. Eager to clear the cobwebs from her mind, she took Brandi's advice and headed into the bathroom to take a shower. She slinked out of her clothes and let them fall to the floor. She turned the shower knob to make the water as hot as she could take it and stepped into the stall.

Within a minute, she began to cry. Then her sobs came hard. Harder. She slumped onto the floor and hugged her knees to her chest, but in the end, she knew hot water would never erase the chill that clutched her soul. She cranked off the shower and dried herself with a towel as another memory of her husband scudded through her mind. Zach. Lying dead on the floor. Wearing only a towel.

Shivering with sorrow, she slipped into one of the white terry cloth guest robes, cinched it at the waist, and returned to the bedroom. She lifted the remote controller, perched on the end of the bed, and tried again to find news somewhere. She toggled through channels until she caught a *LATE BREAKING NEWS* press conference underway.

Her heart skipped a beat as the camera focused on Detective Tallchief who was standing on a podium speaking into a microphone attached to a lectern. His weathered face vibrated with anger as he listed the names of the deceased at the massacre site: Yukiko Kimura, Steven Spitzer, his wife.

Chessa wrapped her arms around herself. Spitzer's wife must have been Snow White. Her body had shielded Chessa from the bullets.

Eight doctors were dead, too, according to Tallchief.

When asked a question about Chessa Paxton, he said, "She has not been apprehended. Yet." He related the story of her escape, how her boat ran out of gas, and how she abandoned ship. He didn't mention anything about a shooter causing the boat to lose fuel.

A worrisome notion struck her. Maybe it wasn't one of Tallchief's people that had shot at her. Maybe the redheaded guard anticipated that she would go to her stepfather's and stationed himself on the bluff below. Who was he? Why had Zach gotten involved with him?

The news aired a few pre-recorded testimonials. The first from Wally Evert; he knew one of the doctors. The second from Senator Jeremiah Wolfe; he was sick about losing his respected colleague, Ms. Kimura, and horrified at the loss of the doctors and Spitzer, and even more distraught about Chessa being on the run. He concluded by saying he was pretty sure she hadn't done this.

Chessa gagged. *Pretty sure?* Did he honestly believe she might be guilty?

A pang stabbed her as she realized her life and the career she had built were ruined. Even if she proved herself innocent, people would still have doubts. She would be a pariah like her father, untrustworthy and unemployable. A lifetime of effort was threatening to slip from her grasp. She had worked so hard to rise to her current position. If the Happily Ever After Ball had gone off without a hitch, she would have been promoted to events coordinator and would have overseen the Gala Galore Show, the most popular nightly event at the casino. She had already started a list of changes she'd hoped to implement.

A brittle-looking woman appeared on the television screen, a microphone in her hand. She spoke on behalf of Spitzer's daughters who were avoiding the press. Chessa didn't blame the young women. Reporters would hound them for comments the way they had harassed Chessa after her mother's death, their tape recorders out and video cameras at the ready. She recalled the stupid questions they asked. *Do you miss you mother?* Of course. *Did you see it coming?* Never, in a million years would Chessa have dreamed her mother would die in a car explosion halfway around the world. *Are you upset with the investigation?* Investigation. That was a laugh. Jeremiah had taken the Swiss police at their word; they had called it an unfortunate accident—a faulty gas leak in an aging vehicle—and offered no follow-up investigation. *Are you grieving?* Grieving didn't cover it. In truth, Chessa had felt like crawling into a hole to curl up and die. For weeks, she had clung to Zach and cried herself to sleep. Weeks merged into months. Her sleepwalking grew worse. Even a year later she felt the piercing memory of her mother's death. With Zach dead...

*Crackle!* Tallchief took the microphone out of the woman's hands and stared at the camera. "If Ms. Paxton surrenders," he said in his booming, gravelly voice, "I promise she will be treated fairly, to the fullest extent of the law."

Tallchief pointed to a picture on a computer monitor that resembled Chessa with her current look: spiky hair and anxious eyes. Even though she was more wrung out than the picture, nearly unrecognizable, she knew she would have to change her appearance again. How else could she slip into the casino unnoticed? She had to go there. Helena, a self-proscribed worry-wart, wouldn't dare meet Chessa anywhere else.

Chessa rose from the bed and paced the room as she pondered the victims. They were an eclectic bunch. The state's director of business and industry, a nanotech genius, his wife, a cosmetic surgeon, and more. Was one of them the intended target or were they all? Why?

Fatigue pressed at Chessa's temples. Her head felt heavy, hazy. She needed sleep. Her eyes started to droop, but she snapped them open when a redheaded man in uniform joined Tallchief on screen. He wasn't the security guard that had given the orders at Spooner Meadow. He was too short and too wide. But seeing him made Chessa wonder whether she could draw a picture of him like the sheriff's artist had drawn a picture of her. Though she had only seen him for a short time, his face was etched into her brain. She picked up a pencil and pad of paper by the telephone and drew a basic oval. She added a square chin. Hooded eyes. Ragged hair, short on top and long at the back. She drew ears but erased them. The guy didn't have Dumbo ears. His were smaller at the top with big lobes. His nose was flat. His cheeks were gaunt, his neck scrawny. He had a tattoo. She started to draw it and flinched; the pencil nib skittered across the paper. *The tattoo*. It was very detailed and weblike. It twisted up the right side of his neck. How had she not remembered this before? In the middle of the web was an image of a quasi black widow spider. She loathed spiders. Feared them. His was missing the distinctive red hourglass marking. Did it represent something?

As Chessa attempted to sketch the image, she felt the impulse to contact Tallchief, but she squelched it. Hadn't he said some of his buddies moonlighted at the ball? What if the redheaded guard was a member on the force, a sheriff who would kill to protect his identity? She opted to stick with her plan. Contact Helena. See if she recognized the guard. If she did, then Chessa would go to the sheriff. But not to Tallchief. To Newman. Yes, he had chased her and almost caught her and, from the get-go had thought she was guilty, but for some reason, she trusted he would do the right thing.

Chessa lifted the receiver again and dialed the number for the Boardwalk Casino and Hotel. A receptionist answered. Chessa said, "Helena Gorzinski, please."

Orchestral music played as she waited. Then Chessa heard a *click* and Helena's voice mail. "You have reached Helena Gorzinski. I am sorry I cannot answer your call," she said in her precise, accented English, "but if you will please leave me a message."

Helena shouldn't have gone home for the day yet; it was only late afternoon. After the beep, Chessa said, "Helena, it's me." No name. She hoped Helena would recognize her voice. "I need to track down a couple of people. A man who might have been either a security guard at the ball or a guest, and a woman who was dressed like a witch." She described their costumes. "I'll explain when I see you."

Chessa hoped Helena understood the last part of her cryptic message. She would slip into Helena's office and they would steal out for their weekly scheduled lunch. Same time, same place. She didn't add that Helena shouldn't let on to anyone that she had called, but she hoped—*hoped*—by not stating her name, that was implied.

# CHAPTER 27

Tallchief punched open the door to Incline Substation, stormed down the hallway, and marched into the homicide room. Man, he needed a cigarette, but he wouldn't light up. A year and two months ago, he had promised Ruthie he would never pick one up again. The smell of stale coffee and microwaved popcorn in the station was making him nauseous. The upside to the whole Paxton mess? His appetite was half what it used to be. His waistline was shrinking.

"Happy, Ruthie?" he muttered as he tossed his Glock on his desk. Ruthie always told him his eating habits would kill him. It was because of her that he planned to leave law enforcement, enter politics, and make a difference for Washoe people in the Tahoe region. How he missed her. He knew how angry she would be if he messed up the current case and kissed his sorry mayoral bid goodbye.

He swore under his breath and refocused. An afternoon of interviews and press conferences, and what did he have? Not much more than a few crank calls and minor clues. A local developer, Billingsley, disliked one of the victims, Yukiko Kimura. Another victim, Dr. Smith, had hosted an all-night gambling party the night before he died, and his safety deposit box held over eight million dollars. The nanotech's daughters were suitably devastated. Good thing. Tallchief didn't want to consider them suspects. There was the matter of the missing shuttle van, too. Had anyone boarded it by mistake?

"Garbage, people!" he yelled at the folks in the station. "What we have is garbage. What is slowing the wheels of progress?" No one looked up. He hadn't expected anyone to. He was ranting. His children, both grown, hadn't understood his zeal for the law. Back when they were in high school, when he had become an activist for the Tahoe Purists, they'd cringed. To them, their dad had turned into a freak, a radical. Today, they understood. Their father was a member of a group that wanted Lake Tahoe returned to its rustic glory. No cars within twenty miles of Tahoe, no boats other than those propelled by oars, and no casinos. They were pacifists not aggressors, and Tallchief was one of many who ensured the group stayed that way. He planned to base his political platform on what the Purists believed. Ruthie was the one who had made the children understand. *Your father is passionate,* she told them. *Dedicated. You should count yourselves lucky to have such a father.* Ruthie. She had made him happy to be alive.

Tallchief stomped across the room and stopped short of Newman who was standing beside his desk, brandishing a document at a woman wearing a red silk blouse, skirt, and pumps. Real upscale. The kind of woman who wouldn't take a second glance at Tallchief. Just looking at her made him realize how lonely he was. He talked to Ruthie's spirit every night before falling asleep, but that didn't cut it. Her side of the bed was cold and empty. Recently he'd turned to the Internet to chat with women. Just chat.

"Newman, what're you doing?" Tallchief asked.

Newman tucked the document under his arm and held up a finger to the woman in red. She glanced at her watch as Newman strode to Tallchief.

"How's your run for president coming?" Newman quipped.

"Don't get cute."

"City councilman?"

"Mayor."

"How many steps from president is that?"

"Too many. What're you up to?" He hitched his chin at the visitor.

"I'm questioning a legal assistant from the firm that drew up the Szabo/Paxton divorce papers." Newman handed a copy of the document to Tallchief.

He whistled. "Bring her into the interrogation room."

"She's only got five minutes."

"Let's make them count."

Newman seated the woman on a hardback chair beside the table in the interrogation room. Tallchief sat in the chair opposite her. Newman remained standing.

Newman said, "Ma'am, this is Detective Tallchief."

Tallchief cleared his throat. "Do you have other documents on file with Chessa Paxton's signature?"

"We do. Many, in fact." Her speech was as polished as her look.

"Do the signatures match?"

"There are slight variations, but under stress, a signature can change."

"For example?"

"The loop on the P is too big."

That was what Chessa Paxton had said, but Tallchief had discarded the notion. A handwriting expert would determine the truth. "You had the documents delivered to her home?"

"Hand delivered. She received them and signed for them."

"She said she didn't. Are you sure it was her?"

"Our delivery man might know."

"Call him please."

"My cell phone has lost its charge."

Tallchief fished his iPhone from his pocket and placed it on the table.

"Look." The assistant blew out a stream of air. "I'm only here because someone from the firm had to come down to the station. I don't want to get Chessa in any trouble. She's such a nice gal. I can't imagine—"

"Please, ma'am, we need to know when Ms. Paxton knew the existence of those divorce papers."

"The delivery guy is on his route."

Tallchief leaned back in his chair and folded his arms.

The assistant took the iPhone, stabbed in a series of numbers, and pressed the cell phone to her ear. After a moment, she explained the problem to her deliveryman and listened to his answer. "Are you certain?" She ended the call and returned the cell phone to Tallchief. "The woman who received the papers had dark hair and sharp cheekbones. That doesn't sound like Chessa."

Tallchief looked at Newman. "She could have been wearing a wig."

"Or Szabo could have had a lover with excellent penmanship," Newman countered.

Tallchief hated snappy comebacks.

~ * ~

Glad to put distance between himself and Tallchief's foul mood, Marcus showed the legal assistant to the substation exit.

As the door was about to swing shut, his foster mother Zelda hurried in, her wide cheeks flushed and her razor-short gray hair standing on end.

"Hi, Mrs. Newman," a clerk shouted.

Zelda acknowledged him and bustled toward Marcus. "I was hoping you'd be here. Whew, this heat!" Her shorts and oversized golf shirt were soaked with perspiration. She had probably been speed walking, a ritual she'd taken up to shed the postmenopausal weight that had grown around her middle. She hugged him and said, "You look like crap." Zelda never bothered with decorum. Too much fuss.

"Why are you here?" Marcus asked. "Is something wrong?"

"Brubeck's acting a little odd." Brubeck was Zelda's golden retriever; Zelda loved jazz. She had introduced Marcus to it. "He's been lost ever since you-know-who passed."

She was referring to Beauty, one of the friskiest retrievers Marcus had ever known.

"Brubeck will be fine." Marcus broke free and braced her shoulders. "It's only been six months. Grieving takes time." He was acutely aware of how much time. "Sorry, I can't chat. I've got to get back to work."

She batted his shoulder. "Are you taking care of yourself? Have you eaten?"

"Why are you really here? The Paxton case?"

Zelda shifted feet. Marcus grinned. He could read his foster mother as easily as an eye chart. Not to mention, every morning Zelda listened to NPR for two hours. She followed it with local news until lunch. Of course she wanted an update.

"I'm not the lead on the case," he said.

"Who is?"

"Tallchief."

Zelda harrumphed. "Is Chessa guilty?"

"You're calling her Chessa?"

"You know me. I'm informal."

Marcus would never forget the day the preacher introduced Eddie and him to Zelda. She understood their pain but told them to put their past behind them. Then she lovingly forced them to clean up and eat. That night, she hid tracking devices in their shoes. Marcus was savvy to her ploy, but he never told her because, for some odd reason, he appreciated her dedication to keep his brother and him safe. From that day on, jazz music and a steady dose of hugs had kept him out of trouble.

"Well, is she?" Zelda pressed.

"Who the heck knows?" Marcus cocked his head wondering for a fleeting moment whether Zelda had picked up a hitchhiker—say Chessa Paxton—and was harboring her. No way. She wouldn't be able to keep that juicy tidbit from him. He blew out a long stream of air. "Why are you interested?"

"Don't be a dolt. Let's walk."

"I don't have time."

"Nonsense." Zelda ushered him outside. "Three minutes of fresh air will do you good."

Even though the late afternoon sun warmed his face, Marcus felt edgy. The temperature had cooled to a comfortable high of seventy-eight, but he would gladly take a cold winter day that could numb him to the core.

"Is she pretty?" Zelda asked. "I've only seen her in news clips."

Until that moment, Marcus hadn't realized how much Chessa had been in the news: during her life with Senator Wolfe, after her mother's untimely death and father's imprisonment, and now this mess.

"Is she pretty?" Zelda repeated.

"Beautiful."

"Intelligent?"

"Resilient."

"You're pulling for her. I like that."

Marcus grinned. Good old Zelda. The reason for her visit was to make sure he didn't make up his mind about the case too soon. Her all-time favorite hero was Supreme Court Justice Ruth Bader Ginsberg. *Get the facts,* Zelda always said.

She looked at him sideways. "Something is bothering you."

"Chessa says she can't remember anything after midnight."

"So, there. You call her Chessa, too."

"What else am I supposed to call her?" he demanded, aware how defensive he sounded.

"Does she have amnesia?"

"She's a sleepwalker. She takes diazepam."

"That's Valium, right? I had a friend who took that and lost an entire week." After a long moment, Zelda said, "I heard on the radio that someone at the marina heard Chessa yell that she's being framed right before she tore off in Evert's boat. Do you think that's possible?"

Marcus jammed his hands into his pockets.

"Her father claimed he was framed, too," Zelda went on. "He said someone high up in the sheriff's office manipulated his case. You've had experience with bad upper management. So did your brother."

Marcus growled. He didn't want to think about Eddie. "I'm not discussing this with you."

"Who said I'm discussing anything? I'm stating facts." She eyeballed him. "Do you have a lead on where she might be?"

"If I did, I'd be there."

"Don't get snippy."

Marcus frowned. Whoever had helped Chessa when she surfaced from the lake, if she had surfaced, hadn't come forward.

"I repeat, do you think it's possible she's being framed? You should find out. I've got vibes."

Marcus rubbed the back of his neck. "*Vibes*."

"Yep."

Through the years, Marcus had been on the receiving end of Zelda's vibes. She'd known when he lied about a taking a road trip with the varsity baseball team. She had sensed every time he got a below-average grade on a test. She had even told him Ginnie was bad news.

"Go back to her house," Zelda ordered. "Revisit the crime scene. I'm not saying anything you don't know, of course, but you've got to get a feel for her. She fled because she's scared and wants answers. Who can provide those answers? Draw on that intuitive sense you have." She laid her hand on Marcus's shoulder. "And pray."

Marcus grumbled. Zelda was the most spiritual person he knew. She didn't go to church regularly, but she prayed daily, lit incense, chanted, and read the Bible. She was forever reminding him to seek the best in people. He wished he could.

"By the way, tomorrow, Saturday, I'm taking the kids to the Happily Ever After Convention," she said. "Do you want to come?"

*The kids*. Zelda had sixteen grandchildren, all from the foster children that she had taken in prior to assuming responsibility for Marcus and Eddie, her last two wards.

"I can't commit." Marcus was surprised that the MASK organization hadn't canceled the remaining events, but a spokesperson told him that a horde of requests had come in begging the group not to do so. Besides, she couldn't be certain the massacre was related to the event. Yes, all of the dead had been guests at the ball, but that didn't necessarily—

"Marcus," Zelda said.

"I'll see. I've got a ton of things to do first."

# CHAPTER 28

Chessa paced the motel room wondering whether Helena had gotten the message and contacted the sheriff. She also wondered what she would do next if Helena refused to help her. The fear that mushroomed inside her reminded her of the way she had felt when she was eight and ran away from home. She ended up somewhere in Incline Village, trapped in an alley behind a restaurant with no way out except to climb over a rickety, ten-foot chain-link fence or to head back to the street past a dog scavenging through the garbage. A rat crossed her feet as she deliberated. At the same time a beggar with a knife turned into the alley. He rushed toward her. Before she knew it, she had climbed the fence.

Someone knocked on the door. Chessa's breath snagged.

"Girlfriend, open up," Brandi said.

Keeping the chain in place, Chessa unbolted the double lock and opened the door an inch.

Brandi eyed the chain. "Do we need a code word?"

Chessa's cheeks warmed. She removed the chain.

Brandi sashayed inside carrying a tray set with a white cloth, cutlery, Saran-wrapped juice, and a covered plate. "You look better." She pulled a newspaper from under her arm and tossed it on the bed. Then she placed the tray on the bed and took the lid off the plate. Beneath was an assortment of celery sticks, orange wedges, chicken wings, cheese and crackers. "Voilá. Nibble food."

Chessa appreciated the effort, but her stomach felt as sore as if she'd eaten tainted meat. "I can't."

"You're going to eat." Brandi snapped her fingers. "Stinger."

"Stinger?"

"Our code word. My favorite drink is a brandy stinger." She held out a carrot stick.

Chessa took it and ate half-heartedly.

"What's that?" Brandi jutted a finger at the drawing of the guard.

"There was a redheaded guy at the ball. He and Zach… They argued… This guy"—Chessa shuddered—"drove the van."

"Maybe he was blackmailing Zach. You know, he found out Zach had a hazy past and promised to keep quiet if Zach helped him this one time. Zach balked and threatened to go to the cops, and the guy had no other option but to kill him."

Chessa couldn't fathom why Zach would agree to help someone kill eleven people. That wasn't the man she had married. It simply wasn't.

Brandi wiggled the pad. "Ever think about switching careers and doing those caricature thingies? Artists around here make a good nickel."

Chessa had never considered herself an artist. She was good with needle and thread or spit and glue. Her father was the artist. His pen and ink drawings were exquisite. He could do wonders with metal, too. Chessa savored the times when, as a girl, she had hovered in a corner and watched sparks fly from the welder hitting metal, not that her father's finished pieces looked like much. Her mother had called them avant garde.

Chessa moaned. *Mother*. If Adriana were here, would she tell Chessa to turn herself in or to continue on her path to the truth?

"Girlfriend, draw that witch you mentioned."

"I only saw her from across the room—"

"Try."

Chessa attempted another sketch, but everything about the image was wrong—the eyes too wide-set, the nose too angular. She wadded up the drawing and tried again. And again. Six sketches later, she still hadn't captured the witch's face. She flicked the pencil in frustration. "It's the cheekbones. I can't seem to get them."

"Hey, talking about that, did you know that one of the dead doctors, the plastic surgeon, was a high-stakes gambler?"

"Where did you hear that?"

"Everybody around here is texting everybody else the latest scoop."

Chessa froze. "Are you texting? Do people know I'm—"

"Listen to me. I will not turn you in, hear me?" Brandi perched on the bed. "But I will tell you some of the gossip. Talk is, Yukiko Kimura was in the midst of a bitter feud with some developer in town, and, get this, she was dating Wally Evert."

Chessa thought of the scene between Yukiko and Wally and Jeremiah.

Yukiko stormed away from them, but then she, too, wound up on the shuttle van. Had the killers drugged her like they had Chessa? Did they incapacitate Spitzer and the others?

Quickly Chessa wrote down her list of suspects and victims on the sketchpad. She drew lines connecting names: Yukiko to Evert, Zach to Evert, Yukiko to Spitzer, Zach to Jeremiah. As she took in the shape of what she had drawn, she gasped. The lines formed a web, a spider's web, just like the tattoo.

# CHAPTER 29

Marcus parked the truck at the end of the Paxton-Szabo driveway. Keegan exited first and stretched. Marcus remained seated and took in the view. Earlier in the day, when he'd approached the cabin, he had searched for indications that a murderer lived inside. Now, as evening set in with no daylight to distort his view, he looked for signs of the woman herself. The A-frame house was typical for a home in a heavily wooded area. It was Tyrolean in style, with scalloped eaves and heart-shaped carvings in the window frames. A pair of ceramic gnomes stood guard on the porch. Pansies crowded the dozen or so clay pots. Bird feeders hung from shepherd's crooks. Birdhouses, the old-fashioned wooden kind, were mounted on posts. Hollowed seeds and mounds of feathers had collected beneath them. An image of Chessa leaning out the window and singing like an animation princess made Marcus smile. Sure, it was an inappropriate response, but c'mon, was this the home of a cold-blooded killer? Or was Chessa Paxton on the run because, like Zelda said, she was scared and truly wanted to prove herself innocent?

Before entering the house, Marcus turned to the young officer standing by the front door. "Any visitors?"

"None, sir."

"How long have you been here?"

"I came on duty an hour ago."

So why, upon entering, did Marcus feel like someone, other than his team, had been inside? He didn't detect a scent; nothing looked disturbed. Had Chessa returned and slipped in unnoticed?

Marcus donned a pair of latex gloves and approached Frita Gutiérrez, a handsome Hispanic mother of three and Marcus's favorite colleague. She was standing in the entryway, rubbing her cross necklace, which meant she was frustrated. Prayer and Gutiérrez went hand in hand.

"Hey, boss," Gutiérrez said. "Lots to explore."

Marcus stepped past her and did his best to separate the normal from the murder scene. The house smelled stuffy yet sweet. Cut flowers drooped in their vases. A pair of wadded socks stuck out from beneath the sofa.

"Everything is tagged"—Gutiérrez led the way into the kitchen—"and going to the lab after you review it."

"Found any clues to the identity of the woman who accepted the divorced papers?"

"None. Neighbors are clueless. No signed receipt."

In the kitchen Marcus spied a half-filled bag of birdseed on the counter. An empty coffee cup sat in the sink; a crumpled napkin, on the kitchen table. Certain items had triangular plastic numbers beside them, indicating the techs believed they were important to the crime scene.

"There are Post-it notes on the fridge," Gutiérrez said. "To pick up milk and bread, call the doc, the usual. I think a couple might be missing."

"Why?"

"Because they're neatly arranged except there are a few blank spots. Of course, Ms. Paxton could have removed them."

The suspicion Marcus had experienced a moment ago returned. Had an intruder stolen inside? Why swipe Post-it notes?

"Moving on." Gutiérrez said, cutting into his thoughts. She was all business. No time for slowing down. She had ten years more experience in the sheriff's department than Marcus, but Marcus held a higher rank than she did simply because her family life came first. "We have bird feathers, acorns, et cetera. On the floor and elsewhere. Lake Tahoe is God's gift to nature. There are thread fibers and sequins, as well. Remember, the gal used to be primarily a costumer, so many of these things could be insignificant, brought in on bolts of fabric, masks, yada-yada." Gutiérrez often talked in shorthand.

Marcus followed her into the living room and paused. Chessa's gold purse was stuffed into the cubbyhole of the desk. Who had put it there? He had left it on top of the desk after rummaging through it. The difficulty of maintaining chain of evidence really ticked him off.

But was that what was really infuriating him? No. He was irked because he had made a mistake. He should have kept a better watch on Chessa. Sure, the case was Tallchief's, but ever since Tallchief had thrown his hat into the political arena, he had been slipping up.

Marcus marched to the guest bathroom. His gaze landed on the ball gown sitting in a heap on the floor, and he wondered again what Chessa's participation had been in the massacre. Was she a killer? There was no doubt she had been at Spooner Meadow. Footprint analysis had proven that.

He blew out a long stream of air and returned to the living room. He gazed at the desk with the cubbyholes. "Can I see those address books?"

Gutiérrez handed them to him. "Chessa's is the blue one."

*Figures.* Judging by the cabin's décor, Chessa had a thing for blue. Marcus flipped through the address book. Pretty empty.

"FYI," Gutiérrez said, "one of the names in there, Helena Gorzinski, is the chief human resources officer at the Boardwalk. I interviewed a few of the casino staff earlier, but Gorzinski wasn't available. Most of the ones I questioned said Chessa is a loner."

"Is Gorzinski a friend?"

"Couldn't say. Coworkers said Chessa changed after her mother died. One claimed she used to hum a lot, but she doesn't anymore."

Marcus made another visual pass of the room wondering if, after her mother died, Chessa bottled things up and finally exploded. Crazier things had happened.

"Szabo's passports," Marcus said. "Forged or legit?"

"Can't tell right off the bat. I called Homeland Security. They don't have him on their radar."

Marcus eyed Keegan who was standing between the sofa and coffee table and thumbing through a picture album. "Got something?"

"Wedding album." He flashed a page at Marcus. "No honeymoon."

"You're telling me," Marcus cracked. He pointed to Szabo's Android cell phone. "Gutiérrez, have you scoured that thing?"

She nodded. "The guy didn't use a password, so maybe he had nothing to hide." She palmed the Android and turned it on. "He only has four client phone numbers listed. By the way, one is Wally Evert."

Marcus whistled, yet another connection to good old Evert.

"I called Evert," Gutiérrez went on. "He said he was introduced to Szabo by Senator Wolfe. He said he'd given Szabo a half million to invest. Because Szabo turned a profit inside three months, Evert was ready to give him another wad of cash."

"Who else is in the contact list?"

"Paul Tarantino."

Marcus cursed under his breath. Evert and Tarantino were at the cash game with one of the dead doctors and both were Szabo's clients. Coincidence?

"The other two contacts are a Nevada real estate developer and an architect," Gutiérrez said.

"Which developer?"

"Carter Billingsley. By the look on your face, I'd say you've heard of him."

"Tell me something," Marcus said, a notion niggling at the edges of his brain. "Why did Szabo live in Lake Tahoe? Don't these venture capitalist guys live in big cities? You know, financially happening places like Los Angeles or New York?"

"I'm not sure there's one city that lures all of them. And remember, for many, these are second or third homes."

"This was no man's second home."

"True." Gutiérrez clicked open a file and showed Marcus printouts of what looked like savings accounts. "Szabo didn't have much available cash. He was tapped out."

"He might have gambled it away," Keegan said.

Marcus mulled over that angle. Maybe that was why Chessa and her husband were getting a divorce. Szabo, like his clients, gambled to excess, and Chessa gave him the ultimatum, but then, after the ball, he went on a toot, returned home empty-handed, and she lost it. However, that still wouldn't explain the massacre.

"On the other hand, he could have diversified," Keegan said.

"Explain."

"Let's say he established a corporation to stave off taxes. People do it all the time. I read a story on the Internet about a guy who channeled money through dozens of accounts. It took the feds a long time to prove it."

Marcus groaned. Call him archaic, but he hated the electronic age. Give him a good old paper trail any day. "Gutiérrez, what about gunpowder residue on Szabo's hands? Did we get results yet?"

"Yeah, it's there. How did you know?"

"Gut feeling. Did you run him through typical channels? Any priors?"

"Actually he doesn't have much of a past. He might have reinvented himself."

"Could he have been in the witness protection program?"

"We've made the call."

Keegan said, "Sir, there are no pictures of the groom's side of the family in the wedding album. Just Chessa's mother and the senator, that therapist pal of hers, Fairchild, plus Evert and Reverend Diggs."

"That man," Gutiérrez muttered. "He gives religion a bad name."

According to Gutiérrez, anybody who wasn't the Pope gave religion a bad name.

"His father was a pretty popular preacher," Marcus said.

Gutiérrez grimaced. "Wild Bill. What kind of name is that for a man of the cloth?"

Marcus grinned. He'd seen the preacher once. A huge bull of a man. Always wore a cowboy hat. On more than one occasion, he was known to arrive at his destination on horseback. Marcus took the photo album from Keegan. Chessa and Zach were married on the pier at Wolfe's house. In each of the pictures, Szabo looked content. In one, the two of them were squeezed between the handsome senator and his equally stunning wife, the brilliant blue of Lake Tahoe an idyllic backdrop to a memorable day. Chessa's smile was broad, her cheeks rosy, her skin glowing. She had loved Zach Szabo. That was no lie.

The therapist, on the other hand, didn't look pleased with the arrangement.

Marcus slapped the album shut. "Keegan, what's the scoop on Ferguson Fairchild?"

"The officer that interviewed him said he was a stuffed shirt. He believes the doctor might be in love with Chessa."

"Interesting," Marcus said.

Gutiérrez cocked her head. "What's going on in that miserable brain of yours?"

"There had to be two killers at the massacre. What if Szabo and Fairchild worked as a team?"

"Motive?"

"Not sure. But what if, once the deed was done, Fairchild decided he wanted Chessa all to himself, so he killed the hubby? Motive: love. Or how about this? What about the developer Billingsley as one of the shooters? He did business with Szabo. He had a temper. Supposedly, a few weeks ago, he got so angry that he tried to run Yukiko Kimura off the road."

Gutiérrez folded her arms across her chest. "I can't see either Fairchild or Billingsley using scissors to kill Szabo."

Marcus agreed. Most often scissors were a woman's weapon of choice, but a male killer could've used them on purpose to cast doubt.

Tabling theories for the moment, Marcus jogged up the stairs and surveyed the bedroom again: flowers in a vase, photos on the bedside table, intricate thimbles and pin cushions stored in a memory box, an antique sewing machine in the corner, dream catchers and masks on the wall, marionettes with frozen smiles.

*Frigging home sweet home.*

Surprisingly, Marcus found himself worrying about Chessa. How was she? Was she facing whatever demons might have provoked her? Or worse, facing the impossibility of proving herself innocent? He couldn't imagine finding a spouse and eleven people slaughtered. Zelda said that children didn't deserve to wander in the restless world alone. They needed an anchor. Spirituality was Zelda's anchor. She had been Marcus's. Who was Chessa's? Certainly not Senator Wolfe.

## CHAPTER 30

While Chessa waited for Brandi to return to the motel room, she reviewed the items lying on the bed: the drawings of the guard, the tattoo, and the witch—the eyes still weren't right—plus the weblike list of suspects. In frustration she shredded the list.

A tap on the door made her jerk around. She hurried to the door and put her ear against it.

Brandi said, "Stinger."

Chessa opened the door.

Brandi sped past her, arms full. She dropped items on the bed, including a box of Clairol Chocolate Velvet dye, three wigs, makeup, eyeglasses, sunglasses, and lots of clothing and accessories. "Spy look number one"—she lifted an oversized Hawaiian shirt and walking shorts with lots of pockets—"or number two?" She plucked a stretchy black denim skirt from the pile, black tank top, wide belt, ankle-high boots, black leather satchel, and gaudy beaded jewelry. "Put on the dark-haired wig, add heavy eye liner and shadow, and you'll look like a working girl."

Chessa smiled for the first time in a long time. Brandi was right. Nobody would expect her to dress like that. She typically wore jeans and buttoned-down shirts.

"I'm afraid the boots won't be good for running," Brandi said.

"I can walk from here to—" Chessa jammed her lips together. She didn't want Brandi to have to lie if the sheriff questioned her. "To where I'm headed."

"It's cool. I understand. You don't have to tell me. Look, I also brought you a can of mace and my spare cell phone." Brandi grinned. "I've got an extra because my new boyfriend is a jealous type."

"Unlike your old boyfriend?"

"Cut me some slack." Brandi plopped onto the bed. "So tell me, why did you marry Zach? I don't mean to be bashing him seeing as he's dead, but—"

"He made me feel safe." *Safe and loved,* Chessa thought. The words made her shiver.

"You barely knew him. I mean, I could sleep with someone I didn't know, once, maybe twice, but I couldn't marry him."

Chessa glanced at her ring, the single diamond and the simple gold band. Zach had chosen it because, he said, it was elegant and uncomplicated like him. Another lie.

Brandi rose and crossed to Chessa. "I always figured you'd go for that producer in Los Angeles. Remember him? He hired you for your first casino gig."

Chessa winced. "He turned out to be gay."

"Or that designer."

"He had a wife and two children. Surprise." Chessa wiggled her fingers.

"Wow."

What Chessa couldn't admit until now was that, after her many bad choices, she had been too scared to delve into Zach's past even though she had an inkling that something wasn't right. She hadn't pressed him for answers because they had enjoyed the same things: walks by the lake, wine tasting, crossword puzzles. She dreamed they would travel the world, parasail in Acapulco, balloon over the south of France. Have kids.

"Hey, girlfriend, are you okay?"

Chessa wasn't; she felt sick to her core. "I'm fine," she lied. "You'd better leave or your employees will wonder where you are and send out a search party."

"True."

"Meanwhile, I'll get to work on the new me." Chessa reached for the hair dye and faltered. Her mouth felt dry, her throat hot.

Brandi rushed to her.

"It's not fair," Chessa whispered.

"You've had it tough. Your dad going to jail. Your mom dying. Zach turning out to be someone you never knew. But we make our future. We choose to act. Hear me?"

Tears flooded Chessa's eyes.

"Uh-uh. Buck up. I do *not* have enough tea bags in the hotel to fix puffy eyes." Brandi chucked Chessa on the chin. She turned to go.

"Computer?" Chessa asked.

"I forgot. I'll be right—"

Someone pounded on the door. "Open up!"

# CHAPTER 31

Fear spiraled up Chessa's throat.

"Hide in there!" Brandi pointed.

Chessa edged behind the bathroom door and peeked through the crack.

Keeping the chain in place, Brandi inched the room door open. Chessa could only see part of the man in the hall, but he was gigantic with long wavy hair. She didn't recognize him. He wasn't wearing a sheriff's uniform.

"Where is he?" The guy's speech was slurred.

"There's no *he* in here." Brandi started to close the door.

"Hold it, girlie." The man slammed a beefy palm against the door while he gazed at the passkey in his hand. "Is this 202?"

Brandi pointed. "Next room over."

He hiccupped. "Hey, you're the hot chick who owns this joint, aren't ya? Yeah, I saw you when I checked in. Say, there's some crazy redheaded dude demanding to see you in the office."

Chessa's heart rate skyrocketed. Was it the guard? How could he have found her?

"Thanks." Brandi slammed the door.

Chessa stumbled out of the bathroom.

Brandi clasped her by the shoulders. "Breathe."

"I've got to go."

"Hold on. There are lots of people with red hair in Lake Tahoe. Heck, one time, I dyed my hair red. Lie down. Rest. I'll deal with him." Brandi exited.

But Chessa couldn't rest. She put the dye down and eyed the clothes. Tourist or hooker? The motel room phone rang. Chessa picked up but didn't say a word.

"It's me," Brandi whispered. "Nothing to worry about. The guy was looking for his wayward teenage daughter."

Even so, Chessa was ready to get moving.

~ * ~

Marcus hadn't driven through the town of Stateline in quite a while. Thanks to the community leaders eager to preserve the integrity and historical glamour of Lake Tahoe, the streets were cleaner than during the days of his youth, the small business fronts repainted, the handful of casinos less offensive.

"The place looks pretty good," Keegan said from the passenger seat. He was scrolling through email.

"Yeah, it does."

As the sun rose over the western string of mountains, Marcus steered his truck beneath the banners for the Happily Ever After Convention that spanned the street. He pulled into the Boardwalk Casino and Hotel's parking lot. The eco-friendly place, unlike its rivals, wasn't bathed in dramatic neon lights and glitter. In keeping with Lake Tahoe's latest building restrictions, requiring new construction to blend into the landscape, the casino favored a more Old West style with a rustic exterior.

"Do you think Helena Gorzinski is going to be straight with us?" Keegan asked.

"If we play straight with her." On the way over, Marcus had been trying to form his first question. He didn't want the head of HR to freeze up. "Follow my lead."

Families with children clad in fairy tale costumes swarmed the plaza between the hotel and the surrounding A-framed shops and pricey condominiums. The area also teemed with visitors wearing Glory to God T-shirts, all eager to attend the revival that would take place at the top of the mountain on Sunday. Signs strung around the mini mall pointed the way to the Heavenly Mountain Gondola that would take the crowds on the first step of their spiritual journey. Marcus had ridden the gondola. The view of the lake would be breathtaking as long as people looked straight out and not down at the parking lot which was cluttered with revival event trailers and Winnebagos.

"Get a load of him," Keegan said.

Reverend Diggs, still in the blue suit he had worn earlier in the day, stood in the middle of the plaza on a temporary stage. He held a Bible in one hand. His other hand was raised high in a fist. Something about him irritated Marcus. The remarkable melodic tone of his voice didn't ring true. Was oration a gift or a skill learned from years of practice? Marcus couldn't remember

Diggs's father having the same gift; he had been stern and gruff. On the other hand, Marcus was nothing like his father.

"Friends, a pure life is God's life," Diggs proclaimed. "God doesn't care about the external parts of your life, only the internal." He rapped once on his chest with his fist. "The heart. That's what matters."

Marcus had heard Diggs's spiel before. On TV. He wondered if the topics for Diggs's sermons stemmed from his personal suffering. He recalled reading somewhere, maybe in a magazine at the dentist's office, that Diggs had little, if any, family. His sister had suffered a horrible fate; his father died in a boating accident.

Keegan said, "If I preached as often as he did, I'd be hoarse."

Diggs's voice blended with the rest of the noise as Marcus strode into the casino with a mix of convention goers and early evening gamblers. He paused inside the door, blown away by the interior. That was where the opulence began.

In the center of the main hall stood a mini-theme park complete with bumper cars, a Ferris wheel, and a child-sized roller coaster, all created with the city's authorization because the theme park was fenced in, keeping children separate from the poker tables. Marcus didn't approve, but he didn't get a vote. The hotel boasted six casual restaurants, two five-star restaurants, a high-end coffee shop, a comedy club, shows with dancing girls, and a bar with nonstop live music.

"Hey, isn't that Wally Evert?" Keegan asked.

Evert, in signature black, sat perched on a stool at a blackjack table. Sitting next to him was Paul Tarantino looking Wall Street-efficient in an understated suit, his hair dyed and coiffed to make him look young and hip. The creases around his eyes betrayed him.

Marcus grinned. "Let's have some fun, deputy. Keep up." He sauntered to the men and put a foot on the rung of Evert's stool. "Evening, gentlemen."

Keegan drew alongside Evert, who laid down his hand of cards and signaled to the dealer to leave them alone. The two other customers at the table cashed in and exited.

"May I help you?" Evert asked.

"As a matter of fact, you can," Marcus said. "Have you heard anything from Chessa Paxton since she fled your marina?"

"No, sir."

Marcus wished he could wipe the smug smile off of Evert's face. "Did you hear about the massacre at Spooner Meadow?"

"How could I not?"

"How could he not?" Keegan echoed, picking up the rhythm like Marcus hoped he would.

"What is Lake Tahoe coming to?" Tarantino *tsk*ed.

Marcus gave him a withering look. The guy recoiled.

"The lake attracts all kinds of people nowadays," Evert said. "Riffraff, my daddy would have called them."

Marcus leaned toward Tarantino and suffered the guy's cloying scent. "Speaking of riffraff, Mr. Tarantino, I heard you were at a private poker game the other night with one of the dead doctors and a famous actor."

"Uh-uh. The Stud didn't stick around." Tarantino winced, realizing he'd acknowledged his presence.

Marcus grinned. "Afterward where were you, say around midnight to two A.M.?"

"Collecting a few debts."

"That late?"

"I get people to respond better when it's dark."

"Does a redheaded guy work for you?" Marcus asked. "Someone who moonlights as a security guard?"

Keegan gawked at Marcus, who shrugged. Yes, he was trolling.

"Lots of guys work for me."

"I'm looking for an enforcer," Marcus said, "possibly a hit man."

"Hit man? Whoa." Tarantino's hands flew up. "I might charge a hefty fee, but I'm legit, and I don't use muscle."

"Do you know Zach Szabo?" Marcus asked.

"Sure. The guy's a whiz with numbers."

"Szabo's dead. Murdered."

Tarantino paled. "Man, I mean *officer*, I had no idea." He whacked Evert on the shoulder. "Did you know?"

Evert nodded once.

Tarantino's cheek ticked. "Look, I swear I had nothing to do with it. Nothing. Like I said, I don't use muscle. People either pay debts, or I ruin their credit. They lose face, not their life."

"The poker game," Marcus said. "Fill me in."

"I lost, but it was no big deal."

"A million is no big deal?

Tarantino snuffled.

Marcus eyed Evert. "What about you? You were there. Did you lose a million, too?"

Evert rubbed his strabismus eye. "Everyone lost a million."

"People kill over losing that kind of dough," Keegan said.

Evert shot him a nasty look. "Not me. I'm very wealthy. I can afford to lose. To me, it's all in a day's fun."

*Fun,* Marcus thought. *Yeah, right.* No one, not even Donald Trump, liked to lose a million bucks in one sitting. Switching gears, he said, "I hear you and Yukiko Kimura were good friends."

"We had our moments."

"Kimura's housekeeper said you and her boss fought."

"She's lying." All the muscles in Evert's neck tensed; his bad eye flickered with a vengeance.

Marcus glanced at his watch. "C'mon, deputy. Let's hit it."

"Yes, sir." Keegan smiled, obviously happy with his supportive role.

As they passed a bank of one-armed bandits, a raw feeling crawled up Marcus's spine. He glanced over his shoulder. Tarantino was glaring at Evert as if he wanted to carve a hole in Evert's skull.

## CHAPTER 32

Marcus entered the Human Resources office and sucked in a breath at the sight. The fire engine-red walls and art deco décor must have been chosen to wake up any employee who came to work sleepy. As tired as he was, he felt instantly energized.

A perky receptionist with stick-straight hair who was shutting down her computer looked up. "Hiya."

Marcus flashed his badge. "Detective Newman. I called a half hour ago. Did I speak with you?"

She nodded and pressed the intercom. "Ms. Gorzinski, that sheriff is here to see you."

Within seconds, a bony woman-child with a moon-shaped face and limp brown hair opened her office door. She seemed the kind of person who might blend into the background, not take the helm of a huge department.

Marcus prepared himself for more surprises. "Ms. Gorzinski—"

"Helena, please. Ms. Gorzinski makes me feel so old." Her Polish accent was faint, the D sounding more like a T. Clipped, precise. She had worked hard on her speech.

"I'm Detective Newman and this is Deputy Keegan of the Washoe County Sheriff's Department. I'm sorry to detain you just as you're about to get off work."

Helena Gorzinski smoothed the front of her beige suit and beckoned the two of them to join her inside her office. With a graceful gesture, she offered them the blue-and-white striped armchairs.

After they were seated, Helena strode across the bold checkered carpet to her desk. She straightened a picture frame and the blotter before taking a seat in the cherry red desk chair. "What do you want?" She didn't look afraid or contentious, just noncommittal. And strong. Maybe she dressed in beige because the office décor was so loud.

Marcus perched on his chair, elbows on the armrests. "I'm here about Chessa Paxton."

Helena tilted her head to one side, as a bird would when assessing a worm.

"Ms. Paxton is a person of interest in the murder of her husband and the massacre at Spooner Meadow," Marcus went on.

Helena sat straighter. "This is not possible. Chessa is not capable of such a thing. *No way*, as you Americans say."

"I'm not sure she's guilty, either, ma'am, but we need to question her."

"Do you know about her mother? She's dead. And now Zach, too? This can't be happening to her. Poor Chessa."

"Who are her friends, ma'am, besides you, of course?" Marcus asked, wishing Chessa had logged more names in her address book.

Helena folded her hands on her desk. "Her friends are none of my business."

"But they are mine. And you were her friend."

"What is a friend, really?"

Marcus chewed on that ambiguous answer for a moment. "I'm assuming you've gone to lunch together?"

"Once or twice." Again, ambiguous.

"You've talked about family, ma'am, and about your jobs. Maybe you've had her over to your house for dinner, or you've been to her house."

"Never to her house." Helena's jaw twitched. "Her husband. He did not like having friends over."

Marcus exchanged a look with Keegan. Zach Szabo didn't like socializing, he had four passports, and he and Chessa had a quickie wedding and a divorce in the works. What was up with the guy? How had Chessa gotten wrangled into such an arrangement? Marcus blew out a long breath. Love could be blind, but Chessa's lack of curiosity was eating at him.

Helena fingered the collar of her blouse. "Marriage. It is time to be lost in love, no?"

Marcus had been lost in love with Ginnie. He hadn't dated anyone since she walked out.

"I met Zach for the first time at the ball," Helena continued. "He seemed nice and so proud of Chessa."

"Have you heard from her?"

She licked her lips. "No."

Marcus cocked his head. Keegan cleared his throat, indicating he had noticed the hesitation, too—Helena Gorzinski was lying. But bullying her wouldn't get her to open up.

Marcus leaned back in his chair. "Was Chessa a good worker, Helena?"

"Absolutely. Mr. Belden—he owns the casino—loves her." Helena's cheeks flushed. "Not *loves*...he *likes* her. No"—she searched for the right word—"he *appreciates* her." She nodded, nailing it. "Mr. Belden *appreciates* Chessa. He promoted her to her current position. She is very creative and smart." She tapped her head. "And she is kind."

*A regular Girl Scout,* Marcus mused.

"You know, she gives much of her time to volunteer work. After her mother died…" Helena touched the picture frame on her desk. "To lose a mother so young. It is horrible. Chessa still believes in God, but even faith does not make it easy."

Marcus nodded supportively. "Has she had any fights with co-workers lately? Something that might have prompted her to lash out at her husband?"

Helena's mouth drew thin. "I tell you, Chessa did not kill her husband. She loved him very much."

"What about the others who were killed?"

"There were eleven, no?" Helena toyed with her hair again, as if trying to keep herself together. "How could Chessa possibly kill eleven people? She is only one woman."

"We have evidence that she was at the crime scene. We believe two people might have been involved."

Helena laid a hand on her throat and crisscrossed her other arm protectively over her chest.

"Ma'am, Chessa could be in danger. If she isn't the killer, then whoever is might be after her." Marcus thought again about the vibe he'd gotten when he entered Chessa's cabin. Was an intruder after Chessa and one step ahead of Marcus? "Please. Do you know where she is?"

Helena shook her head.

"Would you tell me if you did?"

"It is simply not possible."

Marcus wasn't sure if she meant she couldn't or wouldn't.

The telephone on Helena's desk lit up. The intercom crackled. "Ms. Gorzinski," the receptionist said, "you're wanted in Mr. Belden's office."

Helena rose, her body vibrating with pent-up energy, and offered a forced smile. "I'm sorry, gentlemen. I wish I could be of more help. Please excuse me."

Marcus screwed up his mouth and rose from the chair. "If Chessa Paxton contacts you, call me. I would like to help her." He meant that. If she was guilty, he would help her into jail. If she wasn't…

He handed Helena a business card. The card shook in her fingers.

# CHAPTER 33

Jeremiah paced his library, his insides roiling. He pressed the cell phone firmly to his ear. "I need help." He fully expected Phoenix to chastise him. When that didn't happen, he felt his heart rate settle down.

"Just because Chessa hasn't come running home, doesn't mean you've failed. She's had a shock to the system."

"A shock? That's what you call this, a *shock?* She woke up next to her dead husband."

"Where do you think she might have run to?"

"I don't know."

"Think, Jeremiah. Her hiding places."

"The beach. She loves the beach." Jeremiah massaged his neck. "She never should have run. She should have trusted me. Her mother would have been able—"

"Enough! Don't rehash the past."

Jeremiah sucked in air through his nose and blew a long stream out his mouth. Why did he have no comeback? He was always in control. He knew how to manage people, to get his way. But not with Phoenix. Never with Phoenix.

"I appeared on camera," Jeremiah went on. "I pretty much said she was guilty."

"She'll know you didn't mean it. She'll call you."

"Will she?"

~ * ~

Night set in with a heaviness that made Chessa's chest ache. She took stock of herself in the mirror above the motel room dresser and struggled for breath: black denim skirt and ribbed black tank top gripping her body, black floral scarf fashionably tied around her neck, eyes outlined with heavy gothic makeup, the dark wig framing her face like a stage curtain. Through high school and college, teachers and counselors had encouraged her to act, but she had preferred working backstage, making costumes and transforming other people. Now? She was acting with a vengeance.

Chessa whipped off the wig and scratched her newly dyed hair. Costumes were simple to live in for a few hours on stage, not for a lifetime on the run. Sighing, she replaced the wig and transferred the cash from the swim trunks to the skirt pocket. Afterward she slumped on the bed, consumed by thoughts of Zach's deceit. Had he been having an affair with the witch? Why did he have so many passports? Had he been a spy, skilled at disguise and deception? Had he killed of his own volition, or had he obeyed the witch's or somebody else's orders?

Aside from the passports, Chessa wasn't sure, even if she had been forewarned, that she could have seen the signs of Zach's duplicity. If she asked him how she looked in an outfit, he gave her an honest opinion. Sometimes he told her she looked fat or her hair needed work. Dishonest people didn't do that.

When had he started lying to her?

In January, he began traveling more. For *business*, he told her. At times she felt uneasy when he didn't answer his phone after a certain hour, but he always gave her a logical reason.

Frustrated to distraction, she picked up Brandi's spare cell phone and called her. She asked if Brandi had forgotten Chessa's request for a computer. She had; a water heater had busted.

Minutes later, Brandi knocked on the door. "Stinger."

Chessa opened the door and Brandi whistled. "Girlfriend, you look hot and totally not like the old you."

"Thank you, I think."

Brandi handed Chessa an Apple laptop. "Here. Remember to eat. I'll check back later."

With only the ticking of the clock for company, Chessa locked the door, set the computer on the bed, and turned it on. As she waited for it to boot up, she nibbled on carrots and thought again of her mother, her father, and Zach. She had suffered so much pain and loss, and though she knew none of her tragedies were related, somehow she blamed her stepfather for all of it. Jeremiah Wolfe was a powerful man. He could have helped her father. Somehow he should have saved her mother. Most importantly he ought to have foreseen what Zach was up to. When he had the chance on the news, why hadn't he said that Chessa was incapable of killing anyone?

A chilly thought struck Chessa. Was Jeremiah involved? He hadn't liked Yukiko Kimura. She had fought his Nevada isolationist policy: *Nothing new; stick with the tried and true.*

*Stop it, Chessa.* Just because he wasn't Yukiko's champion didn't mean he was guilty.

She wiped her fingers on a napkin then opened the Internet browser. When the launch page for Google came into view, she typed in PASSPORTS > VERIFICATION. Various sites arose, none of which pertained to official passports. She keyed in GOVERNMENT > PASSPORTS and found sites showing her how to apply for a document. She added the word: FORGED, and articles about forged documents materialized, but none of them led to official government sites.

Stymied, Chessa turned her attention to researching the spider web tattoo. Links to over two hundred thousand sites emerged. Her mind reeled as she perused discussions in chat rooms. Though a spider web tattoo could mean nothing more than a guy wishing to imprint himself with his greatest fear, something in her gut told her there was more to the guard's tattoo. He wore it boldly on his neck. He wanted people to ask him about its significance.

Not one picture of the quasi black widow spider in the tattoo looked like the one Chessa remembered. There was always something wrong. The legs of the spider were too long, the color too black. Her hopes rose when she landed on a site for a tattoo artist in South Lake Tahoe who specialized in spiders, but she couldn't find a match to the guard's tattoo among the artist's renderings.

Chessa changed her search words yet again and came upon more than four hundred thousand sites about spider mythology. People considered a spider a weaver of fate or a trickster or even the creator of the universe. In some folklore, witches took the form of spiders to steal young females for sacrifice at harvest time, which made Chessa think about the witch again. Who was she? Was Chessa to be her sacrificial offering?

## CHAPTER 34

The first thing Marcus did when he got home was head to the back porch. His house didn't face the lake. Like Chessa's, it was tucked in the forest, although he could see his neighbors. Light from the crescent moon cast long shadows through the pines. He set twenty coals in the barbecue, squirted the coals with fire starter, and lit the pile with a match. Gently and steadily he blew on the small flame. When he was satisfied the fire had taken, he plodded into the house.

He switched on a lamp, dropped his keys, cell phone, and badge on the kitchen counter, and fetched a steak from the freezer. After unwrapping it, he grabbed a Heineken from the refrigerator.

Before he could pop the top, the landline telephone rang. Marcus scowled. The last thing he wanted was a call from Tallchief, eager to rehash the day's findings. He ignored the jangle and opened the beer. He took a long pull of it. The telephone continued to ring.

"Pick up, answering machine," Marcus muttered. The fickle thing rarely did its job right, but everyone in the department had to have one. Cell phone reception wasn't reliable. After two more rings, he snatched the telephone from the cradle. "Newman."

"Marcus?"

The sound of Ginnie's voice caught him off guard. He set the beer on the counter.

"Marcus, are you there?" She sounded frail, edgy. "Did I catch you at a bad time or are you barbecuing?"

"Fire's started."

"Steak or chicken?"

"What do you want, Ginnie?" Back when they were together, she never cared about chitchat. She was intense. Big issues mattered. Why was she acting like nothing had happened between them, like no time had passed?

Marcus cracked open a container of steak seasoning and liberally sprinkled the steak with it, then returned the jar to the cupboard, and slammed the door.

"I thought I'd say hi, Marcus."

"Bye, Ginnie."

"Wait!"

"Why?" The last time Marcus had spoken to her—a week after she walked out—she had started with: *My therapist said I should call you and admit that I'm frigid*. Like Marcus hadn't known? She had revealed her history many times. Her father had preyed on her big sister. Her mother, who lived in a sanitarium—if she was still alive—never had a clue, and Ginnie, too small and defenseless to fight her father, had never interceded. No matter how Marcus had tried—and he'd tried—he hadn't been able to break through Ginnie's emotional armor. He had loved her. He had wanted to make love to her. One night, Ginnie got drunk on purpose and let someone at a bar screw her, just to force Marcus to break up with her. He didn't. The next morning, Ginnie moved to Reno. A year later, she informed him in one of her Christmas cards that she had married a doctor; they had a little boy and another was on the way.

Ginnie said, "I can smell barbecue. May I come up?"

"Very funny."

"No, really, may I?" She laughed softly.

Marcus missed that sound, missed sitting on the porch and counting shooting stars; Ginnie on her chair, he on his. "Is this part of the therapy?" he said, his voice husky with longing. "Toying with old boyfriends?"

The roar of an engine followed by the crank of brakes cut the silence. A car door slammed. Footsteps crackled on the gravel along the driveway.

Seconds later, Marcus spotted Ginnie through the window. She stood at the base of the back porch steps, hand on hip, her silky dress clinging to every luscious curve, her honey-colored curls fluttering in the breeze.

Marcus pressed through the screen door. "What are you doing here?" His heart was pounding, but he forced his voice to come out flat.

Ginnie ascended the stairs, mouth slightly open.

Marcus stepped aside, rubbing his scruffy face as she slipped past him onto the porch and plopped onto the weatherworn sofa, instantly at home.

"Where are your boys?" he asked.

"Back in Reno with the nanny."

Zelda promised if Marcus ever got married and had kids that she would babysit. She hoped he would have a dozen. He wasn't sure how good a father he would make. Better than Ginnie's.

"I'm getting divorced," Ginnie said.

"Sorry to hear that."

"He left me, but he wants me back."

"Then why are you here?"

"Because I want you."

"Ginnie—"

"I've changed, Marcus." She leapt to her feet and threw her arms around him. "I love you. I've always loved you."

Marcus pried her off of him and held her at arms' length. He wasn't used to the new and improved Demonstrative Ginnie.

"I'm ready to love you like you want," she whispered and licked his ear with the tip of her tongue.

Marcus's mouth grew thick. His groin pulsated with desire. "No, Ginnie."

"Please, Marcus."

He tried to quell the driving urge, but he couldn't. He swept her into his arms and carried her into the house, down the hall, and into the bedroom. He placed her on the bed and shed his clothes.

"Strip me." She raised her arms.

Marcus knelt beside her, his breath catching in his chest as he lifted the stretchy dress up over her full hips and her lily-white breasts. She wasn't wearing a bra. A groan of desire escaped his lips.

For the next half hour, he caressed and kissed her. She responded like a woman in the throes of passion should, but as he neared the *moment*, she stopped. Everything. No push, no thrust.

"Ginnie?"

She rolled to the far side of the bed and curled into a fetal position. "I apologize, Marcus. I…" Her shoulders heaved.

Marcus flopped onto his back, not mad, not frustrated. He simply felt sorry for her. "How did you"—he grappled for the words—"have children?"

"Insemination. Both times." A shudder rippled through her. "I started therapy six months ago. I thought I was healed, so I wanted to try again with you, not him, because I thought we had what it took, but I guess I was wrong."

Ginnie slid off of the bed. Moonlight spilled through a break in the drapes and bathed her in a soft glow. Marcus watched as she slung on her dress and pumps. He was surprised that he felt nothing, and even more surprised that he was thinking about Chessa Paxton, wondering what she would look like with nothing but moonlight for clothing.

When Ginnie finished dressing, she turned and smiled. "I'll go back to him, of course."

"You should. For the boys' sakes."

"He loves me with or without sex."

Marcus did, too, but Ginnie never believed him.

"Just so you know, Marcus, you are the most splendid man I've ever known."

Without another word, she tiptoed out of the house and drove out of his life.

For a long time, Marcus lay on his back, staring at the ceiling, thinking about Ginnie's parting words. When he had been with her, he had been a good man. He had risen above the pain of losing his brother. He had paid attention to civic efforts in Lake Tahoe. He had dared to make a difference. Nowadays he just worked.

After a long while, he slipped into a pair of boxers, fetched the beer and the steak from the kitchen, and returned to the porch. He slapped the steak on the grill. As the meat charred, he sat in the hickory rocker that squeaked with every trundle and contemplated life, death, Ginnie, the fate of Lake Tahoe, and Chessa Paxton, not necessarily in that order.

## CHAPTER 35

"Police! Open up!"

Chessa startled awake on the motel bed, her cheek sticking to the top of the computer's keyboard. The digital clock read 9:00 P.M.

*Crack!*

Metal on wood.

Chessa jumped off the bed and raced to her door.

*Crack!*

Someone was trying to break in to the next room. Not hers. She heard the static of walkie-talkies and knew it wouldn't be long before the police found her.

Quickly she grabbed the leather satchel that she had stuffed with items Brandi had given her and dashed to the sliding door at the rear of the room. She flipped the latch, pushed the door open, and bolted into the dark.

~ * ~

Marcus finished dinner on the porch and leaned back in his chair. The sky was a blanket of stars. He had never wished on one. He was a realist, too jaded from his formative years to believe that dreams came true.

The steady thrum of the breeze through the pines made him yawn. His eyes grew heavy. As he drifted off, he thought of Zelda. She dreamed of visiting Italy. Ginnie had wanted to take a trip to New York on New Year's Eve. Had she done so? Marcus would never know. As his eyes grew heavy, he wondered what Chessa Paxton's dreams were, but he drifted off thinking of Eddie who would never dream again.

*Rat-a-tat. The sound of gunfire. Bullets ripping through flesh. Bodies crashed to Marcus's left and right. Eddie was ahead. Running fast. Faster. Toward a building.*

*Marcus ran after him. His army boots sank ankle-deep in the dissolving sand. He dropped his rifle and reached for Eddie. His fingertips touched the back of Eddie's uniform, but he couldn't grab hold. "Eddie!" he screamed.*

*Eddie ran into the building with heart-shaped windows. He slammed the door.*

*Glass blew from the windows. Shards of burning wood exploded.*

*Marcus dashed to the front door and pounded. It splintered. He charged inside. "Eddie!" No response.*

*He hurried to the second floor. In the hallway, he skidded on the jute carpet. At the doorway leading to a bedroom, he froze. He stared at the bodies on the floor. Not Eddie's. His mother's and his father's. Face up, eyes carved out.*

*He looked past them at pincushions and puppets and masks. On the bedside table was a stack of books. On top, the Bible. Beside the books stood a framed photograph of a bride and groom.*

Marcus woke with a start, his body drenched in perspiration, the morning sun stealing over the mountain, the screech of the rocker on the porch as loud as a salvo of bullets.

## CHAPTER 36

Helena Gorzinski gazed at herself in the employee bathroom mirror. Was it only Saturday morning? Why did it feel like a week had passed since Chessa left yesterday's voice mail message? Helena sighed. She was—how did the commercials on TV say it?—tired and on edge. She hadn't slept well, so she had come in early. She still pondered why she had lied to the sheriff. Would they create problems for her family because she didn't fall in line? She loved America. She treasured citizenship. She enjoyed her job. By not telling the sheriff everything, had she jeopardized all she had worked for?

Helena pulled a tube of gloss from her jacket pocket, unscrewed the wand, and slashed her trembling lips with a soft pink sheen. When she deposited the gloss back in her pocket, her fingers grazed the list of Happily Ever After Ball employees and guests. She didn't need to inform the sheriff about Chessa's call, did she? Chessa hadn't asked her to do anything illegal. The name of a guard; the name of a guest. It was not a big deal. When Helena's little brother got sick, it was Chessa who had kept a cool head and driven him to the hospital. Helena owed her.

"You will not tell," she told her reflection. She drew in a deep breath, entered the toilet stall, and slid the latch shut.

~ * ~

Over a cup of morning coffee, Marcus tried to figure out why he had dreamed of a framed picture beside a bed. It was clearly Zach Szabo and Chessa Paxton, but it wasn't the one he had seen in Chessa's bedroom. In the dream photograph, there was an aura about Chessa, like she was ecstatic that her knight in shining armor had finally come to take her away. Zach, on the other hand, was beaming like a man with an expensive new toy.

Over a second cup of coffee, it dawned on Marcus where he had seen the photo. Keegan had been thumbing through Chessa's wedding album and flashed a page at Marcus. Why had he conjured up that photo?

*Think.*

Zach and Chessa were standing in front of a hotel. Keegan said: *No honeymoon.* Marcus replied: *You're telling me.*

Had they skipped taking a honeymoon? Had they gone someplace local for their wedding night? The hotel. What was the name of it?

Marcus rang Keegan; his voice mail picked up. Marcus left a message and took a shower. As water rained down on his head, he remembered. It was a motel, not a hotel. He had driven by it numerous times. The Cloud 9 located in South Lake Tahoe.

Quickly he dressed and grabbed a slice of days'-old cold pizza for the car ride. On the way out the door, he called Keegan again. This time he reached him.

Twenty minutes later, Marcus met up with the deputy in the motel's parking lot.

"Someone having a party?" Keegan joked as he climbed out of his mud-splattered Jeep. A number of South Lake Tahoe Police Department vehicles idled near reception.

Marcus approached one of the officers. "What's going on?"

"Porn ring bust. We've been here all night. Motel owner's over there."

The officer pointed to a gorgeous black woman. Beaded cornrows framed her face. Short-shorts and a tight tank top highlighted her figure. She was leaning against one of the columns near the motel's lobby, a cigarette pressed between her lips. She looked rattled, like she might tell Marcus anything he wanted to know if he would help her get out of this mess.

Marcus strode to her and introduced himself. Ten minutes later, eyes brimming with tears, Brandi Hayden escorted Marcus to the room to the right of the porn ring fiasco. She inserted a key in the lock of the motel room door and pushed open the door.

"Chessa's gone," Brandi said. "I already checked."

Marcus entered; Keegan followed. The room was cool. Sheer drapes fluttered in the morning breeze. The sliding glass door leading to the rear patio stood open.

"Look, I'm telling you, she's innocent," Brandi continued. "I never would have given her a room if I hadn't been one hundred percent certain of that. I've got good instincts."

*Except when it comes to identifying porn ring operators,* Marcus mused.

"Got a clue where she went?" he asked.

"No, although she said she wanted to figure out the identity of a security guard she saw at the Happily Ever After Ball."

*Again with the guard.*

"Mind if I leave you two here?" Brandi said. "SLTPD want to grill me further."

"Sure, go ahead," Marcus said, then, "Wait! What was Chessa wearing?"

Brandi eyed the pile of clothing on one of the beds. "A T-shirt, skirt, and boots."

Marcus checked the bathroom and noticed an empty hair dye kit. "Her hair?"

"Short." Brandi shifted feet. "Can I go?"

Marcus released her with a gesture and positioned himself in the middle of the room. He turned in a circle, trying to get a feel for Chessa's mindset: a tray of snack food, partially eaten, rested on the bureau; a mess of clothes was piled on one of the unused beds. She must have heard the raid and fled.

"Sir," Keegan said. "Got something." He held up a notepad with a drawing on it.

# CHAPTER 37

Inside the toilet stall, Helena reviewed the list of ball attendees, top to bottom. It included casino VIPs, entrepreneurs, real estate moguls, corporate sponsors' guests, MASK bigwigs, and Senator Wolfe plus his entourage. A few guests had cancelled; some had brought guests who weren't included on the list. At Ms. Kimura's insistence, Helena had noted the description of the costume for each guest. That way Helena and she would be able to greet people by their real names as they encountered them. No guessing games.

*Creak.*

The bathroom door opened. Someone with squeaky-soled shoes entered.

"Ms. Gorzinski," a man said, moving stall to stall.

Something about the tenor of voice made Helena's heart wrench.

"Ma'am, are you in here?"

Helena stifled a moan. Why, oh, why was she sitting in such a compromising position? She tugged on the waistband of her pantyhose, silently cursing for choosing to wear them. So what if they made her calves look better? Who was she trying to impress?

Running shoes and the hem of jeans became visible at the lower rim of her stall door. Helena drew her feet off the ground. Maybe if the man couldn't see her…

"I'm sorry to bother you, ma'am. Your assistant said you were in here. I'm with South Lake Tahoe PD. It's urgent I speak with you."

The sheriff yesterday; the police today. HelenaeHelHelena couldn't bear the pressure any longer. "Yes, Chessa Paxton called me. She wanted to see a list. I've got it. Give me a—"

The door burst open. A wiry man with shocking white hair lunged at her.

~ * ~

For hours, Chessa had hidden in the shadows between a liquor store and a natural health store. Shivering. Frantic.

When the sun crested the mountains and hundreds of tourists started arriving for a day of fun, many dressed in shorts and flip-flops and others in jeans and wild T-shirts or outfits as revealing as hers, Chessa hoisted Brandi's satchel higher on her shoulder and joined the throng.

As one of the herd heading toward the Boardwalk Casino, she reminded herself that in her new costume and wig she was unrecognizable.

A line was forming outside the casino for those willing to wait for the opening of the Happily Ever After Convention. Chessa's heart snagged at the sight of little girls and boys in their costumes: princes and princesses, dragon slayers, Tinkerbells, Peter Pans, and more. How she wished her fantasy world was still intact. Tears sprang to her eyes when she caught sight of one smiling girl who was twirling beneath the arms of an adult. Chessa had twirled like that with her father before he was yanked from her life.

Beyond the eager fans, a group of revival devotees listened attentively to Reverend Diggs, who was pacing on a small stage. The man rarely slept.

"Gambling, my friends, is the work of the devil." Using his hands, Diggs worked the crowd like a skilled conductor. "Turn to Him for your salvation."

Still hesitant to seek the reverend's help, Chessa detoured to the left and strode into the casino. Once inside, she veered right, away from the gambling area. Bells and whistles echoed through the cavernous casino, but they didn't lure her. She sped past the curved bars and the sea of poker tables, the banks of slot machines and the bleary-eyed customers with buckets of change in their laps, and raced toward the Human Resources office.

As Chessa entered, the receptionist, a young woman Chessa had met on occasion, glanced up from her chore of tearing casino ads from magazines. Helena Gorzinski always arrived early to work. It was her family's work ethic. She expected the same of her staff.

"Help you?" the receptionist asked. She didn't seem to recognize Chessa.

A memory sparked in Chessa's mind, the period in her life when her mother and she watched the movie *Working Girl* every week for a month. Adriana said, like the protagonist in the movie, she had changed her pitiful life by being bold. In the span of twelve years, she had risen from a poor Arizona gift shop girl, to mother, to a Nevada senator's popular wife.

"Help you?" the assistant repeated.

Restraining from whipping off the wig and confessing everything, Chessa jutted a hip and in a lousy New Jersey accent, said, "Is Helena Gorzinski in? I've got an appointment."

"Name?"

"Tess." Like the character in the movie.

"I'm sorry, Tess, but Ms. Gorzinski is um…indisposed."

"Do you mean she's in the bathroom?"

She nodded. "Please have a seat."

Chessa darted from the office.

"Miss," the receptionist called. "Tess!"

Chessa didn't slow down. She raced toward the employee restroom. The sooner she could talk to Helena the better. Halfway there, she saw the door to the restroom opening. Helena wasn't exiting; a man with shocking white hair was. Chessa swiveled toward a drinking fountain. She had blended into the crowd in the casino, but in the solitude of the stark hall, she stood out. Using peripheral vision, she watched the man draw nearer. He ducked his chin and trudged past her, probably embarrassed by his mistake. His silver-and-black running shoes squeaked as he rounded the corner.

When Chessa was sure he was gone, she continued on. However, the moment she entered the bathroom, she tensed. It was too quiet and all the stall doors hung open. "Helena?"

No answer.

Chessa hustled past the stand of cleaning supplies and peeked beneath the lower edge of the stalls. In the third one, Helena lay slumped on the floor, mouth and eyes open, throat sliced.

"Helena!" Chessa hurried to her, removed her floral scarf, and pressed it against Helena's neck, but it was too late. Helena was motionless; her blood was streaming down the drain behind the toilet.

Through tears, Chessa spied a small piece of white paper in Helena's hand. She pried it free. A few guest names and costume types were printed on it in columns. It had to be part of the list Chessa had requested. Where was the rest?

The door to the restroom slammed open. Chessa peeked below the stall's rim. A person in silver-and-black running shoes entered—the man that had passed her in the hall.

Chessa scrambled to her feet, but before she could pull the can of mace from her tote, the stall door flew open and knocked into her. She stumbled backward. Her feet slipped in Helena's blood, but she didn't loose her balance.

The man lunged at her with a sturdy looking plastic knife, the kind that would be easy to slip past casino security.

Chessa heaved the stall door at him. Heard him stagger. Heard his knife hit the floor. She whipped the door open and rushed through the opening. Her attacker was bent over, reaching for the knife. She saw the spider web tattoo on his neck and gasped. He was the redheaded guard; he had bleached his hair.

She swung her tote and nailed his head. He lurched forward. She flailed again, but he rolled to his left and dodged the blow.

Why had he killed Helena? To get the list? How could he have known about it?

Chessa tugged the mace from the purse and pressed the button. The mist hit the guard's chin, not his eyes. He kicked upward and knocked the can out of her hand.

Wild to find a replacement weapon, Chessa wheeled around. The guard leaped to his feet and grabbed her hair. The wig came off in his hand. He reeled backward and landed against a sink. He spewed out a string of curse words.

The tirade gave Chessa time to dart to the stand of cleaning supplies. She nabbed a container of Lysol Disinfectant, pivoted, and sprayed. The fluid jetted out. The guard threw up his hands to protect his eyes. As he did, Chessa kicked him in the left knee. He buckled.

Wasting no time, she dashed out of the bathroom and fled to the one place in the casino where she hoped she would be safe. The evening shows wouldn't start for hours.

The stage door to the Wild West Theater squeaked as Chessa pushed it open. A string of running safety lights provided the only illumination. She stole to the costuming room. No one was inside. Her gaze landed on a large wardrobe closet. She hurried to it and climbed in, drawing the door closed behind her. She pressed through the crinoline cancan skirts to the rear, the material scratching her mercilessly, but she didn't care.

In the dark, she hugged her knees to her chest and cried. How had it come to this? Helena was dead and it was Chessa's fault. She had lured her into the madness.

*Creak.* A thin stream of light appeared at the bottom rim of the closet door. Someone in squeaky tennis shoes was entering the costuming room.

Chessa willed herself to become one with the rear wall of the closet. She squeezed her lips together and pinched her nose with her fingertips.

A man said, "What the—"

The closet door whipped open.$

# CHAPTER 38

The bright lights of the dressing room blinded Chessa. She tried to lash out with her fists, but the crinoline skirts made the effort fruitless. Her attacker caught her by the wrists. She twisted to wrench free, but he was too strong. He pulled her out of the closet.

"Whoa, lady, calm down!" he shouted.

Chessa blinked. "Orseno?"

"Chessa?" Orseno Hill's gigantic eyes grew even wider. "Sugar, I can't believe it." He released her. "You look, well, heck, I don't know what you look." Orseno and Chessa had worked together often. He was the costumer for the Wild West Show. "You're in a whole lot of trouble. The sheriff—"

"Helena's dead!" In a gush, Chessa told him about the white-haired guard and the attack.

When she finished, Orseno tugged the hem of his body-hugging T-shirt over his camp shorts and strode to the hotel's house phone.

"What are you doing?" Chessa's voice skated upward.

"Calling security. You need to give someone a complete description of the killer."

"No! Wait!" Chessa raced to him and pressed the disconnect button. "They'll think I did it."

"Don't be ridiculous."

"I'm covered in blood. My prints. My scarf—" Her voice snagged. "I took this from the crime scene." Chessa handed him the shred of paper. "This is part of the list of people who attended the ball. The man who killed Helena took the rest."

"Why would he care about this?"

"There was a witch at the ball, and, wait—" Chessa jutted a finger at him. "You were there. As Robin Hood."

Orseno mimed doffing a cap. "Steal from the rich, give to the poor."

"Maybe you saw her."

Orseno grew serious. "Sugar, there were at least six witches. I remember one in a fabulous costume. Layers of black chiffon and lace and V-neck down to you know where. She had wild white hair and yellow nails. You know who I mean." He snapped his fingers. "She's the crossdresser that performs at the Nugget."

"Not her. I'm talking about a witch with garish red and purple hair. I think her dress was made of feathers."

"Reverend Diggs's guest might fit your description. She was tall. Major reconstructive surgery. Was the witch you saw tall?"

Chessa couldn't gauge the woman's height. She had stood almost eye level with Zach, but she could have been wearing heels. "Did you catch her name?"

"Don't have a clue. Then there was the witchy wife of South Lake Tahoe's finest restaurateur, as well as Wally Evert's date, although I don't think her dress was made of feathers."

"Any others?"

"There was Shawn, of course. How could I forget sweet, beautiful Shawn? Except she wasn't beautiful that night. Big black mouth, disgustingly long fingernails. Her dress was feathers, and she had two-toned hair, red on the tips. What's her last name?" He wiggled a finger trying to conjure it up.

"Spitzer?"

"That's the one. Twenty-two with legs up to here. She and her younger sister are real party girls. Whenever they come to town, they don't stay with their dad and mom. They go to the swanky Montibleau Hotel so they can have their freedom. La-di-da."

"Her father is one of the people who died at the massacre."

Orseno blanched. "Oh, heavens, you don't think Shawn killed all those people? No, no, no. Impossible."

Chessa didn't know what to think. With both parents dead, Shawn and her sister might inherit millions. Money was a great motivator.

"Sugar, I am way out of my league here. I've got to call security."

"I can't stay." Chessa hitched her tote higher on her shoulder, kissed his cheek, and headed for the exit.

"Where will you go?"

Chessa didn't answer. She didn't have a clue.

~ * ~

Chessa weaved through crowds in the casino, her pace brisk but not so manic that she would draw attention. She gazed for any sign of the killer but saw no one acting suspicious.

Fifteen feet from the exit, a hand gripped her shoulder. She pulled free and whipped around.

Reverend Diggs took a step backward, his stunted arms raised to defend himself. "Chessa, darlin', I didn't mean to scare you, but, trust me, if I can see through this disguise, so can the authorities. Talk to me."

How Chessa wanted to trust somebody—*him*—but she couldn't. Not with Helena lying dead in the women's bathroom. No one was staring at the two of them, but someone would soon. Diggs drew crowds. She said, "I've got to go."

"Running isn't the answer. Ask your stepfather for help. He's sick with worry."

"I can't. He'll want me to come home and stay put. I need to be free to find out the truth."

"Listen to me." Diggs clasped her wrists. His thumbs pressed into her so hard that pain shot up her forearms.

Chessa pulled free as a sickening notion came to her a second time. "You. The eight dwarves," she blurted then licked her lips, sorry for her faux pas. Diggs wasn't a dwarf, per se, but he was shorter than the average man. "You were dressed as Rumplestiltskin."

"I'm not following."

"The massacre. What if the killers made a mistake with the other dwarves? You could be in danger."

Diggs brandished a dismissive hand. "I am protected by the Lord."

"No! He doesn't protect everybody. He didn't protect my mother. He didn't protect Zach." She gulped in air. "A friend said your companion at the ball was dressed as a witch. Who was she? What was her name? How well did you know her?"

"There he is!" a large older woman cried and bustled toward Chessa and Diggs. "Yoo-hoo! Reverend." A group of similarly aged women followed her.

Chessa broke free and tore toward the front of the casino.

Diggs caught up to her and looped a hand around her elbow. For a smaller man, he was fast. "Please, don't do this. We'll get you the best lawyer."

"I've got a lawyer."

"Who?"

Chessa wasn't sure. She hadn't asked Ferguson for the name.

"Reverend!" the eager fan yelled.

With the distraction, Chessa wrested free again. "I'm innocent. I'll prove it." She fled through the exit. Warm wind slapped her face as she burst into the open.

"Chessa!" a man called from a white Toyota Tundra idling near valet parking. "Chessa Paxton!"

Chessa's gaze locked with Newman's, and a shiver skated up her spine. Could she trust him? No, she was tired. Vulnerable. She reversed direction.

"Stop, Chessa!" Newman yelled.

Chessa plowed past Diggs's adorers. Near the blackjack tables she glanced over her shoulder. Newman, blocked by Diggs's fans, was hopping up and down. He reminded Chessa of a duck in a shooting gallery. He yelled *stop* again, but Chessa didn't. Couldn't. She sped toward the exit leading to the employee parking lot.

Without paying attention to who might be coming in, she raced through the door. She collided into a young mother wheeling a child in a stroller up the handicapped ramp. The stroller teetered. Chessa reached to steady it. As she did, life hit her one frame at a time. Newman broke through the crowd. The stroller tipped onto two wheels. The mother screamed.

Newman reached for his gun, his eyes warning Chessa to freeze, but she knew he wouldn't draw it. Not with so many people around.

Chessa dove for the stroller. Her hands and knees slammed into the ground. She braced the stroller with her shoulder and nudged it back onto all four wheels. "I'm sorry, ma'am. So sorry."

At the same time, gongs rang out inside the casino.

Chessa glanced over her shoulder. A wave of cheering people blocked Newman's exit. The crowd hoisted a man into the air. The man must have won a jackpot.

Wasting no time, Chessa scrambled to her feet and tore down the steps that led to the labyrinth of employee's cars and delivery trucks. Among the sea of vehicles, she caught sight of a row of motorbikes and an idea came to her. At the head of the row stood a shiny blue-and-black Vespa. Two years ago when she was still a costume designer, months before she met Zach and months after she had ended her disastrous relationship with the married man, a lighting technician whose name she couldn't remember asked her on a date. He tried to win her over by bragging about his cool bike. He showed her how well he had equipped it, with a rear storage compartment packed with an emergency space blanket, bags of dried food, and flares for emergencies. He even boasted about the water bottle holder affixed to the frame. Chessa had acted impressed, but she had turned him down. He said he would try again. Maybe he'd get lucky.

Chessa hoped luck was on her side, and the lighting tech hadn't changed where he kept the spare key.

# CHAPTER 39

Marcus rushed out of the casino and scanned the employee parking lot. He squinted against the midmorning glare caroming off the windshields and looked for movement. Nothing. Chessa was gone.

Keegan joined him, out of breath. "I'm a churchgoer, but that thing back there with the reverend was incredible. My preacher doesn't get a crowd half that big. Not even on Easter."

"Not many do."

"You know, for a second I wondered if Diggs was egging on the crowd so they would block you from catching Ms. Paxton."

The notion had crossed Marcus's mind, as well, but Diggs couldn't have made the one-armed bandit hit the jackpot. No way. Marcus stomped back into the casino and said over his shoulder, "She must have stolen a vehicle. Find out whose and what."

Keegan nodded. "Where are you going?"

"To have a chat with the esteemed pastor." He rammed his way through the masses. He found Diggs near the entrance to the casino and snagged him by the shoulder. "Reverend, I'd like a word."

"Of course." Diggs returned a pen to a woman in a yellow sundress and forged a path through the crowd. "Excuse me, folks. Official business. Bless you, dear. God's peace, darlin'."

Faster than a congregation could say *amen,* fans formed a semi-circle around Marcus and Diggs near the reception desk.

Marcus ignored the crowd's whispering and said, "Reverend, you were talking to Chessa Paxton."

Diggs offered a forceful gaze that made Marcus understand how the man mesmerized people. "I was offering her a safe haven. Is that a crime?"

"Abetting a fugitive—"

"I did not abet. I counseled."

Word games irked Marcus. So did phonies. He had the impression that he was looking at a big phony despite what all the pundits said about Diggs being a good guy.

"I offered to find her a lawyer," Diggs went on. "Chessa said she had one already and that she would prove she was innocent."

"Did she say where she was headed?"

"No."

"To her stepfather's?"

"I seriously doubt it."

"Why is that?"

"Because she doesn't trust him."

"Do you?"

"We're friends."

"I've got a lot of friends that I don't trust."

"Then you should consider changing friends. Is there anything else, Detective?"

Marcus grunted.

Diggs grinned. "Are you wondering whether I, with God's help, made the jackpot happen?"

Marcus shifted feet. Was he that easy to read?

Diggs winked. "All things are possible with God. Now, if you don't mind, I should get back to my congregation."

Marcus scrubbed a hand through his hair. Why had Chessa risked coming to the casino where many would recognize her, disguise or no disguise? To seek out Diggs or someone else? Marcus ran after him. "One more thing, Reverend. Did Chessa say how she's going to prove she's innocent?"

"No."

Marcus fished in his pocket for the sheet of motel notepaper with Chessa's drawing on it and displayed it to Diggs. "Do you recognize this guy?"

Diggs gave the sketch a cursory glance. "Should I?"

"Does this mean anything to you?" Marcus showed him the page on which Chessa had scribbled names that included her stepfather, Evert, and Kimura.

Diggs shook his head.

As Marcus shoved the paper into his pocket, an alarm rang out. Gongs and whistles were good sounds in a casino; warning bells were not. Two security guards darted past and disappeared around the corner to the right. A nasty sensation cut through Marcus's gut. "We'll continue this conversation at another time, sir," he said and chased after the guards. When he found himself in the hallway near Human Resources, he tensed. He pulled his ID from his pocket and flashed it at one of the guards. "Washoe County Sheriff's Department. What's going on?"

"The head of HR was found dead in the women's restroom."

Marcus groaned. Chessa Paxton had been in the vicinity of another body. What were the odds?

## CHAPTER 40

Chessa grasped the handlebars of the Vespa tightly. How she wished she had a helmet for anonymity. She sped from the casino, her thoughts choppy, her movements erratic, and tried to block out the fear, but she couldn't. She wanted to prove herself innocent, but how could she? Helena was dead. The authorities were probably dissecting the crime scene and charging Chessa with the murder. Not to mention, she had doubled down and stolen a vehicle.

Veering toward the highway, she wondered where she was headed. She couldn't go back to the Cloud 9 Motel. Couldn't go to Ferguson's. She turned right out of habit, her home lying to the north.

Seconds later, she was forced to draw to a halt. Traffic had stalled. Panic surged through her and made it hard to breath. Had the sheriff already set up a roadblock? Cautiously she steered the Vespa down the right flank of cars without casting herself onto the scrabble stone shoulder so she could see what the holdup was.

Dozens of picketers were out in force. A handful of men in uniform were keeping them orderly. The group marched single file up a street leading into the mountains, toward Spitzer Nanotechnology. *As if protesting makes a difference,* Chessa thought. Only political bigwigs could make change happen nowadays. She had learned that at the senator's knee.

Chessa glimpsed to the right and gasped when she caught sight of some of the picketers' signs: *Stop nano. Destroy the black goo!* The vision swept her right back to the moment at the ball when Yukiko Kimura got mad at Evert and Jeremiah. She whacked Evert with the butt of her water bottle. At the time, Chessa had thought Yukiko was saying, *You! You!* What if she was saying, *Goo!*? Some people worried that Spitzer's products could turn humans into black goo. Others feared nanobots would creep from new-fangled lotions and fabrics and who-knew-what else into their bodies and turn them into alien creatures. Was Yukiko, who had advocated on behalf of Spitzer Nanotechnology, upset that her boss and his pal were siding with them and using such a derogatory term?

Chessa eased the Vespa forward as a new theory took shape. Had a fanatical group committed the massacre to stop Spitzer's research? Had the killers executed Yukiko Kimura because of her loyalty to Spitzer? Why kill ten other people?

A chilly notion hit Chessa. Could Jeremiah have had a hand in the murders? He didn't want nanotechnology to thrive in Nevada even though the industry had brought a lot of money and new jobs to the state. She flashed on the drawing she had sketched at the hotel. Maybe lumping Kimura, Spitzer, and her stepfather into the mess, especially with the tension surrounding the black goo concept, wasn't as improbable as it seemed. But where did Zach fit in? His involvement kept tripping her up. Why had he joined in the massacre? And why attempt to kill her? Simply because she had seen his passports?

The whoop of a siren made Chessa's pulse spike. She glanced in the side view mirror. An SLTPD patrol car raced toward her from the rear. Forcing herself to stay calm, she hunched over the Vespa, veered left, and eased into the parade of cars.

As the patrol car whizzed past, Chessa's breathing snagged. The patrolwoman driving the car had reminded her of Shawn Spitzer. Was she the witch that was giving the orders?

~ * ~

Though Marcus wanted to blow off the remainder of the day, he couldn't. When murder was priority one, nobody rested. Instead, he decided to revisit Senator Wolfe. Maybe now the man would offer ideas about Chessa's location.

While maneuvering his truck around traffic, Marcus glanced at Keegan. He was sitting in the passenger seat, his face ashen. Marcus couldn't blame him. In the last twenty-four hours, both of them had seen as much death as either could stomach.

"I liked Helena Gorzinski," Keegan whispered, his voice husky with emotion as they pulled into the senator's driveway.

"Me, too." Marcus knew her murder had to be related to the others, but how? Why? Something was definitely not right in Fairy Tale Land. "Did you get a fix on the vehicle Chessa took?"

"I put a guy on it. He's reviewing security footage. He'll call us as soon as he knows something."

They met Senator Wolfe in his office. The windows were closed, the room was stuffy, and the clocks were ticking mercilessly. Wolfe sat at his desk, his face placid although he seemed brittle. Why wouldn't he be? Recent events in his state were spiraling out of his control. Despite his edginess, he looked camera-ready: charcoal gray suit, gray-striped tie. His eyes were clear, as if he'd knocked off the booze. Keegan took a seat and remained quiet. Wolfe's Labrador retriever watched Marcus as he outlined the problem.

When Marcus finished, Wolfe rasped, "Chessa could no more kill someone than—"

"Her father?"

"Don't go putting words into my mouth. She's not capable of the deed."

The dog barked in agreement.

"Hush, Jocko." Wolfe hurled a magazine into the trashcan beside his desk, as if to add weight to his command. The dog cowered. "Chessa ran, Detective Newman, because she's afraid you'll railroad her."

Marcus bridled at the use of the term. He had never railroaded any suspect; he never would.

Patience Troon entered the room carrying a manila folder.

"What do you want?" Wolfe asked.

Troon strutted to the French doors and opened them, letting in much-needed air. The caw of seagulls pierced the silence as Troon strode to Wolfe's side, pulled a sheet of paper from the folder, and placed it on the desk. "This needs your attention."

"It can wait." The senator swatted the paper aside.

Troon retrieved it, replaced it on the desk, and stood nearby, mouth set, perspiration peppering her upper lip.

Marcus cocked his head, trying to size her up. Had she brought in the paper as a diversion? Had she decided Wolfe needed her support? "Sir, let's discuss Ms. Kimura."

"I'm very saddened to hear of her death."

"How was your relationship with her?"

Wolfe placed his elbows on the blotter and tented his hands. "Very good. Excellent. I admired her and supported virtually every effort she made on behalf of the state."

Troon sucked in a quick bit of air.

"Not every effort, sir," Marcus said. "You didn't back her efforts to bring technology to the state. More specifically, nanotechnology."

"You're talking about the Spitzer facility. True. I knew the people of Nevada would put up a fight. We aren't open to sharing our broad spaces."

"I've recently learned that Carter Billingsley wanted the land the facility is on. Ms. Kimura denied his request."

"He's a bully with no bite."

Troon made a snuffling sound.

"Do you know something that I don't, Ms. Troon?" Marcus asked.

Wolfe scoffed. "She doesn't know Billingsley."

"Yes, I do."

Wolfe glowered at her. "How?"

"In passing."

"Then keep your opinions to yourself," he snapped.

Marcus said, "Back to Ms. Kimura."

"Detective." Wolfe sighed. "There were plenty of political factions who wanted our illustrious director of business and industry ousted. She encouraged more than just technology businesses to move to Nevada. She wanted growth. Many Nevadans are anti change."

"Do you know of any death threats made against her?"

Troon, about as subtle as a third base coach, moved her arms from her sides to behind her back.

Wolfe glowered at her. "She had one death threat. It wasn't viable."

"Sir," Marcus said, "I beg your pardon, but she's dead."

"I simply meant that the man is an eco-nut. He wouldn't harm a flea."

Marcus glanced at Keegan, expecting some tart comment from him, hoping for a little of the kid's tag-team style, but Keegan sat idly scanning the titles on Wolfe's bookshelves. Marcus continued, unaided. "Senator, eco-nuts have been known to be anti change."

"Really, Detective," Troon said, "he's not your man. He's only got one arm."

"Are you talking about the leader of the faction known as the Tahoe Purists?"

Troon nodded.

Marcus was familiar with the guy. He was a legend who made two-armed men look like wimps. He could power a canoe or kayak on his own. He climbed ice walls. And he had a well-known temper. He had torn apart campsites of people who didn't obey state park laws. Marcus made a mental note to have Tallchief check out the eco-nut and his vendetta against Ms. Kimura.

"Are you sure there's no one else who might have wanted Ms. Kimura dead?" Marcus asked. "A jealous lover perhaps?"

Wolfe turned his chair to face the window.

"Sir, you're hiding something."

The senator spun around. "Aw, it's going to get out."

"Don't!" Troon cried.

Wolfe glared at her. "Wally can fend for himself."

"We know about Mr. Evert's relationship with Ms. Kimura," Marcus said, pleased he was a step ahead.

"They broke up two weeks ago," Wolfe said.

"I heard Mr. Evert wasn't happy about it."

Wolfe shrugged. "Wally's a practical guy. If a lady says no, he honors that. He's already got a new girlfriend. Anyway, that's all I have to share." He rose.

"Senator"—Keegan bounded from his chair—"one more thing."

Troon's eyes widened. Wolfe's, too.

Marcus had to give his deputy credit. He had timing.

"Sir," Keegan said, "did you happen to know any of the doctors that were killed in the massacre?"

Good question. Marcus had forgotten to ask.

"I met a few at the ball," Wolfe said.

"Two were triathletes," Keegan went on.

"What are you implying?"

"Nothing."

Wolfe's gaze narrowed.

"Another, an eye specialist, was a gambler. You like to gamble, don't you, Senator?"

"On the rare occasion."

"Do you think Mr. Evert might have known him?"

"I can't speak to that, young man. You'll have to ask Wally. If you have nothing further to implicate my stepdaughter—"

"Oh, but we do," Keegan said. "We have evidence."

"Uh-uh," Marcus said. "We're done here." He steered Keegan toward the door to keep him from telling the senator about Chessa's presence at the massacre or about the gold slipper found at the site or that Chessa had fled the site of another murder. The less Wolfe or his staff knew, at this point, the better for the investigation.

~ * ~

After the front door slammed, Jeremiah lurched out of his chair and strode around the desk. "Evidence, Patience. What possible evidence—"

"Calm down."

"Tell me about Billingsley."

"What about him?"

"He's married."

"Your point?"

"Are you involved?"

"Involved in what?"

"Don't be cheeky." Jeremiah raised his hand but stopped short of slapping her.

Patience didn't blink. Her eyes were cold, calculating. Jeremiah hated that about her. Hated that about women. How could they turn off their emotions whenever they wanted?

"You're making mistakes," Patience said. "Speaking off the cuff. The drinking—"

"It's over. I've made a pact with myself." Jeremiah cleared his throat, knowing he was lying. He craved a drink. He yearned to lapse into a drunken fog. "Tell me about Billingsley."

Patience offered a bitter, mirthless smile.

# CHAPTER 41

Seeing the patrolwoman that looked like Shawn Spitzer had helped Chessa focus. She was determined to find out more about not only Shawn and her possible involvement with Zach but also about Shawn's father and his relationship to Yukiko Kimura. Both were dead. Were their deaths random, or had the killer targeted them and the other nine victims?

Chessa faced the clerk at the front desk of the fashionable Montibleau Hotel and felt as if her brain was the ignition and her legs the spark plugs. Thousands of jolts of energy were running between them. She had pretended to be a friend of the Spitzers. The clerk had accepted the claim; she didn't seem to recognize Chessa. Had Newman released a new sketch of her? Had he figured out that she had stolen the Vespa yet?

"Between you and me"—the clerk bent forward and lowered her voice—"the Spitzer girls look pretty ragged."

"Where are they?"

"With their aunt at the Fontaine Funeral Parlor just up the road. They're attending to burial arrangements and, afterward, going to lunch. The parlor offered to do everything for free. Isn't that nice?"

*Opportunistic,* Chessa thought. The place would garner a lot of publicity from its gift.

In less than ten minutes, she arrived at the understated funeral parlor, which was jammed between two tacky wedding chapels, both shaped like wedding cakes complete with brides and grooms on top. Media trucks stood outside the building. A handful of reporters and camera crew were hanging around the entrance.

Chessa parked in the lot beyond and doubled back. Near the front, she overheard two reporters discussing how long they would wait for the Spitzers to emerge.

Head lowered, Chessa hurried past. Feeling as creepy as a ghoul, she entered the candlelit foyer. The scent of sandalwood hung in the air. A glum symphony played through multiple speakers. The parlor's director, a man as gaunt and earnest as his profession, was filing papers in an alcove that served as an office. Chessa introduced herself and once again lied and said she was a friend of the Spitzer family. She asked where they might be. The man eyed her revealing outfit. Chessa defiantly squared her shoulders. Too bad if her clothing didn't meet his standards.

"Follow me." The man led her down a navy blue hall lined with display cases that were filled with decorative urns. He gestured toward a room on the right, the plaque above the door designating it the Planning Room. "They're inside, considering their options."

Though Chessa felt the pressure of time, she elected to sit on the leather bench across the hall. "I won't intrude." From her vantage point, she had a full view of the Spitzer girls. "I'll wait here."

The man nodded and left.

A little voice in Chessa's head urged her to race through the EXIT ONLY door and leave these people alone, but she ignored it. She needed answers.

Shawn Spitzer, who was willowy and exotic and wore her dark glossy hair parted down the middle, stood in profile. Her arm was slung across the shoulders of a younger, shorter, curly-haired girl.

An overly tan woman in her forties, the girls' aunt Chessa assumed, paced in front of an array of urns and caskets. The family resemblance was strong. She had the same aquiline nose and diamond-shaped chin as Shawn and her younger sister. Occasionally the aunt's mouth moved and she swept her hand in front of the options.

Chessa's heart snagged. She had dealt with the same difficult choice. Her mother's ashes were stored in an elaborate blue cloisonné urn with white seagulls flying across it. Chessa told Jeremiah her mother would have preferred the simpler brass urn with the flat top, but he wouldn't hear of it.

Shawn said something to her aunt. The woman nodded. Shawn squeezed her younger sister's shoulder then strode from the room, her cell phone in hand, her fingers tapping keys. Who was she texting? Who was important enough to draw her away from her family at such a heartbreaking moment? Streaks of teary mascara tarnished her pretty face. Her flats made no sound as she stole along the plush carpet and turned in the direction of the ladies' room.

Chessa fetched a couple of tissues from her satchel and followed Shawn. She thrust the tissues at her. "Here."

With a shaky hand, Shawn accepted the tissues, but suspicion swept across her face. "Do I know you?"

"I knew your folks." Not a total lie.

Shawn tilted her head and Chessa stiffened. The witch at the ball had made the same move. Chessa could see Zach having an affair with Shawn and doing her bidding. She was so alluring and young, and yet—

"Are you a reporter?" Shawn asked. "You don't look like one. Are you working undercover? Is that why you're wearing that cheap makeup?"

"Are you always so forthright?"

"Daddy said you can't buy honesty. It's either in you or it's not."

"I'm sorry for your loss."

"If I hear that one more time, I'll heave." Tears pooled in the corners of Shawn's eyes. "I'm sorry. That was rude. I just…" She dabbed her eyes with a tissue. "This sucks. I want my parents back, and we'll never know why, will we?"

"I'm sure the sheriff—"

"Oh, right. They're working so hard. *Not*." Shawn's face pinched with pain. "If you ask me, the world is insane."

*Crazy nuts*, Chessa wanted to say.

"I should get back to my sister." Shawn wadded the tissues in a fist. "Thanks for coming."

"Wait." Chessa grasped Shawn's shoulder. "Your father—"

Shawn stared at Chessa's hand; Chessa removed it.

"What about him?"

Chessa wracked her brain. Would Shawn know her father's enemies? Would she understand the intricacies of his business? "Did your father receive threats to his life?"

"I knew it. You *are* a reporter."

"I'm not. It's the truth. Did he?"

Shawn's shoulders sagged. "You're wondering whether my father was the reason that all of these people were massacred?"

Chessa kept trying to rule out the possibility that one victim was a target. Kill eleven to get to one? It didn't make sense. "The protestors—"

"Daddy said they would never do anything. They're scared of their own shadows."

"None has ever gotten violent?"

Shawn shook her head. "My father said picketing comes with the territory. People don't understand the future. Black goo is sci-fi movie stuff. They lash out." She swept her glossy hair over her shoulder. "Nanotechnology is safe."

"Is it really?"

"The complex structures won't break down like that. I mean, sure, in the early stages, buckyballs have been known to disrupt the membranes of fish brain cells, but researchers have found ways to bond simple chemicals to carbon spheres." She wove her fingers together to demonstrate. "If these people would take a tour of the facility, they'd understand."

"There are tours?"

"Daddy said, 'Open doors lead to open minds.' He wanted everyone to see what we do."

"*We*? Are you a scientist, too?"

A bitter smile pressed at her lips. "Stanford awarded me a PhD saying I am."

"Aren't you twenty-two?"

"I'm a prodigy."

"But you don't work at the facility."

"I work at a satellite location in Silicon Valley." Shawn ran her tongue along her teeth. "You know, two men came to tour the facility in the spring. I think they were government."

A chill coiled up Chessa's spine. "Why would you think that?"

"Let's just say most guys around here don't wear suits like that. They wanted to know what we had in production. Daddy—" Shawn's voice broke. "Oh my gosh. You don't think—" Fresh tears flooded her eyes. "Did they want our research? Did my dad refuse them? Is that why he was murdered?"

Shawn had made a big leap in her deductive reasoning. On the other hand, Chessa was making the same leap. Zach had fake passports. Had he posed as a government agent? Was he a governmental spy? Did he move to Lake Tahoe and marry her as his cover?

"Shawn, dear." Her aunt appeared in the hall and beckoned her.

"Sorry," Shawn said to Chessa. "I've got to go."

"Wait! One more question. I saw you at the ball, right? You wore a witch costume."

Shawn's cheeks tinged pink; the question was obviously not what she had expected. "My mother picked it out. She said someone as pretty as me should see life from the other side. I was darned ugly. The hooked nose, the mole. It's weird, being in disguise and seeing how people look at you if you're deformed. It's…I can't explain it, but it's not cool. I even carried a rotten apple."

The witch with Zach hadn't carried an apple, but that didn't rule out Shawn completely. "Was your costume made of feathers?"

"Yes."

"Black feathers?"

"Red. Can you imagine? They were my mother's decision. The whole thing was so impractical. The ones attached to my shoulders kept hitting people in the face." Her mouth turned up in a smile. "There was another witch who wore an ensemble of black feathers. She was skinnier than a runway model with major cheekbones. Between you and me, I think she had work done. We sort of glared at each other. I mean, how dare she have a gown made of feathers, too." With a quick swipe, Shawn opened the PHOTOS app on her cell phone and tapped a picture of a red-feathered witch and Snow White. She displayed it to Chessa. "This is my mother and I. She—" Shawn fought another bout of tears.

"Don't blame yourself," Chessa said, repeating her own mandate. She couldn't have prevented her mother's car crash. No one could have. "Fate is not ours—"

"Miss Spitzer! Shawn!" A female reporter Chessa recognized from KINC news raced down the funeral home hall, a mini-tape recorder in her hand. "A minute of your time." The woman nabbed Shawn by the elbow.

Shawn looked pleadingly at Chessa, and though Chessa wanted to help, self-preservation kicked in. Before the reporter recognized her and changed targets, she tore out the EXIT ONLY door.

Chessa darted behind the media trucks and waited a few seconds to make sure no one was chasing after her before sneaking toward the Vespa. As she passed the KINC truck, its door wide open, she glanced inside. On the seat lay a notepad, a protein bar, a media credential, a striped shirt bound with a white dry cleaner's ribbon—apparently the reporter didn't ever want to be caught in a soiled blouse—and a sunhat.

Embracing while abhorring her new life of crime, Chessa collected all of the items, tossed everything into the Vespa's storage compartment, climbed on the bike, and sped off.

A minute later, she turned south on Highway 28, but where was she headed? The conversation with Shawn replayed through her mind. Men, possibly government, had visited the Spitzer Nanotech Facility. Should she go there to find out more?

The sound of brakes screeching and tires skidding on the road caught her attention.

Chessa glanced over her shoulder. The green Chevy Blazer that had just flown past her was making a hasty U-turn. Through the windshield, she made out a male driver with a flat nose and bleached white hair.

*No way*, she thought. It was the security guard.

Heart thudding, Chessa sped ahead while checking the side view mirror. The Blazer zoomed toward her. She swerved right to avoid being rammed and skidded on the shoulder of the road. Pebbles splattered upward and hit her legs and the undersides of her arms. She bit back pain and veered onto the road in front of a VW Beetle. The Blazer drew near but couldn't make contact because the VW was in the way. Chessa continued to weave in and out of traffic. The Blazer couldn't maneuver as easily as she could, but she knew she couldn't outrun it forever.

How had the guy found her? Had he seen her stealing the Vespa? Had he viewed security footage at the casino? Even if he had, how had he determined she'd gone to the funeral home?

With a jolt, the realization hit Chessa. The lighting guy must have put a GPS tracker on his stupid bike, and if the guard could find her, so could Newman. She had to get rid of the Vespa or the tracking device.

Where was it? In the compartment beneath the seat? Under the fenders? Without slowing or taking her eyes off the road, she probed each possibility within reach, searching for a disk. Nothing. She flipped open the rear compartment and groped on the underside of the lid while glimpsing in the side view mirror.

The Blazer zipped into the left lane, but an oncoming truck blared its horn, forcing the Blazer to fall in behind a blue sedan.

*C'mon, c'mon.* Chessa's fingers landed on something that felt like a button. She plucked at it, but it wouldn't budge. The tech must have glued it into place. She slammed the lid shut and focused on the road.

Just beyond the tunnel at Cave Rock lay the entrance to Mystic Beach.

Jewel and she had explored every facet of the area during the summer of their sophomore year. As a result, both had suffered royal sunburns. Chessa pictured the layout. The stairs to the beach would be impossible to maneuver on the Vespa, but the access ramp for the handicapped would be manageable and too narrow for the Blazer.

*Do it.*

Chessa shot through the tunnel. To her dismay, as she exited the other end, she spotted a gold Mercedes parked on the side of the road near the entrance to the handicap ramp. Beyond the car trudged an elderly couple carrying a cooler. At the rate they were walking, they would block the entrance at exactly the time Chessa could make the turn. She didn't want to hurt them, but she needed them gone.

She swerved onto the shoulder of the road, beeped on the Vespa's horn, and screamed, "Out of my way! No brakes!"

Responding like a youngster, the old man dragged his companion into the safety of a bush.

Chessa burned past them and tore down the ramp. The railing and hillside whizzed by in a blur. The Vespa hit a rut and bucked, its wheels not thick enough to absorb the jarring impact. Her teeth clacked together, and vibrations rattled the Vespa's frame and shimmied up her arms.

Near the bottom of the hill she saw her next obstacle: the T that dead-ended in the bike path. If she didn't slow down, she would slam into the curb and fly off the bike.

Zach used to love freestyle motocross on ESPN. Chessa would watch with him occasionally. During one event, she'd seen a biker do a spectacular stunt. Emulating the biker, she yanked the handlebars hard to the left and jutted out her left leg. She allowed her foot to drag along the cement, working like a fulcrum. The bike whipped around. The rear wheel spun out. Before the bike could topple to the ground, Chessa jammed her heel into the cement. Pain spurted up her calf, but she held on tight. The rear wheel butted the curb. Chessa's head snapped forward and backward. Her vision blurred but only for a second. Hastily she planted both feet on the ground to keep the bike from tipping, gave a shove, and pelted into the shadows of the manzanita bushes.

When she pulled to a stop, she peeked toward the highway. No sign of the Blazer. Not yet.

# CHAPTER 42

Marcus steered his truck to the front of the trailer at Carter Billingsley's development project and jammed it into park as he ran through the few connections he had accumulated to date. Zach Szabo knew Paul Tarantino, who knew Wally Evert, who might have wanted Yukiko Kimura killed, plus Kimura had a feud with Billingsley, and Senator Wolfe and Patience Troon were hiding something, but what?

He climbed out of the truck and said, "Deputy."

"Sir." Keegan was sitting in the passenger seat, preoccupied with the iPhone and its Internet connection.

"It'll be cramped spaces in the trailer. I'll go in alone and give you a shout if I need backup."

"Yes, sir." Keegan didn't look up.

Marcus mounted the metal stairs to the trailer and, without knocking, opened the door.

The man standing by the sink swung around. He reminded Marcus of a street fighter, his nose crooked from repeated brawls. He wore his surfer blonde hair in spikes. He was holding a half-drunk bottle of Michelob.

"Carter Billingsley?" Marcus asked.

"You found him. Who're you?"

"Detective Newman, Washoe County Sheriff's Department."

Billingsley slugged down the remaining beer and tossed the bottle into the sink with three other empties. He wiped his hand down the front of his checkered shirt and thrust it at Marcus.

Marcus didn't shake. "I'm here to discuss the murders of eleven people at Spooner Meadow."

Billingsley tucked his thumb into the front pocket of his jeans. "I heard the news."

"Yukiko Kimura is dead."

"Heard that, too."

"A few weeks ago, you had an altercation with Ms. Kimura because she nixed one of your projects."

"Altercation. Fancy word."

"You forced her off the road."

"Oh, man." Billingsley slumped against the counter. "I knew that chick would come back to haunt me. Yeah, she and me, we argued. She screamed real loud. I yelled back. It was the liquor talking." He eyed the bottles in the sink. "I don't have a problem, but I can kick back a few. Look, I never laid a hand on her, and I sure as heck wouldn't have offed her."

"Or have her murdered?"

"Just because I'm in construction doesn't mean I know thugs."

"Do you recognize this guy?" Marcus displayed Chessa's drawing.

"Looks familiar. Is he a gambler? I gamble a bit, but everybody does in Tahoe."

Marcus didn't. Neither did his buddies.

Billingsley opened his palms. "Detective, why would I hire someone to kill a slew of people just to get to Yukiko Kimura? That would require a hefty fee, and honestly, I don't have that kind of cash."

Marcus stepped forward. Billingsley dropped his arms to his sides and his shoulders drew in to protect his core. The stink of booze oozed from his pores. At times like these, Marcus considered giving up beer.

Billingsley's nostrils flared. "Have you asked Wally Evert the same questions? He was dating her. That one-eyed piece of junk could hire a hit man faster than I could. Heck, for all I know, he's your killer's brother. I'm assuming the drawing you showed me is a suspect? They both have red hair."

Marcus didn't think the guy in the sketch looked anything like Evert, but not all brothers looked alike. Marcus and Eddie hadn't. Eddie had been slight and pale, the kind of guy people took advantage of.

"Evert's got a heavy hand," Billingsley went on. "I know for a fact that two weeks ago he left Kimura with a shiner. She and me had an appointment, and I showed up at her house ten minutes early. Wally was leaving. She was pressing a frozen bag of peas to her face." He whistled. "There were others with Evert that day. Davey Diggs and some broad."

"What was your appointment about?"

"After our little spat, Ms. Kimura"—Billingsley spit out the name—"asked me to come and talk. Make amends. In the end, we were civil. The road thing, like I said, was a misunderstanding. It wasn't road rage or anything. The steering wheel slipped."

"Really?" Marcus folded his arms. "Two of your exes have filed restraining orders against you." Frita Gutiérrez had dug up that gem. "Did your fist *slip* into each of their faces?"

Billingsley turned pale. "I haven't hit a woman in five years. I'm in therapy."

"Is that so?"

"I see a doctor in Incline Village. Dr. Ferguson Fairchild."

"Fairchild?"

"Yeah. He's like cutting edge when it comes to hypnotherapy."

~ * ~

Chessa tried to peek through the thick stand of bushes, but she couldn't see a thing. The good news: the guy in the Blazer couldn't see her, either. The bad: she didn't have a clue where he was. Had he seen her veer down the handicapped ramp? Was he trying to find a way to her? Or was he on the highway, lying in wait ready to shoot at any sudden movement? Who was he? Who did he work for? Didn't he realize that Chessa couldn't ID him? Except she probably could, with the help of a police artist.

Fifty yards away from where Chessa was hiding stood a public bathroom. She climbed off the Vespa and walked the bike into the building.

A woman with an infant tucked into a Baby Bjorn backpack scowled at Chessa like she had brought a communicable disease into the space. As the woman and child scurried outside, Chessa opened the Vespa's rear compartment and, using the ignition key, pried the GPS disk loose. She raced into a stall, dropped the disk in the toilet, flushed, and watched it spiral into the sewer system. Afterward, she tiptoed to the door and peered out. No one was charging toward the bathroom. The frightened mother and child were nowhere in sight.

But then Chessa heard a rustle. In the bushes beyond the bathroom wall. Was it the guard?

Suddenly a huge bird soared into the air, wings flapping hard.

Chessa shrieked. With her insides in knots, she returned to the stall and relieved herself. Seconds later, she rushed to the sink, snatched a handful of paper towels, wet them, and dabbed at the viscous leg and arm wounds caused by gravel splatter. The water stung. Chessa had to bite her lip to keep from crying, but the pressure stanched the bleeding.

She wadded the paper towels and headed to the garbage can to discard them but paused. She glanced from the wet paper towels to the motorbike. If Newman learned about the Vespa, he would know the license plate number, GPS or not. He would put out an APB.

Speedily Chessa rubbed the bloody towel down the sides of the Vespa. The white stripes turned red. Then she swathed the license plate with blood. Maybe, she hoped, by adding a little confusion, she could buy herself some time.

## CHAPTER 43

Marcus roamed Ferguson Fairchild's living room, and a sour taste filled his mouth. The house was so tidy an OCD person could do a white glove test and not find any dust. The photographs, books, and collectibles were all top of the line. Fairchild, as pressed and fine-edged as his home, sat in a taupe leather chair, eyes placid, thumb and forefinger of his right hand stroking his perfectly trimmed goatee. Was he a murderer? Had he killed those people in the meadow? No, probably not. He would be too worried about blood splatter hitting him.

Keegan perched on the arm of the matching taupe chair while glancing at his iPhone. On the drive over, he had questioned why Zach Szabo had needed so many passports.

At the moment, Marcus wasn't concerned with Szabo and his multiple personalities. For all he knew, Szabo was into fake IDs so he could seduce women by pretending he was a spy. Fairchild, on the other hand, was far more interesting.

Marcus's gaze landed on the suitcase standing by Fairchild's front door. "Planning a trip?"

Fairchild stopped stroking his goatee. "I'm going to see my mother."

Marcus bit back a smile. "Gee, that's nice."

"She's ill. My sister just had a baby; otherwise, she would tend to Mother." He shifted in his chair. "Look, detective, I told the other sheriff everything I know."

"Tell me again. Humor me. What was your relationship with Chessa Paxton?"

"We met in a high school art class."

"You're an artist?" Keegan asked.

"Hardly!" Fairchild grinned. That was the most expression he had shown so far. "It was one of those required classes. We learned perspective by drawing houses and fences. I stunk. I was a math and science guy."

"Go on." Marcus propped his foot on one of the stools. Fairchild frowned, obviously displeased that Marcus was using a stool for the purpose it had been designed. *Tough.*

"We volunteered on a number of projects in town to earn service hours. You know, like reading to children or cleaning up the beaches. Other than that, we were just friends. The three musketeers."

"Three?"

"Jewel, Chessa and me."

"Jewel who?" Keegan cut in. "There's no one named Jewel in Chessa's address book."

"That's because she's dead." Fairchild's face grew dark. "She was mugged and killed."

Marcus said, "Got a last name?"

Fairchild shook his head. "I'm sorry to say I don't. Isn't that awful? It was so long ago. Do you remember everyone you went to high school with?"

Marcus could remember a few faces, a few first names. The guys who were on the football team. The girls who told him to go fly a kite. The girls who didn't. But he believed he would remember the full name of someone who was killed.

"Jewel Jenkins!" Fairchild blurted. "That was it. Chessa and I joined a group to talk about the trauma. Soon after, I decided to become a therapist."

"You're young for a therapist, aren't you?" Keegan asked.

"I've been in practice a few years."

Marcus scratched his neck. "Not sure I'd go to a therapist who's only been practicing a few years."

"That's why they call it a practice." Fairchild chortled.

Marcus scowled. He didn't trust people who laughed at their own jokes. "What happened next?"

"Chessa and I lost touch when we went off to college. She to UNLV, me to USC. I returned to Lake Tahoe a few years ago, and we reconnected. She came to me to discuss the sleepwalking episodes." He swallowed. "You knew about the sleepwalking?"

Marcus nodded.

Fairchild looked relieved that he hadn't divulged some deep, dark secret. He uncrossed his legs and leaned forward, elbows on his knees. "Zach chided her about the problem. FYI, Chessa couldn't kill, not even in a stupor. It's not in her DNA."

"Her father killed someone."

"I'm not so sure."

"Back to Zach Szabo. You don't seem very happy about him having been in Chessa's life."

Fairchild folded his hands. "He wasn't right for her."

"You were?"

"Don't put words into my mouth, detective." Fairchild squeezed his lips together as if he were afraid the truth might pop out. "After Chessa's mother died, she needed someone to talk to. She doesn't seek help on a regular basis. In fact, she's the sanest woman I know. And the most loving. The most giving."

Marcus grunted. Did everybody think Chessa was the next best thing to applesauce?

"Did you know she devotes at least ten hours a week to a variety of causes, like Keep Tahoe Blue?"

"The environmental group?"

Keegan said, "Sir, if you'll recall, Chessa wrote a scathing article about the way developers are ruining the environment."

Marcus removed his foot from the ottoman and started walking around the place, opening doors, sizing up Fairchild as he did. The guy wasn't simply in love with Chessa; he was madly in love with her. But why would he do something as horrific as slay a group of people? What was his motive? Marcus opened the door to a bedroom and was surprised to see a mess. He glanced back at the doctor. Was he neat on the exterior but messed up on the interior?

"She's an angel to so many," Fairchild went on, his eyes bright. "All while she's trying to get ahead in her career."

"Isn't she at the top of her game?" Marcus asked.

"She's talented enough to work in Las Vegas or Los Angeles or even New York, but she stayed in Tahoe to keep close to her family. Since her mother died, moving has been a topic of discussion, but Zach—" Fairchild jammed his lips together. Was he afraid of divulging something that could harm Chessa's plea of innocence? "Zach didn't want to move."

*On the other hand, good old Zach had wanted a divorce,* Marcus mused. Cut ties and run. "Why didn't he want to move?"

"He'd made good contacts here. He felt his business was growing."

Marcus didn't buy that. A handful of clients didn't constitute a growing business no matter how savvy the guy was with numbers. Was forcing Chessa to stay in Lake Tahoe his way of exerting control?

"Chessa's stepfather was introducing Zach to people who were looking to invest," Fairchild said.

"Like your patient Carter Billingsley?"

"How do you know—"

"Did Senator Wolfe introduce Billingsley to Zach?"

"I believe Wally Evert did. Do you know him?"

"In passing." Marcus rubbed the back of his neck. "Billingsley said your specialty is hypnotherapy."

"It is."

"Did you hypnotize Chessa?"

"Occasionally," Fairchild answered. No pretense. If he had tricked her into committing the crime, wouldn't he have lied?

"Did you do so recently while she was seeking your assistance?"

"We didn't have time. She ran in and ran out."

Marcus switched gears. "Did you and Chessa date?"

"What? No." Fairchild's neck flushed red.

"Why not?"

"Are you kidding? She'd never go for someone like me. She likes a man with edge."

"Somebody dangerous?"

"She liked a man that kept her"—he searched for the word—"*guessing*. I never did that. Sad to say, I'm an open book."

If he was, why did Marcus feel the urge to read between the lines?

"Doctor, do you have an alibi for the night of the fourteenth?"

"I was with my mother. As I said, she's ill."

"You didn't go to the ball?"

"Not everybody enjoys fairy tales."

## CHAPTER 44

In the privacy of the public bathroom, Chessa wolfed down the protein bar she had filched from the KINC reporter's truck. Next she donned the reporter's striped shirt over her tank top and plopped the sunhat onto her head. It didn't fit well, so she tugged the grosgrain ribbon tighter to make the hat's brim cup her face. Not stylish, but at least the hat would draw more attention than her features.

Chessa emerged into daylight sitting astride the Vespa. She scanned the area for the guard or the green Blazer. Nothing. Cautiously she rode the bike along the path, gazing up toward the highway. No one—no car—was mirroring her movement. Believing she had, indeed, shaken the tail, she proceeded south in the direction of Stateline.

A short while later, Chessa was sitting in the sales director's office at Spitzer Nanotechnology. She had been granted an interview after claiming to be a reporter eager to check out a story about government interest in the Lake Tahoe region.

Lorna, an unassuming woman with chubby cheeks, didn't offer Chessa anything to drink, not even water. She sat teary-eyed behind one of the two desks in the pine-paneled financial offices. "It's so sad," she said for the second time, referring to her employer's death. "He only went to the ball because his youngest daughter begged him to."

"Tragic," Chessa said. The charade of being a reporter made her feel like a two-bit actor, but she maintained her official pose, reporter's notebook out, pen poised, and did her best to win Lorna's confidence. She noticed a wealth of framed pictures on the bureau behind Lorna's desk. A few included the Spitzer girls. "Were you close to the family?" she asked.

Lorna bobbed her head and mopped her cheeks with a wad of tissues then tossed the tissues into a garbage can and plucked two more from a box on her desk. "They were the nicest people you'd ever meet."

"Mr. Spitzer was a visionary I heard."

"And a true humanitarian. Selflessness is so lacking in today's society, don't you think?"

Chessa offered her most supportive look.

"It's the *me* generation," Lorna went on. "But not him. Nanotechnology, he said, is…*was*…designed to make this world a better place." She stemmed a fresh spate of tears with a tissue. "It won't be the same without him. Or his wife."

Chessa felt herself choking up about Zach, but pushed the memories aside. This was no time to dwell on her personal loss. If she did, she would crumble. "At least his legacy will live on. I'm sure the government men that visited the facility have plans to safeguard all of Mr. Spitzer's research."

"Government men?"

"Men in suits," Chessa said using Shawn's term. "They visited in the spring."

"Oh, *them*. They didn't seem to be interested in safeguarding anything." She leaned forward and whispered, "FYI, I didn't trust them from the moment I set eyes on them. I told that sheriff about their visit, but—"

"Which sheriff?"

"The one who's running for mayor. His picture is everywhere. *Tall*-something."

Chessa grimaced. She couldn't keep crossing paths with Tallchief and his men without getting caught. She offered a collaborative smile. "Tell me about these men in suits."

"It was very hush-hush, but they said they wanted to know more about the technology that helped with fabrics. Flexible fiber technology is one of Mr. Spitzer's greatest accomplishments. There was always something hopping in his brain. Genius." She tapped the side of her head with a finger.

"I'll bet he treasured your loyalty."

Lorna blushed.

"These men," Chessa pressed. "There were two?"

"Mutt and Jeff, I called them. Mutt, the redhead, was as tall and lean as a professional basketball player."

The security guard could have appeared that tall to someone as short as Lorna.

"The other had a crew cut and buffed nails." Lorna tilted her head. "I notice things like that. Men that groom."

Zach had sported a crew cut back in April.

"Did these men present you with credentials?"

"I can't remember. My associate—"

"Are you talking about me, Lorna?" A large woman with short brown hair marched into the office and let the door slam shut behind her. She eyed Chessa with outright disdain. "Who are you?"

"She's a reporter," Lorna said.

"Uh-uh. That's it. We don't discuss our business with anyone who is not approved by Mr. Spitzer. You'll have to leave."

Lorna flicked a finger at the woman. "Oh, hush! Mr. Spitzer cannot approve guests, as you very well know, and in the interim, I'm in charge." She addressed Chessa. "Where were we?"

"Can you describe these men in detail, ma'am?"

"Jeff was very handsome. He had brown hair. Mutt, the redhead, was rough around the edges."

"He didn't have red hair," the associate hissed. "And stop calling them Mutt and Jeff. It's rude." She took a seat at the desk opposite Lorna's and noisily shuffled through a stack of mail.

Chessa said, "Lorna, can you recall if the redheaded man had a tattoo of a spider caught in a web snaking up one side of his neck?"

Lorna shook her head. "Can't dredge up a thing, but they came in April. It was chilly. Both were wearing jackets with the collars turned up."

"Do you happen to remember who set up the appointment for these men?" Chessa asked. "Was it the state's director of business and industry, Yukiko Kimura?"

"No." Lorna gazed at her associate.

"Don't look at me. I haven't a clue."

"Could it have been Senator Wolfe?" Chessa asked.

"No," Lorna said. "Oh, I remember. You know that guy who does all those ads for boats? He's got that weird eye."

"Wally Evert?" A shiver slithered up Chessa's spine.

"He's got his finger in every pie, if you ask me. He's a huge investor—"

"Lorna, enough!" The other woman slapped a palm on her desk. "Miss Whoever-you-are, leave or I'm calling security."

"Don't bother." Chessa tucked her notepad under her arm, and, as coolly as she could, walked to the door while fishing in her satchel for the key to the Vespa.

She weaved through the stream of visitors who were waiting in line for a tour. As she reached the front entrance, a hand gripped her shoulder.

Lorna spun Chessa around. Rosy splotches of embarrassment marred her face. She apologized for her associate's curt behavior. "Just so you know, those guys you're asking about took a tour of the facility. Anybody interested in the company, in any aspect, is required to do so. Mr. Spitzer's rules. He always said, 'Fear is dispelled by knowledge.' Maybe our tour guide would be able to tell you more, but don't ask right here. We don't want Miss Fussbudget to catch you." Lorna ushered Chessa to the head of a group of visitors and addressed a freckle-faced woman in a crisp brown uniform. "Got room for another?"

"The more the merrier," the young woman said.

Chessa noticed a hefty security guard trailing the pack and hoped, when the opportunity arose to ask the tour guide about the men in suits, that he would be far, far away.

# CHAPTER 45

Marcus strode across the Evert's Marina parking lot while working through the details of his interview with Ferguson Fairchild. Toward the end, he didn't consider Fairchild guilty. The guy was too candid. If his mother provided a valid alibi for him, Marcus would cross him off the suspect list. On the other hand, could he trust a mother's testimony? What mother wouldn't stand up for her child? Marcus coughed out a laugh. His mother, for one. His *birth* mother.

"Are you okay?" Keegan strode beside Marcus, his fingers tapping the iPhone screen.

"Yeah," he lied. "What in heck are you researching, deputy?"

"The passports—"

"I told you, bureaucracy works slowly. Leave it—"

A screech of tires made Marcus whip around. Tallchief parked and climbed out of his Explorer and strode across the asphalt toward them.

"Are you expecting him?" Keegan asked.

"Not on a bet."

"You know"—Keegan shut down the iPhone and pocketed it—"with his head bent forward like that, he reminds me of a scrawny hound as if he's trying to pick up a scent."

Tallchief hadn't always been thin, Marcus thought. He had lost over sixty pounds since Ruthie died. He had grown grumpier, too. He charged up to Marcus. "It turns out the one-armed eco-nut is in South America saving some rain forest. He's been there for a month."

"Fine. I'll cross him off the list." Marcus tilted his head. "But that's not why you're here."

"I'm heading up this interview. Captain Armstrong's orders."

"You're not up to speed."

"I'm all ears."

Marcus grumbled. One of the reasons Tallchief and he hadn't worked as a team was that they were both bullheaded. Tallchief didn't look like he was going to bend this time.

"Deputy, remain outside," Marcus said. Three was a bad number in an interrogation. The interviewee, feeling outnumbered, either quit talking or lawyered up.

Keegan hung back as Marcus stomped toward the sales shop while giving Tallchief a twenty-second recap of his meetings with Billingsley and Fairchild.

"Also, thanks to Fairchild," Marcus said, "Chessa Paxton has an attorney at the ready, but they haven't spoken yet. There. You're up to speed." He pushed through the shop door and marched to the marina's sales counter. Two girls in bikini tops and short shorts moved out of his path. Neither made eye contact with him, probably sensing the tension in the air, or maybe because he was more than twice their age. Before he could address the clerk named Missy who had helped him with the boat keys, Tallchief butted in front of him.

"Where can we find your boss?" Tallchief demanded.

The clerk blanched.

*Perfect,* Marcus thought. *One ugly American cop coming right up.* With a gentler tone, he said, "Missy, Mr. Evert is expecting us."

The clerk pointed. "He's in his office, but he's got a guest."

Marcus didn't care if the guy was serving tea to the president. He cut in front of Tallchief and jogged upstairs.

Tallchief caught up to him right before he reached the landing. "Newman, we've got a suspect on the loose. We need to find her. You screwed up, so you follow my lead. The Cap—"

"You know what?" Marcus interrupted. "I'm getting tired of you invoking Armstrong's name."

"It's his call. You'd better fall in line."

"Or what?" Marcus entered Evert's office without knocking.

"Well, well, how do I rate two top dogs?" Evert, in black golf shirt and black slacks, stood behind the bar, a bottle of whiskey in his hand. He poured a jiggerful into a tumbler and pushed it toward his guest, Reverend Diggs, who was also dressed in black. He sat perched on a carved oak stool, his feet dangling.

"You don't rate two top dogs," Tallchief said. "You rate one. Me. Detective Newman is my subordinate."

Marcus huffed. *Fine.* He would cede control. He wanted answers any way he could get them. But the moment Tallchief messed up—

"We've had some interesting developments in our case," Tallchief continued.

"Excuse us for a minute, Davey," Evert said.

"No problem," Diggs responded, but he didn't budge.

Marcus stepped out of the way as Evert came around the end of the bar carrying a drink of his own—clear, no bubbles, with ice. Gin or Vodka? "It's a little early to be tippling, isn't it, Wally?"

"I never tipple, Detective Newman." Evert made a grand gesture for Marcus and Tallchief to join him in the sitting area beyond the bar, an area that only a designer could have dreamed up with a leather two-seater sofa, circular glass coffee table, and a pair of uncomfortable looking barrel chairs. Evert perched on the front edge of one of the chairs and raised his glass in a toast. "Cheers." He took a sip. "It's five o'clock someplace." He smiled, entirely too relaxed, as if he believed he was above the law.

Marcus frowned. With all of Evert's contacts in government, maybe he was.

"Sit, gentlemen."

Tallchief did. Marcus remained standing. Tallchief stared daggers at him, but Marcus didn't flinch.

Tallchief cleared his throat. "I'm getting mixed reports, Mr. Evert."

"About?"

Tallchief hooked a thumb at Diggs. "Can we talk in private?"

"Don't worry. Davey knows everything about me. We go way back. Before I became a sinner." Evert's weak eye wandered. He closed it and reopened it; he wasn't winking. "You can speak freely, detective."

"Carter Billingsley," Tallchief said. "How well do you know him?"

"I don't."

"Why did you set up a meeting between Zach Szabo and him?" Tallchief asked, acting as if he had acquired the intel himself.

Evert grinned. "I learned through a friend that Billingsley needed to invest funds. His reputation was good. So was Zach's. It was just a matter of one friend helping another. No law against it. It's all about money. Heck, even the church is about money, right, Davey?" This time he did wink, using his good eye.

Diggs nodded. "Money helps cure some of the ills of the world."

"Were you trying to help Carter Billingsley because you wanted him to keep quiet about you beating up Ms. Kimura?" Tallchief asked.

Evert's face flushed. "I did no such thing. I—"

"We've got a witness," Marcus cut in.

Evert bolted to his feet and strode to the bar. He slammed his drink on the counter. "Who?"

"Billingsley visited Ms. Kimura's house," Marcus said. "When he arrived, she was pressing a bag of peas to her face. You were there. Reverend Diggs, I believe you were in attendance, as well."

Tallchief shifted uneasily in his chair. Marcus sneered at him. What didn't the guy understand about playing bad cop, worse cop?

"Okay, fine." Evert waved a hand. "I hit her. Once." He rubbed the cheek under his weak eye. "She told me she might be pregnant."

"You hit a pregnant woman?" Marcus lasered him with a look. He'd had enough of this yo-yo.

"You're blowing it out of proportion. See, I couldn't be the father. I mean, yeah, I can get somebody pregnant. All my fish swim, and I might even have a bastard or two."

Evert glanced at Diggs who was staring at his fingernails, looking like he wanted to be anywhere but in the room. Concern flashed in Evert's eyes. Was he worried about what his religious pal might think of him, or was there some reason that Evert needed Diggs in on this particular meeting? Perhaps they had to stay on the same page about the incident. Then again, there were others who had witnessed the punch, including Diggs's date and the housekeeper. So why the panic?

"Look, we hadn't had sex in two months. Yukiko miscalculated on the conception thing, that's all. That day, I'd come over to patch things up between us, but when she told me that she was PG, well, I flew off the handle. I told her we were through. I wanted nothing to do with her."

"If you were so certain the baby wasn't yours, why didn't you say something when I questioned you at the casino earlier?" Marcus asked.

Evert slugged down the remainder of his drink. "Guess I thought I'd muddy the investigation."

"We'll take the mud," Tallchief said.

"Then how's this for dirt?" Evert smirked. "I think Carter Billingsley was having an affair with Yukiko. He could be the father."

"Why would you think that?" Tallchief asked.

"Because I found a shirt with his initials on the cuffs at her house."

Marcus couldn't see someone like Carter Billingsley wearing a shirt with initials. He was a work shirt and jeans kind of guy.

"It was in Yukiko's laundry basket," Evert added.

"What were you doing rummaging through her laundry?" Tallchief asked, going for the obvious instead of the implied.

Reverend Diggs coughed. A signal? Was he there to keep Evert calm? To keep Evert's story straight? Evert threw him a dirty look.

Marcus revisited Keegan's theory about a jealous man staging the massacre to kill a woman who had jilted him. Would Evert have killed ten others in his rage? Maybe Evert's current girlfriend had a jealous streak. He said, "Who was the ash-blonde with you yesterday at the marina?"

Tallchief cut him a look. Marcus shrugged. Tallchief hadn't expected him to bring him up to date on every point of the investigation in thirty seconds or less, had he?

"She's an old friend. A good luck charm, actually." Evert grinned. "She was with me when I won my biggest hand of poker."

"At a private cash game?" Marcus asked.

"At the Boardwalk Casino."

Tallchief said, "Is the Boardwalk your usual haunt?"

"He mixes it up," Marcus said. "Don't you, Evert?" If a gambler gets a reputation for winning all the time, he loses his playmates.

Diggs cleared his throat while plucking at a loose thread in his trouser leg.

"I'm sorry, detectives." Evert glanced at his watch and rose from his chair. "I've got to leave. I have an appointment." He grabbed a set of car keys off the bar.

"Hold it," Marcus said. "Did you take a paternity test, Mr. Evert?"

"No."

"Would you?" Tallchief asked.

Evert splayed his hands. "Yeah, sure. Whatever you need. Are we done?"

"We'll need Billingsley's shirt," Marcus said.

Evert honked out a laugh. "I didn't take it. Do I look stupid?"

Tallchief rose from his chair and stepped toward Evert. "One more question, sir. Where were you on the night of the fifteenth?"

"At the ball."

"And after that?"

"Home in bed screwing my brains out with the ash-blonde. I really must go. Sorry, fellas. You want more of my time, call my lawyer." Evert hitched his head. "Davey, are you coming?" Without waiting for an answer, he exited the room.

Diggs slid off his bar stool and strode to the door. He held it open, indicating Marcus and Tallchief should pass through first. "Sorry for Mr. Evert's gruffness," he said. "He is distraught over the death of Ms. Kimura."

Marcus muttered, "Yeah, the guy is real torn up."

At the bottom of the stairs, Marcus pointed at the beautiful woman standing at the counter chatting it up with the clerk. He put out a hand to stop Tallchief. "That's the ash-blonde."

Tallchief snorted. "I can't see her screwing her brains out with anyone looking like Evert. Think we should get her to corroborate?"

Marcus didn't answer, too transfixed by the floral tattoo on the woman's right shoulder. He had almost forgotten about the sketch he'd taken from the Cloud 9 Motel.

He hustled to Evert before he could leave the shop and whipped the sketch from his pocket. He unfolded it and flashed it at him. "Do you know this man?"

Evert shook his head.

Tallchief drew alongside. "Where'd you get that, Newman?"

"How about the tattoo along his neck, Mr. Evert?" Marcus pressed. "Do any of your workers or clientele sport something like that?"

Evert barked out a laugh. "Everybody has a tattoo nowadays. As for me? I don't want anything invading my body. Pure, the Rev keeps telling me, right, Davey? Keep yourself pure and God will forgive a whole world of sins."

Marcus shook the paper. "The tattoo, Mr. Evert, take another look. It's pretty detailed."

Evert's good eye narrowed. "I told you, no."

# CHAPTER 46

During the first few moments of the Spitzer Nanotechnology tour, Chessa felt like she had been thrust into a scene in *Jurassic Park.* At the beginning of the tour, the guide ushered visitors into a movie theater. Once they were seated, the theater swiveled and offered a view of a laboratory where scientists clad in hoods, masks, ankle-length lab coats, and white boots labored over mixtures, which they then poured into test tubes. Computers registered the variations that the concoctions created. One scientist addressed the crowd. He said the facility was making major strides in a wide field of areas, including environmental, medical, and superficial, or in other words, things that were worn, ingested, or spread on the body. A slide show on the wall behind him displayed the products in further detail.

*Cue symphonic music with the appropriate swell of good vibes,* Chessa thought. Any moment, she expected to see a public service announcement: *Nanotechnology is good for humanity.*

The notion made her wonder again whether the picketers protesting outside the facility could have had something to do with the massacre. But if they did, why would they kill Spitzer, his wife, and some doctors? Why not attack the facility itself? And why kill Zach?

A hydraulic *whoosh* resonated through the hall. A set of double doors to the left opened wide.

The tour guide said, "This way, folks."

Unable to isolate the guide to ask questions, Chessa followed.

~ * ~

Marcus stared after Evert as Diggs and he exited through the shop's front door. The guy was guilty of something, and Marcus was going to prove it.

Tallchief hit Marcus on the shoulder. "Where did you get that drawing?"

Marcus told him.

"Dang it, Newman, this Paxton woman is sending us on a wild goose chase, don't you see that?"

Marcus didn't know what to think. Sure, Chessa could have left it in the motel to throw him off track. For all he knew, the picture could be a rendition of some actor on a television show. He didn't watch much television. But his gut was telling him that finding the redheaded security guard was important because Evert *had* recognized the guy. Marcus was sure of it. Evert's bad eye had blinked like a strobe light.

"I'm telling you Chessa Paxton and her husband did the massacre," Tallchief said, sotto voce, his gaze measuring the other people inside the shop. No one seemed to be listening in. "Then she offed him."

"Why?" Marcus asked. "Give me one good reason why she would kill all those people."

"She's nuts, just like her loony father and mother."

"Her mother?"

"Adriana Wolfe was crazy. Everyone in Nevada knew it. After her religious conversion, she became a proselytizer."

"That doesn't make her crazy."

"Chessa's exactly like her. She wrote inflammatory articles."

"Are you talking about her college assignments?"

"Bingo." Tallchief aimed his finger at Marcus. "Think about the subject matter: cleaning up the environment, ending gambling, and turning back the clocks of progress, and then think about everybody that died at Spooner Meadow."

"How do you explain her husband going along with this subversive plot?"

"Couples believe the same things."

"Do they?" Somehow Marcus had missed that hard and fast rule. Ginnie and he had argued about politics and religion. He couldn't remember a girlfriend he hadn't argued with. Did that say something about him? Perhaps he should address that aspect of himself in the future. Be nicer. See both sides. He glowered at Tallchief. "You're a Tahoe Purist. You're outspoken about its ideology. Are you capable of this kind of carnage? Would your wife have followed your lead?"

"This isn't about Ruthie or me. It's about Chessa Paxton. Her husband did the deed, felt remorseful and panicked, so she stabbed him. She called 911 to make herself look innocent, just like her daddy did."

"Her father didn't call 911; her mother did."

Tallchief grunted. "All I'm saying is the apple doesn't fall far from the tree."

Marcus raked his hair with his fingertips. Using genes as an answer for motive never thrilled him. If he was like his loser parents, heaven help him. And, according to the police report, Chessa's father had supposedly killed in a rage. The massacre at Spooner Meadow wasn't impromptu; it had taken planning. "Why can't you see Zach Szabo leading this brigade? Because then you wouldn't be able to squeeze Chessa Paxton into the scenario?"

"I didn't say—"

"Face it, Tallchief, you are blind with ambition. You want the senator's stepdaughter to be guilty because it will give you front page coverage."

"That's bull."

"You've got no proof she's a killer, only supposition and innuendo."

"Why is she on the run then?"

"Because she's scared out of her gourd."

Tallchief rammed the shop door open. "Fine, if it's not her, who else have we got?" He stepped onto the porch.

Marcus followed and shaded his eyes from the glaring sun. "I'm leaning toward the gambling angle, with Evert as our main suspect. What if he was ticked that he'd lost a million to that doctor? Not to mention, we've got the link between him and Billingsley and Szabo."

"What do you make of Paxton's therapist?" Tallchief headed down the steps.

"I told you before, he—" Marcus tapped Tallchief's shoulder. "Hold up." He jerked a thumb.

Across the parking lot, Reverend Diggs stood in profile to Jeremiah Wolfe, who was seated in the driver's seat of a midnight blue Jaguar, window rolled down. Wolfe was talking while stabbing the rim of the window with his index finger. Diggs looked taut, his jaw set.

Tallchief whistled low and slow. "Where did Wolfe come from?"

"More importantly, what are they chatting about? It doesn't look like Wolfe's seeking absolution, that's for danged sure."

"And where did Evert disappear to in such a hurry?"

"My guess? To the tables. The man doesn't miss a day."

Keegan hustled to Marcus. "See that?"

"It's not like they're hiding. They're in plain sight," Marcus said. "They are old friends, after all. They could be discussing the latest baseball scores." But he didn't believe that for a second. How he wished he had a long-range listening device.

"Do you think they're trying to do damage control on Evert?" Keegan asked.

Marcus was wondering the same thing. "Deputy, see what you can find out about Evert. His books, his personal accounts, any possible safety deposit boxes anywhere."

"Wait a darned second," Tallchief said. "We don't have cause for a search warrant."

"We'll be discreet." Marcus eyed Keegan. "Also find out if Evert's giving cash to anyone. Big lumps of dough. Maybe he's dumping hands at the tables, you know, as a gift to get someone to do his dirty work."

Tallchief said, "If you're right and it's a gambling debt gone wrong, then why were the Spitzers killed?"

"They were already on the shuttle van."

"Anybody find that yet?"

"Nope."

Tallchief exhaled. "And why involve Chessa Paxton?"

"We've established Szabo was at the site. He or the guard in question decided she was expendable."

Tallchief checked his watch. "I'm late." He whacked Marcus's chest with the back of his hand. "Make sure I get a copy of everything you've got. Including that drawing." He stormed to his Explorer and sped from the lot.

# CHAPTER 47

During the restroom break, as tour members formed lines outside the lavatories at the far end of the hall, Chessa seized the opportunity to question the tour guide. Quickly she asked whether the young woman remembered meeting the men in suits. Before the guide could respond, a curly-haired boy came barreling down the hall and bumped into Chessa.

"Sorry," Chessa said, out of habit.

The boy cut her a nasty look, as if the collision was her fault, and then his mouth fell open. "It's you!" He pointed.

"Don't point, son," a woman in her thirties said.

"But, Mommy, she was on TV."

"Not everybody's on TV." His mother dragged him toward the restroom. "Go in there and do your duty."

The boy strained at his mother's strong arm. "It's her, Mommy. I'm not lying. I saw her picture. The sheriff showed it. She killed somebody."

Chessa cursed. The little rugrat couldn't have been more than five. What programs was he watching on TV? She sprinted for an emergency exit.

~ * ~

Marcus crossed the marina's parking lot toward his truck while working the tension from the muscles in his neck. How he wished he had control of the case and not Tallchief, but he wasn't willing to buddy up to Armstrong to get the lead.

Keegan caught up. "Why is Tallchief such a jerk?"

"If he mishandles this case, he could blow his political career. Donors don't contribute if you mess up."

"I'll bet Reverend Diggs reminds himself of that every morning."

Marcus eyed Diggs and Wolfe again. Diggs had one hand on Wolfe's shoulder; the other was raised, palm flat.

"Hey, I almost forgot," Keegan went on. "While you were inside with Evert, a man called the station saying a pretty woman with short dark hair was seen hurtling down a handicapped ramp on a Vespa near Mystic Beach."

"Chessa."

"It's got to be. But, get this, the witness said some guy with white hair in a green Blazer was chasing her. He thinks the guy was a cop."

"How come?"

"The guy got out of the Blazer with a pair of binoculars, and he walked like a cop."

"We have a walk?"

"Guess so."

Marcus smiled. Maybe things were finally starting to go his way. A cop was chasing Chessa. Good. As much as he wanted to be the guy to apprehend her, at this point, he would let anybody get the glory.

The Jaguar's engine revved loudly. Diggs patted the top of Wolfe's car then let his arms fall to his sides, his posture more relaxed than before. As the senator pulled out of the lot, Diggs shouted, "Detective Newman, a moment?" and hurried toward him. He stopped a few feet short and tilted his head back. "About Chessa Paxton. You can't honestly believe she had a hand in any of this"—he twirled his pudgy fingers in the air—"madness. I just want to say again on her behalf—"

"How can you stand to hang around a sleaze like Evert?" Marcus asked.

Diggs sputtered. "I beg your pardon?"

"The guy's a gambler. He drinks like a fish. He sleeps around. Admit it, he's not a cover boy for Christianity."

Diggs smiled a beatific smile that unnerved Marcus, like he knew something about God's Big Picture that Marcus would never fathom. "Detective, my father said every man deserves a chance to change. Every man can undergo a rebirth."

"I heard him preach once. He was pretty good."

"One of the best. He started my church."

Marcus noted the insinuation. *My* church. Not *our* church.

"As for Wally," Diggs went on, "I always hold out hope that those whose company I enjoy will be reborn. I've invested a lot in him."

"How much cash are we talking about?"

Diggs chuckled. "Detective, I'm not implying worldly investments. I'm talking about time. Quality time." He pursed his mouth. "A man as powerful as Wally Evert, once converted, could make a huge difference in my congregation. Think of all the sinners who would come to the Lord because of this one man."

*Think of all the bucks he'll put in the coffers,* Marcus mused. He jammed his hands in his jeans pockets, despising the cynic that lived within him. "What was your business with Senator Wolfe?"

"Jeremiah is distraught about his stepdaughter. He's planning to go on television again and make an appeal to her."

"You're assuming she's taking time out of her busy schedule to watch TV?"

"Whoever she's turning to in her time of need will no doubt inform her."

Marcus wasn't sure Chessa was turning to anyone, which for some reason left a bitter taste in his mouth. "What will Wolfe say?"

"He'll urge her to turn herself in. He'll tell her to trust that the sheriff will treat her fairly. You will, won't you?" Diggs tilted his head. "He'll tell her that he will do everything in his power to see that justice is served."

Marcus frowned. "He came all the way up here to get Evert's approval for this plan?"

Diggs studied his well-groomed fingernails. "Jeremiah came to see me. He wanted me to lay hands on him for strength." He turned his palms up to Marcus. "He believes I have a direct connection to the Lord."

"Do you?"

"Indeed. I must be going. Good day, Detective."

As the diminutive man strolled to his car, Marcus got an itch deep in his gut. The kind he couldn't scratch.

## CHAPTER 48

Chessa dashed down the hall, away from the tour group. The security guard jumped in front of her. Without slowing her stride, she whipped off her satchel and swung it at him. The tail end connected with his shoulder. The guard reeled but revived quickly and clutched the strap of the tote. As much as she didn't want to, Chessa released the bag and darted through the exit door. At least she still had the key to the Vespa.

Sunlight blinded her as she emerged from a side entrance of the facility. Squinting against the glare, she tore down a gravel path lined with white birch trees. She rushed across the grassy expanse beyond the trees, but caught a toe—the ground beneath the grass was rife with potholes—and stumbled. She careened forward and fell to her knees. The key to the Vespa went flying. She crawled toward it.

The guard yelled, "Halt!" and narrowed the lead.

When he didn't add, *or I'll shoot*, Chessa continued on her quest. She nabbed the key, scrambled to her feet, and bolted ahead while chastising herself for being stupid enough to think she could mingle in a crowd and go unrecognized.

The distance to the parking lot was farther than she recalled. Luckily the hefty guard was lagging, the extra weight he was carrying slowing him down.

*Bet you wish you ate a healthier diet*, Chessa thought.

By the time she reached the Vespa, her lungs ached from lack of oxygen. The determined guard arrived at the lot just as Chessa straddled the bike and switched on the ignition. He yelled for her to stop again, but she didn't. Although she was a fugitive, she felt energized and alert and had a good idea where she was headed next. During her Internet search at the motel, she had seen the name of an artist in South Lake Tahoe who specialized in spider tattoos.

~ * ~

Jeremiah opened the windows of the Jaguar and let the warm scent of pine fill the car as he raced toward home. Everything was going to be okay, he kept telling himself. He would call the media. He would make a plea for Chessa to turn herself in. When she did, he would meet with her and make her understand why he had acted the way he had. For Adriana, he would tell her. For your mother. He would beg Chessa to repent, and she would understand his devotion and embrace him and everything he believed in. She would—

His cell phone jangled. The caller's name appeared on the information screen: *Phoenix*.

Sweat broke out on his forehead. His heart started beating fast. The acrid taste of booze crawled up his throat as pressed the button on his Bluetooth device and said, "Yes, I'm listening."

## CHAPTER 49

On the way toward South Lake Tahoe, Chessa stopped at a gas station to purchase a bag of trail mix. She needed fuel. While waiting to pay, she realized she desperately needed a shower, but the luxury of a shower would have to wait. The attendant, a scrawny young male, didn't seem to notice Chessa's odor. He overcharged her for the trail mix by a nickel. She didn't argue; she didn't want to draw attention to herself.

Ten minutes later she arrived at The Alley, a narrow cobblestoned street less than a mile from the casinos. She wedged the Vespa between two huge delivery vans, stuffed the unfinished bag of trail mix into the storage compartment, and gazed down the street. The area was populated with funky clothing shops, fortunetellers, magic stores, and tattoo parlors. During the evening, huge crowds of people fortified with liquid courage, the kinds who embraced the vacation mentality of *what I do in Lake Tahoe stays in Lake Tahoe,* would roam the area. In the late afternoon, however, there were only a few browsers.

Quickly Chessa took off the striped shirt, shoved it in the Vespa's storage compartment, and dumped the sunhat in a nearby trashcan. She mussed her short hair and kept the glasses on. It wasn't a novel look, but it was new. Then she jogged past a candle shop toward the tattoo parlor called INK—all caps—that Chessa had read about on the Internet. She halted when she spied Newman, his deputy, and a frizzy-haired Hispanic woman heading her way. Why were they in the area?

The three ducked through the beaded entry of INK, and Chessa released the breath she was holding. Was it possible that Newman had seen her drawings of the guard at the motel and was attempting to check him out because of the tattoo angle?

Eager to find out whatever they learned but not ready to throw herself on Newman's mercy quite yet, she slipped into All Denim, the clothing store next to INK. The chunky salesclerk was engrossed in a soap opera playing on the TV behind the counter and didn't look up. Chessa hurried to the racks along the far wall and hid among the tightly packed clothing. She pressed her ear against the partition separating the two stores. The noise from the soap opera made it hard to hear every word coming from the tattoo parlor, but Chessa caught snippets.

"...you do this kind of work, these spiders," Newman said.

"Yeah, man, that's mine," a man with a deep, earthy voice said. "I'm particular to the web...the spider's..."

"Know this guy?" Newman asked.

Did Newman have a photograph of someone, or had he figured out she had holed up at the Cloud 9 Motel and was showing a sketch she'd drawn?

The artist must have nodded because Newman followed with, "Did he get this tattoo here?"

"Yeah, man, and a crown of thorns on...I think a cop or military." He said something more but it was muffled.

Chessa cupped her ear to block out ambient noise.

"Can't remember, man," the artist said.

What couldn't he remember? The guy's name? His address?

"My clients don't pour out their life stories to me, detective. I'm not a bartender."

"Did he…cash or credit?"

"I don't accept plastic. Hey, one more thing. I've seen him at the casinos."

Newman said something, none of which Chessa could make out. He must have turned his back to the wall.

The artist said, "Maybe the dude should…Gamblers Anonymous, catch my drift?"

That was the first bit of information Chessa found helpful. The security guard might be a compulsive gambler. If only she had the courage to enter the casinos. She could show a sketch to card dealers.

Newman said, "Keegan, Gutiérrez, let's go."

Chessa tiptoed to the shop's door and peeked out. Newman and his colleagues exited INK and headed toward Lake Tahoe Boulevard.

"Help you?" the salesclerk asked.

Chessa whirled around. "Thanks, I'm good." She threw her hands up to show she hadn't swiped anything.

A news alert rang out on the TV behind the sales counter. Beside the face of a dour reporter appeared a photo of Helena Gorzinski. Chessa's heart snagged. In her haste, she had nearly forgotten about her poor friend.

The reporter said, "It has been confirmed that the woman found dead at the Boardwalk Casino and Hotel earlier this morning was the chief human resources officer. The fugitive Chessa Paxton appears to have been in the vicinity." A sketch of Chessa in a sunhat was displayed on the screen. Someone at Spitzer Nanotechnology must have given the sheriff that tip.

"Have you heard about this chick?" the salesclerk asked.

Chessa willed herself to remain calm and inched toward the exit. "Can't say that I have."

"Yeah, being on vacation, maybe you wouldn't. Are you on vacation? You look like a gal on the go. Me, I've lived in Tahoe all my life."

*Yes, I'm on the go,* Chessa wanted to scream, and she had to go *now*. But where?

"See that guy?" The salesclerk jutted her finger.

A taped interview with Jeremiah appeared on the screen. He was standing beside a reporter outside the casino. His eyes were puffy and red-rimmed. There wasn't any sound accompanying the segment, just a slug line: *Nevada's senior senator, Jeremiah Wolfe.*

"He's, like, the chick's stepdad or something. I heard him talk earlier. A real blowhard, if you ask me. I wouldn't vote for him. He begged her to come home. He said he'd look out for her. Yeah, right." The salesclerk clucked her tongue. "He went on to say she should remember her sophomore year and how he took care of that car mess for her. What do you bet she either stole it or totaled it, right?"

Sophomore year, before she had a license, Chessa had borrowed her mother's car without asking. Around midnight, after a few beers, she crashed the car into a tree. Jeremiah fetched her at the precinct and posted bail, no questions asked. He got the car repaired and never said a word to Adriana. For about six months following the incident, Chessa's relationship with him was better than it had ever been. By mentioning the event on television, was he trying to send her a message? Was he saying he could clean up this mess for her, too?

"You know, you look like her." The salesclerk pointed at the TV.

Chessa glanced at the screen. Her image was gone. The soap opera had returned. An actress with chin-length dark hair and a righteous attitude was telling off her boyfriend. Chessa forced a smile. "I don't see the resemblance."

"Your hair's thick like hers. What products do you use?"

"Suave."

"I use Suave, too."

"Hey, do you know where I can find a pay phone?" Chessa asked, sorry she had surrendered the satchel and lost access to the cell phone and the other clothes Brandi had provided.

"Outside, by the restrooms. Not sure they're working. Are you going to buy anything? Personally, I think you'd look better in blue than that black getup you're wearing—hope you don't mind me saying so—*and* we have a ton of cute purses. Everything's half-off."

Using some of her cash, Chessa quickly purchased a torn pair of jeans, a cheap denim jacket, a pair of Keds, a denim tote, and a frayed baseball cap. She slipped into a dressing room and changed clothes. The jeans chafed the bruises on her legs, but she didn't make a peep. She transferred the remaining money, all twenty-five bucks and change, to the jeans pocket and exited the store.

While she'd been inside, dusk had arrived. Remnants of a brilliant orange sunset streaked the sky. Imitation gas streetlamps flickered along the sidewalks. A family of tourists walked toward Chessa, the oldest son propelling them toward the magic store. A few shoppers lingered by display windows. She pulled the bill of the baseball cap lower. No one took notice of her. She found the pay telephone tucked into the dead-end recess by the entrance to the public restrooms. She slotted in a quarter and dialed.

As she listened to the telephone ringing, her tongue grew so thick she feared she wouldn't be able to talk.

Patience Troon answered. Chessa didn't trust the woman, but she didn't know how else to reach Jeremiah. She swallowed hard. "It's me, Chessa."

"Dear lord."

"I need to speak to Jeremiah." She had never been able to call him Dad. "Don't tell me he's busy. Please."

Silence. Then, "Hold on."

Jeremiah picked up the phone. "Chessa, sweetheart, where are you?" His words were slurred. "Come home and we'll—"

"I didn't kill Zach. I didn't kill Helena Gorzinski. You have to believe me. The sheriff—"

"Of course, I believe you. Come home and we'll work this out."

"I can't. I—"

"It's safe here."

*No place is safe,* Chessa thought. "Jeremiah, remember how you felt when Mom died? How you blamed yourself?"

"Chessa—"

"I blame myself for the massacre. I was drugged, but it's still my fault. If I'd been more alert, maybe Zach"—she gulped in air—"and the others would be alive."

Something clattered on the street. Chessa released the telephone receiver and stole to the corner. Where had all the people gone? The few browsers she had seen earlier had vanished. All except one man. As he passed beneath a street lamp, Chessa stiffened.

It was him. The security guard. With his bleached hair, he looked like a phantom. How had he found her? Did he spot the Vespa? A bottle tumbled across the cobblestone in front of him. He must have accidentally kicked it.

"Chessa," Jeremiah said through the receiver.

The guard didn't turn at the sound. He was staring at something ahead. He hurried onward and pushed through the beaded curtains of INK.

Chessa stole to the telephone and whispered into the receiver. "Jeremiah?"

"I'm here."

Out of nowhere a spider crawled up the handset. Chessa froze. *No sudden movements. Do not make a sound.* The spider skulked across her fingers. She breathed through her nose, short choppy breaths.

"Chessa, what's wrong?"

"S-spider."

"Sweetheart, come home—"

"I c-c-can't."

"Tell me where you are. I'll come to you."

Chessa couldn't stop thinking about what the artist had said to Newman. He believed the guard might be a cop. Or military. Did the guard have the authority to kill her on sight? She needed to hide. Sleep. Work things through. She glanced at the spider again and thought of a place she could go where nobody would think to look for her, but could she do it? She shuddered. For a whole night?

"It's time I face my fears, Jeremiah."

"What are you talking about?"

*Do it!* Chessa flicked off the spider. It flipped to the ground. She jammed it with the toe of her shoe. Then she slipped the telephone receiver into its cradle and returned to the corner. The street was empty; the security guard was nowhere in sight. She mustered the courage to make a run for the Vespa but halted when she heard a spitting sound. A whiz.

Someone groaned.

Seconds later the security guard beat tracks from the tattoo parlor.

Chessa stifled a moan. Had he shot the tattoo artist using a silencer?

A couple of teens exited the shop across the street. Neither of them seemed to care that the security guard was running. He didn't look in their direction, but he did glance in Chessa's.

Did he spot her? She couldn't wait to find out. She flew to the men's restroom. The door was locked. She tried the women's. Also locked. As a last ditch hope, she raced behind the dumpster at the end of the recess. The area stank and trash was everywhere, but that wasn't the biggest problem. If the guard crouched down and peered beneath the bin, he would see her feet. Quietly she placed a discarded, broken-down box over her shoes and held her breath.

~ * ~

Jeremiah Wolfe gripped his desk to steady the blur in his head and leveled Patience with his gaze. When had he lost control of her? Of his life?

"Well?" Patience said, the scowl a permanent fixture on her face since yesterday.

"Well, what?" He heard the laziness in his tone and didn't care.

"Where is she? The sheriff will want to know."

Something clicked in Jeremiah's brain. Chessa had whispered the word *spider*. She said she had to *face her fears*. Was she sending him a message? He struggled to sit a little straighter thinking maybe Fate wasn't out to destroy him after all. He urged his head to clear. What did she mean? The answer came to him in a flash. "She's going camping."

Patience sniffed. "Don't be absurd. She abhors camping."

"It's—" Jeremiah desperately needed a drink of water. He reached for a glass on the desk. It was empty. Why? Because his life was empty. Useless. Adriana would slap him if she knew what a weak-willed man he had become. Thank heaven he didn't have to face her. He rotated his neck to loosen the knots. "It's brilliant. No one will suspect."

"Where will she go?"

"Where she must." Jeremiah nodded; the motion made him slightly nauseous. "Yes, that would make sense." But was Chessa thinking rationally? "Get me Davey Diggs on the phone."

"He'll know you've been drinking."

"Call him!" Jeremiah slapped his palm on the desk.

"You can't possibly think prayers will help in this case."

"Chessa contacted me, didn't she? I prayed for that."

# CHAPTER 50

Chessa heard footsteps. It had to be the guard. He stopped at the entrance to the recess. She breathed shallowly; her heart slammed her ribcage.

After a long moment the footsteps retreated and turned into galloping. The guard was making a run for it.

*Do something! You couldn't help Helena. Help the artist! Move!*

Cautiously Chessa emerged from her hiding place. Assured the street was clear, she hustled to the tattoo parlor and paused at the beaded entryway. Candlelight cast a hazy glow in the shop. A swarthy man with short-cropped hair lay on the floor. Blood pooled beneath his neck and back, but his chest was rising and falling. He was alive. A cell phone rested on the sales counter.

Though Chessa didn't want to enter another crime scene, she had no choice. She sneaked in, snatched the phone, and exited while pressing 911. An operator answered and went into her spiel.

When she finished, Chessa said, "A man's been shot." She relayed the address as she tore off on the Vespa. "He's alive. Hurry!" She turned left onto Lake Tahoe Boulevard and glimpsed the guard walking, not running, beyond a group of burly men. He appeared to be heading toward the plaza between the entrance to the Heavenly Mountain Resort and the Boardwalk Casino and Hotel.

Chessa forged ahead, trying to keep him in her sights, but she couldn't. He blended into a swarm of people. "The killer is still in the area," she said to the operator. She described the guard, gave his approximate location, stabbed END, wiped the cell phone free of prints, and hurled it beneath a parked car.

Seconds later a siren pierced the air. The drone grew louder. An emergency vehicle was headed toward The Alley. Chessa breathed with relief. The tattoo artist had a chance.

Taking care to obey the speed limit, Chessa tucked her head and drove north through Stateline. She wanted to get to her destination and sleep. If she didn't rest, she wouldn't be able to focus. And she needed to focus. Theories reeled in her mind, but none of them made sense. How could she have been blind to what was going on with Zach and his clandestine life? When she found the passports, he grabbed them back. He said he traveled. It was *no big deal*. She demanded to know why each passport had a different name. He promised to tell her after the ball. He said she would laugh.

Chessa shivered as she remembered the moments after that: Zach running his hands through her hair, cupping her chin, and kissing her; Zach abandoning her at the ball and then lifting her into his arms and shoving her into the casino's shuttle van.

His betrayal squeezed her heart. Had he come into her life so he could infiltrate her stepfather's world, or had he been involved with something more sinister? Why had he let her live at the massacre? Why keep her survival a secret from his partner?

Chessa wanted to scream. She needed to know more—*everything*—about Zach.

Out of the corner of her eye, she caught sight of an office supply store. If she did an Internet search on him, could she find out who he really was?

~ * ~

Marcus strode into the tattoo parlor steeled for another bloodbath and was glad when it wasn't. The artist, a Dominican no older than Keegan, lay prone on the floor, his shirt drenched in blood. A skinny emergency tech was on her knees, pressing on the artist's chest. Another was wheeling in a stretcher. Marcus, Keegan, and Gutiérrez had reached the north end of Stateline when they received the alert.

"Can he talk?" Marcus asked the tech.

"I've filled him up with drugs. He's out of it."

"Who called it in?"

"Wouldn't give a name. Female. Said the killer was a tall man with bleached hair."

"As in white?" Marcus asked, recalling that a guy fitting that description had been seen chasing Chessa in a green Blazer. Same guy? What were the odds?

"Sir!" Gutiérrez hurried into the shop, her cell phone pressed to her ear.

Keegan followed.

"Yes, ma'am," Gutiérrez said into the phone and held up a finger to Marcus.

Keegan hooked a thumb. "The salesclerk at the shop next door said someone fitting Chessa Paxton's description bought clothes at the store about fifteen minutes ago."

Marcus couldn't believe it. Chessa was near another shooting? Was she the unidentified female that had called it in? Had she lied about the description of the killer to throw authorities off her trail?

"Also, there's someone outside who saw some guy with white hair leaving the shop," Keegan added. "Could it be the same guy that chased Chessa in the Blazer?"

"Boss." Gutiérrez stowed her cell phone into its clip. "A gal called the station saying she was shocked to see a young woman on a motorbike drive into a public restroom. She said the woman was a mess. Bloody legs and arms. The gal didn't call it in earlier because her baby—"

Marcus stormed out of INK and strode to a group of people standing by the crime scene perimeter. Even though he didn't have jurisdiction, he pulled the drawing of the security guard from his pocket and flashed it at the crowd. "Did anybody see this guy?"

A man with leathery skin raised his hand. So did two teens.

## CHAPTER 51

Chessa noticed a few customers inside the office supply store as she drove past. The bank of computers for public use looked unoccupied. A young man tended the counter. Chessa parked the Vespa on a side street, removed the denim jacket in case the salesclerk at All Denim or one of the tourists in The Alley remembered what she was wearing, and tossed it into the rear compartment. Then she put back on the stolen striped shirt, knotted it at her waist, and pulled down the scoop of her tank top to draw focus to her cleavage.

As hoped, the young man at the counter gazed at her chest as she entered and nothing else. Chessa crossed the worn carpet to the public computers and sat in one of the chairs. She inserted her last twenty-dollar bill into a Pay and Play machine—everything in South Lake Tahoe sounded like a gambling venture—and watched the digital readout. The twenty didn't register any credit for use of the computer. She pressed the eject button, but the twenty-dollar bill didn't materialize.

"Swell," she muttered. She couldn't complain to the clerk. No matter how good her cleavage was he wouldn't refund twenty dollars without asking for proof of identification.

With five bucks and change in her jeans pocket, she slunk out of the store, defeated.

~ * ~

As the moon crested the mountains to the east, Chessa drove up North Canyon Road toward the trailhead to Marlette Lake. She parked beyond a dusty Econoline van at the outer rim of the unpaved lot, threw on the denim jacket, took the space blanket and flashlight from the compartment beneath the seat, and stuffed a bottle of water and the remaining trail mix into her tote. She switched on the flashlight so it cast a wide beam in front of her and tramped toward the lake, although she wouldn't rest there. She would be too exposed.

The scent of pine was heady, but not heady enough to relax her and make her imagine, even for a second, that she was on vacation. It took every fiber in her being to keep from screaming. Adrenaline zipped through her with each pop of a stick or crackle of leaves beneath her tennis shoes. A squirrel skittered in front of her. A second followed. She bit back a gasp and chastised herself for being such a wimp.

Along the way, Chessa realized she couldn't recall the spot where Jeremiah had veered off eighteen years ago to show her the best kept secret in Lake Tahoe. A small, unnamed creek. *My little Eden*, he'd called it.

The sound of babbling water lured Chessa onto a narrow path, but the trip toward the stream took longer than she remembered. When the water's gurgling intensified, she ducked beneath a pine bough. The beam of the flashlight highlighted water and she breathed easier. It wasn't Jeremiah's Eden—the stream was barely two feet wide—but she would settle for anyplace where she could sleep out of sight from other campers.

Chessa searched for a flat spot of dirt and set down the blanket and her tote. Then she listened. She didn't hear human chatter. She didn't see any campfires blazing. A campfire would be nice, she thought, but she didn't know how to light one. Besides, even if she did know how and she had matches, she wouldn't. She couldn't draw attention. The blanket would have to suffice.

A broad-based tree would be the best place to rest her head, she decided. She couldn't imagine lying on the dirt, and she wasn't about to pile pine needles in a stack. They could be infested with spiders.

Before Chessa settled by the tree, she searched for a sizeable stick to use as protection, just in case a creature made its way to her quasi-camp. As she combed the area, a wealth of guilt swept over her. People were dead. More could die. Should she have known the massacre would occur? Had Zach let anything slip that she should have picked up on? A moan escaped her lips. Spending the night in the cold with thousands of wild things as her companions would never be enough punishment for what she had neglected to see.

Maybe the plot had something to do with nanotechnology or maybe not. Eight doctors were dead. Was one of them the target of the massacre? What about the security guard? Had the 911 operator told the sheriff what Chessa said, that he shot the tattoo artist? Had Newman found him yet? If so, maybe the guard had confessed and proven her innocent. Not likely.

*Rest. You can't solve anything if you're exhausted.*

The first stick Chessa found was puny and would be useless if a mountain lion or something larger showed up. She settled for a branch about three-feet long and three-inches thick.

A quarter of an hour later, she sat against the tree, draped herself with the blanket, and tried to get comfortable. The bark jutted into her back. She tolerated the pain and looked up at the dark purple sky, which was peppered with stars. Under any other circumstance, she would think the view was beautiful. Tonight it heightened her loneliness. Her stomach grumbled, but she wasn't hungry; the partial bag of trail mix she had downed earlier was still lumped in her stomach. However, she was thirsty. She popped open the bottle of water and drank a sip.

A cool breeze caressed her face, and Chessa felt almost calm.

Until an owl swooped to a branch ten feet overhead and hooted.

"Go away," she hissed, hating herself for being scared. How she wished that, after her junior year, she had taken the Outward Bound trip her mother had suggested instead of the three-week papier-mâché class. What confidence she would have if she had learned to survive in the wilderness.

*Oh, Mother.* Tears pressed at the corners of Chessa's eyes. She felt foolish yearning for her mother, but she knew Adriana would have been able to make sense of the madness. Adriana would have found some way to prove Chessa innocent.

Chessa would never forget the last day her mother and she had spent together. It was a week before Chessa's wedding and two weeks before her mother's fateful trip to Geneva. They drove to Reno in Adriana's BMW, top down, a crisp spring breeze whipping through their hair. Two girls out for a shopping spree. At the first store, her mother said she never tired of the *ka-ching* of a cash register, even after all those years running the gift shop. She said it was music to her ears, knowing Jeremiah and she could provide for Chessa, implying that Chessa's father hadn't. Chessa kept mute. She didn't want to ruin a good day with her mother, and bringing up the topic of her father invariably started a fight.

They visited three dress boutiques and a fabric store and ended up at an antique store. Its owner, familiar with Chessa's fascination with sewing items, led her to a thimble display. While Chessa fingered each, she changed her mind about discussing taboo topics and asked her mother about her father. Why did he murder that man? She wondered if someday she might snap like he did. Her mother cut her off and jabbed Chessa's chest with her finger, while shouting that she would never, ever be like him. But that didn't satisfy Chessa. She couldn't understand why her father hadn't responded to her letters and why she couldn't visit him. Adriana claimed that it was his rule. He had forbidden contact. In a huff, she paid for the thimble and marched out of the shop.

Over a less than festive lunch at a Mexican restaurant, Adriana proposed a boating outing, a last hurrah with friends before the wedding. Chessa recalled the outing like it was yesterday. Adriana had ended up with a severe sunburn; she had refused to use sunblock. At the wedding, she apologized for her peeling skin. A week later she was ashes.

"Oh, Mother," Chessa moaned aloud and switched her position against the tree. The space blanket crackled with the movement. The owl hooted shrilly, clearly disturbed.

And then the forest grew eerily still and a branch snapped.

## CHAPTER 52

Chessa spied movement. At a distance. Two gleaming orbs as yellow as the owl's stared back at her, except the intruder wasn't a bird, and it wasn't human. But it was walking on two legs—a black bear. Chessa considered scrambling to her feet and wielding the stick, but then she recalled something Jeremiah once told her. Black bears are basically docile animals and are most often looking for food, not a fight.

The bear—male—dropped to all fours. He swung his head to the right and left. He sniffed the air, nostrils flaring, and padded closer.

Chessa's breathing quickened. What in heck had she been thinking, hiding in the forest? Two days of eluding the law had made her cocky. Talk about needing a reality check. She willed herself to stay motionless and sized up the bear. Outlined in dim moonlight, he looked about one and a half times the size of her dog, Jocko. She could take Jocko in a wrestling match.

The bear lumbered closer.

*Don't move, Chessa. Do. Not. Move.*

The bear batted a rock in his path and growled. He eyed Chessa's denim tote and moved forward. He pawed it and turned it upside down. The half-eaten bag of trail mix fell out. Saliva oozed out the sides of the bear's mouth.

*Take it. It's all yours.*

Something crackled off to the bear's right. He craned an ear and grumbled. Whatever it was, was not worth his time. He pawed the bag of trail mix. Nuts skittered out. He bent forward, scooped the morsels into his mouth, and smacked his lips. He leaned down for more, but he drew up short when something crackled again.

A low moan echoed through the woods.

A shiver ran down Chessa's spine. Whatever had made that sound wasn't human, either.

The bear snorted, scooped up the package of treats, and galloped into the woods. At the same time, a hulking form burst through the bushes. Another bear. It charged after the first.

When their sounds receded, Chessa let out the breath she was holding and blinked repeatedly, terrified that if she got up and ran, she would incite both animals to return to her. Little by little she inched deeper beneath the blanket and pulled the top over her head.

Dawn couldn't come soon enough.

~ * ~

Tallchief slammed the telephone into its cradle. It was nine frigging P.M., and he was still getting crank calls about the case. Chessa Paxton had been spotted here, there, and everywhere. A lot of pretty women, it turned out, owned motorbikes in Lake Tahoe. He narrowed his eyes to block out as much of the precinct's fluorescent lights as possible and concentrated on the latest telephone call. Apparently a tattoo artist was in critical condition, and Chessa Paxton had been seen in the vicinity. If someone would bring him a positive ID that she was the shooter and deliver her on a platter, maybe he would be a happy man. Maybe.

"Somebody was shot?" Ferguson Fairchild asked. He sat in a metal chair by Tallchief's desk, looking as pristine as he had when he'd entered the station. He was on his way to visit his mother when Tallchief called him in. Tallchief wanted another pass at him. Newman might have been too lax. "Who was hurt? Chessa?"

"None of your business," Tallchief snapped. Everyone's footsteps echoing on the tile floor was making his head ache. He needed two Tylenol and eight hours sleep. Make that ten. Nighttime used to be his favorite part of the day. At the end of a shift, Ruthie and he would sit out on the porch wearing night vision goggles and watch animals foraging for food. His life had meaning with Ruthie. With her gone, the only way he would find satisfaction would be to get elected. Serve his people. Not solve a massacre that made no sense. He ran a hand down the back of his neck. "Let's continue, Dr. Fairchild."

"What more can I say?" Fairchild smoothed the creases of his shirt. "I already told you Chessa needs medicine on occasion, but so do a lot of people, and it doesn't turn them into monsters. And, no, she hasn't contacted me since she drove off in my car. I went through all of this with the other sheriff and the one before him."

"You retained an attorney on her behalf."

"I haven't paid the lawyer a dime, if that's what you're asking, and Chessa and she haven't spoken yet."

"I hear Ms. Paxton wrote dozens of left-wing articles during college, is that correct?"

Fairchild snorted. "You're kidding me. You think she's a fanatic because she completed some two-bit college assignments?"

"You tell me."

Fairchild slapped the arm of his chair. "She's not an extremist, if that's what you're getting at."

Tallchief grinned. The doctor was excitable. Good. "The two of you took classes together in high school."

"Art. I told Detective Newman that, too."

"And biology."

Fairchild nodded.

"How did Ms. Paxton do in biology?"

"What do you want me to say, that she used scissors to cut up a frog? C'mon, detective, I could dissect a cat with the precision of a surgeon, but that doesn't mean I've gone around stabbing anyone in the back." He jutted a forefinger at Tallchief. "Man, you and the tabloids. You can turn anything around, can't you? I was at the grocery store yesterday, and there was this paper, the *Reno Star*, with this two-headed kid on it and the caption read: *Freak of nature or accident of science?* I'll bet you anything it was a manufactured, computerized picture, but it'll still make people run scared." Fairchild folded his arms across his chest. "I'm done talking to you without benefit of lawyer. I will not give you any more ammunition with which to bury Chessa."

Newman trudged into the station and tossed his keys on his desk. He eyed Tallchief. "Why's he here?"

"Because I wanted a word." Tallchief addressed Fairchild. "Get out of here, but keep your cell phone charged."

As the doctor exited the precinct, Tallchief turned to Newman. "You look like crap."

"Feel like it, too. I need to eat."

Tallchief couldn't remember the last time he'd put anything in his stomach.

"I've got something." Newman waved a slip of paper.

Tallchief took it. The name *Richter* was on it, along with three block letters: *CVD*. "Who's Richter?"

"John Richter might be the redheaded guard Chessa Paxton was talking about. He was seen in the vicinity of a shooting in The Alley in South Lake Tahoe."

"The tattoo artist?"

"You know about it?"

Tallchief hooked a thumb at his desk. "A citizen just called it in."

"It turns out the artist did the tattoo on Richter's neck, similar to the one in Chessa Paxton's sketch."

"Why didn't you contact me?"

"Short version? A witness saw Richter leave the scene and head into the Boardwalk Casino. We went there to follow up."

"And you detained him?"

"Lost him. *But*"—Newman emphasized the word—"we've got more on him. Richter worked as a security guard at the casino."

"Whoa!" Tallchief held up a hand. "Uh-uh. You're not thinking Chessa Paxton is innocent because she fingered this security guard, are you? Besides, she said the guy was wearing black at the ball. The guards at the casino wear maroon."

"Richter, if it was Richter, was probably in costume because he was fired by the casino a week ago." Newman stepped closer, his face close to Tallchief's. "Listen up, Richter was ID'd as the guy that shot the tattoo artist. He has bleached his hair, and a guy with bleached hair was spotted not only at the casino the day Gorzinski was murdered, but he was also seen chasing Chessa Paxton in a green Blazer on Highway 50. Partial plate: *CVD*."

Tallchief flicked the slip of paper and let out a whistle. "And he's in the wind?"

"Didn't pay last month's rent. No forwarding address. Telephone disconnected." Newman ticked the points off on his fingertips. "In addition, the tattoo guy told us Richter is a gambling addict, so we're checking out all the casinos." Newman jammed his hands into his pockets. "Did you learn anything new from Dr. Fairchild, or did you just want to rattle his cage?"

"The latter." Tallchief eyed the paper with Richter's name.

"Don't go thinking about being a hero." Newman wagged a finger in Tallchief's face. "I know that look. You're thinking of tracking down Richter and getting some press for your mayoral bid."

At times, Tallchief hated Newman, but he hated himself more for being transparent.

"I'm going to catch a meal with my team," Newman said, "and run through our findings since we split up this afternoon. Care to join us?"

"I'll pass."

"I'm warning you, leave the hero stuff to the younger crowd."

"Give me a break." Tallchief crossed to his desk, snatched his keys, and stormed from the building. A hero didn't wait for an invitation. A hero acted.

# CHAPTER 53

Marcus met Keegan and Gutiérrez at the Blue Sky Diner, which was kitty-corner from Evert's Marina. It was the kind of place Marcus called a *work-aurant,* a step above fast food joints, but the customer still had to get his own food. Good eats, reasonable prices, no music, and bright enough colors that he didn't feel like he would fall asleep at any moment. He had ordered meat-loaf with a side of macaroni and cheese, hard on the arteries but satisfying. He would run a couple of miles in the morning to work off the guilt.

Gutiérrez sashayed to the table, waving her tray of food under Keegan's nose as she sat. "Mine's better than yours."

"Only if you like onions." The deputy had opted for a burger and fries.

Marcus eyed Gutiérrez's meal. "You got any protein in that sandwich?"

"Tofu." Gutiérrez transferred her plate and glass of water to the table, ditched the tray, and settled into her chair. "Tallchief isn't joining us?"

"He's following up on John Richter," Marcus said.

"How? We have no sighting."

"He'll troll the casinos, like the others. He thinks he's Columbo."

"Swell." Gutiérrez attacked her meal noisily.

"Who's Columbo?" Keegan asked.

"A TV detective, way before your time," Gutiérrez muttered. "Boss, do you think Tallchief will make a good mayor?"

"He'll be okay. He's fair." Marcus ate a bite of his meatloaf, wishing he could drink a beer with it. "He doesn't overheat."

"Except with you." Gutiérrez snickered.

"I push his buttons. We have a long history."

"Which you'll share at some point?" Keegan asked.

"Not likely," Gutiérrez said. "Newman doesn't share anything with any-one."

"He told me about his brother."

"Enough." Marcus pushed his plate away. "Back to business. Let's piece what we have together."

"Where do you think Chessa is?" Keegan asked. They had all taken to calling her Chessa. Ms. Paxton and person of interest were too long, and perp didn't fit.

"I don't have a clue." Marcus wondered if the former security guard had a bead on her and was going after her. He seemed to have a knack of knowing where she was: the chase on the highway, The Alley. It bothered Marcus that the guy was always a step ahead. Had he known Chessa intended to meet up with Helena Gorzinski? How? Sure, Chessa could have called Gorzinski and Richter tapped Gorzinki's phone. On the other hand, what if Richter was the one who filched the Post-it notes from Chessa's refrigerator? Maybe one of the notes mentioned a Saturday appointment with the head of HR. Yeah, that would make sense.

"Boss, are you all right?" Gutiérrez asked.

"I'm fine." Marcus swiveled his chair and straddled it, arms crisscrossed along the top. "Keegan, what did you get on Evert's paternity matter?"

Gutiérrez said, "Is that why we're here? At this diner? To spy on Evert?"

"If we need a question answered in a timely manner, it wouldn't hurt to know his comings and goings." Marcus had a good view of the marina entrance from where he sat. As of an hour ago, Evert was in his office upstairs.

"No results yet," Keegan said, "but you didn't expect any this fast, did you?"

Marcus hadn't.

Keegan went on, "I asked Billingsley to submit to a DNA test, too. He agreed."

"You told him about the shirt with the initials?"

"Nope. The fact that he agreed sends up a red flag, right?"

Marcus grinned. "Gutiérrez, what do we have on the rest of the victims in the massacre?"

"The facial reconstructionist was getting a divorce, but his wife says it was amicable. We didn't uncover any hidden money accounts for him. He's clean. Not a gambler. He and his wife had a settlement hearing. The attorneys for both sides agreed to it. His wife has a solid alibi."

"Convenient."

Gutiérrez raised an eyebrow. "Not everybody is guilty."

"Tell that to the jury."

"Both triathlete doctors were married and beloved," Gutiérrez went on.

"I couldn't get one person to dredge up any dirt on them. They, too, were not gamblers. According to relatives, the surviving spouses are in shock. One has been bedridden since the discovery. Another is in the hospital. She just underwent a hysterectomy."

"Man, that's rough." Keegan downed the last portion of his burger.

"Do we have more on Dr. Smith?" Marcus asked.

"He was hocked up to his eyeballs," Gutiérrez said. "That eight million in the safety deposit box would go a long way."

"Follow the money," Keegan mumbled as he wiped his mouth with a napkin.

"Yeah, it's always a good bet," Marcus said. "We've got plenty of people interested in money in this case. Evert, Billingsley."

"Don't forget Szabo, who had none," Keegan said.

Marcus addressed Gutiérrez. "What about the Spitzer daughters?"

"Interesting you should ask," she said. "It turns out Chessa got to them before we did."

"What?"

"Yep. She tracked them down at a funeral parlor and met with the elder Spitzer girl, Shawn. Directly afterward, according to timetables, is when Richter, driving a Blazer, chased Chessa on the highway. My theory: he must have figured out the GPS before we did. Chessa caught on and dumped it at that public bathroom."

"How did he figure out The Alley?"

"I would bet he didn't, but he guessed Chessa might have seen his tattoo, so he went there to destroy that link. Anyway, back to Shawn Spitzer"—Gutiérrez sipped some water and continued—"a knockout girl by the way. She said Chessa asked a lot of questions about the nanotech facility. Chessa seemed most interested in government people who showed up there."

"Government people?"

"Venture capitalists aren't the only ones interested in what nanotechnology is all about, I guess. So I followed up on that angle, and, get this, Chessa showed up at the facility and questioned a sales director about the visitors. She was posing as a reporter."

Marcus smiled. "Our fugitive is nothing if not industrious."

"Afterward Chessa took a tour of the facility."

"You're kidding."

"A child on the tour recognized her. Chessa bolted. A guard chased her, but he lost her on the dash to the parking lot."

Keegan wadded his napkin and set it on the table. "There sure has been a lot of ill will surrounding Spitzer Nanotechnology. Did you see the line of protesters this morning?"

Gutiérrez nodded. "Change is hard for some to handle."

Marcus flashed on what Keegan had said a moment ago. *Follow the money.* "Was Spitzer's company private or public?"

"As private as the man," Gutiérrez said.

"So the daughters stand to inherit—"

"Sir." Keegan cut him off and hitched a thumb, his gaze focused on something outside the restaurant.

Carter Billingsley had parked his company truck in the Tahoe Kings Court parking lot and was assisting a lady out of a powder blue T-bird. Not just any lady. Patience Troon.

"I'll be right back." Marcus hopped to his feet and marched out of the restaurant.

Warm air radiated off the pavement as Marcus caught up with Billingsley and Troon at the entrance to the motel's reception office. Fluorescent light flooded the planes of their faces. "I don't think your wife would approve, Billingsley."

The guy tensed. His hands balled at his sides. Troon's eyes revealed nothing, but she looked surprisingly sexy in her slinky black dress and strappy heels, and she smelled of an expensive perfume.

Billingsley composed himself and said, "You're following me, is that it?"

"Just lucky," Marcus quipped, though he knew this was better than lucky. "Tahoe's a small place. I see just about everybody I know twice a day. I hear you're giving us a DNA sample."

"I am. I want to be compliant, but I swear to you I never slept with Yukiko Kimura. I never did anything but business with her."

"Then why was a shirt with your initials on the cuffs found at her place?"

"No way."

"Do you own a shirt like that?"

Billingsley squirmed then nodded. "My wife wants me to look polished when we go out, but I did not leave a shirt because I wasn't *there.* Someone must have planted it. Plus I have an alibi for the night of the killings."

"Really." Marcus cocked his head. "What would that be?"

Troon sighed. "Isn't it obvious? Me."

~ * ~

Flashlight in hand, Tallchief paced the parking lot by the Nugget Casino, his fourth casino of the evening. Some of his men had entered the place to look for Richter, but Tallchief had opted to take the more direct approach. He bent to view the license plate on a green Blazer.

A cat rocketed from beneath the vehicle and yowled.

Tallchief startled. He snapped off the flashlight and mopped his sweaty head. He had to relax, keep cool. He fingered the Glock in his holster and reminded himself he was ready. He had run through the arrest scenario a dozen times since he'd left the precinct. Okay, so he hadn't fired his gun anywhere except the range for the past year, but he was ready. He was a pro. The arrest would be as simple as playing two-man basketball. Catch John Richter climbing into his car, detain him, and question him. Slam dunk.

But not quite yet. The SUV's license plate didn't match.

## CHAPTER 54

Marcus worked hard to fall asleep. His body was roasting with pent-up energy. It didn't help that the neighbor's dog was barking incessantly and a squirrel or some other creature he didn't want to contemplate was scurrying back and forth across his attic. He kicked off the covers, pulled them back on, then kicked them off again and stared at the shadows on the ceiling.

Why couldn't he stop thinking about Billingsley and Troon? The two had joined Marcus and his team at the diner and spilled out their life stories, how Billingsley hadn't gotten any sex from his wife for years and how Troon found it hard to meet men in her line of work. They admitted to having an affair for six months. Marcus released them, but a notion cropped up as they drove away. Had they figured out where Marcus was dining and come to the motel specifically so he would see them? If Troon had wanted to keep a low profile, she shouldn't have been flaunting her relationship with Billingsley right next door to Evert's Marina, especially with Evert being so buddy-buddy with her boss. Before heading home, Marcus ordered Gutiérrez and Keegan to dig a little deeper, to see if there were witnesses to the affair and make sure that it wasn't just a ruse planned by Billingsley to blur his guilt.

Squeezing his eyes shut, Marcus tried again to fall asleep, but images of the massacre sped through his mind, the same kind of visions he'd experienced after coming home from the war: blood, gunfire, and victims' faces, all twisting in pain.

*Clack!*

Marcus sat upright. Something or someone was outside. The neighbor's dogs stopped barking. The squirrel in the attic grew quiet.

*Clack!*

On the gravel in the driveway.

Marcus grabbed his Glock and charged down the hall. Midway he stopped at the window. Through the inch-wide break between the drapes, he peered into the gloom. The crescent moon didn't enhance his vision, but he noticed movement. He started toward the door, ready to take on his visitor but froze when a shadowy figure emerged. Female with short hair, her body outlined in moonlight. She took a step toward the house and paused, as if trying to decide whether to disturb him or not. Something was familiar about the woman's shape. Was it Chessa Paxton? How would she know where he lived?

The woman began to move again. She climbed the stairs.

Marcus reset the safety on his gun and switched on the porch light. He swept open the front door. The scent of pine filtered inside. So did the pungent aroma of Chanel No. 5 and scotch. He stiffened. "Ginnie."

Her face was overly made-up and tearstained. Her hair, a poor excuse of a short-cropped wig, sat askew on her head. The V-neck of her wraparound dress fell open too far. Red welts scarred her chest. She was missing an earring.

He guided her into the house and shut the door. "What happened?"

"I got screwed." She spun away and stumbled into the living room, but she didn't sit. "My husband and I thought we'd try a little role playing. You know, change it up a bit. We got a sitter for the kids. Went to a motel." Her body gave way to convulsive shuddering. She sank to her knees. "Oh, Marcus, I'm so messed up. I didn't know where to turn."

Marcus placed his gun on top of the stereo and removed the wig from her head. Her curls tumbled around her shoulders. He enfolded her in his arms. "*Shh.*"

"He wanted me to do things." Ginnie slurped in air. "But I couldn't. I went catatonic. He lost it and hit me. He said, 'What am I paying all that stinking money to a therapist for?' like seeing a therapist makes all the bad stuff in my head go away. He doesn't get it." She hiccupped. "You get it. I know you get it."

He nodded.

Fresh tears streamed down her cheeks. "Why did he make me do it?"

Marcus couldn't answer her. All he could think about was Chessa Paxton. Had her husband made her do something she didn't want to do?

~ * ~

Chessa woke with a start, heart pounding. She had been dreaming about spiders. Hundreds of spiders. Crawling up her legs, her neck, her face. She bounded to her feet and let the space blanket drop to the ground. She rubbed her arms. She needed more sleep, but she was afraid to doze off. She paced in front of the tree and counted backward from one hundred. Anything to get calm.

When she hit the number one and felt her breathing ease to normal, she risked slipping beneath the blanket again.

~ * ~

Around midnight Tallchief, irritated that he hadn't found Richter, got an itch of inspiration. He had read Newman's report about one of the dead doctors participating in a private cash game with Evert and his buddies at the Bella Vista. What if Richter hooked up with them, and the three were playing cards right now? What if Richter hoped to win a big money game so he could leave the country for good?

*Not on my watch.*

Tallchief pulled into the lot at the boutique hotel, cut the lights on his Explorer, and exited. Thanks to the sodium vapor lights, he didn't need his flashlight to see license plates.

Something howled, then out of nowhere, a pack of cats darted across Tallchief's path. His gut tensed until he saw the color of the cats. All three were white, not black. No worries. *What a superstitious fool,* Ruthie would have said. He shrugged off the tension and proceeded up and down each of the narrow parking rows looking for his quarry.

When he found a green Blazer, license plate 4CVD127, tucked between a pair of larger vehicles, his blood thrummed with energy. Sure, if he was one of his deputies, he would chew the guy out for not calling in backup, but this was open and shut. He had the jump on Richter. On the other hand, a call to Newman to let him know what was up was smart. Ruthie would berate him if he didn't do that. He pulled his cell phone from his pocket. There was no signal even though the night was clear. Swell.

A trio exiting the front of the hotel caught his attention. Two were stumbling. The third jiggled the keys and called out, "Designated driver."

Within seconds, an engine roared to life and a sedan sped out of the lot.

A moment later the rear door of the hotel opened. Tallchief swung around. A man in a baseball cap, bent at the waist, staggered out. He stumbled down the stairs and disappeared around the corner, probably to throw up in a stand of bushes. Or maybe not.

Tallchief jammed his cell phone in his pocket and followed the guy, just in case it was Richter trying to get away. He paused when he heard a crackle and a footstep. Behind him. He slipped his Glock from the holster and whirled around.

The man in the baseball cap ran at him and whacked his gun out of his hands. It clattered on the ground.

At the same time, Tallchief made out a tattoo on the guy's neck. "Richter."

"At your service."

Richter elbowed Tallchief in the stomach. Tallchief wheezed; his knees wobbled. Richter kicked karate-style and rammed his heel into Tallchief's chest. Tallchief reeled and landed on his butt. He groped for his gun but came up short.

Richter wedged a foot on Tallchief's hand. "Uh-uh, old man."

The sodium arc lights from the Explorer cast an eerie glow around Richter as he raised a gun fitted with a silencer and aimed at Tallchief's chest. "Shouldn't have come looking for me."

He fired.

Pain shot through Tallchief. Blood oozed from his stomach. Why hadn't he thought to wear a flak jacket? When had he lost his edge?

"FYI," Richter rasped, "we know where Chessa Paxton is. You can't protect her any longer."

Tallchief sobbed. If only he had *tried* to protect her.

# CHAPTER 55

In the dark of dawn, Chessa jolted awake. Not because she'd dreamed about spiders again. She had heard a noise. She felt around for the flashlight, but it wasn't where she had put it. Had the bear scooped it up with the trail mix? Had she bumped it while sleeping? She couldn't make out anything but tree shadows.

*Crack.* A twig or branch broke.

Footsteps. Cautious. Steady. Human.

Chessa threw off the blanket, clutched the thickest part of the stick, and scrambled to her feet. Before she could find her balance, someone from behind grabbed her hair.

"Found you." A man's voice.

He slapped the side of Chessa's head. Heat blazoned her ear. She grasped the stick tighter and jerked her head to the left. The man lost hold; her hair was too short to keep a good grip.

Chessa spun around, stick raised, and glared at her assailant. Bleached hair. Spider web tattoo. It was *him*. The guard.

Alarm sparked inside her. How had he found her?

"Gonna fight me, babe?" His mouth twisted up on one side. "C'mon. Come at me." He wiggled his fingers, beckoning her to take him on.

*Run!* rang out in Chessa's head, but before she could make a move, he rushed her. Caught her by the shoulders. Hurled her to the ground. The stick flew from her hands. He kicked her thighs. Over and over.

Shooting pains coursed up Chessa's body and into her head. She groped for the stick. Couldn't reach it. She scraped a handful of dirt and pine needles and hurled it at his face. He staggered as he brushed the grime from his eyes, giving her time.

Chessa crawled to the stick, got hold, and swung to face her attacker.

He kicked the stick away, hoisted her to her feet, and clenched her by the neck with both hands. His thumbs pressed her windpipe. Breathing became difficult. Her vision blurred.

"I can't shoot you, as much as I'd like to," he rasped. "Can't leave that kind of evidence. I've got to make it look like an ambush."

In the deep recesses of her mind, Chessa remembered watching an Internet video on self-defense. Zach had sent her the link and ordered her to view it. *You never know,* he said. The instructor claimed when an assailant had both hands on a victim, it made the assailant vulnerable, not the victim. Chessa hadn't ever practiced the moves on a real person, only in front of a mirror.

*Please work.*

She thrust both arms upward and clawed her attacker's eyes and nose. He roared. She jammed a foot on his instep, then rammed him in the groin with her knee.

He released her and tumbled backward, one hand on his private parts, the other braced on his thigh. He lifted his chin and cursed her.

She retrieved the stick and lunged at him with force she didn't know she possessed. She nailed his stomach with the sharpest end. He groaned and sank to his knees.

Chessa threw the stick aside, snatched her denim tote bag, and sprinted to the hiking path. She didn't look back.

By the time she reached the trailhead parking lot, her lungs felt ready to explode. She found the Vespa intact where she'd left it beyond the Econoline van and breathed a sigh of relief. Her attacker had pinpointed her, but not her means of escape. She straddled the bike, switched it on, and zipped down the mountain taking the turns at breakneck speed. Often during the long haul, she glanced in the side view mirror, expecting the guard to catch up to her, but he didn't. Maybe he was still incapacitated. Doubtful. Maybe he figured she turned left at the crossroads and headed north to the campground in search of help. That would put him a good half-hour behind her.

At the junction to Highway 50 and 28, a chilling realization hit Chessa. *Jeremiah.* He was the only one who could have guessed where she had gone. He had sent the guard to kill her.

## CHAPTER 56

Marcus made Ginnie spend the night—she took the bed; he took the couch. At seven A.M., he sent her off sober. In her parting words, she thanked him for being the best man she had ever known and promised she would find a new therapist.

When he arrived at the station, he downed a doughnut in three bites. Not his wisest choice, and yet now, even though the doughnut was protesting at the pit of his stomach, he eyed the box of sweets sitting on the interrogation room table and craved another. Gutiérrez, who had shown restraint and chosen a bran muffin, was leaning against the wall looking smug.

"More coffee?" Marcus asked the card dealer from Harrah's Casino who was sitting at the table, munching on a blueberry muffin. Yes, Marcus was being solicitous. Tallchief's claim that the captain was upset with Marcus's performance was having an effect. No matter how irritated he might be, he did not want to be demoted or, worse, fired.

The card dealer shook his head. "As I was saying"—he brushed crumbs from the table into his palm and dumped them into the muffin's empty paper shell—"about a week ago, Wally Evert lost some major hands to Paul Tarantino, and Evert never loses hands. So I figure, Evert was paying off Tarantino for something, right?"

"Go on," Marcus said, learning nothing new so far. Through a source, Gutiérrez had discovered that Tarantino's savings account had recently ballooned.

"See, I've got this thing for reading people. Hey, is that—"

Marcus peered where the guy was looking, out the interrogation room window into the station. Keegan was leading Paul Tarantino to the metal chair beside Marcus's desk.

"Yeah, no worries," Marcus said. "We won't let him know that you ratted him out. Listen, you come up with a list of when and how much Evert scraped together, and you can go. Gutiérrez—"

"I'm on it."

As Gutiérrez ushered the card dealer out the door, Marcus marched toward Tarantino, eager to grill him. After Billingsley and Troon's testimonies, and with corroborating evidence of their affair from the motor court motel staff this morning, Marcus had returned Evert to the top of his suspect list. But Evert wasn't the kind to dirty his own hands. Hence, the search into Tarantino's funds.

Marcus nailed Tarantino with a knowing look. "How's it hanging, Paul?" Rapid fire, he laid out his theory about Evert hiring someone to do his handiwork.

"You can't think it was me." Tarantino squirmed, his fear real. "I'm telling you I don't...I never...I wouldn't."

"Evert lost a number of gambling hands to you. Cash."

"Who told you that?"

"A little birdie," Keegan chimed in. He had tracked down the card dealer at dawn.

"Aw, dude, my nephew needs a kidney transplant," Tarantino said. "My sister lost her job and doesn't have insurance. I didn't have enough to cover it, so I asked Evert for a loan. He owed me."

"For what?" Marcus asked.

Tarantino studied his fingernails. "I located an employee for him."

"I'm listening."

"A teenager who used to work at the marina. The kid emptied the till. I've got a source that can follow up on jerks like that using social security numbers. They caught this one in Utah about a month ago. It was a tit for tat deal with Evert, know what I mean? I'm a good guy. A decent guy."

Marcus frowned. "Get me paperwork on your sister's son—doctors' names, the works—and you'd better darn well keep your nose clean."

"You bet." Tarantino couldn't scramble to his feet fast enough. He hustled out of the precinct.

Marcus gazed at Tallchief's desk. Where was he? Tallchief was never late. And what the heck was Reverend Diggs doing sitting in the chair beside Tallchief's desk? Was he ready to make yet another plea for mercy on Chessa Paxton's behalf?

"Deputy," Marcus said, "would you mind getting me a cup of coffee while I deal with Diggs?" Maybe coffee could curb his desire for another doughnut. His stomach would have to deal with the acid later.

"Sure. I want a cup myself," Keegan said and headed off.

Marcus strode to Tallchief's desk. "Reverend Diggs, what's up?"

Diggs stood and tilted his head back to meet Marcus's gaze. "My Winnebago at Heavenly Mountain was broken into."

"Was anything missing?"

"I don't think so, but whoever tossed it left a message on the mirror. It said: *You got lucky.*" Diggs worried his hands. "Fortunately, I was at a meeting with my church leaders, or—"

"Were there any witnesses? Did anybody see someone enter your RV?"

Diggs shook his head.

"Was the door busted?"

"I don't lock my doors. I trust in the goodness of man."

Marcus chewed his teeth. Wasn't anyone paying attention to the sorry state of the world lately? "Why come to me? Why not South Lake Tahoe PD?"

"I thought it might have a bearing on your case. Chessa warned me that I was in danger. She thought, because of the dwarves that were killed in the massacre, that I was a possible target."

"Why didn't you tell me that when—"

"Newman! Your mom, line one," a deputy yelled. "The dog—"

"Newman!" Captain Armstrong marched into the station looking as commanding as a four-star army general, his silver hair sprayed into place, linebacker shoulders square and strong. "Get over here!" A battalion of men in suits followed in his wake.

Marcus groaned. What had he done this time, and where was Tallchief? "Keegan," he called to the deputy across the room, "forget the coffee and come over here." He turned to Diggs. "Reverend, I'm sorry but I have to go. I don't believe you're in danger, sir. As public as you are, if you were the murderer's target, I believe he or they would have tried again."

"Are you sure?"

"Look, why don't you fill out a report for us, and let's back that up by having South Lake Tahoe PD visit your trailer, sound good?" Marcus hustled across the room and came to a stop in front of his boss. "Sir."

"You're off the Paxton case."

"Why? What did I do—"

"Tallchief's been murdered. A hiker found his body at Spooner Meadow."

## CHAPTER 57

By the time Chessa reached Incline Village, the morning sun had crept over the ridge of mountains and Sunday church bells were chiming. As she neared the Incline Sheriff's Substation, she admitted to herself that she was exhausted. She had no more fight left in her. She was ready to turn herself in. She only hoped her bedraggled appearance would add weight to her claim of innocence. She didn't need a mirror to know she resembled a punching bag.

Twenty yards from the entrance, Chessa pulled the Vespa to a halt and planted her feet on the ground. Reporters with microphones, news crews with cameras, and hordes of people crowded the substation entrance. Even at a distance, she could hear some in the crowd tossing around her name. What had happened? Did a camper find the security guard? Did the guard then lie to his rescuer and say Chessa had attacked the tattoo artist and killed Helena Gorzinski?

Needing to know what was going on before she blindly threw herself on Newman's mercy, she veered into a nearby alley and parked.

A frail homeless man shuffled to her. He held out his tattered straw hat. "Help me." The sign taped to the garbage bag he wore over his clothes said: *Will work for food.*

A new plan formed in Chessa's mind. She pulled out the last of her money. "I'll pay you five bucks plus change for your bag, sign, and hat."

The homeless man removed his things quickly and thrust them at her. Cackling while fanning the singles, he scurried from the alley.

Minutes later, dressed in a disguise that reeked of booze, Chessa emerged from the alley. She shuffled toward the substation parking lot, and keeping a steady pace so as not to draw attention, hid behind a stand of bushes to listen in.

The frizzy-haired officer Chessa had seen with Newman at the tattoo parlor was answering the reporter's questions. "We believe she's a person of interest in the death of Detective Tallchief," the woman said.

Chessa teetered. Tallchief was dead? They thought she had killed him?

A reporter said, "I heard Ms. Paxton left Detective Tallchief a voice mail to meet her in Spooner Meadow."

Chessa felt as if someone was squeezing the air out of her lungs and ratcheting imaginary handcuffs around her wrists and ankles. Someone was framing her. Again. Despite her rising panic, she willed herself to stay put. Running out in the open to tell Newman—everyone—that she hadn't killed Tallchief wasn't going to solve anything. She needed more information.

*Honk!*

Chessa spun to her right. A midnight blue Jaguar with Jeremiah at the wheel swerved into a parking spot and screeched to a halt. The crowd of reporters rushed toward him as he stepped from the car. His hair was mussed, his face drawn.

Why was he here? Chessa raced to fill in the blanks. What if Tallchief figured out something that could implicate Jeremiah in the massacre? What if Jeremiah sent the security guard after Tallchief as well as Chessa? Maybe he had ordered Patience Troon to call Tallchief and pretend to be Chessa.

A side exit door banged open and Newman stormed out. He glanced at the horde surrounding Jeremiah but didn't move in that direction. Keys in hand, he trudged toward his beaten-up truck.

Chessa headed toward him. He was her only hope.

As Newman climbed into the cab and revved the truck to life, Keegan broke through the throng and dashed across the asphalt. "Sir. Hold up."

Chessa froze in the shadow of a parked car.

Newman glared at Keegan through the opened window. "What?"

"Where are you going?"

"My mom's house. The dog hurt his leg."

"Don't you want in on this?" Keegan gestured to the media-feeding frenzy. "Senator Wolfe is here to meet with Armstrong."

"Didn't you hear? Armstrong kicked me off the case."

"No way. But he can't—"

"He did."

"What about Diggs's Winnebago getting robbed?" Keegan pressed. "The incident could be linked."

"Who knows what's real and what's fantasy at this point?" Newman grimaced. "What's bugging you, deputy?"

"Tallchief went looking for Richter. We both know he did. What if he found him? What if Richter killed him?"

Chessa craned an ear. Who was Richter?

"If and when they bring in Chessa Paxton, maybe they'll get answers," Newman said. "Not my problem. Get back to work. And don't mess up."

Keegan turned on his heel. "Tell your mom hello."

Newman ground the truck into gear and backed it up a few feet.

As he did, Chessa knew what she had to do. The tailgate was nonexistent. A tarp, tied at its four corners, covered the cargo hold. Just as Newman neared a speed bump, she bolted toward his truck and dove in the back, hands first.

## CHAPTER 58

Chessa gripped one of the cords attaching the tarp to the truck's frame to keep from flailing around. After a few short minutes of hairpin turns and bumpy roads, she felt as battered as a piñata. The fact that she was wearing a slippery garbage bag didn't help. The heat beneath the tarp grew intense. Dust swirled in where the tailgate should have been. She suppressed the urge to cough and did her best to focus on her impending meeting with Newman, whenever that might take place. For all she knew, his mother lived in New York. Chessa worked through the first words that she would say. *I'm innocent* wouldn't cut it this time. Would he believe her about the attack by the security guard in the forest? Would he believe Jeremiah sicced the guy on her?

Suddenly the truck jolted. Then it bucked and fishtailed. Brakes squealed. Chessa lost her grip on the cord and tumbled backward. Her head grazed the side of the truck bed. She jammed the toes of her shoes against the frame but couldn't stop her slide. She heard a hissing sound followed by metal scraping pavement. A tire must have punctured.

The truck skidded. Chessa groped for a finger hold, in vain. She flew out the rear of the truck. Her heels hit dirt and scrub brush, not pavement. She staggered as the truck hurtled down a steep ravine.

Displaced birds soared into the sky. Rodents scurried to safety.

To keep herself from tumbling down the ravine along with the truck, Chessa pitched sideways and crashed into a manzanita bush. Thorns pierced the garbage bag and ripped her shirt.

Dazed but not knocked out, she freed herself from the bush, ripped off the garbage bag, and scanned the crash site. Below was a cliff. Newman's truck had stopped short of it and was tipped onto the driver's side. The engine was revving loudly. Steam leached from under the hood. The only thing keeping the truck from careening into the gorge was a gigantic pine tree.

A red-tailed hawk keened overhead, as if insisting Chessa do something. She glanced back at the road. What had happened? Had the security guard made his way down the mountain to the station? Had he seen Chessa dive into Newman's truck? Had he blown out a tire on purpose? If he was in the area, he wasn't revealing himself.

The hawk keened again.

Cautiously Chessa sidestepped down the prickly hill, doing her best not to make too much sound and alert the guard if he was in the area. She couldn't avoid stepping on pine needles, but the crunching was minor. When she reached Newman's truck, she noticed the cab's rear window was cracked open an inch. She climbed onto the vehicle, crawled across the tarp, and peered inside. Newman's back was jammed against the driver's door. His eyes were closed. Blood oozed from a gash on his forehead. His head must have hit the steering wheel.

"Detective?"

His eyes snapped open. He glowered. "What the blazes are you doing here?"

"I was hiding in your truck. I was waiting for the right moment to approach you. I'm innocent. I didn't kill Tallchief. I didn't kill Zach or any of those people."

"I'm off the case."

Chessa tried to pry open the window, but it wouldn't budge. "Close your eyes," she ordered then shut her own and jabbed the cracked window with her elbow. The glass gave way. She kicked out the rest of the frame with her foot, which caused the truck to shudder. She tensed. Due to the heavy snows of winter, the roots of the pine could give way any time. "We have to get you out of here. Are you hurt? I mean, other than the cut on your head?"

"My knee."

"Broken?"

"Twisted."

"Take my hand." Chessa stuck her arm through the hole in the window, careful to avoid the sharp edges. Newman hesitated. "Do it!"

His fingers grazed hers, and electricity zinged through her. She was certain she saw something in his eyes that said he believed she was innocent, that he wasn't the enemy, but the moment vanished as quickly as it came. Not wishing to stay in the truck a second longer, she braced a foot against the side of the bed for leverage and pulled Newman free of the cab.

The pine tree creaked.

"Move, move, move!"

They hit the dirt with a thud. Seconds later, the pine tree lost its footing. The truck barreled forward with the tree and dove into the ravine. It struck the bottom with a thunderous crash.

Chessa gasped. "Your head—" The bleeding was worse than she'd imagined. She moved to stanch the cut.

Newman swatted her hand away—"Leave it!"—and pulled handcuffs from his pocket.

"Are you kidding me?" Chessa raised her arms. "I won't run. I promise. I came to you, remember?"

"I have to take you in."

"Give me a break. Hear my side first."

Newman wrestled with the idea. After a moment, he stowed the handcuffs and shimmied a cell phone from his pocket. "Great, no signal. Let's get to the road."

She clutched his forearm. "Wait. The shooter—"

"What shooter?"

"The one that made you swerve off the road."

"I hit something sharp and blew out a tire."

"I don't think so. The security guard. The one I told you about." Words flew out in short, choppy gulps. "He wounded the tattoo artist, and he killed Helena. He found me in the forest."

"The forest?"

"I stayed there overnight. At dawn, he attacked me. We fought. Hard. I escaped and I came to the precinct to—" She drew in a quick breath. "He might have caught up to me. He might be the one shooting at us. We should hide."

"I'm not hiding from anybody." Newman removed his gun from his holster, as if that would be enough defense against a killer with a rifle, and nudged Chessa upward.

"My stepfather might have guessed I was in the forest. I think he sent the guard to get rid of me."

Newman stumbled.

"Throw your arm over my shoulder," Chessa commanded.

He didn't argue. The climb up the hill was more challenging than the descent, particularly with Newman leaning on her, but Chessa refused to buckle.

"I believe I was set up," she continued. "The killer planted the divorce papers and placed the bracelet in my husband's hand to cast doubt on me."

"We found your shoe at the massacre site."

Chessa shuddered. She had come to tell him the truth. She wouldn't stop. "Yes, I was there, but I didn't remember at first, when you questioned me. The last two days, I've been recalling things in bursts, as if a nightmare was interrupted. Zach was in the meadow and the security guard, too. Is his name Richter?"

Newman threw her a suspicious look.

"I was at the precinct. I overheard you talking with Deputy Keegan. Tallchief went looking for Richter. Is Richter the security guard's name?"

Newman didn't answer.

"C'mon, level with me. I told you things have been coming back in flashes. I was supposed to die with the others, but Zach didn't shoot me. I remember seeing him talking to a witch at the ball. And I remember the security guard—Richter. He said the witch said the firestorm will happen in three days. I think the massacre might—"

"What firestorm? What witch?"

"That's just it. I don't know. The witch at the ball—" Chessa described the costume. "She had prominent cheekbones and dark hair tipped with red and purple. Of course, that could have been a wig."

Newman's gaze narrowed; he was weighing the information. "The man who delivered the divorce document to your house said a woman with dark hair and sharp cheekbones accepted it."

Chessa heartened at the news. "Shawn Spitzer said a witch in a black-feathered costume at the ball had major cheekbones, and Orseno Hill, a man I work with at the casino, said Reverend Diggs's date was dressed in feathers. Did you question her?"

"Not me, but someone else might have. Tallchief"—his voice snagged—"put a lot of personnel on this."

"And he's—" Chessa spied something. Up on the road. "Duck!"

# CHAPTER 59

Marcus wasn't sure what to believe. Was Chessa Paxton imagining things? No shots rang out. No one charged toward them. Erring on the side of caution, he steered her toward a stand of bushes. His left knee throbbed, but at least his leg wasn't broken.

Peering through the branches, he aimed his Glock toward the road. No movement. No glint of metal. No vehicles or people of any kind. So why was his gut in knots? Because he sensed danger. He listened for a telltale sound while cursing his fate. How dare Chessa put him in such a precarious career position. If the brass found out he was harboring a fugitive...

Okay, sure. He didn't like how Captain Armstrong had muscled his way into the investigation, but he'd had to, right? Tallchief was dead. Marcus rankled at the captain's inference that he was inept, but that wasn't what was really bothering him. Jeremiah Wolfe had shown up. Why? If the captain followed protocol, he would have gone to the senator's house. Big fish goes to bigger fish.

It was crazy thinking—Marcus had to admit he was starting to see conspiracies in everything—but what if Chessa was right? What if her stepfather had hired someone to kill her? Somebody in a Blazer had chased her yesterday, and she did look like she'd been in a fight. Did that mean she wasn't guilty of murdering her husband and the others? No. She could have double-crossed a partner, and that was who was hunting her.

"Do you see anything?" Chessa whispered.

Marcus swiveled to meet her glance. An inch-long gash paralleled her eyebrow. A bump the size of a walnut marred her cheekbone. Her chin resembled raw hamburger. Thumbprint bruises stained her neck. She had risked her freedom by leaping into his truck. Near the cliff, she had risked her life to save him from a fate he didn't want to contemplate. Maybe she was innocent.

*Keep your distance, Marcus.* Man, seeing Ginnie had messed him up bigtime. All women weren't victims.

"Do you hear that?" Chessa whispered.

"Sounds like a drill. There are workmen a mile east, near Brown's Creek. Look, the truck going off the road was an accident. Like I said, my tires were in bad shape. A nail on the road or a sharp stick—"

"You're wrong and you know it. I see it in your eyes."

Marcus grimaced. Right before he swerved, he had heard a *ping*.

~ * ~

Jeremiah stood by the wall safe in his library, its door hanging open. The painting of Emerald Bay that usually covered the safe rested on the floor against the wall. Sunlight pierced the office window and ricocheted off the frame. Jeremiah blinked. Boozy perspiration soaked his underarms. A riot of emotions swept through him: anger, frustration, relief. The conversation with Armstrong had gone as expected. Adriana would have been proud of the way Jeremiah had conducted himself. He had offered clues as to Chessa's whereabouts, and the captain had praised him for his candor even though Chessa was still on the run. Jeremiah left the precinct, shoulders squared and looking like the epitome of a good citizen.

"What a crock," he muttered.

He was the farthest thing imaginable from a good citizen. He didn't deserve to take another breath. He urged himself to continue with his plan. He pulled a stack of letters bound with a rubber band from the safe, letters he hadn't read for a long time, the last dated over a year ago, and set them on the floor next to the painting. Then he reached into the vault and withdrew the Beretta. His fingers trembled as they wrapped around the cold metal.

He moaned. The two belts of scotch he'd downed the moment he returned home would never give him enough courage.

Jocko whimpered.

"Hush, boy."

Secrets. So many secrets. Only he, Jeremiah Wolfe, Nevada's hero, could stop the madness. He had to confess. He picked up the letters, inserted them into the pocket of his jacket, and slotted his finger through the gun's trigger.

Flooring squeaked. Jeremiah pivoted.

"What are you doing?" Patience demanded from the archway.

Jeremiah glanced at the gun and back at her.

Patience's nostrils flared. She held out her hand. "Give me that."

There were days she could be tough, but today he would be tougher. He had to go through with it. He couldn't keep living the lie. "I'm responsible."

"Not when you're drunk." Patience strode to the telephone on the antique side table. "I'm calling Reverend Diggs."

"Don't. He can't—" A shudder ripped through Jeremiah. All his life he had wanted to do the right thing. When had he become such a fool? "It's my fault. Phoenix—"

"The name's Patience. How much have you had?" She strode to him, hand extended. "You're going to stop drinking. Today. This instant. Do you hear me? You've got to sober up."

Jeremiah's shoulders sagged.

"Remove your finger from the trigger."

He obeyed.

"Give it to me."

He didn't; he wouldn't. "I'm going to my darkroom."

"Good idea. Develop a few pictures. It relaxes you. You always think better in there, but don't do anything—"

"Rash? I won't. Promise."

# CHAPTER 60

Chessa's muscles ached as she negotiated the hill beside Newman. After a moment of silence, he'd felt it was safe for them to move again, but he had warned her to stay low. Perspiration slithered down her back and soaked the waist of her jeans. A bed and a meal, which only two days ago were expected conveniences, would be such a luxury. She glanced sideways at Newman, overwhelmed and grateful for his help despite how ruinous to his career his decision might be. What had tipped the scales for him? She didn't dare ask. He trudged beside her, pensive and not nearly as intimidating as the moment she had first met him. Yes, he was meaty and solid, not rawboned like Zach, but there was something different about him.

He whispered, "Continue with your theories."

"What if only one person was the target of the mass killing and the rest were—"

"Collateral damage?"

"Exactly. They were at the wrong place at the wrong time. The dwarves, I mean the doctors, were already on the van."

Newman narrowed his eyes. "How do you know about that?"

"I was on it."

"You were—"

Chessa put her hand up to pacify him. "Zach carried me onto the van. I was groggy. I think he drugged me."

Newman pushed past her as they neared the highway. "Stay back." He clawed through dense foliage to the edge of the road. "It looks safe." He beckoned her onward.

Chessa slipped on the hardscrabble shoulder of the road, then found her footing on the pavement. She didn't see any vehicles or pedestrians.

"Follow me." Newman strode ahead of her, iPhone in hand. "Dang. Still no signal. Go on. Tell me more." He didn't look at her as he continued to search for a cell phone signal.

"Steven Spitzer," Chessa said. "What if he's the important piece of this puzzle? Have you seen all those people picketing outside his facility?" She plucked pine needles off her torn shirt, caring, oddly enough, how ragtag she looked. "Two men visited the place in April. Spitzer's daughter thought they were government men, interested in the research. I think they were Richter and my husband."

"If they killed Spitzer to hurry a sale along," Newman said, "they failed. With his death, there will be all sorts of red tape to forage through. Next?"

"There's a Big Blob Theory." Chessa explained about the concern that nanobots would somehow invade human bodies, ruining what God created.

"Deputy Keegan ran that idea past me. It's a little extreme."

"The massacre was a *little extreme.*" Chessa heard the edge in her voice. She swallowed hard, desperate to keep herself in check. She didn't want Newman to think she was a lunatic. "There's also the possibility that Yukiko Kimura was the target. She opened up Nevada to tech-savvy businesses. My mother once said that Yukiko was too forward-thinking."

"Why would your mother weigh in?"

"They were friends. Or *frenemies,* if you will. They occasionally went to lunch. About a year and a half ago, my mother said the conversation remained light until they began discussing economic growth. Mom opposed it. Yukiko stormed out of the lunch, and—" Chessa gasped. "Oh, lord."

"What?"

"The authorities claimed my mother's death was an accident. What if Yukiko hired someone to kill her? My mother had a broad base of influence in Nevada. People listened to her. What if Jeremiah was secretly against my mother's narrow views, and he collaborated with Yukiko? But then he killed *her* because he couldn't be connected to the conspiracy—"

"Watch out!" Newman threw his arm out and thrust Chessa off the pavement.

She fell as a red Mustang convertible flew past. It wasn't the security guard out to attack them. It was a young female driver, oblivious to the world, chatting on a cell phone, her hair tangling in the wind. Chessa had been so engulfed in conversation she had blocked out all other sound.

"You okay?"

She nodded, though her heart was hammering in her chest. She scrambled to her feet and drew in a breath, hands braced on her knees.

Newman held up a finger and pressed his cell phone to his ear. "Zelda?

It's me. Can you hear me? Are you there? I've got car trouble on Mt. Rose Highway."

*Car trouble,* Chessa thought. What an understatement.

Newman shook the phone and mumbled, "Crap. Lost the connection." He jammed the phone into his pocket and marched ahead. "Go on with your theories."

Chessa raced to catch up. "What if Spitzer and Yukiko Kimura were killed because they represented the worst-case scenario? Cutting-edge science could change the entire landscape of Nevada. She was Spitzer's advocate."

Newman took a moment to mull that over. "Did you know she was pregnant?"

"You can't think someone murdered her and eleven other people to destroy a fetus."

"It's a theory."

"Who's the father?"

"We're not sure. Maybe Wally Evert."

Chessa said, "Evert, Yukiko, and my stepfather had a fight at the ball. At the time, I didn't think anything of it. Yukiko slammed her water bottle against Evert's chest and yelled at him. It looked like she said, 'You, you.' But I've thought about it since. Maybe she was saying, 'Goo.' Black Goo is what the naysayers call nano—"

An engine roared.

Newman propelled Chessa off the road. A spray of bullets spattered the ground near them.

A dark blue truck zoomed past.

Newman grabbed Chessa's hand and steered her down the hill into a cluster of bushes. "Did you recognize the shooter?"

"I didn't see—"

"Cauliflower ear. Crooked nose. Not Richter."

Chessa shook her head.

"So there's a second guy? I feel like we're caught in a spy movie."

"I've wondered whether Zach was a spy. He was so angry when I asked him about the passports. Later, at the ball, when he talked with the security guard and the witch, he acted like he was part of a cabal."

"Again with the witch?"

"She said the firestorm happens in three days."

"A firestorm is a natural phenomenon. Fire breeding off its own wind. You can't plan one."

"What if it's the name of a plot? If it's supposed to happen in three days, that's—"

"Down!"

Another shower of bullets ravaged the edge of the highway.

# CHAPTER 61

Chessa huddled behind the bushes, her flesh prickling with anxiety. She drew closer to Newman, the need for human contact intense.

Up on the road, tires screeched. A vehicle honked its horn. As the blare retreated to the south, tires screeched again, and an engine cranked into gear.

"He's turning around." Chessa's voice cracked, betraying her fear. "We should run—"

Newman gripped her wrist. "Keep still. I'm hoping for a clear shot."

Through a break in the branches, Chessa caught a blur of dark blue. The truck, heading south in the wrong lane, cruised the edge of the road. Metal glinted. The driver aimed his weapon out the window.

But then a boxy white Element, also in the wrong lane, appeared just north of the truck. It tore ahead and slammed into the truck's rear end. The truck sprang forward. The Element whacked the truck again. Unable to hold the road, the truck skidded forward and came to a halt. It teetered precariously over the edge of the highway. Its front left wheel spun without gaining traction.

The Element pulled to a stop. A thickset female with short-cropped gray hair and a wide, approachable face climbed out. The hem of her golf shirt rose up as she shielded her eyes from the sun. In her other hand, she held a gun.

"Marcus!" Chessa whispered.

"It's cool. That's my foster mother Zelda. She's got a license to carry."

"How did she get here so fast?"

"She's a worrywart. She knew I was coming to the house. If any of us show up late, she goes searching. C'mon." Newman moved toward the road.

Chessa followed. "What about the driver of the truck?"

"If he shifts weight, he's toast. He won't budge. By the way, my mom likes people to think she's crusty. Don't let her fool you."

As Chessa reached the highway, Zelda hurried to her and enfolded her in her fleshy arms, the move dispelling Newman's warning.

"Well, I'll be," Zelda said. "It's you. The fugitive. All bruised and torn. Never mind the *how*. I'm sure you'll tell me in time."

"Your car," Chessa said.

Zelda waved her off. "That's what insurance is for. Marcus, where's your truck?"

"At the bottom of the ravine."

"Guess you can buy yourself that eco-friendly car you've been talking about." Zelda chuckled softly as she flung open the Element's rear door. "Get in, sweet girl."

"I'll be right back," Newman said and ran to the dark blue truck.

Chessa climbed into the Element and a golden retriever sidled to her. He lavished her with wet kisses.

"Brubeck, out of the way," Zelda ordered.

"It's okay. He's fine. I love dogs." Though Chessa had resigned herself to never having Jocko while married to Zach, if she was proven innocent, she wanted him to move home.

*If.*

"I heard your dog hurt his leg," Chessa said.

"He stepped in a gopher hole, silly mutt. He's limping, but he'll heal." Zelda climbed into the driver's seat and slammed her door. "Seat belt, please. I'm Zelda, by the way." She snickered. "Can you imagine giving a child that name? My mother had a fixation for F. Scott Fitzgerald and his loony wife." A wistful look filled her eyes and quickly vanished. "Nobody reads anymore."

"I do," Newman said as he opened the Element's rear door and placed an automatic weapon on the floor.

"Raised you right, didn't I? How's your attacker?"

"Out cold." Newman slammed the door and climbed into the front passenger seat. As Zelda pulled onto the highway, he pressed the numbers on his cell phone, and muttered, "Sure. Now it works. Hey, Keegan, it's me. Listen up." He gave the deputy the location of the accident and a brief recap of the attack. "I handcuffed him to the passenger door. Nah, the truck's stable. It's not going down the hill anytime soon. By the way, the guy's key chain has a grocery store value card on it. See if you can identify him. I put the keys in the truck's bed. Sure, whatever you want, deputy, just don't blow your career." He ended the call.

Chessa smiled at Newman. "Thank you for not telling him about me."

"Why would he?" Zelda asked.

"Because he should arrest me."

"Oh, for heaven's sakes. You're not guilty."

"Mom."

Zelda eyed Newman with something short of disdain. "I've taken in broken children for going on thirty-five years, son. I know children from the moment I meet them. I knew it about you, and I know it about this girl."

"She's a woman."

"Don't get smart with me. She's not guilty. If you look into her soul, you'll see. And don't give me guff about your intuitive gift shutting down when your brother died."

Chessa yearned to know the rest of Newman's story. How had he come to live with Zelda? What happened to his brother?

Zelda petted Newman's cheek. "Yes, I know you suffer, but Eddie was saved. You ask Pastor John. Your brother's soul was clean. He was on the path to a new and happy life. That mess of a war killed him and made him doubt himself and his recovery, but he was saved, suicide or no suicide."

Suicide. Chessa couldn't imagine.

Zelda gently whacked Newman up the back of his head. "Look at this girl and tell me you don't see what I see. Go on."

Newman glanced over his shoulder. Chessa felt a warmth creep up her neck and into her cheeks. Brubeck, as if assigning himself her bodyguard, nestled into her and shoved his head beneath her fingers. His fur felt like warm velvet.

"Even the dog adores her. End of discussion. Now"—Zelda knuckled Newman's arm—"what's this about blowing your career?"

"I'm off the Paxton case. Captain Armstrong—"

"Has had it in for you from the get-go." Zelda glanced in the rearview mirror and smiled at Chessa. "Therefore, you have no reason to take Chessa in."

Newman grumbled.

"That's a pretty necklace you're wearing, Zelda," Chessa said, trying to neutralize the tension in the truck.

"This old thing?" Zelda caressed the heart-shaped silver locket fondly. "It's my string of love. Inside are pictures of the grandchildren. I have to switch them out every month." She chuckled. "I have sixteen. All of my foster children, except Marcus, have blessed me with little loves."

"Don't start," Newman warned.

"I took four of them to the convention yesterday, by the way. They loved it. There were so many interactive things to do."

"Swell."

Zelda winked at Chessa. "You're a mess. We'll have to fix up those bruises when we get home."

"I'm fine." Chessa felt eons better in the safety of the car. "More importantly, I need to get on the Internet. Do you have a computer?"

"Of course. I'm hip, no matter what my son says."

"Detective Newman actually told me you were wonderful."

"Detective Newman? Oh, please." Zelda sniffed. "You call him Marcus. None of this formal stuff. Say it, dear. Marcus."

"Marcus," Chessa murmured, liking the way his name rolled off her tongue.

For the initial portion of the ride, Zelda bombarded Chessa with questions. She answered each, happy to have someone to talk to who wasn't acting like she was Lizzie Borden. Newman—*Marcus*—sat straight, eyes focused on the road, but she could tell he was listening. His mouth turned up occasionally, sending puzzling emotions through her. She liked him and trusted him. Was that appropriate?

When Zelda ran out of mundane questions, she reached back and patted Chessa's knee. "I know what it's like to lose a husband, sweet girl. My first and only love died of lung cancer a few years ago."

Chessa's eyes welled up. She fought the tears. "I wish I'd known more about my husband."

"I'll bet you know more than you think. What was his favorite color?" Zelda cut a sharp glance at Newman. "You make a face like that again, son, and it'll freeze. Go on, Chessa. What color?"

"Blue, like mine."

"Which blue?"

"Tahoe blue, at the deepest part of the lake."

"What food did he like?"

"He wasn't particular but probably enchiladas." An image came to Chessa of Zach and her cooking together. Zach prepared the filling, making it extra spicy, while she shredded the cheese. Before they reached the dinner table, they had eaten half the fixings.

"What about music?" Zelda asked.

"He listened to guitar solos occasionally." At Zach's request, Chessa had bought him a Carlos Jobim CD. He owned a guitar, but he never played it. Why have it, then? That was one of those little secrets she had hoped to uncover during their marriage. "He hated television. Noise, he called it. Come to think of it, he didn't like the Internet or anything current. He preferred to read." Lately, all he'd been reading was the Bible, as if he were trying to memorize it. The recollection gnawed at Chessa. Zach's dedication had become a bone of contention between them. Not that reading the Bible was bad. As a girl, Chessa had read it front to cover. She believed in God. She meditated in private. She understood faith, but Zach's dedication had started to border on obsession. How could someone as religious as he was turn into a killer?

~ * ~

Jeremiah rested his elbows on the metal design table in the darkroom, downed another belt of whiskey, and burped. The stench made his nostrils flare. The eerie red glow over the developing tank grew blurry. He gripped the rim of the table to steady himself. No good passing out. He had a job to do.

Hoisting his empty glass, he toasted the photo of Adriana that he'd clipped to a clothesline where he displayed all his work. "To you, my love. I could never say *no* to you, could I? My downfall. You were never going to love me. And I"—he glanced at the packet of letters from the library safe that were sitting beneath Adriana's picture—"never stopped loving you."

He gazed at a photograph of eight-year-old Chessa, so delicate and despondent after her father was dragged from the house. Jeremiah had hoped that Chessa, with Zach, would learn to trust again. Maybe even find faith. What a stupid dream.

"Chessa, I'm sorry. If only I'd told you the truth. Instead you are a pawn in the horrible game that I should have ended."

# CHAPTER 62

Chessa sat on the dusty green-and-white striped swing on Zelda's front porch, a laptop computer perched on her thighs. An Internet search was underway for SPIDER > TATTOO. She could sense the tension oozing from Marcus even though he stood ten feet away at the edge of the porch. He was gazing at the horizon. The afternoon air was heavy. A gust of wind kicked up tumbleweed. No homes stood within a half a mile. A few cactus plants and native Joshua trees dotted the dusty landscape. Pots filled with purple flowers lined the stairs leading to the porch. An old Ford Bronco stood in the carport.

"Marcus," she said.

He didn't answer. Was he questioning his choice to help her?

"Where's Brubeck?" she asked.

"Probably gone off to visit Beauty's grave," Marcus said over his shoulder.

"Beauty?"

"Our other golden retriever. She passed away a year ago."

Chessa had noticed two dog pillows in the living room. She hadn't wanted to ask after the other dog.

"He was a sucker for her." Marcus whistled and clapped his hands, then whistled again.

A few seconds later, Brubeck limped around the corner of the house and up the stairs. He glanced from Chessa to Marcus and back again, then loped to Chessa and plopped down at her feet. He lifted his head, expecting a pat. She obliged. His fur was dusty but comforting.

The Internet search stopped and a number materialized: 425,343 SITES AVAILABLE, even more sites than the ones Chessa had discovered when she'd scoured the Internet at the motel. She switched the order, typed in TATTOO > SPIDER, and over three million sites became available.

"Swell," she muttered.

"Striking out?" Marcus turned to face her, his gaze filled with concern.

"Worse." She clicked on a site about spider mythology and how that related to tattoos and hit ENTER.

Zelda pushed open the door to the porch "Problem?"

"No," Chessa said louder than she had intended. "Sorry, Zelda."

"No worries." Zelda set a tray loaded with food and drinks on the white resin table next to the swing.

"You didn't have to go to all that trouble."

"Nonsense. Neither of you will let me put more than balm on your wounds. I can at least tend to your nutrition." Zelda indicated the computer monitor. "What's that?"

"An article about spider mythology."

"My. I never realized so many countries had different myths. Fascinating." She pointed at the food. "Eat. And there's more if you need it." She returned inside the house.

Chessa forced her attention back to the screen. "What did she just say?"

"So many countries had—"

"Why did Zach need four passports?" Everything—the massacre, Helena's murder—came back to Zach. "They couldn't all be real, right? Have you traced them?"

"We're on it."

She scowled at him. *We're on it* meant sometime in the next century they might have an answer. She wouldn't hold her breath. She typed Zach's name into the search engine line: ZACHARY X—X for his middle name Xavier—SZABO > FEBRUARY 22, 1980. Only thirty sites registered a hit. All of them turned out to be newspaper articles about the Zach she had known and loved. As a freshman in high school, Zachary X. Szabo of Flagstaff, Arizona won a math contest and kicked a game-winning goal in a statewide soccer competition. In his sophomore year, Zachary X. Szabo volunteered with a dozen other boys who called themselves the Royal Rebels to build houses for the poor in Honduras. There were no listings about Zach prior to his high school years and only Chessa's and his wedding announcement after that. How was that possible?

Simply to compare, Chessa typed in her own name, which drummed up over a thousand references. Granted, she had made the news with her recent promotion and those articles she had written back in college had garnered a few e-rebuttals, but how could Zach have so little history? Was his whole life a lie?

Chessa stopped, hands hovering over the keyboard. "Marcus, what were the names on the other three passports? I skimmed them too quickly."

"Sven Swenson, Sergei Lebedev, and Roberto Aguilar. Look, Keegan has our guys looking into whether they are forgeries, but the wheels of bureaucracy...you know."

Chessa quickly typed in the first name: SVEN SWENSON. Thousands of mentions emerged. "Any middle initial?" she asked.

Marcus shook his head. Just in case, Chessa added an X for Xavier and up popped dozens of articles about Sven X. Swenson. He existed from 1980 to 1994, the fourteen years before Zach came into being. She typed in SVEN X. SWENSON > OBITUARY but found none. The same happened when she typed in: SERGEI LEBEDEV. Thousands of mentions for the general name. A more limited listing for Sergei X. Lebedev, and he, too, vanished from the scene after 1994.

"Do you think they could be aliases for Zach's younger years?" she asked.

"Why would he need aliases as a child?"

"I don't know. Maybe his family was in the WITSEC program."

"I considered that."

"Maybe they had to move secretly and Zach Szabo wasn't his real name, either."

Chessa typed in: ROBERTO AGUILAR and another set of entries emerged. When she entered: ROBERTO X. AGUILAR, however, nothing came up. Not one article.

"That ruins your theory," Marcus said.

Chessa threw him a scathing look and changed the search string to: ROBERTO AGUILAR > XAVIER. A few articles appeared. When she spotted one written in the *Gila Bend Times*, she paused.

"What's up?" Marcus said. "You gasped."

Chessa pointed to the article about Roberto's brother Xavier dying in a poisoning incident. "Gila Bend is in Arizona. Zach used to live in Flagstaff."

"So?"

"He had a younger brother named Jav. I teased Zach about the name. Was Jav short for Javelin? Java? Jarvis? He wouldn't tell me. What if Jav was a nickname for Javier"—she pronounced the J like an H—"the Spanish equivalent of Xavier? I never met him. He lived overseas, or so Zach said. I didn't press him. I hate that I wasn't more curious." She ordered herself to stop second-guessing her past with Zach. What happened, *happened.*

"Okay, you've hooked me. Go on."

"What if Zach was really Roberto Aguilar at birth?" Chessa thought of her conversation with Zelda earlier. Zach preferred Mexican food and Spanish guitar music. He often said, *Te amo* to Chessa: *I love you.* "What if—"

She typed in ROBERTO AGUILAR > XAVIER AGUILAR > OBITUARY. A picture of Roberto and Xavier Aguilar appeared in the *Gila Bend Times.* Chessa sucked in a breath. Roberto's hair was darker than Zach's, but there was no doubt that he was her late husband. They had the same skin tone, smile, and eyes. Those deep brown eyes.

Marcus said, "Wait a sec. Go back to the previous article."

Chessa did.

"Scroll up," Marcus ordered. "Hold it. There." He pointed. "That doesn't say Roberto's brother was poisoned. It says that Roberto Aguilar *alleged* that Xavier had been poisoned. By sunscreen. He held a nanotech company called Kellerton Tech responsible."

Chessa typed in another search string: STEVEN SPITZER > KELLERTON TECH. Nothing came up. She entered ROBERTO AGUILAR > KELLERTON TECH. A number of articles popped up. Aguilar was one of thousands that claimed Kellerton Tech injured a family member. A class action suit was launched.

A reporter for the *Gila Bend Times* wrote:

*One source told this reporter that a favorite aunt mysteriously died. In her teens, the aunt had been a die-hard sun worshipper, but in her thirties, the aunt became a devotee of Kellerton sunblock. Ten years later, she passed away from a bizarre form of cancer that doctors said was untreatable.*

Chessa said, "So Zach was one of a bunch of angry relatives?"

"Seems like it. Open that next article." Marcus pointed at the monitor. "In the *Denver Chronicle.*"

Chessa read the first few paragraphs. At the end of the third, her mouth went dry.

*A fringe group calling itself the Rebels of the Republic united today outside Geo-5Tech, a startup group in the Denver area. The anti-tech group…*

"The Rebels of the Republic," Chessa whispered.

"What about them?"

"One of the first articles referring to Zach said he went on a missionary trip during high school with a group that called itself the Royal Rebels. It was a do-gooder trip, building houses for the poor. What if his group morphed into this political faction, the Rebels of the Republic, dead set against technology companies? What if this is the group that will carry out the firestorm?"

"Firestorm," Marcus mumbled.

Chessa summoned up information about the Rebels of the Republic. She found one that sucked the air out of her lungs.

*Jalapa, Guatemala, August 24, 1998*

*The Rebels of the Republic, formerly known as the Royal Rebels, have once again rebuilt a town ravaged by a hurricane. However, this time when the work was done, the group marched back into town and delivered Bibles to every survivor, newsworthy because the magnanimous Reverend Davey Diggs was the pastor coordinating the charge.*

# CHAPTER 63

Chessa set the computer on the swing and rose to her feet. "I knew there was something suspicious about Diggs."

"Hold on." Marcus nabbed a half of a tuna sandwich from the tray. "All we know—" Brubeck gave his master a pitiful look. "Not on your life, buddy. Human food." Marcus took a bite of the sandwich and swallowed. "All we know is that he led this group when Zach was in high school."

"Davey Diggs infiltrated my family."

"*Infiltrated* is a strong word. His mission is to get people to believe."

"His popularity borders on cultlike status."

"A few rock celebrities are just as popular. That doesn't make them evil."

"So what do we—*you*—know about Diggs? I assume you've done some research on him."

Marcus polished off the sandwich and brushed crumbs off his hands. "Keegan checked him out. Diggs doesn't rate a blip on the feds cult radar screen. His father, Wild Bill, started the church in a town outside of Reno. When he died in the boating accident, Diggs took it over and, thanks to the power of television, grew the church to international proportions."

"That adds up to a lot of donations."

"True. The Glory to God church must have a sizeable bank account, but any church that size would."

"What about Diggs's personal accounts?"

"We never looked into them. We've had no cause. Let's set Diggs aside for a moment and refocus on Zach."

But Chessa couldn't. Diggs had wielded power over Zach. Over her mother. Over Jeremiah. How much influence did he have over his other followers? Had he instigated the massacre?

Chessa returned to the swing, set the computer on her lap, and started another Internet search. In seconds, she pulled up the official website for Davey Diggs, PhD, subtitled: *Leader of the Glory to God Christian Revolution*. She had never visited the site before, never felt the need, not even when her mother had urged her to reexamine her faith. But as she read, the hair at the nape of her neck prickled. Aside from links to Diggs's sermons about purity, there were numerous quotes encouraging his believers to embrace the literal translation of the Bible. One commanded them to actively rid the world of manmade scientific horrors.

On the right of the website was a hyperlink leading viewers to chat rooms where they could discuss Diggs's principles. Chessa wondered whether, if she looked long enough, she would find comments from Zach among them. Below that, there were hyperlinks that would open to film footage of Diggs preaching at his revivals as well as Diggs's performances as a young actor. Beneath those, there was an icon with hyperlink that read in all caps: *DONATE!* Across the bottom of the site were multiple links to opinion articles written by Diggs.

Chessa read a few and her stomach soured.

Marcus joined her on the swing. "What's wrong?"

"Diggs had an older sister."

"I know. She suffered a horrible fate."

"According to him, she was destroyed by earthly poisons." Chessa indicated the reference. "He hates science and its power to corrupt the cleanliness God intended. Listen to this. 'Creation is steeped in purity, but man continues to mess it up. God does not care about science and progress. God wants us to return to our natural state.' I remember my mother saying those exact words after her conversion."

"That doesn't mean—"

Chessa thrust the laptop into Marcus's hands and leaped to her feet. "Diggs's revival meeting is tonight. What if he intends to ignite a revolution? By utilizing the code word *firestorm,* his flock will know it's time to wipe out all nanotech facilities."

"People wouldn't—"

"This could become a war pitting the zealous against nanotechnology around the world. That's why Zach had those passports. He traveled under aliases to spread Diggs's vicious gospel."

Marcus shook his head. "Why kill Steven Spitzer ahead of schedule?"

"I heard he was a solitary guy. He rarely went out in public. Maybe the Rebels of the Republic realized they had to strike when they could."

Marcus ran his finger over the track pad on the laptop and moved the cursor around the website. "Chessa, hold on. There's no mention on the website of the Rebels of the Republic or the Royal Rebels. Granted, way back when, Diggs might have led Zach's do-gooder group in Guatemala, but I repeat, there's no mention of any group with rebels in the name on his website." He set the computer aside and stood up. "I'm sorry, but I can't wrap my head around Diggs urging his followers to kill masses of people."

Brubeck barked.

"I agree, boy." Chessa bent to pet him. "Davey Diggs scares me. He always has. I could never put my finger on why, but he is a master of manipulation. The way people blindly follow him makes me think of the Jim Jones or Heaven's Gate fiascos."

Marcus pulled his cell phone from his pocket.

Chessa tensed. "What are you doing?"

"Calling Keegan."

"To turn me in?"

"I'm way past that. I want him to examine Diggs's financial records. I don't think this case is about religion."

Chessa returned to the swing and picked up the laptop.

"What?" Marcus said into the cell phone. "Are you kidding me? No way."

While he paced, Chessa reviewed more articles about the Rebels of the Republic. In the past ten years, they had done good deeds in Brazil, Germany, and Sweden. When she reached the end of one article, she saw a picture of the group and gaped. All of them were men in their early twenties. In the middle stood a man with a severely damaged ear, what some would call a cauliflower ear. His arm was slung over the shoulders of a redheaded man with a spider web tattoo up his neck. Richter. There was no doubt.

"Marcus." She beckoned him.

He ended the call. "You won't believe this! The guy that attacked us in the truck downed a cyanide pill. He's dead."

"And you won't believe this." Chessa pointed to the screen. "We've got to find Richter. He's key. The tattoo artist said he was a compulsive gambler."

"I told you we have guys trolling the casinos."

"C'mon. We've got to try, too."

Marcus deliberated then yelled, "Mom, I need to borrow the truck!"

# CHAPTER 64

For five minutes they argued, but in the end, Chessa won. She was going to South Lake Tahoe with Marcus. While he coordinated via telephone with Keegan, Chessa climbed into the Ford Bronco that was parked in the carport.

Before she could shut the door, Zelda raced from the house. "Wait! I want you to have this." She handed Chessa a yellow sweater. Chessa wasn't cold; a warm breeze was blowing in as afternoon turned to dusk, but she accepted the sweater gracefully. "And this." Zelda held out the heart-shaped locket she had been wearing. "It'll bring you luck."

"I couldn't."

"I insist." Zelda clasped the locket around Chessa's neck. "Yes, it suits you." She petted Chessa's cheek. "May the Lord watch over you."

A lump lodged in Chessa's throat. She battled her swelling emotions, shocked at how attached she had become to Zelda in such a short time.

"Promise to come back soon, with or without my cantankerous son."

Marcus kissed his mother on the cheek, slid into the driver's seat, tossed his cell phone into a cup holder, and geared the truck into reverse.

"You look smug," Chessa said.

"Keegan's meeting me at Harrah's Lake Tahoe."

"Meeting *us*." Chessa smirked, pleased that she had found her backbone. "Why Harrah's?"

"A card dealer ID'd Richter's picture. The guy plays there regularly. If we don't find him there, we'll go casino to casino."

"Don't compulsive gamblers hang out at the same place?"

"Not necessarily. If their luck runs dry at one, they move on to another. We also have eyes at emergency clinics. He might have sought treatment after your attack." Marcus veered left out of the driveway, heading in the opposite direction from how they had entered, and sped through a neatly trimmed residential area as he explained what Keegan had discovered. "It turns out Davey Diggs has established a family trust, which is about five layers deep, the first layer established in the Cayman Islands. Its value is upward of seventy million dollars, none of it earmarked for churchly needs."

"Seventy million?" Chessa smacked her palm on the doorframe. "Let's hear it for believers who donate."

"Guess who else is included in the trust? Wally Evert and a woman named Constance Edwards."

"Why?"

"Turns out they're all related. They had the same father."

"The preacher?"

"The same. It seems good old Wild Bill sowed his seed without benefit of marriage. Davey Diggs officially changed his surname to Diggs *after* his father died, probably to cloud the truth. His real surname is Brady."

"Wait. Isn't the sister dead?"

"Nope. If you'll recall, Diggs stated earthly poisons *destroyed* her. He didn't say she was dead. I've seen her picture. It's hanging in Evert's office. She has a severely deformed head."

"Man, Keegan's good."

Marcus grinned. "The kid's definitely pleased with himself."

"Can you arrest Diggs?"

"For what, being born out of wedlock?"

"For scamming unsuspecting converts or, I don't know, *something*. What if Diggs leaves the country before you can prove he orchestrated the upcoming raid on nanotechnology facilities?"

"We don't know that's going to happen."

Chessa huffed.

"We'll extradite him." Marcus whipped the car around a sharp turn.

"What if he gets a new identity? What if he gets his face reconstructed like the woman he dates? Hey, do you think she might be his sister? The picture on Evert's wall could be old. Maybe the sister is the witch who will give the order to start the firestorm."

"We don't know there's going to be a firestorm."

"Don't you see? It's a ruse to drum up more cash, but it's disguised as this nanotech conspiracy so no one will suspect." Chessa swiveled to face Marcus. "The revival will be televised. Diggs will have a rapt audience. The witch or he will make one last plea to wipe out nanotechnology, to preserve God's pure creation, and a whirlwind of donations will come in. Maybe the goal is to rack up a tidy one hundred million dollars. After the money gets transferred to the offshore account, Diggs and his siblings will split the country."

Marcus looked dubious.

"Diggs flies private," Chessa added. "He rents a Gulfstream."

"How do you know that?"

"Jeremiah and my mother flew on it numerous times. At least have Deputy Keegan check to see if the pilot has set a flight plan to somewhere outside the U.S."

~ * ~

Richter—he despised his given name John, though he didn't mind his initials, J.R.—hated taking orders, but after the screwup by his colleague on Mt. Rose Highway, he had to follow up personally this time. He exited the casino where he had spent the afternoon, attached Sierra Pacific Power Company magnetic signs to the doors of the Blazer—the signs were always handy in case of emergency—and sped to Zelda Newman's house.

A white Element was parked on the street. Detective Newman, his mother, and Chessa Paxton weren't outside on the porch, enjoying the evening. They had to be inside.

An owl soared across the open land, its silhouette backlit by the rising moon. *It's an omen*, Richter thought. *A good one.*

He climbed out of the Blazer with a Walther P38 in his hand and stole to the side of the house. He peered through a window. The television was on. Some idiotic commercial was playing. Nobody was sitting on the couch. A pile of knitting lay on an easy chair. Two dog pillows sat empty against the far wall. Where was everyone?

Richter crept to the rear of the house thinking about where he was going after he finished this job. Back to the poker table. Back to his good luck. He'd hated leaving. His cards had been hot, hot, hot. He hoped the streak would continue. After the attack he had suffered at Marlette Lake, he deserved a big payoff. But first, he had to pop these three.

~ * ~

Chessa gazed out the Bronco's front window and watched the lines of the road disappear beneath the tires. The monotony lulled her into a drowsy state. Traffic flowed smoothly. The neon glow of Stateline lit up the horizon.

"When we get to the casino, you stay in the truck," Marcus said without taking his eyes off the road.

"But if Richter has changed his look, I'll recognize him."

"So will I. Do as I say. I'm out on a limb. If anybody sees you, I'm toast."

Chessa couldn't think of a comeback. She offered a tiny salute.

"Don't be cute," Marcus said. "Life and death is not cute."

His jaw ticked. Was he thinking about Tallchief and whether he could have prevented the man's death the same way Chessa was thinking about Helena and Zach and the others?

"What if Deputy Keegan sees me?" she asked.

"I'll explain."

"That I'm innocent."

"Allegedly innocent."

*Allegedly* was better than nothing. For the remainder of the drive, Chessa was drawn to Marcus's face, the set of his jaw, the way he chewed his teeth. He glanced at her occasionally, his conflicting emotions obvious.

When they arrived at the tall black casino and hotel, Marcus parked the truck and pocketed the keys. "There's Keegan. Stay," he ordered, as if he was talking to the dog. "Keep out of sight."

Chessa hunkered down and waited.

Minutes passed before Marcus returned. He swore under his breath as he slammed the door.

"No luck?" she asked.

"Nope." He switched on the ignition and roared out of the casino parking lot. "He's not at his dump of an apartment, either, or any of the medical clinics getting treatment for injuries you inflicted."

At the next two casinos, Marcus repeated his routine. Park, pocket the keys, meet up with Keegan, search.

By the time they arrived at the Boardwalk Casino and Hotel, Marcus was cussing loudly. "An hour. We've wasted an hour."

Chessa touched his wrist to calm him. A riot of emotions coursed through her. She removed her hand quickly.

Marcus snarled and climbed out of the Bronco. "Down!" he barked and slammed the door.

Chessa stretched out on the front seat and was surprised to see keys hanging from the ignition. Either Marcus trusted her or anger was making him careless. She waited a moment, as she had at each previous stop, and dared to peek out the window. Twinkling Christmas-style lights hung across the outdoor shopping mall plaza, from the entrance of the casino to the Heavenly Mountain Gondola. Glory to God revival attendees strolled the mall in droves as did Happily Ever After Convention goers. A pair of towheaded teens that Chessa recognized as children of a MASK volunteer stood in line. She ducked down, hoping they hadn't caught sight of her. Seeing them made her heart ache. How she wished she could return to her old life. Or did she? She never wanted to be that naïve again.

Blinking back tears, she risked peeking out a second time. Her stomach lurched when she spied Diggs and Evert among the throng approaching the casino. With them was a leggy blonde with prominent cheekbones. As she walked, the woman toyed with her long hair using her thumb and forefinger, a mannerism so familiar that Chessa suffered a stabbing pang of loss. Of course the woman wasn't her mother, the cheekbones too high, the skin too pale, the hair all wrong, but Chessa was certain that she was looking at the witch—*sans wig*—who had chatted up Zach at the ball.

# CHAPTER 65

Refusing to watch another connection to the murders disappear, Chessa crept from the truck and hurried into the casino after Diggs and his friends. She averted her face as she passed the line of people entering the convention. Nobody would notice her raggedy clothing—lots of people wore worse, on purpose—but her bruised face was another matter. The balm Zelda had applied had only taken away the sting.

The activity on the main floor of the casino was chaotic. Bells and whistles rang out. The repeated *clatter-whoosh* of the mini rollercoaster in the theme park located at the center of the room made Chessa's ears throb, but she didn't slow down.

Diggs, Evert, and the woman neared a small bar, its stools filled with patrons. The woman put her hand on top of Diggs's head and manipulated it to the right. She was making him look at something.

No, not something. *Someone*. Richter. He had dyed his hair black and was wearing funky glasses, but it was him. He was standing beyond a sea of people at a craps table, not a poker table.

Adrenaline caromed through Chessa. Where were Marcus and Keegan? Probably scouring the poker table section on the far side of the theme park.

Diggs said something to Evert, who nodded and took the arm of the blonde. They continued to stroll through the casino while Diggs made a beeline for Richter.

Chessa didn't dare go in search of Marcus; she might lose track of Richter. She hustled after Diggs.

Richter was oblivious to Diggs's approach. He raised his hand overhead, shook the dice, and hurled them onto the table. Fellow gamblers cheered the toss and clamored for their winnings.

In the uproar, Diggs slinked close to Richter and whacked him on the shoulder. Richter swung around, eyes blazing. Diggs thrust a finger into Richter's chest and said something. For all Chessa knew, he was telling the guy not to miss the revival meeting, but she didn't think so. She crept closer and peeked over the shoulder of a customer in a plaid shirt.

Richter looked agitated. He knocked Diggs's hand away.

Diggs grinned and said loudly enough for the crowd to hear, "God does not appreciate failure, right, folks?" Then he lowered his voice and said to Richter, "You have doubts? Take them up with the senator. He's the genius of this operation."

"But Evert said—"

"Listen to me. Jeremiah Wolfe is the brains, got that? If this goes the wrong way, he's taking the fall, not me and not Evert."

Chessa stiffened. Was Jeremiah, not Diggs, the driving force behind the firestorm plan? He had sent Richter after her in the forest. Had he masterminded the massacre? Did he want the nanotech people destroyed? Maybe he'd paid Diggs millions to make him his pawn.

Anger burned inside Chessa as she sprinted out of the casino. She climbed into the Bronco, twisted the keys, and jammed the gear into drive. Marcus would be steamed when he realized she absconded with the truck, but she couldn't stop. She had to confront Jeremiah.

# CHAPTER 66

Marcus stormed out of the casino, fists clenched. A dealer said Richter had been playing poker earlier in the day, but he was pretty sure Richter had left around dusk. "Thirty minutes wasted looking for that jerk," he groused. "The guy is a ghost."

"Sir," Keegan said. "Where's your vehicle?"

Marcus gazed at the spot where he'd left the Bronco and cursed under his breath. He squinted to lessen the glare of neon lights and took in Lake Tahoe Boulevard. It was packed with cars, trucks, and trailers, but not the Bronco.

"Call the station." He raised a hand. "No, wait." He couldn't very well admit that he had left a fugitive in his truck along with the keys. He whipped open his cell phone and dialed Zelda. The telephone jangled.

Two times. Three, four, five.

*C'mon, Zelda, pick up.*

Six, seven.

Why hadn't she purchased an answering machine like he told her to? A sinking feeling cut through him. Had he endangered her by bringing Chessa to the house?

"Hello?" Zelda answered, out of breath.

"Where've you been?" Marcus demanded and instantly despised himself for taking out his frustration on her.

"Brubeck came home with dirt all over his nose. He'd been nuzzling Beauty's grave, of course, so he and I went back to, you know, say a prayer. When we returned, there was a note from the utility company on the door, so it slowed me down. I needed my glasses to—"

"Utility company!" Marcus shouted. "Get out. Grab the dog and go to the neighbors."

"Why?"

"Mom, utility men don't show up at night. He could be the killer."

"Nonsense. He wrote a note. He said he'd be back tomorrow and signed it J.R."

*John Richter.*

Marcus willed his voice to remain calm. "Humor me, okay? Leave. Now."

When she agreed, Marcus nearly ended the call, but then he remembered why he had rung her in the first place. "Mom, did you put a tracking device in that locket you gave Chessa?"

"Would I do a thing like that?" she said, all innocence.

"You put one in my shoe when I first moved in."

"I did no such—"

"C'mon, Mom, no more games."

Zelda sighed. "Don't tell me you lost her."

"She drove off in the Bronco."

"What did you say that made her—"

"I didn't say a darned thing."

"Language, son."

"Sorry," Marcus muttered. "I promise I was as kind as possible to Chessa Paxton. Please, Mom, this could be a matter of life and death. She might have seen the killer and gone after him in the truck."

"Dear heaven. Yes, I installed a tracking device."

"Do you still access the device with the radar equipment hidden in your bedroom closet?"

"Oh, please." She snorted. "I use something much more up-to-date than that old junk."

# CHAPTER 67

Chessa knew the hike along Glenbrook Creek with only the crescent moon for light would challenge even the most expert hiker, but she didn't think going through her stepfather's security gates and alerting the press to her presence was a good idea. And, yes, the media was there. She had driven into the community and seen the trucks camped on the street and the bored crews leaning against the outsides of the vehicles.

During the summer as a teen, Chessa regularly sneaked out of the estate and swam parallel to the shore to a spot where friends would be waiting and provide dry clothes for her. When she returned, she would steal into the boathouse, don her clothes, and tiptoe back to bed.

Today she would do the reverse. She removed everything she was wearing except her bra and panties—her shirt and jeans would drag her down in the lake. She tucked everything beneath a bush, out of sight. As an afterthought, she took off Zelda's heart-shaped necklace and stowed it beneath the pile. She didn't want to damage the photos inside. Not to mention, if anything happened to her, she wanted Zelda to have the locket back.

Ten minutes later, chilled, but not as cold as she was after her escape during the storm, Chessa crept from the water and shuffled to the side of the boathouse. She edged along the walls to the front.

Before rounding the corner, she took in the scene. Everything about the grounds looked perfect. Like the senator. Like his house, his car, and once upon a time, his family. And everything looked empty. No guards paced the back lawn. Nobody sat on the lanai.

Chessa dashed to the front of the boathouse, stabbed the security code on the keypad, opened the door, and tiptoed inside. From a closet on her right she fetched her mother's sleek wind jacket and wind pants, the royal blue ones that Adriana always put on before going boating on a chilly day. Jeremiah hadn't been able to part with any of Adriana's clothes.

When Chessa's body warmed again, she crept to the boathouse door, pushed it open a crack, and peeked out. No one lurked about. Lights were on in the kitchen, but nobody appeared to be inside. She raced across the grass and started up the steps of the lanai. As she reached the top, the kitchen's exit door opened.

Heart banging in her chest, Chessa backtracked and dove behind a cluster of azaleas. Through the branches, she watched as Jocko plodded out of the house and lumbered to the far edge of the garden.

Chessa remained still, hoping the big lug wouldn't be able to smell her. His senses had grown dim in the last year. If he did detect her, he would alert the rest of the household with his joyous barking.

Jocko sniffed a few plants and did his business. After a while, he returned to the house and entered the kitchen. Within a minute, the old guy would fall asleep on his pillow just inside the door.

Chessa waited for someone to close the door, but no one did. Knowing that the maid had a habit of letting Jocko out and forgetting about the door for a while, she decided to risk climbing the lanai steps again.

Just as she reached the top stair, Patience Troon said, "What are you doing, Rosa?"

Chessa dashed to the exterior wall of the kitchen and pressed herself against it.

The maid said, "Fixing a meal for the senator."

"You know he doesn't wish to be disturbed when he's working in his lab."

"But he hasn't eaten. He shouldn't skip meals."

"That's not your concern. It's mine."

When Chessa was twelve, Jeremiah became a photography fanatic, imagining himself the next Ansel Adams. Everywhere he went, he took his Nikon. No digital cameras for him. He loved to lecture her about the way light played on people's faces or filtered through the trees at certain times of the day. Chessa stifled a moan. If he was responsible for the horror over the last few days, those fond memories spent with him would be obliterated.

The kitchen went quiet. Chessa waited for what seemed like an eternity. Once she was certain the women had left the vicinity, she retreated down the steps of the lanai and cut around the house to the left.

Cautiously she opened the door to the garage. A sensor beeped once, signaling an exterior door had opened. She tore inside and hid in the broom closet. She pinched her nose to block the scents of cleaning fluids and listened to the thrum of air conditioning. Each area in the house, including the garage, was fitted with an AC unit even though simply opening a window would provide the best fresh air known to man.

When no one entered the garage to search for an intruder, she exited the broom closet and weaved around the Jaguar and Mercedes toward the developing room. She grabbed a peen hammer from the tool bench as she passed.

The developing room door didn't have a lock. No one dared disturb the senator if he was in the lab, except the maid with an occasional meal when Patience wasn't playing watchdog.

Chessa whipped open the door and tried quickly to adjust her eyes to the dim red light. The long and narrow room looked as it always did. The racks above the stainless steel sinks were stacked with photography paper and mementoes Jeremiah had collected on trips. The shelves below were cluttered with containers of fluid and cleaning essentials. Basins were drained of putrid-smelling developing fluid. Photographs, secured by rubber-tipped metal clips, hung from the clothesline.

Jeremiah sat eerily still at his finishing desk, body bent forward, head resting on one arm. Why wasn't he moving?

Chessa crept closer and realized why. A half-empty bottle of Jack Daniels and an empty tumbler stood on the table beyond him. Furious that he would dare to get drunk at a time like this, she said, "Jeremiah!" He didn't budge. "Jeremiah, wake up!"

He made a snuffling sound but didn't rouse.

She laid the peen hammer on the table and lifted her stepfather by the shoulders. She sucked in a breath when she realized the hand resting beneath his drunken head held a Beretta.

Carefully she unpeeled his fingers from the butt of the gun, set the gun on the shelf beside a bundle of letters, and struck him hard on the back.

He muttered something. His head lolled.

Chessa pushed him upright in the chair and pressed her palm against his chest to steady him. "Look at me," she ordered.

He opened his eyes. They were rheumy. His face was tearstained. He groped the table.

"I moved the gun," she said.

"I don't deserve to live. I don't deserve..." His words slurred together. "Phoenix has risen from the ashes."

"Make sense, old man."

"Your mother—"

"Is dead. Focus! What's going on?"

Jeremiah burped.

The stench made Chessa's nose flinch. "Did you hire John Richter?"

"Who?"

"Richter. The security guard that killed all those people. The massacre."

Jeremiah rubbed his eyes with the heels of his hands. "Yukiko. It's my fault."

Chessa pried his hands from his face. "Are you confessing?"

"Yukiko figured out—" He coughed. "And you—" He sobbed. "You saw—"

"The passports. Zach belonged to the Rebels of the Republic. They traveled the world. They rallied people to wage war against nanotech companies."

"I'm so sorry. Your mother—" Jeremiah waved a hand and babbled something indiscernible. "I had to obey, don't you see?"

"I don't see anything." Chessa's voice vibrated with rage.

"She loved you, but she—" He reached up and touched the lower rim of one of the pictures that were drying. "She is so beautiful."

*Not is,* Chessa wanted to shout. *Was.* She *was* beautiful.

"We fought, your mother and I. All the time. That's why she wanted to leave me."

"Did you order her murder? Did you cause her car crash?"

"No! What? How could you think—" Jeremiah picked up a tiny lace doll from the shelf. "She bought this for you. She was going to give it to you, but—" Tears streamed down his cheeks. "Take it." He thrust it at her.

Chessa's hands shook as she realized what it was. Not just any doll, but *the* pincushion doll her mother had bought for her in Geneva. *You're going to love it,* her mother had said.

Something—a sensation—drew Chessa's gaze to the picture clipped to the clothesline above Jeremiah's head. It was a close-up of a woman. Not her mother. The nose wasn't right, the cheekbones too sharp, the skin too pale, and the hair was blonde not dark brown, yet the eyes were her mother's, and suddenly Chessa understood. Hot, bitter anger cut through her. Diggs's date at the ball, the woman Chessa had seen walking with him at the casino, wasn't Diggs's sister. It was Adriana. She was alive.

Years of cloistering herself from hurt scudded through Chessa. "Mom survived the explosion?"

Jeremiah groaned. "Your mother was never in the car. She staged it. She told me it was better for you if she didn't contact you. She said if she died it would be easier for me, too. The media wouldn't say she abandoned me for Davey."

"She left you for Diggs?"

"They're a couple."

"People get divorced, Jeremiah. They don't run off and fake a death."

"My career was flagging. Her demise, heaven forgive me, gave me a boost in the polls. I was reelected in a landslide. Widowers often are. It was her last gift to me." The resentment in his voice was unmistakable. "She wanted a holy marriage with Davey. She wanted to start fresh, like the Phoenix, but that wasn't enough for her. She came to me again. To carry out Firestorm."

Chessa teetered. "It's a revolution, isn't it?"

Jeremiah nodded. "She said I had to help her. She blackmailed me because I covered up the murder years ago."

"What murder?" Chessa couldn't string his drunken logic together.

"When your mother and father were married, she and I had an affair. A man named Gustavson found out."

"The car salesman that my father killed?"

"He didn't do it."

Chessa's breath caught in her chest. Jeremiah had to be mistaken. It was the liquor talking. Of course her father did it. He went to jail for the man's murder.

"Gustavson learned that your mother and I were—" Jeremiah swallowed hard. "He realized it could damage my political career if word got out. I was running on family values. He demanded money. He came to your apartment for payment. You were there at the time. Your mother went wild. How dare he, in front of you! She stabbed him again and again. Then she called me, and I waited for your father to come home. I knocked him out and put the knife in his hand. Your father is innocent. Your mother made me swear not to utter a word or"—Jeremiah keened like a wounded animal—"she would implicate me, and I'd be ruined. I loved her. I would have done anything for her." He started to hyperventilate. His eyes rolled in their sockets. He fell forward, and his forehead hit the desk with a thud.

"Jeremiah!" Chessa felt his wrist. He had a pulse. She released him and eyed the pincushion. Could her mother really be the monster Jeremiah described?

*Creak.*

Someone was outside the door. Chessa ducked behind Jeremiah.

The door handle turned slowly. Very slowly. Patience Troon wasn't gutsy enough to come after Chessa herself. She would have called one of the security guys at the gate.

Chessa snatched the peen hammer off the table and grabbed a can of finishing spray, prepared to use it if she had to.

The door swung open and something low and dark poked its head inside. Jocko.

Fighting back tears, Chessa laid her weapons on the countertop and held her arms out. Jocko waddled into them. "Hey, fella." He licked her cheek. Chessa nuzzled his forehead with hers. "Yes, I missed you, too." She scratched him behind his ears and hugged him harder.

From her new vantage point, she noticed something lying on the floor beneath her stepfather's chair: an article carefully cut from a magazine with a photograph at its center.

She collected it and tilted it to the light. Davey Diggs and her reconstructed mother stood on a ski slope in Aspen, mugging for the camera.

Up until now, Chessa had thought Zach's betrayal had wounded her more than anything she could bear. But this? Her mother's duplicity slashed her heart in two. Adriana had let Chessa believe she was dead. She had sent Chessa's father to jail for a crime he didn't commit.

A siren wailed in the distance. Chessa froze. Was Newman after her? Had he guessed where she had gone? No way would he believe what her stepfather had told her. She would have to prove it herself. She would have to track down Adriana and force her to confess.

"Where is she, Jeremiah?"

"The revival," he mumbled.

"But, of course." Chessa's voice was bitter with hostility. "She's such a pious soul."

# CHAPTER 68

Marcus pressed the accelerator on Keegan's Jeep and urged it to go faster. Keegan hadn't forfeited his keys readily. He had shown some backbone and demanded to know what was going on. Marcus explained quickly. To his credit, Keegan didn't condemn Marcus for not hauling Chessa into the station, but he didn't look happy, either. Why should he? Marcus was involving him in something that could destroy his career. "You can bow out, deputy. You're not an accomplice."

Keegan grunted and continued searching for a location on Chessa's tracking device via Google Earth using the radio frequency Zelda had provided. The iPhone's screen glowed hot blue in the dark.

"Got anything?" Marcus asked.

"Not yet."

"Dang, I thought that stuff worked fast."

"It all depends on signal strength. In Tahoe—"

Marcus slammed the steering wheel with his palm. The knee-jerk reaction sent a riot of pain up his arm, but he was ticked. What if Richter had been at the casino? What if he kidnapped Chessa? He could be taking her someplace to kill her, though that didn't seem Richter's style. He had acted rashly when he'd attacked Helena Gorzinski and the tattoo artist, and, Marcus was pretty sure, when he'd murdered Zach Szabo, scissors or no scissors.

Keegan whooped. "All right! I've got a signal. Head north."

"Narrow it down, will you?" Marcus couldn't drive north forever.

"Looks like Glenbrook Golf Course."

"That's near the senator's house."

A mile up, Keegan said, "Turn left. Here."

"Wolfe's house is farther north."

"The blip isn't moving. The remote frequency is accurate to two-point-five meters. Chessa is due west."

~ * ~

For the return swim, Chessa kept on her mother's wind jacket and pants. Back on shore, her skin prickled with gooseflesh as she shimmied out of the wet clothes. Quickly she redressed in her jeans and shirt and raced to where she had hidden the Bronco. She tossed the wet clothes onto the floor by the passenger seat and seconds later was on the road.

Moisture from her hair dripped down her spine and chilled her, but the cold was nothing compared to the subzero emotions clutching her heart. Her mother was alive. Her mother—the witch—wanted her dead. All because of Diggs. Prior to meeting him, Adriana had attended church on typical holidays. After her conversion, occasional worship became daily worship, daily worship turned into double sessions, and doubles turned into multiples. When had the love affair with Davey Diggs started?

Chessa cut around a stalled car, her fingers squeezing the steering wheel in a death grip as bitterness crawled up her throat. She would never understand why her mother had abandoned her—not when she fell in love with Diggs, but, before, when she killed someone in cold blood and let Chessa's father go to jail for the crime. Chessa recalled a very tense Christmas when she was six years old. Her father beckoned her mother into the living room. He said he had a surprise. Chessa crept into the room and hid behind the sofa. She peered around the corner expecting to see her mother open a beautiful present. Instead, her father shook a charm bracelet at Adriana and demanded to know who had given it to her. Adriana seized the bracelet and, with tears streaming down her face, tossed it into the fireplace. Chessa's father shouted horrible words. He shoved his hand into the fire to retrieve the bracelet. Chessa screamed, *No, Daddy!* Her mother, outraged that Chessa had been spying, ordered her to her room. Ear pressed to the door, Chessa listened to them argue for another hour. The next day her mother gave Chessa the fire-ravaged charm bracelet and asked her to keep it for her. It would be their secret.

Chessa's heart wrenched as she realized Zach must have been clutching the bracelet to signal that her mother was alive.

## CHAPTER 69

Marcus continued driving, his jaw locked tightly. "Are you sure about that GPS?"

"Positive," Keegan said.

There was no reason for Chessa to have stopped at the lake's edge. Was Richter ordering her at gunpoint to get out of the Bronco? Had he already killed her? Was he intending to dump her body in the lake? It was a perfect burial ground. According to legend, members of the Mafia had dumped bodies in the lake during the 1950s. In warmer water, gases in a decomposing body would make it buoy to the top, but since Lake Tahoe was icy cold, bodies didn't decompose, gases didn't form, and bodies stayed submerged.

"Turn right," Keegan ordered.

Marcus obeyed. A half-mile later, he whipped to a stop and sprang from the car. Moonlight slashed a walking path that led to the creek. "Let's go."

Marcus tramped along the creek. Keegan aimed his flashlight at the uneven terrain. Other than burbling water, Marcus didn't hear a sound. No motorboats on the lake. No roars from the highways. He itched with frustration. Had they been sucked into a giant wormhole? How could Chessa have come this way without leaving a trace?

He stretched the kinks out of his neck. "Deputy, you seem to know this area pretty well."

"I spent a lot of time here as a teen working on a Boy Scout badge, sir. We did soil sampling missions and that kind of thing."

At Zelda's insistence, Marcus had tried to take part in the Boy Scouts, but at the time he couldn't embrace the structured program.

"Hold up." Keegan pointed to a set of footprints.

Marcus crouched down and inspected the prints. One set. Narrow tennis shoes. Chessa was wearing Keds. He felt a surge of hope. Unless Richter was walking in the water, Chessa was alone. But why come here? What was she up to? And why, for Pete's sake, had she run off without confiding in him?

"There! She's right there." Keegan pointed to the mouth of the creek where the water flowed into Lake Tahoe.

To the right of the mouth stood a large boulder. Marcus raced to the far side and spotted more footprints going in and out of the water.

A flicker of something sparkly on the ground caught his eye. "Deputy, hit that with the flashlight."

The circular glow outlined Zelda's heart-shaped necklace. Chessa must have figured out it had a tracking device and removed it from her neck.

~ * ~

Jeremiah had wanted to do so much good in his lifetime, but love had interfered and made him weak. With shaky fingers, he reached for the telephone and dialed the number that was etched on his brain for *Phoenix*. When Adriana picked up, he said, "Chessa knows. I told her everything. She's coming to get you."

As usual, Adriana berated him. He didn't care. He set the phone on the desk, found the Beretta where Chessa had placed it, clasped it tightly in his fingers, and thankful he had finally drummed up the courage, placed the tip against his head.

~ * ~

Marcus studied the shoreline. The Bronco was nowhere in sight. No tracks. Nothing. Maybe Chessa parked it a mile back, swam to here, got rid of the necklace, and continued on to her stepfather's house. As fit as she was, she could probably make the distance in ten minutes. Maybe less. But why go there? Because something led her to believe her stepfather had a hand in either the massacre or her husband's death. Had she chosen to confront him?

"Keegan, get in the Jeep."

"Where are we headed?"

"The senator's house."

Marcus drove at breakneck speed, the cool of night blasting through the open windows. At Wolfe's estate, he displayed his badge to the gate guard. Reporters hanging by the entrance clamored for a story, but Marcus ignored them.

As he pulled up the driveway, a shot rang out. He tore ahead, heart thudding, disastrous scenarios coursing through his mind. Either Wolfe had fired at Chessa, or she had fired at him, or Richter, if he was part of the equation, had pulled the trigger.

Patience Troon answered the door, hands shaking, her skin devoid of makeup. Her bathrobe was cinched so tightly Marcus wondered how she could breathe. "Did you hear that?" she cried.

"Where's Senator Wolfe, ma'am?"

"This way." Troon burst out the front door and raced to the garage.

Marcus and Keegan followed her down a breezeway and through the pedestrian garage door.

Troon switched on the light. It popped. "Crap," she said, a word Marcus never thought he'd hear coming from her lips. She pointed. "He's in his developing room. Over there."

The garage was eerily silent. Shadows clung to the walls. Cars loomed like monsters. A dim red light glowed from a room on the opposite side.

"Keegan, flashlight."

Keegan switched on his torch.

A whimpering sound came from inside the developing room. Marcus tensed. Was Chessa injured? He eased around the Mercedes and Jaguar and pushed open the door.

Jocko sprang to his feet to stand sentry in front of Wolfe, who sat slumped forward in a chair, his head and arms on the table, his hand clinging to a Beretta. Blood seeped beneath the senator's head onto the desk. A cell phone and a piece of stationary lay beyond.

"It's okay, boy." Marcus stuck out his hand out so the retriever could catch his scent.

Jocko took a tentative step and sniffed, then rotated his head and gazed at Wolfe.

Troon inched into the room and cried, "No!"

"I'm sorry for your loss, ma'am." Marcus turned to Keegan. "Call it in."

Troon wagged a finger. "What's that wadded under the desk?"

Marcus retrieved the paper and unfolded it. It was a picture from a magazine of Diggs and a blonde woman. Although the woman had altered her features and changed her hair color, Marcus knew the truth. She was the same woman he had seen in photographs in the senator's office—Adriana Wolfe.

## CHAPTER 70

Davey Diggs gargled minty mouthwash and spit in the bathroom sink. As he began his vocal exercises, his cell phone buzzed in his pocket. He didn't like cell phones. He was convinced that a friend of his, a daytrader, had died from a brain tumor because the guy used a cell phone twenty-four / seven. Yet cell phones were necessary evils. Up until show time, Davey kept his switched on. Last minute emergencies took him out of the spiritual moment, but they had to be averted.

He pulled the phone from his pocket and glanced at the readout from Adriana: *S.O.S.!!*

She was not typically given to drama. He dialed her number.

"Jeremiah just committed suicide!" she blurted. "With me on the line. Chessa knows about me. About everything. She's coming—"

"Calm down, darlin'. I'll handle it." Davey hung up and dialed Richter. "Chessa Paxton is on her way to see her mother. Do not mess up."

~ * ~

Rage roiled inside Chessa as she drove past casinos, their neon lights garish and vulgar and traffic a tangled snarl. She wanted to blame her mother for everything that had happened, but deep in her heart, she knew she couldn't. She was to blame. She had been naïve. When exactly had she relinquished control of her life? When her father was taken away? Or before, when she bought into the lie that her mother loved her and would take care of her? It crushed her to think how she had let her mother manipulate her. Now she was convinced that her mother had lured her into a relationship with Zach. Blithely Chessa had married him and ceded even more control over her life. Not only had she passed on the job in Las Vegas, but she had also cut friends out of her life.

That ended now. No more therapist. No more fairy tales. She would face reality. She would say *no* when she had to. Not *yes*. Not always *yes*.

Chessa searched for parking spots near the Boardwalk Casino, but they were nonexistent. The Glory to God Revival crowds had taken all of them. People swarmed the sidewalks heading across the plaza to the gondola's base station. A few blocks farther along, she veered into the Cloud 9 Motel parking lot. She squeezed the Bronco into a narrow slot, scrambled out of the truck and, in too much of a hurry to think about disguises and stealth, dashed back to Lake Tahoe Boulevard.

Revival attendees were marching along the boulevard chanting Diggs's favorite slogan, "Give me grace. Give me peace."

Chessa's skin crawled as a trio of people linked their arms through hers and urged her to join in their rapturous din. Wriggling free of them, she raced headlong to the Heavenly Mountain parking lot. Winnebagos and media trailers stood at the far end.

~ * ~

Richter paced the parking lot trying to shake off the way Diggs had talked to him, like he was a peon not good enough to lick Diggs's boots. How dare he? Since the age of thirteen, Richter had been one of the devoted. Thanks to the Rebels of the Republic—no, thanks to *him*—God's work had been accomplished around the world. Diggs needed to appreciate that. Richter would make sure he did. He pulled his Walther P38 from beneath the waistband of his jeans and marched onward.

## CHAPTER 71

Staying in the shadows, Chessa darted to the far side of the first Winnebago. The echo of footsteps made her whirl around.

"Hello, baby." Up close, Adriana's rebuilt face was hauntingly beautiful, her skin pale with no visible wrinkles. Witch costume or no witch costume, Chessa wouldn't have recognized her mother had Jeremiah not forewarned her.

Anger swelled inside her. She attacked her mother, lashing at the eyes first. She missed and struck cheekbone. Adriana yowled and grabbed Chessa by the wrists. As strong as Chessa was, her mother was bigger and stronger.

"Chessa, please, let me explain—"

"There's nothing you can say that will stop me from hating you." She writhed against her mother's hold. "You're a monster. You let my father go to jail for a crime you committed."

Adriana slapped her. Hard. Chessa twisted free and elbowed her mother in the chest, and then roundhoused her with her other arm. Adriana reeled and crashed into the Winnebago with a bang.

Hands fisted, Chessa stalked her mother. Adriana held up her arms to protect herself, but Chessa didn't strike. Yes, she wanted to break her mother's perfect Aquiline nose, but first she wanted the truth. The whole truth.

"I should have realized before," Chessa hissed. "I'd visited Jeremiah in his developing room a couple of times over the past year. The pincushion doll you brought back from Geneva was there the whole time, sitting on the shelf. You shouldn't have left it, Mother." She said *Mother* on purpose. Adriana hated the word. Chessa understood why. Adriana wasn't a mother; she was an aberration. "I might not have believed Jeremiah otherwise."

Adriana rose to her knees and pressed her palms together, a picture of pious humility. "I need you to understand what happened."

"I don't care."

"I'm with Davey because we want to enlighten—"

"Don't!" Chessa jabbed a finger at her mother. "Do not try to put a religious skew on this. You wanted me dead." She sucked back a sob. "Zach messed up at the massacre, didn't he?"

"I wept with joy at the news that you had been spared." Adriana struggled to her feet and reached out.

Chessa knocked her mother's hands away. "I was targeted when I saw the passports, because one day I would be able to connect Zach to the Rebels of the Republic and the horror that they have done and will do."

Tears pooled in Adriana's eyes. "Zach loved you, baby. He instigated the divorce so you wouldn't be associated with him after—"

"It was *you*. You were the person who accepted the divorce papers at the cabin." Chessa forced Adriana backward. "You signed them. That loopy handwriting. The letter P. I'd tried to copy your signature so many times that yours became mine." Chessa inhaled as everything became clear. "Oh, lord. The charm bracelet."

"What charm bracelet?"

"Yours. The one Daddy and you argued about. Jeremiah gave it to you, didn't he? I told Zach it was a symbol of your betrayal. He wasn't holding the bracelet to give me a clue that you were alive. He wanted me to know that you killed him."

"No."

"You murdered him and let me take the blame. Did stabbing him feel as good as stabbing Gustavson?"

"I didn't kill that man."

"Why did you execute Zach, Mother?"

Adriana's nose flared. "He messed up. That night at the ball, it got out of hand. He would have—"

"A massacre isn't something that gets *out of hand*, Mother. That cult of yours—"

"It's not a cult."

"Diggs sets the dogma; the rest fall in line." Chessa stepped forward, ready to strike. "What do you know about Davey, Mother? Why is he qualified to lead?"

Adriana edged along the wall of the Winnebago. "You never liked him."

"Why should I? He orchestrates death."

"God justifies the killing."

"God doesn't approve of murder, Mother."

"The Rebels of the Republic are holy. We all have relatives or friends that have died because of nanotech inventions."

"You don't. Nana and Poppa died of old age. Your brother drank himself into his grave."

"We worry about the seepage of microscopic technology into the environment," Adriana went on, not bothering to counter Chessa's reasoning. "Davey says if we get rid of the nanotech geniuses of the world, we will put an end to the abomination they create. We will prevent them from tainting our world. We will return to the purity of—"

Chessa smacked the Winnebago. "Do you hear how crazy you sound?"

"Doctors keep explaining these deaths as natural causes, but Davey and I know it's the tech companies' products. Davey says we must never back down. The devil is at work. Man, by rearranging molecules, is perpetuating evil. It's true." Adriana nodded, as if convincing herself. "Davey's older sister died from poison generated by—"

"She's not dead, Mother. She's alive and filthy rich like Davey. Like their brother."

"That's impossible."

Chessa choked back a laugh. She thought she was naïve, but her mother was the queen of naiveté. "Do you know why she's rich? Because of donations that Davey's phony enterprise receives."

"No."

"It's true. Davey and his siblings have stashed seventy million dollars in a private trust fund, and, surprise-surprise, the name of his church isn't included in that trust." Chessa enjoyed the shock in Adriana's eyes. "Take me to him, Mother, and let's ask him about it. The truth will set you free."

"Don't move!" a man yelled.

## CHAPTER 72

Chessa pivoted and raised her arms to defend herself. Richter rushed her and slammed into her with something hard, metal—a gun. She thudded into the wall of the Winnebago. Her vision grew hazy.

"You should learn to keep your voice down, babe." Richter pointed his gun at her face. "You gave yourself away." He whacked her with the back of his hand. Bone crunched in her ear. He grabbed the neck of her shirt and dragged her past the trailer.

"Don't!" Adriana screamed.

Richter ignored her and kept dragging, but then he lost his grip and pitched forward onto his knees. Adriana had mounted him from the rear. She raised something silver overhead. Scissors. She stabbed him between his shoulder blades. He elbowed her and bucked her off and walloped her with the butt of his gun. She tumbled backward.

Chessa rammed her heel into Richter's jaw. Blood spurted from his mouth. He plunged to the right. His head struck pavement. He wasn't dead, but he was stunned.

Adriana scrambled to him and retrieved the scissors. "This way."

She scurried between two Winnebagos. Chessa followed. On the far side, Adriana threw out her arm. Two women in white gowns with gold sashes and official-looking strides were heading toward the media trailers.

"We'll hide in there." Adriana hitched her chin in the direction of the Winnebago to their right, the largest of the three.

Chessa didn't have time to argue. Richter could have revived. Adriana climbed the metal stairs and tugged the door open.

The moment Chessa entered, she knew where she was. Diggs's dressing room. She couldn't have felt creepier than if she had joined him in the shower. A rainbow collection of robes and vestments hung on a metal wardrobe stand. A baker's rack held a sewing kit and boxes of exotic masks. Two white hats—a pope-like miter and a feather headdress—sat on the top shelf. Scepters topped with ornamental knobs stood in a pool cue holder beyond the rack.

"He's a regular costuming nightmare, isn't he, Mother?"

Adriana didn't respond. She slumped despondently into a chair. Was she wondering how she could ask her beloved about his precious seventy million bucks?

"Mother, let's call the sheriff. He'll help you—"

"I don't think so." The bathroom door pushed open and Davey Diggs walked out in a white robe. "Hello, Chessa, darlin'." He aimed a gun at her. "You did well, my love."

He wasn't talking to her. Adriana had recovered with lightning speed and was rushing to the exit door, scissors in hand, to block Chessa's escape.

## CHAPTER 73

Leaving Douglas County sheriffs to handle the details of the senator's suicide, Marcus gunned Keegan's Jeep and headed south. The package of letters he'd found in the developing room rested in a cup holder. He envisioned the last lines of Wolfe's suicide note:

*Chessa, sweetheart, your mother couldn't help herself. She's a woman ruled by righteous zeal. Do your best to show compassion when you see her.*

Marcus knew where Chessa would look for Adriana. The revival was tonight. No doubt her mother would be by Diggs's side. Marcus couldn't help feeling sorry for Chessa. She had been her mother's pawn for far too long. He hoped she could control herself when she met up with the woman.

"You okay, sir?"

"Yeah," he lied then ordered Keegan to call SLTPD and get some units to the trailers stationed in the Heavenly Mountain Resort parking lot.

~ * ~

Chessa couldn't believe she had fallen for Adriana's act one more time. *So much for wising up.* Adriana had stabbed Richter in order to convince Chessa to follow her into this pit. She needed to get the gun away from Diggs, but how?

"Love is a crazy thing, isn't it, Chessa?" Diggs moved nearer.

"You don't love my mother. You used her. You knew she was weak. You knew she would do anything for you. You're a phony, for God's sake."

"For God's sake. Yes, indeed." Diggs glanced at the wall of photographs and chortled.

Chessa followed his gaze and saw a gold-framed photograph of Diggs with Evert and a disfigured woman, and in an instant, she understood everything. "You had to preach for a long time to pull off this scam, didn't you, Davey?"

"What scam?" Adriana asked.

"He's not a believer. He's a fraud."

Adriana gazed at Diggs.

"I told you, Mother. He and his half-brother and -sister are in this for the money." Chessa inched toward the stand of scepters. What perfect weapons to bring down a phony king. "I'm assuming, Reverend, that those pictures on the wall represent your not-so-handsome family." Diggs was height-challenged, Evert was sight-challenged, and Constance Edwards was beauty-challenged. "His sister wasn't poisoned, Mother. That was baloney. She suffers from cranial disfigurement. How do I know? Because I did some research before the MASK ball. See her forehead? It's abnormally large and her eyes are at odd angles." Chessa glowered at Diggs. "Nanotech products didn't cause that, Davey. Admit it. You three inherited your challenges from dear old dad's defective genes, didn't you?"

Diggs's face turned hard.

"As a group," Chessa continued, "you decided that you wanted retribution not only against your father, who made all of you bastards, but against God's hatefulness. Am I warm?"

"Darlin', you have no idea how hot you are."

"Along the way, you realized you had a good mind." Chessa moved closer to the stand. "Not just good, *great*. And you had a flair for the dramatic. Thanks to your acting ability, you took revenge against your reprobate father and God in one fell swoop. You falsely dedicated yourself to God's work, and in the course of the work, you earned money."

"A ton of money."

"Once the world learns of your plot, Davey, the house your father built will be destroyed. They'll call him a fraud. They'll vilify him."

Diggs grinned. "That's the plan."

Chessa was within reach of the scepters, but she didn't want to make a sudden move. Diggs's finger was still poised on the gun's trigger. "I told my mother about the seventy million, Davey. I told her none of it is earmarked to support the cause. The sole owners of the trust are your siblings and you."

"You said Constance was dead, sweetheart," Adriana whispered.

"I never said that. Wise up."

"Davey, we need money to pay our soldiers. They are the first line of offense." Adriana's lip quivered. "They won't act without payment. Firestorm will fail."

"Mother, you still don't get it. Firestorm is a diversion. If it works, terrific.

If it doesn't, Davey doesn't care. He will be out of the country."

Adriana's face turned pale.

Chessa eyed Diggs. "Gee, Davey, didn't you tell her? Mother, listen up. Only family gets to go on this trip, and by the absence of a ring on your finger, I'm assuming you never got around to consecrating your vows."

Adriana's mouth trembled. "Davey, you said you wanted me to go to San Francisco and rest after our success, and next week we would get married."

"I've made a change in the itinerary, Addie. Get that through your head." Diggs dismissed her with a wave of the gun. "As for you, Chessa—"

"God's purity must be preserved!" Adriana lunged at Diggs, scissors jutting from her fist.

Diggs threw an arm up to block a blow. They struggled.

Adriana screamed, "You are our leader!"

Chessa grasped a scepter, but she didn't have an angle to attack, not without hurting her mother.

"God needs us, Davey!"

"Wise up, woman. I used you. And Zach. And all the others. God doesn't exist."

"Don't say that." Adriana dropped to her knees. She placed the scissors on the floor and folded her hands in prayer. "Please say He exists. Beg His forgiveness, my love. He will forgive us our sins."

Diggs cackled. "Are you nuts? You can never be forgiven. You're a murderer."

"It was an accident," Adriana sputtered.

"One murder, maybe, but two? You'll never be redeemed. But what does it matter? Nothing exists after this."

"Don't say that. Eternity—"

"There is no eternity, Addie. This is it. This is our hell, and I am not going to spend mine in prison." He leveled his gun at her.

## CHAPTER 74

Marcus and Keegan hurried toward a team of South Lake Tahoe police that was standing in a semicircle by one of the Winnebagos. On the ground beyond them lay Richter, his breathing labored. Blood pooled beneath him. He wouldn't last an hour. Marcus flashed his badge to the tallest of the group and quickly explained his mission.

"Do you mind if we search for Reverend Diggs?" Marcus asked the tallest officer.

"Be our guest."

Marcus yanked his Glock from his holster and stole to the first two trailers. He peered between them. "All clear."

Keegan raced to the next opening. "Clear."

A gunshot rang out.

Marcus's pulse kicked into overdrive. He ran toward the largest of the Winnebagos just as a second gunshot rang out.

~ * ~

As much as Chessa didn't want to care about her mother, she did, but she couldn't save her if she didn't save herself.

The first bullet struck Adriana in the chest.

Chessa trained the scepter on Diggs and charged.

Diggs pivoted and fired. The bullet went wide and slammed into the trailer door.

Chessa thrust the scepter at him. The trailer lurched beneath her feet, which threw her off balance. She was barely able to connect with the gun barrel as he fired a third time. The bullet pierced the trailer's ceiling. She flailed again and knocked the gun away from Diggs.

He roared and yanked the scepter from her hands. She stumbled into the baker's rack and pitched forward, landing on her hands and knees. Hats and other gear flew off the rack.

Diggs tossed the weapon aside and threw himself at Chessa. Like a wrestler, he reached around her, as well as beneath her, and strapped her chest with his arm.

Chessa eyed the opened sewing kit that had fallen off with the hats. She groped for a safety pin and popped it open. She jabbed the pointed end into Diggs's face. He cursed. His hold weakened. Chessa elbowed him and sank to her belly. From that vantage point, she spied her mother's scissors beneath the baker's rack. She stretched her fingers, retrieved them, and wriggled onto her back. She thrust the pointed end at Diggs's core. The thickness of his robe prevented a good strike. He struggled to his feet.

Chessa seized a handful of the hem of his robe and tugged.

Diggs teetered. He fell sideways. She crawled on top of him and hauled back with the scissors. "Say your prayers, Reverend."

The trailer door whipped open.

"Chessa, don't!" a man yelled.

Chessa didn't turn and look at Marcus. She didn't dare give Diggs an edge. "He deserves to die, detective."

"Not like this. Let the system—"

"The system doesn't work. My mother killed Gustavson, but my father went to prison."

"No," Adriana said from somewhere behind Chessa. "Gustavson hid in the apartment. He came at me with a knife. He tried to rape me. Your father showed up and stabbed him twenty times. He couldn't stop."

"Liar!" Cold bitter rage cut through Chessa. For a nanosecond a moment ago, she had pitied her mother for falling for someone as slick as Davey Diggs, but now, she felt nothing but hatred and, in an odd way, relief. She didn't need to care about her mother any more. Adriana was a fiend. She had sent Chessa's father to prison. She had pretended to be dead so she could change her life's path, never once thinking about what her death would do to Chessa or her stepfather.

Through clenched teeth, Chessa said, "Jeremiah told me the truth, Mother. You stabbed that man and let Daddy take the blame."

Adriana whimpered. "I've asked for forgiveness."

Chessa twisted her head and glowered at her mother who lay in a pool of blood. "For heaven's sake, Mother, you will never—"

Diggs reared up and wrenched the scissors from Chessa. He slashed at her. She dodged the blow and held up her arms to protect herself from another attempt.

"Stop, Diggs, or I'll shoot," Marcus yelled.

Before Marcus could make good on his promise, a piercing wail sliced the air.

Adriana dove at Diggs and took hold of the scissors. Diggs backhanded her, but she didn't lose her grip. She wrestled the scissors away, flipped them in her hands, and stabbed Diggs in the neck. Over and over.

"Mother, no!" Chessa leaped to her feet.

Marcus rushed into the melee and gripped Adriana by the shoulders, but she twisted free and jabbed Diggs again.

Chessa hauled her mother away from Diggs. "Stop!"

Adriana shuddered. Her hands shook. Blood oozed from the hole in her chest.

Diggs slumped to the floor, his gaze disbelieving.

As a final breath wheezed from his punctured body, Adriana dropped her arms to her sides. "Sweetheart, I'm so sorry." She wasn't talking to Chessa. She was addressing Diggs. "What have I done?" She crept to him, lay beside him, took his hands in hers, and started to murmur a prayer. After a moment, her words faded and her breathing ceased.

"No!" Chessa crouched beside Adriana and caressed her hair, stunned that she still had an ounce of feeling left for her. Grief squeezed the air from her lungs until she was gasping for breath.

Marcus knelt beside Chessa and slipped his arm around her shoulders. "Let her go."

She slogged to a stand. "My father is innocent."

"I know. Your stepfather left a note."

Chessa pushed away from Marcus. "Left a—" Her hand flew to her mouth. "Oh, no."

"He also left these." Marcus pulled an aging stack of letters strapped with a blue rubber band from inside his shirt, the letters Chessa had seen in Jeremiah's developing room. "I think your stepfather wanted you to have these."

Expecting to read correspondence from her mother to Jeremiah or to Davey, Chessa was shocked when she read the topmost letter:

*My darling Chessa,*

*I think of you every day while I'm in prison, and I pray for the day when we will be together and you will know the truth. ~ Daddy*

A drawing of Chessa and a puppy was included in the letter, a puppy she had long forgotten because her mother put it up for adoption the day after Chessa's father was taken away.

A heavy weight lifted from Chessa's shoulders. She felt as if she had been trapped in a windowless castle tower for years and was just beginning to see the beautiful world she wanted to explore.

With shaky fingers, she opened the second letter.

## CHAPTER 75

**TWO MONTHS LATER**

Chessa rose from the chair by the patio table in Zelda's backyard and stretched, her skin warm from the August sun and her stomach full with ribs, bean salad, and homemade cornbread. Afraid to trust the good feelings rushing through her, she wrapped her arms around herself and watched as Zelda's foster children and their spouses bussed empty serving dishes to the kitchen, the screen door squeaking with every entry and exit. The flock of grandchildren, each under the age of twelve, played tag. Brubeck chased the kids, yipping as if he was an integral part of the game. Jocko sat on the porch, longing yet too old to join the fun.

At the far end of the yard, Chessa's father, Philip, chatted easily with Zelda and Deputy Keegan, who was oiling down the hot barbecue grill. Her father looked happy, his hair sun-bleached, his skin tan, which was so different than the day of his release. Chessa would never forget the drive to his new apartment and the angry, sad, and confused emotions spewing out of him. Therapy with a doctor that Ferguson had recommended was helping her father deal with the betrayal. The next step: helping him find the courage to display his passionate artwork. Zelda knew an art gallery owner in Incline Village. Philip wasn't quite ready to approach the owner. He had found a job at Home Depot. He was overqualified, but he was okay with that.

A squeak drew Chessa's gaze to the house. Marcus pushed through the kitchen's screen door. He looked in her direction and a tide of feelings flowed through her. After Marcus had assisted in arranging her father's release as well as getting her charges of theft and more dismissed, Chessa hadn't communicated with him, not because she was afraid he would dredge up bad memories—they were fading fast—but she had wanted to concentrate on her career, wherever that might lead her. Oddly enough, seeing Marcus on occasion, even though it was in his official capacity, had clouded that perception.

When the invitation for a picnic came from Zelda, Chessa posted the note on the refrigerator in her cottage and stared at it for a week. In the end, she agreed to come so she could thank Zelda in person for all she had done.

"Chessa, help me put away the folding chairs," Marcus shouted.

She smiled. How could she say no to such a sweet request?

In silence, they loaded chairs onto a flatbed cart. They wheeled the cart to the garage and parked it in the far left corner.

"I don't know anyone who has a cart of folding chairs," Chessa quipped.

"Zelda's a party animal. She likes the family to get together every couple of months."

Once they returned to the sunshine, Chessa said, "You look good, Marcus. Rested and healthy."

"You, too, and tan."

She smiled. "Beach time is heaven for the soul."

"I heard you closed the sale on the cabin."

Chessa nodded. Selling her dream home had broken her heart, but after what had occurred there, she hadn't been able to sleep in her bedroom. The couch in the living room hadn't proven any better. She put the cabin on the market at a fire-sale price, sold it a week later—all cash with a thirty day closing—and moved into a rental cottage in the hills with a minimal view of the lake. She enjoyed sitting on the porch at night, gazing up at the stars.

"I heard your stepfather's place sold, as well."

"Mm-hm." Jeremiah had left Patience Troon and Chessa a tidy sum. Patience had resettled in the Bay Area. Chessa wasn't sure how to invest her portion.

Marcus shifted feet. "Did you hear about Diggs?"

"I keep up with the news," Chessa replied, the emotional wounds too fresh to say more.

Despite the proof that Diggs was a crook, over three thousand people attended his funeral. What his followers would never know was that his death ensured the safety of nanotech geniuses around the world. The message to destroy all of them was never transmitted. Diggs's siblings and key members of the Rebels of the Republic were awaiting trial. The government was keeping tabs on others in the group. Followers needed a leader, and in the absence of one, they would search for another.

"Zelda tells me you're going back to church," Chessa said. "Are you suffering a crisis of faith?"

"Just because there's one bad pastor, doesn't mean they all are. I like going, believe it or not." Marcus laughed, a hearty belly laugh. The sound warmed Chessa. "I feel calm when I'm there."

"Well, it suits you. The lines on your forehead and creases around your eyes have softened. You're actually quite handsome, Marcus." The flirtation in her voice surprised her. A flush of heat rose up her neck and into her cheeks. "Well…it's been nice seeing you," she murmured and set out across the yard.

"Hey, hold up." Marcus jogged to her side and clasped her elbow, not tightly, just enough. "You've been avoiding me all afternoon."

"There are so many people to see."

"Liar." He released her elbow.

She folded her arms in front of her. "You've got a great family, and Deputy Keegan is a hoot. He said you're a tough partner, but he respects you and the way you handled yourself with Captain Armstrong."

"The guy was pulling a power trip." Marcus massaged his neck and worked his tongue inside his cheek, deliberating over something. Finally he said, "Zelda thinks I should ask you out."

A flurry of emotions swirled through Chessa.

"Are you dating Dr. Fairchild?"

"What? No." Chessa hadn't dated anyone. When she wasn't working, in her free time she took long walks with Jocko or gardened or read. She hadn't seen Ferguson since he'd announced his plans to move his practice to Southern California. "What do you want to do on this *date*?" She tilted her head, this time deliberately flirting.

Marcus grinned. "First off, no foot races."

Chessa bit back a smile. "Deal."

"And no long swims in the lake."

"Sensible."

"No high-speed boat chases."

"Doesn't leave us many choices, does it?"

"Not really."

"Hmm." She looked up into his face, ready to abandon all pretense. "What if we ride in the same boat?"

~*~

If you liked this book, please do me a personal favor and review it. I would be grateful!

~*~

## AUTHOR'S BIO

Agatha Award-winning and nationally bestselling author **DARYL WOOD GERBER** ventures into the world of suspense with this debut novel, *GIRL ON THE RUN*. Daryl writes the bestselling ***Cookbook Nook Mysteries***. As **AVERY AAMES**, she pens the bestselling ***Cheese Shop Mysteries***. Fun tidbit: as an actress, Daryl appeared in "Murder, She Wrote". In addition, she has jumped out of a perfectly good airplane and hitchhiked around Ireland by herself. She absolutely adores Lake Tahoe, where ***GIRL ON THE RUN*** is set, and she has a frisky Goldendoodle named Sparky. Visit Daryl at www.darylwoodgerber.com.

Zappos

Made in the USA
Las Vegas, NV
08 January 2021

15456235R10171